loving DEEP

TRACEY DEVLYN

STEELE RIDGE
www.SteeleRidgeSeries.com

TEAM DEVLYN
Edited by Gina Bernal
Line Edited by Deborah Nemeth
Copyedited by Martha Trachtenberg
Beta Reads by Amy Remus, April Renn, Cricket McGraw,
Isabel Seligstein Hofmann, Karen Grage, Kym Fullen Amaral,
Michelle Steffen and Tara Kingston
Cover Design by Killion Group, Inc.
Interior Formatting by Author E.M.S.
Author Photo by Lisa Kaman Kenning, Mezzaluna Photography

This is a work of fiction. Names, characters, places, and incidents either are the product of the author's imagination or are used fictiously, and any resemblance to actual persons, living or dead, business establishments, events or locales is entirely coincidental.

Print Edition, November 2016, ISBN: 978-1-944898-09-0
For more information contact: tracey@traceydevlyn.com

BOOKS AVAILABLE BY CO-AUTHORS OF THE STEELE RIDGE SERIES

BOOKS AVAILABLE BY KELSEY BROWNING

PROPHECY OF LOVE SERIES
Sexy contemporary romance
A Love to Last
A Passion to Pursue

TEXAS NIGHTS SERIES
Sexy contemporary romance
Personal Assets
Running the Red Light
Problems in Paradise
Designed for Love

BY INVITATION ONLY SERIES
Sexy contemporary romance
Amazed by You

THE GRANNY SERIES w/NANCY NAIGLE
Southern cozy mysteries
In For a Penny
Fit to Be Tied
In High Cotton
Under the Gun

JENNY & TEAGUE NOVELLAS
Contemporary romance
Always on My Mind
Come a Little Closer

BOOKS AVAILABLE BY ADRIENNE GIORDANO

PRIVATE PROTECTORS SERIES
Romantic suspense

Risking Trust   Negotiating Point
Man Law   Relentless Pursuit
A Just Deception   Opposing Forces

HARLEQUIN INTRIGUES
Romantic suspense

The Prosecutor   The Defender
The Marshal   The Detective
The Rebel

JUSTIFIABLE CAUSE SERIES
Romantic suspense novellas
The Chase
The Evasion
The Capture

LUCIE RIZZO SERIES
Mysteries

Dog Collar Crime   Dog Collar Knockoff
Dog Collar Limbo   Dog Collar Couture

CASINO FORTUNA SERIES
Romantic suspense
Deadly Odds

JUSTICE SERIES w/MISTY EVANS
Romantic suspense

Stealing Justice   Cheating Justice
Holiday Justice   Exposing Justice
Undercover Justice   Protecting Justice

To Canis rufus
And to all the brave wildlife warriors protecting this critically endangered and important species

loving
DEEP

TRACEY DEVLYN

CHAPTER ONE

Kodiak Island, Alaska

STOMACH DOWN, LEGS SPREAD WIDE, he steadied his breathing and waited.

His heart pumped a steady cadence achieved only through years of experience. Anticipation tingled along every nerve ending, though he did not allow it to break his control.

The snow-tipped mountains, with their glacial valley and emerald ridges, failed to break his concentration.

The profusion of chocolate lilies, wild irises, and monkey flowers painting the wet meadow below failed to break his concentration.

The gang of bachelor river otters carousing in the clear stream cutting through the valley failed to break his concentration.

As his guide had promised, an enormous, lumbering Kodiak bear came into view, rewarding his patience. He'd been tracking the adult male for three days, enjoying the hunt almost as much as he would the kill. Almost.

A Kodiak in his prime. One that stood ten feet tall on his hind legs and weighed in around fourteen hundred pounds. A behemoth among giants.

Click by slow click, he rolled the scope's dial until the blurry image sharpened into distinct objects. A small adjustment to the left was all it took to place his target in perfect alignment with his Ruger's sights.

He released the safety, and the pad of his finger slid over the cool metal trigger until both dovetailed into a perfect grip. For several seconds, he followed the brown bear, admiring the male's sure-footed gait around thick tufts of grass and over Mini Cooper-sized boulders. Muscles rippled beneath the bear's dense fur, hinting at the beast's incredible strength.

The hunter's pulse spiked at the thought of conquering such a powerful animal. Only one other bear on earth could topple the Kodiak from his throne—the magnificent polar bear, the largest of them all.

Slowing his heartbeat, he waited until the Kodiak presented the broadside of his shoulder. A clean lung shot.

Releasing a slow breath between his lips, the hunter pulled the trigger. The bear dropped. Dead before he hit the ground.

Blood roared through the hunter's veins. Another victory. Another milestone met. Another good kill.

"Fine shot, sir."

"Indeed."

To experience this second in time again, he would pay double the five thousand dollars he'd shelled out for this honor. He nodded toward the dead Kodiak, and his indispensable guide flicked a hand at the nearby porters, who rushed to prepare the bear for transport.

Soon, the fallen Kodiak would occupy a space of honor opposite the polar bear in his trophy room. Two giants standing sentinel in his sanctuary, welcoming their master, warding off his enemies. Warriors protecting a warrior.

Five hundred ninety-nine kills. Only one more to go before his name would be featured in the Master Marksmen book—or, as it was known in the more elite inner circles, the Kill book. A status achieved by few others.

One more.

The rarest of them all.

Canis rufus. North Carolina's red wolf.

CHAPTER TWO

Steele Ridge, North Carolina

CRESTING A THIRTY-FOOT RISE, BRITT hiked to the overlook he used to spy on the red wolf den. He paused about twenty feet from the edge to peel off his backpack and retrieve his binoculars. Not taking any chances, he crouched low to avoid detection by his quarry below.

A sharp pin pricked his neck. Britt swiped at the mosquito. The bloodsucking bastards had been especially bad this summer, and he could do nothing to protect himself other than wearing long everything. If he applied bug spray, he might as well flash a beacon, notifying the wolves of his arrival, so keen was their sense of smell.

He set his pack and walking stick aside and lowered himself onto the grassy, rock-strewn ground. He inched forward commando-style until the ravine came into view. Dense stands of tulip, maple, and oak protected the understory and blocked out much of the Carolina sun. Even so, large shiny-leaved rhododendrons filled empty spaces, as did longleaf bluets, frostweed, and snakeroot.

North of his position, where one side of the creek bed rose twelve feet high before leveling off to create a shrub-laden shelf, a familiar pile of dirt led into a shadowed nook. Low branches made it difficult to see the den with the naked eye. But Britt knew what to look for and where to look for it.

Setting his binoculars in place, he focused in on the nook, which was two foot wide by one and half foot high. The small, dark cavern provided shelter to the breeding female and her four-week-old pups. Given the lateness of the hour and no sign of adults outside the den, the breeding male must have taken his small pack hunting.

Five pups—three females and two males. Before he'd left for a construction conference, he, his mentor, Barbara Shepherd, and friend Deke Conrad had flushed the breeding female from the den, so they could check on the pups and take blood samples. Although earlier tests had confirmed that the breeding pair were full-blooded red wolves, Britt had wanted to remove any lingering doubts about the pups.

Movement just inside the den caught his attention. The pups were stirring. He wondered if their floppy ears had gone erect yet.

The breeding female, Calypso, poked her broad nose outside the den, sniffing the air. Then she eased through the opening until the upper third of her body was visible. She glanced inside the den and soon, one by one, the pups tumbled out of their protective shelter.

Sensing their untethered freedom, yet too frightened to venture far, the pups loped along the creek bed shelf, tackling each other, relieving themselves, and chasing unsuspecting critters. Their ears were a mish-mash of one ear up, one ear down. Two ears down, two ears up.

Calypso watched over her brood like any long-suffering mother who'd given up on teaching her children how not to pick their nose at the dinner table. He'd seen the expression on his own mother more times than he could count.

Britt pulled his phone from his pocket, zoomed in to take a couple still shots, then hit the record button.

Before long, the tension that had riddled his body began to fade and he found himself smiling at their antics.

Now he wished he'd taken the time to stop by Barbara's place instead of coming straight here. She would have loved witnessing this milestone. After several days of conference head, all his mind had been able to manage was a simple list of instructions: airport—home—equipment—den.

His senior by twenty-odd years, Barbara could out-trek him and had more guts and grit than most men. After one lively conversation about coyote management, Barbara had adopted him as her unofficial student. She'd volunteered hours of her time toward his education. To this day, he couldn't fathom why someone with a PhD in Animal Behavior from Duke would spend a second of her precious time with a rough-around-the-edges country boy like him.

He'd asked her about it once and got a simple answer in reply. "Passion is worth a thousand PhDs. I can teach you how to transect a study area. But I can't teach you how to care about the findings." She'd tapped the left side of her chest. "That kind of wisdom comes only from the heart."

Britt stopped the video recorder and stared down at the wolves. A sense of overwhelming helplessness seeped into his good mood, melting his smile back into its familiar no-nonsense lines. Would he and Barbara and Deke be able to do right by the wolves? They needed constant monitoring to make sure they weren't overcome by disease, shot by farmers, or caught by trappers. The odds of surviving extinction in the wild were already stacked against the red wolf and now, for this isolated pack, the odds had hit hope-killing proportions.

He followed the pups' movements for a while longer, then backed away from the edge of the bluff. Collecting his gear, he headed out. He could have stayed and observed the wolves for hours, but the sun had begun to dip below the canopy and he'd left his flashlight in his truck.

Britt didn't mind being out in the woods at night, when he was assured of a clear night sky. But the clouds had grown thicker and would block the moon's light. Which meant it would be hard as hell *not* to break his neck.

Careful not to create a footpath leading to the den, Britt hiked a different route back to his truck. Barbara's property lay in this direction, and he would use the opportunity to stop by her place and fill her in on the pups' progress.

Unlike many large tracts of land in Western North Carolina, this property hadn't been logged to death. Stands of towering, thick-waisted oaks and hickories dotted the landscape, proclaiming this an old growth forest.

He still couldn't believe how much his life had changed since his baby brother, Jonah, developer of the blockbuster Steele Survivor video game, bailed out their on-the-brink-of-financial-collapse hometown.

"Meddling billionaire." Britt dug his walking stick into the ground as he ascended a steep incline. "Why didn't he stay out west and tear up some lives in Seattle?"

After years of helping raise his five brothers and sisters, Britt was finally able to concentrate on his own career and happiness. Though he still had his sixty-year-old mom and his little sister, Evie, to watch over.

Then his brother Jonah came home, bored and flush in the pockets, and proceeded to reprioritize Britt's world once again. By saving the town, Jonah, along with the entire Steele family, became the custodian of twenty thousand acres, a law enforcement training center under construction, and a mountain of headache-worthy decisions.

Britt thought about the application sitting on his kitchen table, ready to go. So much for his promise to

Barbara and his sister Evie. He couldn't mail the paperwork now. Spending a few weeks in a foreign country was unthinkable. He needed to stick around to coordinate the training center's contractors. And he couldn't leave the pups. Couldn't miss another day of their development.

Regret closed his throat, suffocating him for an alarming period of time. He wallowed in the unfairness of setting aside his dreams yet again. But only for a minute. He'd learned long ago about how resentment ate at a person like a starving lion, leaving behind nothing but a hollow shell.

He swallowed hard, forcing the ache and regret to release their hold and slither back to their compartments where they roiled 24/7.

And that's when he saw her.

CHAPTER THREE

TINY NEEDLES PIERCED RANDI'S SKIN—one at the base of her neck and one on her left shoulder, right through her thin purple stonewashed tee. She smacked at the mosquitos with greater force than necessary, causing herself more pain than the bites themselves. She checked her palm for bug fragments or blood smear. Nothing. "Freaking mosquitos! Do I have a neon sign over my head that reads 'Eat Me'?"

Randi fingered the bite on her neck and felt the welt already forming. "*I. Hate. The outdoors.*"

She hadn't always disliked the outdoors. There was a time when she enjoyed traipsing around these grounds more than playing with dolls, eating candy, and tormenting boys.

But that was ten *Star Trek* movies ago.

Randi reached the stream and followed it until she heard the rushing current of a waterfall. Excitement made her reckless, and she barreled forth. Limbs whacked her face and brambles scratched her arms. One moment she was on her feet and the next she was on her knees. She didn't look down to see what had tripped her, just scrambled to her feet and continued her mad dash to solace.

The understory opened and the sun shone through a hole in the canopy. Randi halted as if she'd reached the end of her leash. She blinked, unable to believe her eyes. The Landing, as she and her family had dubbed it two and a half decades ago, looked the same. Absolutely the same.

A three-tiered waterfall dominated the area. The clash and gurgle of water echoed off the bluff walls, surrounding Randi in unrivaled serenity. She loved this place. Missed this place. Longed for this place.

At the base of the waterfall, a small pool of clear water formed before narrowing down to a six-foot-wide stream that separated her mother's property from the newly formed Steele Conservation Area. She had spent many hours in the heat of the summer flopping around in that pool. Her inner child goaded her to shed her clothes and jump in.

But the rushing water seeped into her subconscious, bit by bit, reminding her of the large vanilla latte she'd consumed an hour before. How long had it been since she'd peed in the woods? So long ago she couldn't remember. At one time, she'd perfected the squat and shake method. Could she still drop trou in the open?

Randi glanced around. In all her years of coming to the Landing, she'd never seen another soul.

She'd never make it back to her mother's farmhouse. The more she thought about peeing, the worse her urge became. *Just do it, Shepherd. All this dithering over two minutes of your life.*

Randi ducked behind the largest tree she could find. She unbuttoned her fashionable skinny jeans and tried to shuck them down to her knees. It was like peeling off a layer of wet skin. After a good ten seconds of wrestling with them, she assumed the position—and waited. And waited. "Pee shy? Really?"

The tight jeans gathered around her knees began to cut off her circulation. If she didn't relieve herself soon, she'd be stumbling around on lifeless nubs. A slow trickle began—and that's when she felt the first needle prick. "Not now. For the love of Pete, not now." She smacked her bare bottom, only to be attacked by another needle and another and another. Everything was free flowing now, so she couldn't stop or she would be in worse discomfort than before.

She pushed, hard, forcing herself to go faster while she continued to slap the disease-transmitting bitches landing on her ass. When it was safe to do so, she closed off the spigot, stood, and performed a rusty shake-jiggle before pulling her panties up, then wrenching her jeans back into place. Or at least she tried. Inch by slow inch, she slid her pants up, giving herself a wedgie when the rough denim caught on her cotton panties.

Perfect.

"An interesting feat of acrobatics," a deep, masculine voice said from behind.

This can't be happening. Surely, I haven't been so awful as to deserve this sort of humiliation. Dread seeped into every pore, every muscle, every nerve ending. Randi whipped around. Oh, yes. She'd ticked off the Almighty in a big way.

Dressed in greens and tans and browns, from head to boot, Britt Steele strode toward her with a confidence that could only come from spending decades in the woods. His wide shoulders and broad chest filled her line of sight, massive, imposing, breath-stealing. Thick dark-blond hair framed a shadowed square jaw and intelligent brown eyes.

Eyes that had just caught her copping a squat.

So much for clearing her mind. This moment would be etched into her long-term, short-term, quarter-term, three-quarter-term memory, and every fraction in between.

Fixing a nonchalant smile on her face, Randi fastened her jeans. "Show's over, Mr. Tom. Enjoy your hike." She brushed past him. Humiliation roiled deep in her chest, upheaving the anger that constantly fought for release. Good God, she didn't need this. Didn't need the hottest guy in town catching her urinating in the woods and observing squished bug bits all over her bare bottom. And the wedgie. She needed to pull her underwear out of her crack in a bad way.

"Tom?" he asked.

Don't answer. Don't turn around. Don't acknowledge. "As in Peeping." *Gahhh.*

He chuckled. "I don't think this particular setup qualifies for Peeping Tom status. Not when the *show* was there for all to see."

Randi turned to face him. "Mind telling me what you're doing on Shepherd land?"

The softness around his eyes disappeared, returning his handsome face to its normal forbidding expression. This was the Britt Steele she was accustomed to. The one who came into her bar every Friday night and lounged at a corner table while sipping a whisky. The one who watched everyone around him with the keenness of a wolf and the temperament of a bear.

"I needed to cross the creek. This is the best place to do it."

"Interesting, but your explanation doesn't really answer my question." She eyed the antenna strapped to his back and the handgun at his side. "Tracking something?"

"Bobcat." This time, he brushed by her.

Bobcat? "There's no hunting on Shepherd land." A statement that hadn't always been true. At one time, her mother's family had owned over five thousand acres of gameland where hunters could pay to harvest bear, deer, fox, grouse, turkey, and more.

"That's good, because we're out of season." He didn't bother stopping, kept an even gait as he wound around various trees and shrubs and fallen trees.

"Why are you tracking bobcat?"

"Nothing nefarious. Just a simple wildlife survey of the Steele Conservation Area." His gaze raked a hot path down her body. "As for being on Shepherd property, I couldn't resist the show." He resumed his hike.

Randi's jaw locked at his callous reminder. She recognized his maneuver. Scratch at an open wound and maybe your opponent won't realize you've duped them. She knew this. Yet she couldn't stop herself from spinning around, unzipping her pants, tugging them down a few inches, and waggling her mosquito-bitten ass at his retreating back.

"How's that for a show, Steele?" She bit out the challenge beneath her breath and had her jeans back in place in under three seconds. Damned if she hadn't fixed her wedgie in the process.

No doubt she would be horrified by her impulsive actions later. She always was. But right now, the only emotion she could muster was an immature satisfaction for a well-executed *up yours.*

"Randi?"

No, please no. Not two self-imposed humiliations in one day. "Nothing more to see. Have a good day."

He sighed. Loudly. "Is your mom home?"

The change in topic was so abrupt that she failed to find an appropriate response. So she said the first thing that came to mind. "You knew my mother?"

"We've collaborated on a project or two over the years."

A fact Randi should have known, would have known, had she seen her mom more than a handful of times in the past decade. She recalled them talking at his mother's birthday party a few months ago, but she didn't realize their relationship went beyond acquaintance.

The hollow ache in her chest made speaking difficult. It was as if a knowing hand had ripped all the important parts out, leaving only air behind. "You've been away?"

"Just got back from a conference in DC. Came straight here. Why?"

"My mom's dead."

A hush fell over the woods as if every mammal, every insect, every gust of wind silently wept.

"Dead?" His voice shook. "I don't understand." His

harsh brown eyes bore into her skull as if he could siphon the knowledge from her brain. "Barbara was healthy."

"Such a stupid accident." She rubbed a hand against her stomach to quiet the tremors growing there.

"How?"

Randi really didn't want to do this now. She'd been living off coffee and a busy schedule since receiving *The Call*. To relive it all again…*Sheesus*.

Britt's tortured, knowledge-needing gaze pushed back her pain. She dove into her Shepherd Survive It mode and turned this unpleasantness into another one of her kajillion tasks that needed to be completed.

"It's time for me to get back to work," she said. "I'll walk with you as far as the sharp bend in the stream."

Randi led the way until the understory opened up and they could walk side-by-side. He remained quiet while they navigated the uneven terrain.

The story of her mother's death seemed packed in her throat. She didn't know why. Although her mother's passing saddened her, grief did not overwhelm her. In life, their relationship had been complicated, distant, there but not. Why would her death change that fact?

"Of all the ways Mom could have died," Randi began, "rolling down the side of the mountain was the kindest end."

"Kindest?"

"Better than a wild animal attack or a long, debilitating exotic disease or a swarm of killer bees."

He lowered his voice, as if he thought a higher volume would shatter her into oblivion. "Head, neck, or back?"

"Neck." Randi pressed her forearm against her stomach. "No one can tell me for certain what caused her fall. Some have suggested foul play. Others believe she got too close to the edge. And the bolder ones have speculated alcohol was involved."

She stepped onto a log. Her mother's advice echoed in her head.

"Never step over a fallen tree trunk, Miranda. Copperheads tend to take refuge under decaying logs and can be startled into striking out. Step onto the log, then off, out of striking distance."

"I've never seen your mother drink anything stronger than iced tea."

"Neither have I."

"I'm sorry. Not having closure must be difficult."

"Yes, but I consider myself lucky."

He eyed her for a moment. "How so?"

"She could have gone on one of her long hikes and simply disappeared." Randi stared straight ahead. "I know it sounds morbid, but at least I don't have to contend with that horrible situation."

"So, you're a could-be-worse kind of girl."

"Guess so."

"Dammit, I don't know what to say other than I'm right sorry." Concern carved into his grief-torn features. "How are you holding up?"

"Good as can be expected, given the circumstances."

"When's the funeral?"

"We put Mom to rest two days ago."

"Two days ago? Her accident must have happened the same day I left for DC."

Randi nodded. He was struggling with the knowledge that fate had denied him the chance to say good-bye to his friend. She recognized the signs, because she'd experienced a similar torment the day she learned her mother had died.

"Do you need anything?"

"No, thank you. I'll be occupied for the next week, getting the farmhouse spruced up."

Randi prayed the property would sell quickly. With the land in such pristine condition, except for the hundred acres her mom leased to a local farmer, Randi expected a developer to snap it up in a heartbeat. At a premium price.

The land held stunning long- and mid-range views of

the Blue Ridge Mountains and it had never been timbered. Couple the views with the moderate winter and summer temperatures, and one had the perfect enticement for people flocking into the area from the cold, flat regions of the North and Midwest.

"So you've decided to put the property on the market?"

"My life is downtown. I don't have the time or resources to maintain Sagebrook."

"Don't feel like you need to do anything with the house right away," Britt said. "Give yourself time to grieve. I don't plan on moving in for quite some time, if ever, so any cleaning or refurbishments would be wasted."

Randi's pace slowed. "Pardon?"

He stopped a few feet ahead of her, pivoted, and studied her face. Whatever he saw there, he didn't like. Granite crackled along his jaw line, and his nostrils flared. A curse split the air between them.

"Are you telling me you don't know the full details of your mother's will?"

Why would she? It's not as though her mother had ever invited her over for dinner to discuss the matter. Frankly, Randi was shocked her mom had bothered with such tedious, familial matters. They had never been on her radar. Or so Randi had thought.

"It's not a topic we'd ever discussed."

"Who's her attorney?"

"Virgil Carlisle."

"Carlisle? Please tell me you're joking."

"She trusted him."

"I take it Virgil hasn't discussed your mother's will with you either?"

Her mother's cousin could barely recall his middle name most days. A hard-as-nails lawyer for nearly two decades, Virgil's career had taken a nosedive five years ago when booze became more important than legal briefs.

"We spoke briefly after the funeral, but I haven't been able to reconnect with him since then. What do you know that I don't?"

Britt scrubbed a hand over his face. "It's not my place." Beneath his breath, he said, "I'm going to skewer that drunken bastard."

"It's not your place? What a crock." She moved toward him, forcing her anger to stay at a low boil. "My mother's work associate knows more about her will than I do. Sounds like your *place* was secured by dear ole Mom."

"Look, all I know is what Barbara told me before she died."

"Which was?" Had her mother willed the property over to Britt Steele? Could she have done something so outrageous? She and her mother hadn't been close, but they'd loved each other in their own way.

"Dammit, Randi. Go get the details from Virgil, then we'll talk."

Despair bubbled to the surface. What would she do if this property wasn't hers to sell? Where else could she get that kind of capital? In such a short time span?

"If you're not going to share what information you have, get back on your side of the creek."

He stared at her, incredulity lining his perfect forehead. "You're kicking me off Shepherd land?"

"Sounds that way to me." Her long strides carried her away. Away from his knowing eyes. Eyes that logged her every failure.

CHAPTER FOUR

BRITT WATCHED RANDI'S TIGHT ASS storm away. He'd been watching that ass for months. Ever since their brief encounter at his mom's birthday party. A sixty-second introduction had been enough to entice him into her bar—a place he'd been avoiding.

From the outside, Blues, Brews, and Books appeared too civilized for his tastes. He preferred drinking holes that didn't scowl at a man for putting his boots on a chair. Holes that served eat-your-liver whisky and greasy tater tots.

But Blues, Brews, and Books had proved to be a comfortable, tater-serving place, one he and his brothers frequented every Friday night.

He followed Randi's angry strides until the dense foliage swallowed her figure. A worm of concern curled around his chest. What if Barbara hadn't followed through on her promise?

The wolves couldn't lose access to this property. It would be devastating to the pack. Barbara understood their vital role in the ecosystem, the importance of preserving the swiftly dwindling species.

A developer wouldn't.

A farmer wouldn't.

A hunter—

"Dammit." Britt didn't need this complication now. Once he finished his part in Jonah's grandiose plans for the town, Britt would get his life back on the track he'd set for it. Not the one his father had forced him down for the past two decades.

Recalling his commitment to be at his mother's for dinner, he glanced at his watch.

Shit. If he didn't double-time it back to his truck, he'd be late.

He rolled his head from side-to-side. *Pop, pop, pop, pop, pop.* Now if he could only do that a few dozen more times. Harboring this kind of tension around his brothers, especially pain-in-the-ass Reid, wouldn't bode well for his mother's happiness. Or his.

Britt made sure his equipment and weapon were secure before settling into a ground-eating jog. The rapid pace compelled him to keep his mind on the space before him, rather than on the desperation he'd seen in Randi's almond-shaped eyes.

Barbara had assured him that her daughter wanted no part of Sagebrook. So what had been the cause of Randi's despair? Her reaction seemed volatile, something far different than a daughter grieving for the loss of her mother.

He couldn't allow himself to care. Right now, the wolves needed someone to protect their habitat. And that someone was him.

A while later, Old Blue rumbled toward his mother's dream home, Tupelo Hill. A large, white, in-need-of-a-good-paint-job house with an immense wraparound porch. For years his mother had gazed longingly at this home while making do with a three-bedroom, one-bath house for a family of eight.

When the baby boy billionaire saved the town, Jonah had also fulfilled his mother's long-held secret wish by gifting her with the enormous five-bedroom, four-bath house. Of course, his mother had protested the purchase, claiming the home was far more than she and Evie needed. True, but that was before Jonah, Reid, and Grif had set up residence there.

For a short spell the country house had busted at the seams with Steeles. His mother, in her element, had happily cooked and cleaned for her grown-up boys, and his brothers were content to let their sixty-year-old mother do it.

Luckily for them, Grif and Reid hadn't overextended their welcome. They were Carlie Beth's and Brynne's problems now. With Evie away at university, she couldn't be labeled a burden to their mother. His little sister had always been self-sufficient anyway, like him.

Jonah was another story. If Britt found out his mother was washing the little shit's underwear, the two of them were going to have words. Or fists. Whatever it took to make him grow up.

All three Steele brothers lined the porch, each with a longneck in their hands. Shaggy-headed Jonah rocked in a chair, his pale face plastered six inches from his phone. Sleek and unshakeable Griffin cradled his two favorite girls—Carlie Beth and their fourteen-year-old daughter, Aubrey—under each arm, swaying in the porch swing. And hell-raiser Reid lounged on the wide porch railing, his broad back propped against a support beam and one denim-clad leg stretched out before him. An I'm-going-to-fuck-with-you glint sparked in his blue eyes.

"Well, well, well, look who made it after all."

"Not tonight, Reid," Grif warned.

"Hey, Britt!" Aubrey said with a big grin.

"Hey, Aubrey. Come and give your almost uncle a hug."

She pounced on him like Tigger, all long legs and skinny arms and twitching tail. Aubrey had taken to him, more so than his younger, more dynamic brothers. Few adults knew what to do with him, which made his connection with Aubrey, an awkward boys-are-my-world teenager, all the more puzzling.

Setting her away, he said, "You look real pretty tonight." He nodded toward Grif and Carlie Beth. "Got a heartbreaker on your hands."

Carlie Beth smiled and Grif groaned.

"Bro," Jonah said without looking up.

"Jonah." He dropped into the rocker on the opposite side of the door, close to trouble. He knew how to deal with Reid's nonsense. When it came to the genius gamer, he had no idea.

"Is Brynne coming?" Carlie Beth asked.

"Nope." Reid pulled a hefty swig from his longneck. "One of the shop girls called in sick, Brynne has to close up. She sounded tired. I told her to go home afterward."

"Shop girls?" Britt asked with a pointed look.

"What the hell else do you want me to call them? They're girls and they work at Brynne's clothing shop. Shop. Girls."

"Employees, staff, ladies…Take your pick."

"Oh, thanks, Mom."

"I know. I never let you have any fun. Deal."

"Aubrey, let's go see if Grammy and Evie need any help." Carlie Beth ushered her daughter inside, but not before sending Reid a bad uncle glance.

"Ballbuster, that one," Reid said.

"If your pie-hole had any manners, she wouldn't have to bust anything." Jonah's thumb slid across the five-and-a-half-inch screen with dizzying speed.

"The vampire speaks," Reid said. "Do you even know what day it is?"

"Fuck you Friday."

Reid barked out a laugh and nearly fell off his perch. Once he recovered, his laser focus zeroed in on Britt.

Here we go.

"Why are you so long in the face this evening?"

"Reid," Grif warned again. "Mom's been looking forward to tonight all week. Don't start your shit."

"What? Are you his protector?" Reid asked in his typical take-it-too-far way.

"No, I'm yours."

"I'm merely voicing some concern over my big brother's grumpy mood."

Britt knew better than to engage Reid while tension continued to coil in his neck and back like an anaconda crushing the organs of its prey.

Ignoring Reid, Grif asked Britt, "How was your conference?"

"Good keynote speaker and the field excursions were interesting. The five days could probably have been cut down to three, though."

Of the three brothers, Britt was closest to Grif. They shared the same level-headedness and take-charge attitude. However, their careers were worlds apart. Grif's revolved around sports and making money. A lot of it. Those with that kind of mindset rarely understood the value of safeguarding the natural environment. Something that often swallowed up money rather than making it. Eco-tourism being the one exception.

"Any issues here?" Britt asked.

"Much better now that no one is trying to kill Brynne," Reid said.

After finding a woman who could put up with his dipshit ways, Reid had almost lost Brynne in a drug scheme. Although Britt knew crime existed in every dark corner of the world, he hadn't been prepared for its close proximity to those he loved. Seeing Reid, fearless in ways he couldn't fathom, afraid for Brynne tore at that space in Britt's heart that was brother, father figure, protector.

Reid eyed him. "So fierce, Tarzan. Do we need to find you a Jane?"

"This is gonna be so great," Jonah said to his screen.

Britt stopped rocking, his hands wrapped around the arms of his chair.

"Oh-ho!" Reid taunted. "Could it be the ape-man's found a Jane?"

Grif cursed.

Jonah pointed his phone toward the oncoming storm.

Britt sprang forward, clamping his arm around Reid's neck in an unbreakable band before the troublemaker knew what hit him. He hauled his brother into the house amid a plethora of curses and fist slams. "I'm thirsty. Let's see what Mom has to drink."

Britt cut the corner short, ramming Reid's shoulder into the doorjamb. The ladies weren't in the kitchen, which suited Britt fine. He wasn't interested in humiliating Reid—much—he just wanted to teach the little pecker a lesson in moderation.

He crowned his captive with the refrigerator door before grabbing a longneck.

"Sonofabitch! I'm going to rip your balls—"

"Reid," Joan Steele called from the dining room. "Language, young man."

"I am going to kill you for this," Reid said quietly, so only Britt could hear. Then he raised his voice. "Sorry, Mama."

"Don't forget Evie and our guests," Mom said. "I didn't raise heathens."

"Sorry, ladies."

"Britt," she said. "Not in the house. And be careful of your brother's injured knee."

Rather than release his squirming brother, Britt tightened his hold and retraced his steps. "Just needed to get something to drink, Mom."

Jonah stood in the open door, still recording. He pressed his back against the screen door to let them through. The moment Britt stepped outside, he released his brother, who nearly tumbled off the porch in his haste to get away and right himself.

Angling his head toward Jonah, Britt warned, "That had better be for your own amusement."

"Seriously? This video gem could get me a million likes in less than an hour."

Britt did not break his Do and Die stare.

"Shit, man. We've got to get you into the twenty-first century."

"Tarzan—"

A pillow to the head cut off Never Learn Reid's next

taunt. "If he doesn't finish kicking your ass," Grif said, "I will."

Lean arms curled around Britt's waist from behind. He peered over his shoulder to find an impish Evie smiling up at him.

"Take pity on the Green Beret," she said, her sapphire blue eyes twinkling. "He's lost when not hunting bad guys."

Britt's dark mood lifted at the sight of his baby sister. Some people had the ability to brighten a room—or a heart—just by making an appearance. That was his Evie. Other than the occasional annoyance with her brothers, she never appeared anything but happy. Never had a harsh word for another person. Never let life defeat her.

"When did you get home, Squirt?"

"Fifteen-twenty minutes ago. I would have been here sooner, but my friend Kathy got dumped by her quarterback boyfriend. She was a mess. I fed her chocolate and gave her a book to read."

Jonah snorted. "One about how real men should act?"

"Don't mock, boy genius"—she released Britt, but didn't move from his side—"until you've sampled the wares."

"I've read one. A bunch of Romeo and Juliet nonsense. I'll stick with action-adventure."

"*Romeo and Juliet* is a tragedy, not a romance." Evie's blue eyes sparked. "Most action-adventure movies have an underlying love story."

"Do not. They're about the chase and blowing shit up."

"Indiana Jones and Marion, Katniss and Peeta, Han Solo and Princess Leia, Clark Kent and Lois Lane, Neo and Trinity, Four and Tris, King Kong and Ann Darrow." Evie ticked off on her fingers. "Every one is about a guy and a girl fighting evil forces while giving in to their growing attraction."

Reid's eyebrows shot up and his hand swiped the air toward Evie in an age-old gesture of "What the hell?"

Britt ignored him. Explaining the nuances of when to use and when not to use "girl" to a bonehead would require more energy than he cared to expend.

Jonah eyed her with disbelief while his computer circuit of a brain analyzed each movie Evie named—and found she was right. "Dammit, Evie. Why'd you go and ruin them for me? King freaking Kong? Seriously?"

"Time for you to break free of la-la land."

For a moment, Jonah appeared to want to pounce on Evie and show her he spent as much time in the gym as he did with his video games. But his hard gaze flicked to Britt, then back to Evie, then to his telephone, taking the self-preservation path.

Britt bumped Evie's shoulder with his. "I have a present for you."

"You do? What?"

Glancing around, he found his brothers watching them. "Let's take a walk."

He led Evie to the side of the house where an old tire swing hung from a gigantic oak tree. He pulled out his phone and scrolled through his photo album. "Take a look."

She peered at the screen, saw the frozen image. "You got them?"

He winked, then nodded toward the phone. "Hit play and find out."

She did, and the screen came alive with wolf pup antics. Evie followed the pups, her excited expression transforming into one of wonder. Although she'd assisted him, Deke, and Barbara before, this was her first glimpse of the pups.

No one else in his family knew about his work with the red wolves. Only Evie. It wasn't that he didn't trust the others. The Steeles were notorious for keeping family secrets within the clan, but none of the others had the same affinity for the environment as Evie.

Being able to talk about his work with someone who did more than nod at his words was...Hell, he didn't know what it was, but he liked it.

"Oh, my gosh. They're amazing!" She handed him the phone. "When can I see them in person?"

"Soon. Let's give them time to acclimate to their new world before visiting again."

"Gah." She whacked his shoulder. "I knew you would torture me."

"My favorite pastime."

She sent him a dirty look. "I'm still amazed by how this breeding pair found each other."

No one would have guessed that any of the unaccounted-for wolves from the defunct Great Smoky Mountains National Park reintroduction program would have survived and remained true to their species. The odds had been stacked against them to a suffocating degree.

But the Steele-Shepherd breeding pair had beat the odds. Clobbered them, in fact. No doubt the two were several generations removed from the original reintroduction group. But somehow, they—and their ancestors—had managed to retain their purebred red wolf status. Truly amazing and inspiring. Britt wondered how many more might be roaming the Eastern Tennessee-Western North Carolina landscape.

"Me, too."

"Theirs is a modern-day love story," Evie said with a grin. "No distance has been too great, no starvation has stopped them, no coyotes have tempted them. Epic."

"You *have* been reading too many romance books."

"Not possible. Imagine what a happier world we would live in if more people read *those* books."

"The men would be happier for sure."

"Reid's rubbing off on you."

"Bite your tongue, woman."

"You know, if you spent more time with him, he wouldn't harass you so much."

"Not true. I've spent hours with him on the training center renovation. He's as much of a pain in the ass now as ever."

"Hey, Friends of the Flowers," Reid called out. "It's time to eat."

Evie's eyes twinkled. "I see what you mean."

"Never doubt your big brother." He draped an arm around her neck and headed toward the scent of barbecue and roasted potatoes. Saliva drenched his mouth. No one could top his mom's BBQ pulled pork. Tender, melt-in-your-mouth pork dipped in a spicy-tart sauce authentic to generations of North Carolinians.

Everyone took their normal seats at the dining room table. Mom at one end, and Britt at the other. For a long time, Britt had refused to take the end chair, his dad's spot, believing the old man would return. But he never did, so Britt had assumed the head-of-the-household position in mind and body and chair.

Grif, Carlie Beth, and Aubrey sat to his left and Reid, Evie, and Jonah to his right. If any more siblings found their mates, they would need a bigger table. Randi Shepherd's image floated across his mind, laughing and sharing stories with his family. The scene was so clear, so real that Britt's gaze turned to his right, expecting to see her beautiful face shining with laughter.

Instead, he found Reid waving a hand inches from his nose. If Britt had a machete, he would hack off the damned thing at the wrist.

"Yoo-hoo, Tarzan. Mom asked you a question."

"Reid," his mother scolded. "Stop calling your brother that ridiculous name."

"Why ridiculous? He spends all his time in the jungle."

"Save your sass for the playground, not your mother."

Reid's cocksure expression crumbled.

Britt shared a look with Grif, whose lips twitched before he concentrated on filling his plate. No one dared to push their mother once she delivered a setdown. Not even Reid.

"How are the renovations going for the training center?" Evie asked Reid into the silence.

Reid stabbed a potato with his fork. "Slow."

After Jonah saved the town, the newly constructed sports complex needed a new purpose. Jonah in his understated wisdom deemed it a perfect location for a regional law enforcement training center. Given Reid's injury and the unlikelihood that he would be able to return to the Green Berets, he had been the perfect candidate to coordinate the refurbishment of the state-of-the-art facility.

With Britt's construction experience.

They would both be lucky to get through the project without maiming each other.

All the brothers played their part to give Reid this golden opportunity. Jonah supplied the cash, Grif executed the agreements, Reid provided the vision, and Britt dealt with the contractors. Rather than show some appreciation, Reid had turned into an even bigger turd.

Although it wasn't the best timing, Britt had welcomed the distraction of attending a conference in DC. He'd needed a break from...everything.

"Any issues at the construction site while I was gone?"

"If I had five hands," Reid said, "I still wouldn't have enough fingers to tick off all the crap I had to deal with while you were vacationing."

Britt allowed the vacation comment to slide. "I guess now you'll appreciate my presence a little more."

"What the hell does that mean? I appreciated you before."

"You have an interesting way of showing it, bro," Jonah put in.

"Did they finish the firing range?" Britt pressed.

"Another day or two. Why? You getting itchy?"

"Just tired of dropping lead on my own property."

An accomplished archer and rifleman, Britt liked to keep his skills sharp between hunting seasons. Many years ago, as a young hunter, he'd clipped a deer with a bullet. He'd followed the blood trail for over three hundred yards before he lost it. The thought of that injured deer's suffering had haunted him for years. Still did, from time to time.

Since then, he'd learned patience and kept his skills fine-tuned. He'd never missed his target again.

The others managed to wheedle Reid out of his miff long enough for Britt to learn that everything was progressing well enough, despite Reid's whining. Britt was glad. Although he'd needed the break, he would have felt guilty had things gone to hell while he was away.

An hour later, Evie walked him out to his truck. "You were patient with Reid."

"Years of experience, Squirt."

"No, he's more obnoxious than ever. Something's bothering him, and you seem to be the focus."

"He'll figure it out."

"Do you know what's going on with him?"

"Not a clue."

"He does love you. But he's in an odd place. Almost losing Brynne messed with his disposition."

Britt suppressed a grin. "*Disposition?* You sound like Mom."

"Quit trying to distract me." She rubbed her fingertips together in a gesture he recognized as anxiety. "You'll keep that in mind, right? About Reid."

"Don't worry." He slid behind the steering wheel and shut the door. "I won't kill him. Today."

She shooed away a mosquito floating by his chest. "Did you mail your application?" Her face lit with guarded excitement.

He would have loved to say yes. Just to make her happy. Instead, he turned over the engine. "Not yet." He set the truck in reverse.

"You're stalling. Why?"

"It's called commitments, Evie. Maybe there'll be time once the renovations on the center are done."

"You have been preparing for this moment for over two years."

"Looks like I'll be preparing for a while longer."

"Reid and Jonah will understand a few weeks' delay."

"Like Reid understood my conference delay?" He nodded toward her feet. "Watch your toes, Squirt."

CHAPTER FIVE

RANDI BENT OVER HER DESK in the rear office at Blues, Brews, and Books. Burning eyes stared at the small digital clock in the upper-right corner of her computer screen. *8:17 a.m.* She rubbed her temples to ward off the oncoming headache. Waiting until a decent hour to call Virgil might be the hardest thing she'd had to do since learning how to tie her shoes.

Numbers, words, and columns blurred together like a bad game of Scrabble. She'd slept little the previous night, making bookkeeping near impossible this morning.

Her attention moved to the stack of condolence cards, opened and read, but not answered. She really needed to send out thank-you letters before too much more time passed. The muscles in her chest tightened. Tomorrow. Tomorrow, she would find the words.

She reached for her latte, hoping the sugar and caffeine mix would slap her into her normal alert, on-the-go self. When she tilted the cup toward her mouth, she misjudged the sippy hole, and creamy coffee dribbled down her chin and onto her desk.

"Why am I not surprised?" Pulling several tissues from the box, she mopped up her mess and pitched the soiled tissues into the trash. A discarded white envelope in the recycling bin next to her trash caught her eye.

Gaviston and Swink, Attorneys at Law.

Randi straightened, pushing receipts to the side until she found the crisp white vellum. Its message—salvation. So why did the words make her stomach cramp like a runner's muscles after hours of dehydration?

A tentative knock provided a much-needed interruption. "Come in."

"Morning, Randi. Sorry to bother you." Petite, with sleek black hair streaked with bright purple highlights, Kris McKay entered her office, confusion evident in her normally impish Asian eyes. "Jed's around back with a delivery. He needs to speak with you."

"Would you mind handling it, Kris? I'm in the middle of something here."

Although small of stature, Kris had a backbone made of titanium. Randi had witnessed her assistant manager slash barista slash waitress talking down a drunken miner three times her size. Like all of Randi's employees, Kris wore many hats. However, Kris had been with her since Blues, Brews, and Books first opened and she loved the place as much as Randi—and was fiercely protective of the shop and her employer.

"I tried," Kris said. "When I started discussing the details of our next order, Jed insisted on speaking with you."

The worry that had been flowing like slow-moving lava in her gut since her discussion with Britt Steele fired to life, searing her chest. "Is there a problem?"

"He wouldn't discuss specifics with me."

Randi nodded and made her way to where Jed waited for her in the empty bar. One deep blue awning stretched across two distinct storefronts, signaling to patrons they had arrived at Blues, Brews, and Books. One side of a soundproof moveable wall housed a bar and restaurant. The other, a coffee shop with an oversized Little Free Library. Staff flowed freely between the two via a back corridor, and both businesses shared a dry and cold stock area.

So many people had advised her against such a peculiar arrangement. But Randi had conceived the idea of Blues, Brews, and Books in her early days at university. An all-in-one gathering place. Most people liked simplicity and familiarity, along with great service and exceptional product. Her business delivered all of that and more.

The unique configuration allowed Randi to manage both businesses efficiently and, once inside, her customers weren't even aware of the operational aspect. Most of the locals distinguished their meet-up place as Triple B bar or Triple B restaurant or Triple B café, which suited Randi just fine. She didn't care what people called her establishment as long as they continued to buy her product and enjoy the service.

Although unconventional, Triple B had become popular with folks of all ages and interests. Now, she had to do everything within her power to save it.

"Hey, Jed," Randi held out her hand. "Kris said you wanted to speak with me."

He returned her handshake. Bordering six feet and more on the pretty side than masculine, twenty-two-year-old Jed Decker spent a good deal of time on the road, delivering his family's locally brewed beer.

"Sorry to hear about your mama, Randi. Daddy sends his condolences."

"Thanks, Jed. The flowers your family sent were beautiful."

"I know this isn't a good time." He shifted his stance, planting his feet farther apart. "But Daddy asked me to tell you that we can't make any more deliveries until your current balance is settled."

The fire flared into her throat, cutting off her words. She'd been expecting this. For the past three months, she'd paid only a portion of each bill that had rolled in. Hoping to give herself enough time to figure something out.

She did a quick calculation. "I can give you a check now for half, then the rest next month."

Shaking his head before she even finished, he said, "Daddy said all or nothing." Regret tinged his tone, though his gaze remained steady.

Randi briefly wondered how many times he'd been forced to have this conversation with other customers. Decker beer was one of her best sellers, so canceling her order was out of the question. Which meant something else would have to be sacrificed.

"I understand. Tell Avery that I'll have the bill settled within the week."

Jed smiled. "Will do."

After Jed left, Randi stood motionless, her arms hanging like useless iron weights at her side, her gaze inward, frozen by the images of failure scoring her mind. Fingers gone numb rubbed her temples again, fighting off the building implosion. She had to get control of this situation. So much more than her livelihood was at stake.

Blues, Brews, and Books employed fourteen people besides herself. She paid her staff well. Some said too well, but Randi believed in rewarding extraordinary performance. She asked a lot of her employees, with having to become familiar with different product lines and, for that matter, clientele. They juggled many hats and deserved to be paid for their efforts.

Everything had been going great. In the last six months, profits had exceeded the projections she'd established in her long-term business plan. Blues, Brews, and Books had become *the* hangout place.

Then she'd made a fatal decision, one that had gone against her gut, but she'd trusted someone she shouldn't have. Now she would have to tread water until this mess with Britt Steele was sorted out. And look forward to many more awkward conversations like the one she'd had with Jed.

The entrance door to the bar side rattled. A man in a tailored suit set down his briefcase to cup his hands against the glass and peer inside.

She held up a finger and made her way to the front of

the bar. Unlocking the bolts, she opened the door and was momentarily stunned into silence. The guy was Henry Cavill gorgeous. Expensive suit, broad shoulders, and emerald green eyes set off by the blackest hair she'd ever seen. Blacker than Kris's. Neatly trimmed dark curls were kept under control with just the right amount of hair product.

"Good morning," she finally managed. "Are you looking for the coffee shop?"

"In a sense," he said in a deep, velvety voice. "I'm looking for the owner, Miranda Shepherd."

Her day just got a whole lot brighter. "I'm Miranda."

He flashed her a megawatt smile. "Then I'm at the right place." Holding out a business card, he said, "I'm Keith Gaviston of Gaviston and Swink. Am I calling at an inconvenient time?"

Randi debated sending the handsome lawyer away; she was completely unprepared for this conversation. However, her curiosity had her opening the door and gesturing for him to enter. "Can I get you something to drink, Mr. Gaviston?"

"Thank you, no. Please call me Keith."

She led him to a booth and scooted into one side.

"Given your response to my name, I assume you received my firm's letter."

"Yes."

"When I didn't hear back from you, I feared the envelope went astray."

"I only received it yesterday. It's a lot to absorb."

"Indeed, it is." He drew two file folders from his briefcase. "Perhaps I can set your concerns to rest, if you'd care to share."

"Well"—Randi fidgeted with her watchband—"for starters, what type of organization is Carolina Club?"

"A club that caters to the refined tastes of some of North Carolina's most influential gentlemen."

Refined tastes? "Your first attempt to set my concerns to rest has failed, Mr. Gaviston. I watch enough *Criminal*

Minds to know that *refined tastes* can cover any number of perversions."

"Don't you get nightmares from watching that show?"

"Oddly, no. Not sure what that says about me."

"Tremendous intestinal fortitude, I suspect."

"Sounds like a fancy way of saying I have guts." She sent him an I-know-what-you're-about smile. "Are you trying to distract me with compliments?"

"Do I look like a man who would resort to such underhanded tactics?" He rounded the question off with a grin that would have stopped the most dedicated of wives' hearts.

Although Randi wasn't immune to his smile's effect, she'd worked in and around bars since college and had either seen, heard, or been the recipient of sexy smiles, sensual once-overs, and even a body brush or two. She knew how to shrug it off and get down to business.

"Refined tastes, Mr. Gaviston?"

"Keith, remember?"

"I remember."

"The Carolina Club's primary interest is in wildlife conservation and education. Something your mother was quite passionate about, as I understand."

"How did you come by this fact?"

"Word travels fast in these parts. Especially when the owner of such a large parcel of pristine land passes away."

"How much property does the club currently hold?"

"In North Carolina?"

"Yes, and in total, I guess."

"The club holds title to approximately thirty-five hundred acres in the state and a little over twenty-five thousand acres in other parts of the world."

World?

"And you're preserving all this land?"

"Yes. The membership is quite passionate about conservation."

"A private club stowing a large amount of land away," she mused. "There has to be some benefit to the club."

"Are you always this suspicious?"

"Only when something has a bit of stink to it."

He slid a crisp white sheet of paper in front of her. The expensive vellum carried the same Gaviston and Swink letterhead as his previous communication.

"This is the amount I've been authorized to offer for your property. As you can see, the figure is more than fair."

Randi stared down at the zeros that seemed to go on and on and on. Sweat broke out on her palms and prickled heat rushed up her neck. Blood pumped in her ears, drowning out logic, lifting up hope. She had no idea what the fair market value was for her mother's property. But the club's offer far exceeded anything she'd considered.

However, her bullshit detector was firing off the charts. If she hadn't been so preoccupied with calling Virgil this morning, she would have done a quick Internet search on the club. Randi stared at the zeros rolling across the paper. The desperate side of her mind wanted to accept so she could get a full night's rest for the first time in weeks.

But something seemed fishy about the offer—and the organization. The idea of a group of rich men, with *refined tastes*, banding together to set aside tens of thousands of acres for protection didn't ring true.

Guys weren't that altruistic. Although there were exceptions, most men expected a return on their investment. Something besides warm and fuzzies.

"Do you not agree the club is offering a fair price?" Gaviston pressed.

"More than fair. Maybe too fair."

"Is there such a thing?"

Irritation simmered beneath the surface of her play-it-cool facade. "Do not mistake my gender or hair color as signs of weakness, Mr. Gaviston. It won't bode well for our continued association."

He did that chin-roll thing men did when their necktie was too tight. "You're right, of course. I took our banter too far." He closed his briefcase. "Why don't you take some time to consider the club's offer? I'll check back with you in a few days." He slid out of the booth. "How does that sound?"

Randi thought it was a great plan. She hadn't spoken to Virgil yet, so she didn't even know what her rights were, related to her mother's property. With a little time and breathing room, she could make a sound, logical decision. She really disliked doing anything on the fly, especially with something so important.

Standing, she held out her hand. "I'll review the club's offer and have an answer for you when you return."

On the way back to her office, Randi's best friend and sometimes employee, Carlie Beth, caught up with her. "Hey, Randi. Register three is low on ones."

"Already?"

"What can I say? Coffee business is brewing this morning."

"Clever. Thanks for filling in again for Amy." Randi opened her office door. "She sounded horrible over the phone."

"Any time. It's good for me to get out of the forge and talk to actual people rather than scraps of metal."

Randi produced a limp smile. Normally, Carlie Beth's wisecracking could pull her out of any funk. But not today. Too many worries weighed on her mind. "I'll replenish register three in a second."

"Something wrong? You seem distracted."

She debated whether to share her current debacle with Carlie Beth. Any other time, she wouldn't have hesitated. However, Carlie Beth's being engaged to Griffin Steele made Britt her family. Randi didn't want to put her friend in a position of having to choose sides.

"I'm fine, thanks. Just a lot on my mind."

"You always have a lot on your mind. Running a coffee shop, bar, and restaurant has a way of keeping your brain in hyperdrive." Carlie Beth rested her bottom on the edge of Randi's desk and gave her an I'm-not-leaving-until-you-tell-me look. "Spill it."

"I can't. Not to you."

Hurt speared across Carlie Beth's features. "Why not?"

"Because part of my dilemma has to do with one of the Steele brothers. I don't want to put you in the middle."

"Is it Grif?" Carlie Beth asked.

"No."

"Then spew. I have experience navigating through all that testosterone. Let me help you."

Randi hesitated only a second more before laying out the details of her and Britt's encounter in the woods. For self-preservation purposes, she left out the ass-eating mosquitos and squat-catching humiliation. After she finished her story, Carlie Beth remained quiet for several long, thoughtful seconds.

"Have you spoken to Virgil yet?"

Glancing at the clock for the hundredth time, Randi said, "No, I'm waiting until nine before calling him."

"You're a better woman than I am. I would've called him over and over until he dragged his hungover butt out of bed."

"Believe me, I was tempted."

"What are you going to do if your mother cooked up some deal with Britt?"

"I don't know." Randi chewed on her bottom lip. It was dry and peeling in places. She grabbed her purse and dug into a side pocket for her little tub of cherry Vaseline. After dabbing the pad of her ring finger into the petroleum jelly, she smoothed a thin layer onto her lips. Better already. She recapped the tub and dropped it into her purse. "Under normal circumstances, I would be relieved not to have to worry about what to do with the place. But my financial situation has changed and I could use the influx of capital."

"I'm sorry, Randi." Carlie Beth squeezed her shoulder. "I wish I had a magic solution. Let's hope Britt soaked up too much fresh air and it affected his recall of his conversation with your mom."

"What do you know about him?"

"Who? Britt?"

Randi nodded. "Although he's a regular on Friday nights, I've probably only said ten words to him in all that time."

"From what Grif has told me, Britt spent his teenage years and twenties making sure his mom and siblings had what they needed. I suspect that kind of sacrifice has a way of making a guy grow up quickly."

"He's not exactly approachable. Does he resent the lost years?"

"I don't know about the resentment. At family functions, they like to poke at each other until they make their target crazy. But they're a loving, protective bunch."

Randi tried to envision a carefree, joking Britt, but the only image that came to mind was his stern, watchful expression. Until she recalled his comments about her *show* in the woods. His unsmiling features had softened the teensiest amount, enough to give her a glimpse of the true man beneath.

Even so, Randi had a hard time believing her mother would give her birthright to Britt Steele. "What about his integrity? Could this be an elaborate scheme?"

"To do what? Steal your inheritance?"

"I know it sounds farfetched. But I can't figure out why my mother would put me in this position. We weren't close, but we weren't enemies either."

"For Britt to engineer something so elaborate, he'd have to be in league with Virgil. Would you trust your mother's cousin to pull this off?"

"Hmm, you have a point."

Carlie Beth's voice took on the soothing tone of a mother trying to calm a distraught child. "Britt seems like an honest guy. Don't think the worst until you hear it come out of Virgil's mouth. Positive thoughts."

Artisan to the core of her being, Carlie Beth survived potential disasters by not giving them a lick of her energy. But Randi couldn't operate that way. She needed a backup plan. A plan B and sometimes C and D. Having something to focus on in times of crisis was essential to her peace of mind.

"I shall fill my mind with rainbows and fairy dust...and chocolate. Lots of chocolate."

"That's my girl."

"Let me get those singles."

Randi took care of the cash issue, then headed back to her office to call Virgil. He didn't answer. "Virgil, this is Miranda Shepherd. Please call me when you get this message. We need to talk about my mother's will."

Ending the call, Randi propped her head in her hand, rubbing at the tightness in her chest and fighting the despair pulling at her mind.

CHAPTER SIX

TRIPLE B SUPPORTED THE REGION by serving top grade, locally brewed beer and farm-raised fruits and vegetables along with hosting talented, homegrown bands. All of which entertained Britt, but none of which kept him coming back, week after week after week.

Masking his interest in the woman across the room, he sipped his favorite adult beverage, Defiant, a locally distilled whisky. Wearing a red wraparound top and skintight black jeans tucked into a pair of short-heeled black leather boots, Randi Shepherd lifted up on her tiptoes to draw down a blue bottle of 1800 from a high shelf behind the bar. Her top stretched with her, revealing an expanse of silken flesh and a round, firm bottom.

Britt stuck the red straw back into his mouth and resumed his chewing while eyeing the other guys in the bar. Men ranging from twenties to sixties gawked at her curves, some openly and some more discreetly. The latter included Deke.

His tumbler hit the wooden table with a hard, dull thud.

"What's got your undies in a bunch tonight?" Deke asked.

"How about I give you something to worry about besides my undies?"

An inch taller than Britt's six-foot-three frame, but slighter of build, Deke had one of those deep masculine voices that made every woman—and some men—take notice. They'd been friends since grade school. Deke had gone on to earn a master's in wildlife biology and then nabbed his dream job with the U.S. Fish and Wildlife Service.

Britt was jealous as hell of his accomplishments, but that didn't stop him from being proud of Deke. His friend had pulled himself out of a rough childhood, then worked two side jobs while going to school full-time. He deserved every bit of his success.

"How many more Friday nights is it going to take before you get up the nerve to ask Randi out?"

"I don't know what you're talking about."

"Don't give me that bullshit. You've been struck stupid by her since the first night we arrived." Deke's attention dropped to Britt's mouth. "If you wind that straw up any faster, you could power up a car engine."

Britt tossed the ratty straw onto the table. He couldn't argue with Deke's blunt assessment. Before walking into Randi's bar six months ago, he'd only met her one other occasion, though he'd seen pictures of her dotting Barbara's living room. Most were of her as a small child, a few revealed a young teenage Randi, none captured the adult she'd become. She had…matured in the intervening years.

"I don't feel right about dating Barbara's daughter."

"I figured that's why you were playing it cool." Deke dipped a chip into a bowl of salsa. "Look man, I'm not trying to be an uncaring hardass, but Barbara's gone. The coast is clear, though I never thought you dating your friend's daughter was much of a roadblock."

"It was for me. Besides, given our current predicament regarding the property, I don't see us hooking up any time soon, if ever."

"You've got to get out of your Dr. Doom and Mr. Gloom funk. It's Friday night. We should be dancing."

Deke caught the eye of a brunette. She sent him a slow, welcoming smile. "Behold, my moody friend. I'm about to show you what fun looks like."

Britt watched Deke stroll away, a devil-may-care smile on his face. Deke loved chatting up folks. His easygoing charm could win over the most closed-minded, cantankerous farmer. Unlike Britt, who found most social interactions painful and annoying.

He made a mental note to have Deke sweet-talk the conservation area's neighbor, Harvey Griggs. The sixth-generation farmer had a cargo load of complaints that could line the French Broad River. Anything from the conservation area's deer eating his wife's flowers to the Steele family's takeover of the town to the effects of the barometric pressure on his joints.

He finished off the last of his whisky and looked around for their server. A few were working other tables, but he found no trace of the lanky redhead named Tiffany. Or was it Tricia? Tina?

Shifting his attention back to Randi, he debated all of three seconds before heading in her direction. He needed another whisky and they needed to talk. He parked himself at the end of the bar, straddling the last open stool.

"What can I get you?" the bartender asked.

"Another Defiant and a chat with your boss."

Older than Britt by a good ten years and sporting Mr. Clean muscles, the bartender asked, "What do you need with Miss Shepherd?"

Britt held the man's gaze. He'd been in enough visual pissing matches to know how to hold his own. "A chat."

"It's okay, Grady." Randi patted the big man's shoulder. "I got this." She pulled a narrow rectangular bottle from a wide assortment on the counter and poured two fingers in one smooth move, then set the tumbler of amber liquid on a square napkin before sliding it toward Britt. "Virgil hasn't returned my phone call, so there's nothing for us to discuss. Unless you'd like to tell me what you know."

Even though she said the words softly, Britt felt them reverberate through the room. He didn't feel comfortable sharing his and Barbara's conversation. Randi should hear it from her mother's attorney. But with the weekend in front of them, who the hell knew when Virgil would get in touch.

"I didn't think so." Randi started to turn away.

"Wait."

"Change your mind?"

Grady continued to eyeball him from the opposite end of the bar, and several others seemed to be hovering in anticipation of his next words.

Britt stood, dropping a ten-dollar bill onto the bar. "Is there someplace we could talk in private?"

After a short hesitation, she finally nodded. "Give me a sec." She stopped next to the bartender and whispered something to him.

"This way," she said to Britt as she brushed by. "Feel free to bring your drink."

Grady's keep-your-hands-off-her glare followed them out of the bar.

If the bartender's distrust hadn't been focused on him, he would've admired the man's protectiveness of his employer. Feral loyalty like that didn't exist in the business world these days.

"Grady doesn't seem to care much for me."

"He's determined that no female on his watch will ever be molested by horny fools."

"Including his boss?"

"Especially his boss."

"Ex-military?"

"Marine. He still trains with them on occasion."

She zigzagged her way into the bowels of Blues, Brews, and Books before stopping at a locked door. Inserting a key, she led him into a spacious, clutter-free office. One side of the room contained a desk with a computer and printer and several mounds of neatly stacked papers. A utilitarian guest chair stood nearby.

The opposite side appeared to be a sort of temporary living space. A television was nestled in the corner, framed by a plush purple recliner and a long brown pleather sofa. Atop the sofa sat a folded blanket and plumped pillow. A door leading into what appeared to be a bathroom separated the living and workspace.

Did she live here?

Given the fact that she managed three businesses in one, it wouldn't surprise him if the answer were yes.

"Have a seat." Randi grabbed a ginger ale from a small refrigerator next to her desk. "Can I get you anything?"

Britt held up his glass. "Thanks, I'm good." Not sure which side of the room she'd invited him into, he waited for her to make the first move. She sat on the sofa, so he made himself at home in the purple contraption. The cushioned *rocking* recliner enveloped him in masculine heaven. Tension oozed from his body and a low moan tumbled out of his throat.

"It's a beautiful thing, isn't it?"

"Hmm-mmm. If it wasn't purple, I might try to steal this away."

"Eggplant."

He opened his eyes. *When had they closed?* "What?"

"The color is eggplant, not purple."

"Why do women insist on embellishing basic colors?"

"To annoy the male species, I suppose."

"Mission accomplished."

They shared a smile, and the impact of that brief connection made it seem as though one of his brothers had wrapped him in a bear hug. He was used to thinking of her on occasion, a byproduct of his Friday night visits and growing attraction. However, after their encounter yesterday, he'd thought of little else. He told himself that worry made him recall every word, every expression, every feeling from their time together.

However, Britt tried not to bullshit himself. Others, he could talk nonsense to all day to avoid an issue.

"What do you know, Britt?" Randi asked into the silence.

He knocked back the last of his drink, gathering his thoughts. "Didn't you think to track down Virgil at his office?"

"I spoke to his assistant this afternoon. She wouldn't share his whereabouts."

Britt sat forward, resting his forearms on his knees. He met her gaze. "Should you decide to sell the Shepherd property—in whole or in part—your mother promised me right of first refusal."

Her eyes flared, and some emotion he could not read tracked across her features.

"Barbara never said anything to you?"

She shifted her attention to the corner of the room, her jaw firming and her chest rising on a deep inhalation. "Is there anything else?"

Dammit, Barbara! What were you thinking?

Anger swelled inside Britt for the pain he was causing Randi. Although Barbara's life had been cut short far too early, she should have verbalized her intentions to her only daughter.

"Only that if you decide to sell the property and I want to buy it, the purchase price would be at twenty-five percent below fair market value."

"I see. Did you and my mother concoct any other limitations on my inheritance?"

"We didn't concoct anything. Barbara wanted the land preserved and she indicated you had no interest in it. When she suggested this arrangement, I assumed you were in agreement. As I understood it, the house and ten acres would be carved out for you. No conditions attached."

"How generous." She shot from the sofa and began pacing the small confines of the office-apartment. "Tell me something, Britt. Why would I agree to sell a thousand acres for below fair market value when I could get double that amount?"

Britt set his empty tumbler on a side table and rose. "Double? Is that wishful thinking? Or do you have an offer on the table?"

"I can tell you it's not wishful damn thinking."

"Who?"

"None of your business."

Dread seeded his thoughts. If Barbara failed to mention any of this to her daughter, Britt wondered what else she hadn't done as promised. What if she'd never gotten around to amending her will to include a right of first refusal? If she hadn't and Randi sold the property to a developer, the Steele-Shepherd pack would not survive the intrusion. Red wolves valued their privacy and were frightened of humans—more than any other wild canid.

He wouldn't feel settled about any of this until they heard from Virgil.

Britt studied Randi's profile. Beneath her bravado, he knew she was hurting. Knew she felt betrayed by her parent. A feeling Britt understood all too well.

Making his way over to her side, he said, "I'm sorry this has happened."

"If it's as you said, the apology isn't yours to give." She folded her arms across her middle. "It's simply another disappointment added to a very long list."

When it came to soothing emotions, especially feminine ones, Britt sucked at the task. He could never find the right words and made things worse when he tried. But seeing Randi weighed down by pain propelled him to make the attempt.

"Listen, I don't know why Barbara never mentioned her intentions. But what I do know is that she loved you."

She sent him an appreciative yet sad smile. "I know." Unfolding her arms, she headed to the door. "My mother's love for me has never been in doubt. Nor was my position in her pecking order." She opened the door. "Good night. I will track down Virgil tomorrow, even if I need to go to his house. I'll let you know what I find out."

Stopping beside her, he ached to soothe away the resignation now blanketing her features. It was far worse than the pain.

"Would you like company?"

Her gaze dipped to his mouth and lingered there for a heartbeat. Britt's body reacted to the small sign of her interest. He sensed the same yearning in her that he'd fought every day since walking through Triple B's doors. How long had he waited for her to send him one lingering glance? One I-caught-you-staring moment? One subtle brush of her body against his?

Of their own volition, his nostrils opened wider, searching for her scent, for something of her he could hold on to through the long hours of the night. He canted his head until he located the faint trace of jasmine…and feminine musk.

"What are you waiting for?" He whispered the words against her lips. Not touching, but close. Achingly close.

She opened her mouth and her ginger ale-laced breath fanned over his face. If she didn't kiss him in the next five seconds, he would take the decision out of her hands.

"For you to leave," she said.

Lust-taut muscles turned into slabs of concrete. "Leave?"

There, on her upturned face, he read her desire and her decision to ignore her body's needs.

Unable to simply walk away, Britt skimmed the underside of her chin with the back of his forefinger. Her skin was soft, smooth, satiny. More so than he'd ever envisioned.

"See you tomorrow."

As he strode away, Britt wanted to look back and see if she was watching him, or his rear, walk down the hallway. Something to tease her about later. In the end, he didn't give in to his curiosity, though he made sure her gaze traveled down his back to his ass.

CHAPTER SEVEN

RANDI NEVER MADE IT TO Britt's on Saturday. It took her most of the day to track down Virgil. By noon, she'd made up her mind the lawyer was avoiding her on purpose. The thought cramped her stomach for hours. If he was dodging her attempts to speak with him about her mother's will, he must have bad news.

Through word of mouth, she finally located him at his gun club. Not out on the range, but gambling and drinking in one of the back rooms of the lodge. From the smell emanating from his disheveled body, she'd bet this was where he'd been holed up for the past few days.

It took her the rest of the afternoon and part of the evening to sober him up enough to have a competent conversation.

"Would you like another cup of coffee?"

"Hell, no." Sitting at his kitchen table, Virgil grasped his head with both hands. "Can we do this tomorrow?"

"Hell, no." Randi pushed away from the wall where she'd been lounging, waiting for the semblance of a clear mind to appear. "It's well past time I heard the details of Mom's will. And I'm not letting you out of my sight until you read me the contents."

"Didn't we discuss this already?"

"No. At the funeral all we talked about was setting up a meeting."

He made a snuffling sound. "Why'd you wait so long to contact me?"

The pounding in Randi's temple expanded to her left eye. If she didn't fear going to hell, she would curse her mother up one side of her coffin and down the other.

"Are you serious? Did you already forget how I had to haul your sorry hide out of that gambling cave today?"

Red mottled the area near his receding hairline, and his gaze dropped to the tabletop. "Dammit, Miranda. I don't even know if I have the paperwork here. More than likely it's at my office."

"Then we'll take a ride to your office." Randi poked her head into Virgil's refrigerator to find him something to eat. A half-eaten sandwich partially wrapped in Big Abe's Deli paper, three dill pickles in a jar, a full bottle of ketchup, a slice of cheddar cheese, and five large eggs. She'd worked with worse. "After you eat."

Drawing what she needed from the fridge, she piled everything onto the counter.

"What are you doing?"

"Making an omelet."

Randi pulled thin slices of ham from the leftover sandwich and tore them into pieces before dropping the tortured mess into a bowl of egg whites and yolks. Then she speared a pickle and chopped it into cubes. They joined the ham and eggs, along with the cheese.

"That's not like any omelet I've ever seen."

"That's because you pollute your body with junk food. This is gourmet."

"Putting pickles in my omelet is considered gourmet?"

"Don't forget the ham."

"I'll pass, thank you."

"We're not leaving until you put something into your stomach. And this little delicacy is all we've got."

"No wonder you're not married yet," he grumbled. "Bossy as all get-out."

"Virgil, my dear. You have yet to see my bossy side."

"What do you call shoving that gourmet crap down my throat?"

"Friendly fire. If I were being bossy, you would be making your own meal."

Virgil attacked the meal with the gusto of a man who'd lived off pretzels and hard liquor for several days. The omelet barely made one circle in his mouth before he swallowed. Just as well. Who knew if the concoction was even palatable? She sure as heck hadn't sampled the dish before serving it.

As it turned out, Virgil had her mom's will buried on the desk in his home office. The moment he put his glasses on, the disheveled drunkard transformed into a polished attorney. He read the document, word for word, pausing at moments to explain a difficult clause or answer an unasked question.

For thirty minutes, Randi sat in surreal disbelief, brought on by both Virgil's transformation and her mother's wishes. She walked away, numb and unsure of her next move.

The next morning, armed with a leaded, Grande vanilla latte, Randi idled in front of Britt's cabin. She hated visiting him on Sunday, but she wanted to get this business over with so they could both move on. She hoped he was a morning person.

A scattering of large, thick-branched trees encircled Britt's one-story, no-frills cabin. The large logs appeared hand-hewn, old, imperfect. Not so with many of the new log homes popping up all over the Blue Ridge Mountains. Many looked like replicas of their neighbors, assembled out of a box like a paint-by-number portrait, replete with a butt-ugly green metal roof and natural stained wood from corner to corner to corner to corner.

Few had character like this cabin. This cabin had seen decades of harsh winds, brutal sun, and driving rain. It had character and had obviously been looked after by caring owners over the years. Not one broken window or termite-infested log. Not one overgrown weed in the yard. The rustic cabin suited Britt. Both were rugged, sturdy, pleasing to the eye.

She strode up the two steps to knock on his screen door. Nothing. Opening the door, she rapped her knuckles on the wood panel. Still nothing.

Her gaze dropped to the doorknob. She hesitated only a moment before curling her fingers around the iron knob and twisting. Locked. A stream of relieved breath slipped between her lips. What would she have done if it had opened? Walked inside his home, nosing into each room until she found him? What if he'd been in bed? Or worse, the shower?

An image of Britt's big naked body standing beneath a shower spray misted her vision. Steam billowing all around him. His dark blond hair almost black when wet. Droplets sliding down his broad chest, his hard stomach, his long, thick...Randi shook her head, blasting away the moment. She couldn't be distracted by hot images of Britt during their talk. She'd never be able to get an intelligible word out.

Before she thought the worst of his silence, Randi decided to check around back. Maybe he was working on something and didn't hear her drive up. Like chopping wood for the winter. Shirtless. Sweaty. *Gah!* She hopped off the porch and quick-walked around the side of the house.

What on earth was happening to her? She had admired his good looks before—what woman in her bar hadn't? But never had she been plagued by sensual fantasies of the man. Maybe she needed more coffee. She took a big swig, pulling at the sippy hole like a babe at her mama's teat.

Her search behind the cabin revealed no half-naked bear of a man, or otherwise. Returning to the front porch, she sat in one of the Adirondack chairs to wait him out. He was either ignoring her, had wandered off into the woods, or someone had picked him up. She would sit here and check her e-mail while enjoying the rest of her latte until he emerged.

She prayed he wouldn't arrive with a girlfriend. Talk about awkward. In all the weeks he'd been visiting her bar, she'd never seen him come in or leave with a woman. Many had made themselves comfortable at his table, especially if he was accompanied by one or more of his brothers or male cousins. Few single women could resist such a tempting buffet of masculinity.

A light breeze tickled the fine hairs on her cheeks. Randi lifted her nose to the wind like a dog tracking a curious scent. Calm rushed over her, burrowing past the stress and heartache to open a path to her senses. The shuffle of a thousand leaves reached her ear as well as the laser gun song of a lone cardinal in the distance. The scent of loamy damp soil hung in the air like an invisible fog. An early June sun warmed her eyelids.

Several minutes filtered by before she broke free of her trancelike state. She sipped her latte while scanning her e-mail. Five messages—two e-newsletters, one e-mail from Aunt Sharon filling her in on the antique clock she found for Randi's coffee shop, one social media notification, and one letter from a Russian gentleman in need of a good, obedient wife.

She deleted all but Aunt Sharon's and debated whether or not to respond. Since her sister's passing, Aunt Sharon had made it her mission to make sure Randi didn't feel lonely. If more than a few days went by without her hearing from Randi, her aunt would send her an e-mail or text or call or stop by.

Randi appreciated the gesture, but her aunt had to know that her sister and niece hadn't been close. Why she thought Randi would feel lonely was a mystery. She'd been on her own for years. Her mother's passing had changed nothing when it came to Randi's day-to-day activities. People surrounded her every day, all day.

Hitting Reply, Randi began composing a response. She and her aunt had a close relationship. More of a friendship these days than anything else. No one could match Sharon's energy or giving nature. Everyone loved and respected her. As they had Randi's mother, but for entirely different reasons.

The cursor on her phone blinked a silent, challenging rhythm. A memory of her and her mother nursing a small litter of orphaned red fox surfaced. The care with which her mother had tended the month-old kits, and how she'd instructed a seven-year-old Randi not to cuddle the babies because they would be released back in the wild, rose in Randi's memory with perfect clarity.

An ache started deep in her throat, growing thicker and taller with each breath. She closed her eyes and fought back the nostalgia. For every precious moment with her mother, Randi had ten instances of neglect and heartache.

When she opened her eyes, she spotted a figure emerging from the tree line. *Britt.* Dressed in black running shorts and a white T-shirt, he jogged toward her, muscles bunching and stretching. Sweat soaked his shirt and hair, and his face glistened from his exertions.

Randi's breath stopped flowing through her lungs, her windpipe, her nose. The breeze buffeted her unblinking eyes, drying them out. Foreign cravings stirred low in her, seeking the source of their awakening.

The second his gaze connected with hers, his steady gait hitched before slowing to an unhurried stroll. He used the dry end of his T-shirt to mop the moisture from his face. The move revealed the most amazing abs. Britt Steele was ripped. Not a single ounce of fat.

Randi blinked several times to unstick her eyelids and sucked in her middle. She drank far too many lattes and ate way too much pasta for the same to be said about her body. What she wouldn't give to run her fingertips over such perfection, especially the long trail of hair that disappeared beneath his shorts.

The T-shirt dropped back in place, and Randi rose to greet him. "Good morning, Britt. I'm sorry—"

"Have a seat." He climbed the stairs. "I'll be back in ten minutes." Unlocking the door, he strode inside. The screen slammed shut. The interior door stood wide open.

Randi blinked. *What the heck?* She stared at the screen door, cocking her head to listen. Comprehension dawned, along with irritation. Could he not have postponed his shower until after she'd left? She'd already lost thirty minutes waiting on him. For most people, a half hour was a blip of time. For her, it was a trip to the grocery store or a load of laundry or an oil change. All the things she had to pack into her Sunday that she couldn't do during the week.

She contemplated storming inside after him, but that would mean coming into contact with a nude, wet Britt. She contemplated harder. And harder.

"Arghh!" Randi plopped back in her chair, her normal boldness failing her on an epic level. She'd already mooned the man. She couldn't bring herself to shock him into a heart attack.

By the time she'd tapped out a response to Aunt Sharon and answered a new text from Kris McKay, Britt rejoined her, wearing a gray tee and jeans and carrying a bottle of water, his feet bare.

Taking the seat beside her, he set his water on the wide, flat arm of his chair. "Good morning."

Tension drained from her shoulders, though an anticipatory wariness remained. "Did you have a nice shower?"

"Yes." He lifted the water bottle to his mouth, keeping his gaze on the distant landscape. "What can I do for you, Randi?"

"I've brought news about my mother's will."

"As I recall, you promised that information yesterday."

"I know, and I'm sorry. It took me all day to track down Virgil, then I had to sober him up."

He glanced down at her hand. "Phone broke?"

"No, but I left your card at the office."

"Do you have Carlie Beth programmed into that smart machine of yours?"

Randi's jaw locked. He'd found the gap in her logic in less than ten seconds. She tried to tell herself that she didn't want to further involve Carlie Beth by asking her for Britt's number. But deep down she comprehended that avoidance was her main motivator.

What would it have been like to speak with him on the phone? His deep, calm voice flowing into her ear. Close. Intimate. Tantalizing.

"What reason should I have given Carlie Beth for wanting your number?"

"None at all. If she was unsure, she could have cleared it with me."

"Men might work that way, but there's no way I could have called Carlie Beth and asked for your number without some sort of explanation. If you and I'd had a friendlier association, she might not have thought it strange. But serving you drinks doesn't buy me anything more personal than a drive-by hello."

"What's the worst that could have happened?" His brown eyes held hers. "Carlie Beth might get the wrong idea about your intentions? Maybe think you're infatuated with me?"

Try as she might, Randi could not stop the blush from burning up her face. Again.

Rather than break his visual hold though, she held tight. Let him make of her fiery cheeks what he would. He couldn't have known what direction her imagination had taken her these past few days. Even if he had, he'd shown little interest in her.

Except for that brief caress in her office the other day.

"I attempted to apologize for not stopping by yesterday, but you seemed more interested in running inside."

His full lips curved into the slightest smile before he picked up his water and took a drink. "I think better when I'm not covered in sweat."

The statement landed between them like a jumbo jet taxiing down Main Street. What would it be like to see this calm, controlled, elusive man come unhinged by pleasure? Unable to think, unable to breathe, unable to stop.

Randi cleared her throat. "Good to know. Now, how about we get to what I came here to discuss?"

"I'm all ears."

"In my office, you mentioned that Mom had offered to put a right of first refusal in her will for you if I decide to sell the property."

"That's correct."

"Virgil read Mom's will to me, word for word." She took a fortifying breath. "There's nothing in there memorializing such an agreement. The property is mine to do with as I like."

"Virgil read it wrong." The insane comment was out before Britt had time to think about it. But what other reason could there be? Barbara had been the one to propose the clause. Had even badgered him until he'd agreed.

"For the red wolves," she'd said. *"My daughter wants nothing to do with this land. She'll sell it to the highest bidder. You and I both know that won't be an organization who will give a rat's ass about those wolves."*

So he'd agreed, knowing that even at twenty-five percent below fair market value the property would put him so deeply into debt that he'd have to put in eighty-hour weeks for the rest of his life in order to make ends meet.

"No, he didn't," she said in an even voice.

"He must have, Randi. There's no other explanation. Barbara was very clear to me about her wishes."

Anger sparked in her green eyes. "Then she either

changed her mind, or never got around to amending her will."

"I want to see it."

"See what?"

"Barbara's will."

"You think I'm lying?"

"No. But I don't trust that drunken bastard's reading skills."

"Neither did I. That's why I asked for a copy."

Fear splintered his gut. Barbara's mistake would mean the end of the Steele-Shepherd pack. A land-hungry developer or a group of unscrupulous game hunters would wipe them out. Or scatter them across the countryside, where landowners mistaking them for coyotes would peg them off. All because a two-sentence wish never got added to a fucking document.

He shot out of his chair, unable to sit still any longer. Options thundered through his mind like a nonstop locomotive. He dismissed each one as fast as they arrived. As a general tradesman, he made good money because of his versatility. He refurbished kitchens and bathrooms. Built decks and garages. Tracked down electrical problems and waterline leaks. And even changed a porch lightbulb when old Mrs. Zigfield couldn't reach the outlet. That one he'd done pro bono.

But he didn't make enough to win a bidding war. And there would be one.

He sure as hell wasn't asking his baby brother to spot him the dough.

"Would you consider selling to me anyway?"

Silence.

Facing her, he noted the tension radiating along her brow line and the ridge of her shoulders. Her hands gripped each other in a hold that scattered every ounce of blood from her skin, leaving skeletal white fingers behind. She stared at him, but he didn't think she really saw him. It was as if she looked inward, searching.

"Randi?"

Her eyes fluttered until they refocused on him. Regret fractured the air between them, then she stomped out the last of his hope. "You're welcome to make an offer."

Glancing away, he fought to control the low quakes of desperation, of helplessness, deep in his gut. "What about half?"

"Half of what?"

"Half to me and half to whomever you have lined up?"

"Who said I had anyone lined up?"

"You indicated as much earlier. Besides, why else would you go against your mother's wishes? Someone has offered you a deal too sweet to pass up."

Her squared shoulders lost their stiffness, curling inward like a protective shield. "I think it's time for me to go." She dug into her purse and pulled out a stack of papers. "Here, read for yourself."

Britt took the papers. "What's this?"

"A copy of my mother's will. I sense you don't fully trust my word on this. Normally, I wouldn't care a flying fig. But, in this case, I believe you deserve to see for yourself."

Unfolding the papers, Britt scanned the lines of legal jargon until he reached the clause that discussed the property. Each word ripped at him like the cutters of a chain saw tearing through wood.

Barbara hadn't kept her word. Her land, the wolves— none of it was protected.

When he lifted his eyes, the world around him blurred into one indistinct background. Dammit, why hadn't he seen this coming? Barbara had been scatterbrained at times, jumping from one project to the next. But it had never occurred to him that she would leave something this important for another day.

He held out the papers for Randi, but she was gone. A door slammed in the distance, and he spotted her wrapping a seatbelt across her chest. Jogging down the steps, he caught up with her before she could turn the ignition.

"Where are you going?"

"Home. Why?"

Britt almost said, "There's something I'd like to show you." But he couldn't take her to the wolves. The fewer people who knew about them, the better. Besides, given her disinterest in her mother's environmental causes, he doubted she would appreciate the rare treat, or grasp the importance of his work. Like so many others.

The Jeep's engine snarled to life and the fan pushed a wave of cool air out the open driver's side window. Randi's unique scent floated on the current, tunneling into his senses. He could breathe her in all day and never tire of her scent. Bold woman mixed with a hint of jasmine.

"I'd like to try and persuade you to hold off on selling your property."

"For how long?"

Britt hedged. "Until I can raise the funds to meet your asking price."

"From your brother?"

Jonah's billions were no secret in Steele Ridge. His brother's wealth had saved the town when it was on the brink of bankruptcy. But it still rankled that she thought he needed to ask his little brother for money.

Britt considered the potential price tag for the Shepherd property and had to concede Jonah might be his only option if he wanted to save the wolves. He just couldn't stomach the asking, the owing, or the debt that would go far deeper than financial. Who knew? He might have a miracle still left up his sleeve.

"No, I'll be doing this on my own."

"I don't have that kind of time." Regret crept into her expressive eyes. "I'm sorry." She began backing up.

Her choice of words puzzled him. Up to this point, he'd assumed her decision to sell had more to do with disinterest and the need to move on.

"What kind of time do you have?"

The vehicle slammed to a halt. "Pardon?"

"Time. How much can you give me?"

She stared at him a moment before asking in a low voice, "Why do you want this land so badly?"

Sweat pebbled between his shoulder blades. How could he explain his interest without giving up the wolves? An explanation she would believe. He could tell her that it would make a nice, contiguous addition to the ten thousand acres of Steele Conservation Area, but he didn't think that would earn him any extra time points. So he stuck with the truth.

"Keeping the land in its current, natural state was important to Barbara. After all she's done for me—did for me, I owe it to her to preserve what she loved."

Shifting her attention to the distant tree line, she gripped the steering wheel as if it were the only thing grounding her in place. Or maybe it was a handy substitute for his neck.

"You have until the end of this week." She stabbed him with a warning look. "No more."

Britt's heart plummeted like the ever-changing temperatures on Mt. Everest.

Five days.

That was all the time he had to develop a relocation plan for the wolves. He'd been putting away every cent he could for the past decade and had managed to save a respectable amount. But it wasn't anywhere close to what he needed to purchase Randi's acreage.

So relocation was the only answer.

Britt's fingers curled into a tight fist and he lowered his head as frustration and sorrow welled up in him. The wolves had finally found a safe haven, one he and Barbara would have protected for years to come.

Now they had to be uprooted just when this batch of pups had begun to explore their surroundings. He would have to move them farther inside the conservation area and hope they would accept their new home. Which meant he'd have to tell Jonah.

Although the family called the large tract of land a

conservation area, no long-term plans had been developed, or even discussed. The family had been focused first on bailing out the town, then on building a world-class training facility. No one had yet given a thought to the excess acreage, except Britt.

"Thank you."

She nodded and backed down the drive.

The jagged stones beneath his bare feet began to register. He stepped off the gravel drive and slid his soles across the grass before heading back inside his cabin. Doing a quick calculation in his head, he figured he had at least three to four weeks, maybe a little more, before the paperwork was executed and the new owner took possession. It would have to be enough.

Five days to plan, three weeks to implement. Months to worry. Wolves had a mind of their own. There was no guarantee that they wouldn't find their way back to the edge of Shepherd land, to the farmland they used as a corridor for hunting. To potential danger.

CHAPTER EIGHT

"WHEN DID YOU EAT LAST?" Aunt Sharon gave Randi a fierce hug upon her arrival.

"Probably breakfast." Although Randi couldn't actually recall what she might have shoved down her throat before heading off to speak with Britt. Maybe nothing.

"Have a seat while I heat up a bowl of chicken noodle soup." She closed the front door. "I made it yesterday, so it'll be good and fermented."

Auntie never served soup, stews, or chili the same day she cooked the dishes. She believed they tasted their best after a day or two of *fermenting*. Randi had to agree with her, but she wished her aunt would use a different word so it didn't sound like a lab experiment, with her niece as the guinea pig. Lord knew Auntie liked to mix things up with her recipes.

"Don't go to any trouble, Auntie. I'm really not hungry."

"What nonsense!" Auntie flapped her hand in the air. "With Glen gone and the kids scattered all over God's green earth, you're the only one nearby I can dote on. Now, turn on the TV. *Wheel of Fortune*'s on in fifteen minutes."

Randi groaned. *Wheel of Fortune* turned her aunt into a screeching madwoman. Shouting out words and nonsensical phrases until she hit on the right combination. Then she crowed like a five-year-old for having beaten her unfortunate opponent to the finish line. Lord forgive anyone who solved the puzzle before her aunt.

The only time Randi had ever received her aunt's death stare had been the time she'd called out the winning puzzle first. She'd never made that mistake again.

Grabbing the remote, Randi hit the power button, then panned through the guide until she found the right channel. Directive accomplished, she joined her aunt in the kitchen to search for her favorite cookies.

Auntie made the best oatmeal and raisin cookies in all of Haywood County. Soft and moist and never-ending. Raisins on their own—disgusting. Raisins in oatmeal cookies—delish.

She went straight for the mouse-shaped ceramic jar smiling down from the refrigerator top. The mouse's blue chef's hat and red apron appeared as good as new. Not a single chip anywhere.

Drawing it down, she peered inside. Nothing. Disappointment made her shoulders sag. Replacing the lid, she set the jar back in place.

A low laugh sounded behind her.

"What's so funny?"

"Thirty years old, and you still go right for the Jerry jar."

As in the Tom and Jerry cartoon featuring a wily mouse forever on the run from the not-so-witty cat. Appropriate, given the number of greedy hands that had pounced on the cookie jar.

"Creature of habit. Besides, your cookies are the best."

Auntie nodded to a large Tupperware-type bowl on the counter. "I made two dozen oatmeal to take to the children's ward at the hospital. Help yourself to a couple."

Randi's mouth watered at the mere thought of fresh-baked cookies. "No thanks, Auntie. I'm not going to steal treats from sick kids." She grinned. "No matter how much I'd like to."

"Such a good, unselfish child." Auntie set a steaming bowl of soup on the table. "If it'll make you feel less guilty, I'll make up another batch tomorrow before I take it over."

"You're too good to me. And your cookies are too yummy to pass up." She picked two cookies from the plastic container, then another three before closing the lid. A nicer person would have decided against snatching those last three, but not Randi. If not for her, the kids would've only gotten two dozen cookies to share. Now they were going to get more. No guilt at all.

Randi placed the cookies next to her bowl, then unwound the twist tie holding the cracker bag together. She crumbled two crackers into her chicken noodle soup and stirred them around before scooping a big spoonful into her mouth.

After the third bite, Randi's eyes started watering and her mouth burned. "Auntie," she croaked out. "Have you been experimenting again?"

"Why, yes. I added pepper jack cheese to make it pop." She dried her hands on a hand towel. "Do you like?"

Her aunt's hopeful smile forced Randi to check her reply. Never in a million years would she hurt this woman's feelings. Instead, she winked. "Popping accomplished." She stood and dove for the refrigerator. "A tall glass of milk will complement the soup nicely."

Auntie's eyes danced with mirth. "Help yourself, dear."

Five minutes later, the soup bowl and glass of milk sat empty, and Randi was busy blowing her nose. Adding the cheese turned out to be a nice touch—after Randi got over the initial shock. She actually loved spicy food, but it wreaked havoc on her sinuses.

"Thanks, Auntie. That hit the spot."

"Not too spicy?"

"No, ma'am." When Randi made to clear her place, Auntie waved her off, grabbing the dishes herself.

"Did you have something on your mind?" Auntie asked. "Or did you come over to keep an old woman company?"

"Fifty-eight isn't old."

"Someone should tell my body that in the morning." She sent Randi a sideways glance. "And you didn't answer my question."

"A little of both, I suppose." Randi broke off a section of her cookie and held it beneath her nose. When she detected no foreign matter, she shoved it into her mouth. "Hmm. Delicious."

Auntie slid into the chair across from her. "What's bothering you so much to make you run here for an ear and a cookie?"

"Mom's will."

"What about it?"

"Did she ever talk to you about the details?"

"Of course, we shared everything." Auntie frowned. "Has Virgil not met with you yet?"

"Yesterday." Randi decided to spare her aunt the play-by-play. "Do you recall Mom ever mentioning Britt Steele?"

Auntie sat back. She studied Randi's face long enough to set her nerves on edge. "She did. Quite often, in fact. Why?"

"A few days ago, Britt told me that Mom promised him right of first refusal on the property should I wish to sell." Randi waited for her aunt's acknowledgment or outrage. She got neither reaction. "But Mom's will made no mention of such an agreement."

Auntie shook her head in disgust. "Barbara never liked dealing with 'tedious paperwork.' Doesn't surprise me that she left this undone. Though it does disappoint."

"So it is true."

"I'm afraid so." Auntie reached across the table and grasped Randi's hand. "She thought you'd fallen out of love with the place, dear. Sometime last year she told me she'd tried to entice you out for a hike during one of your rare visits, but you had no interest in it. Not long after that she made the proposal to Britt Steele."

Randi recalled the incident. Her mother had invited her over for Easter brunch, which had been unusual, in and of itself, because Barbara Shepherd had never been much of a cook. If a hot meal had made its way to the table, she'd had her father to thank for the occasion.

But the real shocker had been her mother's confession about missing her and wishing they could spend more time together. Excited but wary, Randi had arrived on her mom's doorstep with a bottle of her restaurant's best wine and a box of her mom's favorite candy. Graham crackers loaded with melted marshmallow and a layer of creamy caramel—rich milk chocolate blanketed the entire concoction, creating chocolatey s'mores.

The moment her mother answered the door with a familiar vacant, harried expression, Randi had known their makeup luncheon had been sacrificed to the newest injured animal or environmental catastrophe. She'd ushered Randi into the house with instructions on when to take the meatless lasagna out of the oven. It was then her mother had encouraged her to go for a hike and explore her old haunts.

However, the only thing Randi had been able to decipher in those few minutes of rambling explanations was...*again*. She'd allowed her mother's persuasive words to work their way into her heart until she'd yearned for reconciliation. But her mother had let her down once more.

Barbara had promised to be back in two hours. Randi had waited four, then she'd never returned.

"The story's a little more complicated than what Mom told you."

"So you're not going to sell?"

For a stomach-churning moment, Randi wondered if she would keep the property if her circumstances weren't what they were. She honestly didn't know. Blues, Brews, and Books was her life now. The bar demanded her every spare minute. How would she keep things afloat there if issues at Sagebrook kept pulling her away?

"I can't manage both."

"Then sell the property to Britt Steele and be done with it."

"According to Britt, Mom promised him twenty-five percent below fair market value."

"Now that does seem generous."

"Agreed." Randi pressed the palm of her hands over her eyes. "I can't figure out why she wanted him to have the property so badly."

"Did you ask Britt?"

Randi's palms moved to her temples. Her fingers cradled her skull. "He said something about Mom wanting to make sure the land was preserved in its current state."

"Even at twenty-five percent below fair market value, you'll be getting a nice nest egg."

"If he had the money—which he doesn't. I'm sure when he agreed to this arrangement, Britt expected to have another decade or two to save up."

"Why save up when you have a billionaire in your pocket?"

"He has no interest in asking his brother for money." Something Randi found intriguing. He didn't want to be indebted to his younger brother. Even though it would be a hundred times harder, he preferred to raise the funds on his own. She tried not to admire his determination, but how could she not?

"Since Barbara failed to put their agreement in writing, there's nothing preventing you from signing with the highest bidder."

"Even if it means going against Mom's wishes?"

"Wheel. Of. Foortuune."

Auntie stood, hooking a finger beneath Randi's chin and lifted. "I loved your mother dearly, but she's gone. Now it's up to you to clean up the mess she left behind. The property is yours."

CHAPTER NINE

BRITT STORMED OUT OF HIGHLAND Bank & Trust located on the corner of Main and Buckner Streets. Because of the noon hour, he'd had to park several blocks away. After the meeting he'd just had, he welcomed the distance.

Although he'd held little hope for a better outcome, he still steamed at being denied the size of loan he would need in order to purchase the Shepherd property. Especially when the word came down from Harrison Clinewater. The guy had been an arrogant prick in high school, and time had not improved the silver-spooned shit.

If Mrs. Grafton hadn't been sitting ten feet away, Britt would have leaned across Clinewater's desk and reminded him of the time he'd locked him inside the music teacher's supply closet. In his skivvies.

That's what he got for stealing Reid's jeans out of his gym locker during the kid's first week as a freshman. Britt's jaw hardened at the long-ago memory. Clinewater had gotten off lucky. He should have thrown Reid's tormentor into the closet bare-ass naked.

Caught up in his thoughts, he almost missed today's chalkboard message outside the Mad Batter Bakery.

Brothers are like devil's food cake. Rich, devilish, steadfast.

Britt's innards did an X Games-worthy triple

backflip. Glancing around, he searched for Jeanine Jennings, baker's assistant and author of the eerily prophetic chalkboard signs.

When the messages had started appearing twenty years ago, Britt hadn't believed all the hubbub. Superstitious people, believers in ghosts, and mob squads all had one thing in common—gullibility. One whisper in their ear, and they took off like a lightning bolt. Reason be damned.

After a few people he trusted got Jeanined, Britt had become a believer, but this was the first time she'd set her prophetic chalk stick on him.

"Whoa!" a guy said, sidestepping the two-hundred-pound steamroller.

"Sorry, man—" Britt looked up to find his brother Grif. "Why the hell are you standing in the middle of the sidewalk?"

Grif raised an are-you-kidding-me brow. "Where are you stomping off to?"

Britt scrubbed a hand down his face. "I have a job in Maggie Valley."

"What's going on? Something's obviously distracting you."

"Nothing a few hours of hard labor won't cure."

"If you need to talk something through, let me know. I'm damned good at finding solutions to issues."

His brother had earned such bragging rights. He represented some of the most successful, wealthiest names in sports. He'd fought for them at the boardroom table, wiped drool from their drunken mouths, and bailed them out of jail for racing their new hotrod down a California interstate. Even so, Britt had no idea where he'd even begin explaining this situation with Randi, so he fell back on his best tool—silence.

A shade of disappointment crossed his brother's face, but Grif knew him better than most and shrugged it off. "Got time for a bite to eat?"

Britt checked the time. "Sure."

Grif jabbed a thumb over his shoulder. "This place is as good as any."

Britt stared at the stenciled logo on the window, not believing his eyes.

Blues, Brews, and Books Restaurant and Bar.

How the hell had he wound up here? He glanced down Main, looking for his truck. There it sat, opposite him, on the same side of the street as the bank. Not only had he crossed the street, he'd gone a half block farther than needed.

A large hand waved in front of his face. "Yo, bro. This okay?"

"Big Abe's Deli down the way might be better. I've only got thirty minutes."

"The acoustics in that place suck. You can't hear the person sitting across from you." Grif motioned for him to follow. "Come on, we'll ask them to put a rush on our order."

Tension rippled across Britt's shoulders as he stepped inside. He did a quick inspection of the tables and behind the bar. No beautiful blonde in sight. His muscles relaxed enough for him to slide into a corner booth.

"Hey, handsome, what can I get you to drink?"

Grif smiled in surprise. "I didn't know you were helping Randi out today."

Carlie Beth set down two ice waters and gave Grif a quick hello kiss, then came around the table to hug Britt. "What are you boys up to today?"

"Lunch." Britt glanced at his phone clock again. "Any chance I can get out of here in twenty-five minutes?"

"No problem." She pulled a notepad from her apron pocket and flipped it open. "Know what you want?"

"Cheeseburger, medium rare. Everything but onions."

"Anything to drink?"

"I'll stick with the water."

"Make it a double," Grif said.

"Alrighty. I'll be back in ten with your order."

Both he and Grif followed Carlie Beth's progress

across the room. Where Randi seemed to prefer sleek, skinny jeans and tight-fitting tee, Carlie Beth favored loose clothing and steel-toe boots. Blonde versus strawberry blonde. Short versus tall. The two were opposites in so many ways, except their unwavering friendship.

"Quite the catch, that one."

Grif shook his head and sat back. "Who knew it would be possible to fall in love with a woman fourteen years after a one-night stand?"

"Got me. I haven't managed to do it once in thirty-four years."

"You'll find your Carlie Beth."

Britt scanned the bar again. "I'm not worried about it." He melted back into the booth. "How are things at city hall?"

"Infuriating as hell. I assumed government politics wouldn't be that much different than sports politics. Everyone wants something. It would just be a matter of figuring out those wants and using them to my advantage."

"Not so cut-and-dry, I take it?"

"I swear, they must supply politicians with a regular dose of crazy pills. There's no anticipating what strange bullshit they'll come up with during a council meeting." Grif began spinning the water in his glass, round and round and round. "I can spend hours, *days*, before a meeting talking to each of them, laying out my plan and getting their nods of approval. Then, *voilà*! They throw out some crazy shit that no sane person could anticipate, and expect me to have a logical answer. That I can come up with one probably says something about me that I don't want to explore."

"Probably all those years of keeping hacker Jonah out of trouble. Excellent training ground."

"Anyone who willingly goes into this kind of public service must be half batty. Every day, I'm fielding dozens of constituent complaints, some legit, some not.

But they all have one thing in common—they're impossible to make happy." He stopped swirling his water. "It's enough to drive a man to knitting."

Britt raised a brow.

"You're right. Nothing's that bad. Maybe crossword puzzles."

"Amen, bro."

Britt stared down at the black line of God knew what embedded beneath his fingernails. No amount of Lava soap could remove the signs of manual labor from his hands. "Will you stay?"

Grif had spent the past decade in California as a high-performing sports agent. He'd made multimillion-dollar deals and rubbed elbows with the biggest names in sports. And if that wasn't impressive enough, the overachiever had earned his bachelor's degree in accounting and an MBA in three years.

After Jonah had saved the town, he'd wrangled Grif into helping him get Steele Ridge back on its feet, financially. Grif had agreed to become the city manager, a decision that still puzzled Britt.

Had his brother gotten tired of the high life and yearned for a slower pace? Had something gone wrong and the city hall gig had come at the right time? Or had Grif's generosity simply been the pull of familial bonds?

Britt might never learn the reason behind Grif's return. However, seeing the way his brother's eyes followed Carlie Beth around the room, it was clear why he stayed.

"We're still working through the logistics. Commuting back and forth from Los Angeles is exhausting as hell and moving Carlie Beth's forge to California is out of the question." Grif crunched a cube of ice. "Then there's the question of whether or not we should uproot Aubrey."

"My buddy Deke transferred here in the fifth grade. Tough in the beginning, but he adapted."

"If anyone could adapt, Aubrey could. No one is immune to her sweet heart."

"It'll work out."

"Here you are, boys." Carlie Beth slid a plate first in front of Britt, then Grif. "Ketchup's on the table. Can I get you anything else?"

"No, thanks," they said in unison.

"Enjoy your burgers. Jessica's going to take over from here."

"Are you headed to the forge?" Grif asked.

"No, Grady's wife fell and broke her hip. He's on his way to the hospital." She untied the short apron from around her hips. "Several shipments arrived today. I'm going to help Randi in the stockroom for a while."

"Are there no other guys here?" Britt asked.

Carlie Beth smiled. "You do know that I move heavy iron pieces around all day long, right?"

Britt's gaze drifted toward the bar, and beyond, to where he assumed the stockroom would be located. An image of Randi hefting heavy boxes onto narrow shelves left him feeling uneasy. A ridiculous reaction given she'd likely performed such labor many times before. She didn't strike him as the type of woman who played the I'll-break-a-nail card.

"Keep my seat warm, will you, Carlie Beth?"

"Sure. Where are you going?"

"To help Randi."

"What about your burger?"

"I'll eat it when I get back."

"But it'll be cold."

"Nothing a thirty-second nuke can't handle."

He wound his way deeper into Randi's domain, navigating on instinct and a familiar pull he always experienced when in her vicinity. Easing down a narrow hallway, he caught the faint sound of clinking glass. He spotted a half-opened door down the way. Light fanned through the opening, spotlighting the opposite wall and wooden floor planks. A shadow moved from inside, back and forth, forth and back.

Not wanting to startle whomever was inside, he

paused in the doorway to see if he'd found his quarry. Dressed in bootcut jeans and a white V-neck tee, Randi Shepherd bent over to pick up one of the numerous boxes lined up by the back door. Britt decided she looked amazing from all directions—north, south, east, and west.

"Bend with your knees."

The box she was in the process of lifting rattled, and she set it back down with a clank.

"What are you doing here?"

Her long dark-blond hair was somewhat tamed in one of those messy ponytail bun things women liked to wear. The style revealed her slender neck, wide cheekbones, and delicate jawline. Dangly gold earrings glinted in the fluorescent light, and olive-green hiking shoes capped off her ensemble. She was a tempting combination of feminine tomboy. The kind a man like him wouldn't fear breaking in half or mussing up.

"Having lunch with my brother."

She brushed loose strands of hair off her forehead, leaving a small streak of dirt above her right eyebrow. Britt ached to brush away the smudge with his thumb and soothe the area with a long line of soft kisses. Would she gasp and smack the shit out of him? Or would she tremble and whisper *more*?

"Is there something I can do for you? Or were you planning to stuff me in my own cooler?"

"Nothing so hypothermic." He shoved his hands into his jean pockets. "I understand Grady's not here. Thought I'd give you a hand."

"You want to help me? Why?"

"Despite our current predicament, I've nothing against you, Randi. I've been in the bar and coffee shop many times, and you're always here, working. You're going at it as hard as anyone else. Harder, actually." The more he spoke the wider her eyes got. *Shit.* He'd said far too much. But he wasn't done. More words were forming on his tongue. Words he hoped would set her at ease and release the tension knotting his guts. "Even the strongest need help, from time to time."

Instead of making things right between them, he'd managed to shock her into speechlessness. *Brilliant, Steele. Truly your best one-liner with a woman yet. Freaking moron.*

An awkward silence filled the stockroom's stale air. A damned flush began to creep up the back of his neck. He couldn't recall the last time he'd made a fool of himself to the point of embarrassment. And wouldn't you know, he'd picked Miranda Shepherd to witness his colossal comeback.

What the hell had he been thinking? It wasn't like they'd been friends before the will debacle. He tried to put himself in her shoes, seeing a big guy like him stalking into her stockroom while she was alone. No wonder she turned wary on him. She didn't know him, or what he was capable of.

"I can see my offer is causing more harm than good." He turned to leave. Tail tucked between his ass cheeks and all. He would send Grif and Carlie Beth to her—exactly what he should have done to begin with, rather than running in here like a schoolboy, eager to please the prettiest girl in the class. If Grif, or his other brothers, ever figured out what he'd been about today, he'd never live it down.

"I would love some extra muscle."

Not quite believing his ears, Britt glanced over his shoulder and caught her tentative smile before she bent—at the knees—to pick up a carton. After her initial instructions, they spent the next twenty minutes in relative silence. A companionable silence. Britt wasn't much of a small-talker, so the lack of conversation suited him fine. The glimpses of her smooth midriff and the study of her striking profile kept him well motivated.

"All done." Randi pulled off her gloves. "Thanks for your help. I admit I wasn't looking forward to this project."

"Anytime."

Peering down at his hands, she said, "I'm sorry I couldn't find a pair of gloves for you. Did your hands survive?"

He rotated his hands around. A few scrapes marked his knuckles, and dirt covered his palms. "I torture my hands far more than this on a daily basis. And besides, I could have grabbed a pair from my truck."

"Let's at least get you washed up before you leave." She led him into a cramped utility room housing a washer, dryer, water heater, furnace, and sink. Turning on the water, she held her finger beneath the stream until she was satisfied with the temperature. She dropped the bar into his palm as if afraid to touch him. "Lather up."

While he began a vigorous, no-nonsense lather, she remained beside him, watching. An aura of intimacy fell over the small, dimly lit room. Beyond the smell of soap and damp concrete, Britt zeroed in on Randi's unique scent. Jasmine mixed with perspiration, the intoxicating combination wrapped around him until his heartbeat pulsed through the air, adding heat and need to an already charged atmosphere. He slowed his utilitarian scrub to a languid, thorough wash.

When her breathing turned as ragged as his, he held out the bar in his soapy palm. "Next?"

With his hand relaxed, there was no way she could take the bar from him without skin-to-soapy-skin contact. She stared at his outstretched hand for several seconds before meeting his gaze.

"What are you about, Britt Steele?"

"Damned if I know, but I'm going with it."

She laughed, and a giant foot pressed on Britt's chest at the joyful note. He tried to come up with another witty remark, so she wouldn't stop. But unfortunately, one witticism per millennium was his quota. While her smiling mouth consumed his attention, she found a way to retrieve the soap without touching him. Dammit.

Spell broken, they rinsed and dried their hands and rejoined Grif in the dining room. Seeing their arrival, Carlie Beth finished up with her customer, then grabbed Britt's plate and headed to the kitchen.

"Thanks for lending me your lunch date," Randi said. "It would have taken much longer to organize the stockroom without him."

Grif sent Britt one of his I-could-make-life-really-bad-for-you-now grins. "He's starting to go soft around the middle, so a little physical exertion is good for him."

Randi's gaze slid down to Britt's stomach, hopefully noting the absence of any paunch. Didn't stop him from contracting his muscles, though.

The restaurant door opened, drawing Randi's attention away. Her features scrambled into a mixture of confusion and excitement and maybe a bit of dread.

Britt angled around to see who'd caused such a shift in her mood. Two men in suits and ties paused just inside. Both carried an air of money about them, though the older gentleman with the receding hairline looked as though he'd walked into a warren of maggots. The younger of the two appeared more comfortable, and a grin broke across his face when he located Randi.

Without conscious thought, Britt straightened his spine and expanded his chest. His territorial radar was zinging off the scale. The guy was Superman good-looking, right down to a blinding white charm-your-granny smile and slicked-back black hair.

"Well, I'll leave you gentlemen to your food." Randi's gaze skimmed over Britt. "Thanks again."

She met the duo halfway across the room, shaking Clark Kent's hand first, then his arrogant friend's. After a few more words between them, Randi waved her guests over to a red leather booth tucked in the corner by where the local bands set up. Grif whistled. "Bro, you got it bad. When did that happen?"

Tearing his gaze away, Britt sat. "Don't start. Nothing's happened—happening."

"Then you're an idiot. Randi's got her head screwed on straight and she's a beauty to boot. What's the obstacle?"

"I'm not one of your players, Grif. You don't need to broker a deal on my behalf."

"Here you go," Carlie Beth said. "Careful, the plate's hot. Let me know if there's anything else you need."

"Thanks, this will do." When she turned to leave, he said, "Actually, one more thing."

"Shoot."

"Any idea who Randi's meeting with?"

Carlie Beth peered at the booth before glancing in Grif's direction. Eyes twinkling, she gave Britt a mischievous smile. "You mean the hottie?"

"I mean the dude in the suit."

Both Grif and Carlie Beth chuckled.

"Haven't a clue."

Britt scowled at Carlie Beth's retreating back.

"Didn't you have someplace you needed to be?" Grif asked.

"Looks like I'll be a little late." Britt bit into his hamburger, fighting the urge to gawk at the trio huddled behind him.

"About that obstacle."

Unable to speak without spitting food all over the table, Britt settled for sending his brother a scorching glare. This was why you never wanted Grif Steele pissing around in your pot. He never let anything go. Not even after threats of bodily harm.

"There's an issue with Barbara Shepherd's will, and Randi and I are on opposite sides of the field."

"Not an ideal situation for a blooming romance, I'll admit. What's the issue?"

"Don't you have some ledgers to balance or something?"

"Probably, but your love life is much more interesting." He wiped his mouth with a napkin. "Spreadsheets and financial software."

"What?"

"Most businesses stopped using written ledgers twenty years ago."

"I still use a ledger book."

"Dear God." Grif tossed his napkin on the table. "I'm coming over to your cabin next weekend to hook you up with QuickBooks."

"Quit Books?"

"*Quick*Books. Small business financial software."

"The hell you are."

"I bet Randi uses it."

"Her business is a bit more complicated than mine."

"We'll work on getting you into the twenty-first century later. Let's get back to your love life—or lack thereof."

Britt grabbed three french fries and dipped them into a blob of ketchup. He stabbed the bloody potatoes into Grif's direction. "If I tell you, you can't go blabbing it to the family."

"Deal."

"Or Carlie Beth. She's friends with Randi, and I don't want to cause trouble there."

Grif's response was much slower in coming. "Carlie Beth knows Randi better than you or I. Let's keep that door open. She won't do anything to jeopardize her friendship."

Between mouthfuls of hamburger, fries, and coleslaw, Britt spent the next five minutes explaining to his freaky smart brother about the will and Barbara's promise.

By the end, Grif looked equal parts shell-shocked and intrigued. "Any idea who made the offer to Randi?"

Britt glanced over his shoulder at Randi and her guests. "She's not even hinting at their identity."

"You think those two guys made the offer?"

Turning back to his plate. "No telling."

"What are you going to do?"

"I'm not exactly sure. But I have five days to figure something out." Britt set his half-eaten hamburger down, no longer hungry. "If I knew why she wanted to sell the property so badly, I could tackle the problem from that angle."

When Grif didn't comment for a long while, Britt studied his brother's face. Indecision rode his features. A foreign emotion for his take-charge sibling.

"What?"

"A couple weeks ago, I had lunch here with the president of one of the local banks. He let a comment slip about it 'being a damned shame what's going on with this place.' Then he caught himself as if he'd said too much." Grif rapped the tips of his fingers against the table. "I didn't unload any questions on him, thinking Carlie Beth might have the scoop, but she had no idea what he meant."

Double damn shit! Britt chanced another glance over his shoulder. The trio had disappeared. How the hell had they left without him hearing? Had her meeting with two guys in expensive suits been a coincidence? "If Randi's business has suffered a financial setback, she'll fight like a wildcat to protect it. As near as I can tell, Triple B is her life."

"I agree." The irritating, rhythmic rap of Grif's fingers halted. "You could talk with Jonah."

"No."

"If it's important to you, it'll be important to him."

"He just paid millions to bail out this town, and now he's funding a renovation of a failed sports complex to keep Reid busy. I won't be another one of his charity cases."

"The training center will impact far more lives than just Reid's."

"That may be, but you and I both know Jonah wouldn't have bothered if Reid was still with the Green Berets."

"I get that protecting the Shepherd property is important to you," Grif said. "But what I don't understand is *why* it's so important."

"The land's gone untouched for over a century, maybe more. Outside a few acres, the land hasn't been impacted by farming, logging, or aggressive hunting. The diversity of plant and animal life is incredible."

"All the more reason Jonah would want to add the acreage to Steele Conservation Area."

"Why would he care? He's been cooped up behind a computer for the last two decades. The kid's so pale he could be mistaken for a vampire."

"Have you played any of his games?"

"Not since Steele Survivor."

"Do yourself a favor—go check them out."

"There's no point. I don't have time to play games and I won't go to him for money."

"Then you'll lose the Shepherd property."

CHAPTER TEN

RICHARD NORWOOD TILTED HIS HEAD back and released a stream of fragrant cigar smoke into the mahogany-stained timbers above. The even, controlled action muffled the relentless chatter in his head. His mind never ceased its thinking, analyzing, searching for new ways in which he could challenge himself. Something membership in the Carolina Club demanded on a constant basis.

Made up of wealthy, competitive gentlemen, the club had been in existence for over a hundred years, providing exclusive recreational opportunities for men willing to pay a fortune for the privilege of such rare pleasures. The need to reinvent oneself, over and over and over, was as addicting as sugar or heroin. Taste, crave, repeat. Taste, crave, repeat. Taste, crave, repeat.

"What news do you have for us, Mr. Gaviston?"

The attorney settled into one of the many comfortable leather chairs strewn about the Canid Chamber—so called for the many wolf, wild dog, and fox trophies decorating the room. Gaviston nodded to each of the five men gathered.

"I presented the club's generous offer to Miss Shepherd on Friday. Unfortunately, she was not ready to make a final decision."

Gaviston believed the club's interest in the Shepherd property revolved around its rich gameland. A truth, but not Richard's sole motivation. Only a select few knew the full scope of why he wanted the property. Why they wanted the property. The Marksman League.

Several of his close colleagues and he were within a few kills of making Legend status. The last kill on the list seemed impossible to obtain until club member Neil Watters overheard a conversation between Barbara Shepherd and Britt Steele, revealing the state's rarest mammal—*Canis rufus*—had settled on Shepherd property, making the land invaluable to the exclusive Marksman League.

"How can this be?" Angus Ferguson, a vascular surgeon from Asheville, snapped the newspaper shut, his ruddy Scottish complexion more pronounced than normal. "We offered the girl a fortune."

"Indeed, sir." Gaviston remained unruffled in the face of Ferguson's outburst. "However, Miss Shepherd is a savvy businesswoman and she's proceeding with caution."

"I share Mr. Ferguson's confusion." Jun Ito advanced his black rook into an offensive position against a ghost player. "By accepting our offer, Miss Shepherd would become a millionaire."

If Jun Ito's designer clothes and polished manners weren't enough to label him as old money, the gold family crest he always wore around his neck would clinch it. Although the real estate tycoon had grown up in the United States, he'd spent each summer in Japan, the country of his birth and the resting place of his ancestors.

"The amount offered far exceeds fair market value, and Miss Shepherd realizes that fact."

"So?" Samuel Taylor drawled in his thick Texan accent. "Money's money. I sure wouldn't balk if any of my overseas shipping accounts tried to give me more, I'll tell you that right now."

"Miss Shepherd indicated the club's offer might be too good to be true." Gaviston held Richard's gaze. "I gave her a couple days to think about the matter."

Richard nodded, not happy with the delay, but he'd learned to trust Gaviston's instincts.

"Thank you for the update, Mr. Gaviston. Contact us once you have Miss Shepherd's answer."

Gaviston rose. "Should I update the president?"

"Not necessary. I'll be meeting with Mr. Bennett later today."

The moment the door closed behind the lawyer, Chicago investment banker Neil Watters said in a quiet, lethal voice, "We need to devise a Plan B. The Shepherd girl is going to be a problem."

"The girl *is* Plan B," Richard reminded him, giving Ferguson a pointed look. "What we need is a foolproof plan should Miranda Shepherd not accept our offer."

Although Watters neared Legend status, he had more trials to complete before Richard could bring him into the League's confidence. Completing Carolina Club's Kill List proved an effective recruitment tool for more cultivated, select tastes.

A wave of fury burned over his scalp. Their original plan had been a good, solid strategy, though the Shepherd woman had proved to be a strong adversary. One who'd refused to back down.

But the memory of her stubbornness wasn't what put Richard in a rage. It was the damned hotheaded Scot. Angus Ferguson had a tendency toward impetuous, not thought out, or approved, actions. And more importantly, he'd anticipated Richard's next move, something that wouldn't happen again.

"She'd be a bloody fool not to," Angus blustered. "It's the only way to save her business."

"Be careful of absolutes." Richard released another column of smoke. "Operating in black and white always proves disappointing."

"What do you propose?" Jun asked.

"It's quite simple. If she will not sell us what we want, then we'll have to take it."

"By whatever means possible?" Sam asked.

"We didn't allow her self-righteous mother to stand in our way. The grieving, financially ruined Miranda Shepherd will either bend or break to our will."

"Your preference?" Jun asked.

"The latter, of course."

CHAPTER ELEVEN

THEN YOU'LL LOSE THE SHEPHERD property.

Grif's words continued to haunt Britt for the next four days. Losing the property meant failing the red wolves. Something he couldn't do.

Although he suspected it would be a long shot, Britt had contacted several national and international conservation agencies to see if they would be interested in purchasing property inhabited by red wolves. Many had been quite intrigued, but none would commit funding until their biologists could verify the wolves' authenticity. Not one of them would accept the tests he'd collected. Once again, time wasn't on his side.

He hadn't bothered notifying the North Carolina Wildlife Resources Commission or the U. S. Fish and Wildlife Service. Both were useless to him. The combination of the Commission renouncing the red wolf as a distinct species and an independent report revealing the Service's lack of adequate support for the Red Wolf Reintroduction Program had once again thrown the program into a tailspin of impending failure.

The numerous papers and handwritten notes on his desk blurred in front of him. Between working on the Shepherd property issue, refurbishing Ronnie Smith's kitchen, and checking in on Reid's contractors, Britt had slept less than four hours a night in the past week. He rubbed his tired eyes, wondering how the hell he was going to fix this thing with Randi.

Considering the amount of business flowing through Blues, Brews, and Books, Britt had a hard time believing her company was in financial trouble. But he trusted his brother. The guy had his nose up everyone's business. Grif had only been back in North Carolina for a few months and he knew more about the inner workings of the town than Britt, who'd been here his whole life.

So what had happened? How had a thriving business taken a dive? Lawsuit? Bad investment? Poor bookkeeping? More than once, he'd seen on Gordon Ramsay's show tales of how a bad chef could have a disastrous impact on a restaurant—ordering too much inventory, allowing a decline in the quality of the food, not having control of the kitchen. Britt recalled his recent lunch and couldn't fault the service or the food. But maybe Carlie Beth had something to do with his positive experience.

As closemouthed as Randi was, he'd probably never find out the exact reason behind the bar's imminent collapse. The realization bothered him more than it should.

A knock sounded on his cabin door, jerking him out of his thoughts of Randi's financial crisis. He glanced at his phone—9:20 p.m. He rarely got visitors and never any after sunset.

He moved toward the window and looked out. A red Jeep sat in his drive. Britt's heart slammed against the wall of his chest before sliding into a freefall toward his stomach. He stared at the door for a confused moment, unable to reason out why Randi Shepherd would be at his door at this time of night.

Another knock, this one more forceful, compelled him into motion. Bracing one hand on the doorframe, he eased opened the door. "Randi." He peered behind her. "Can I help you?"

"Am I interrupting anything?"

He shook his head. "I needed a break." He waved her inside, though he didn't move aside.

Wearing a sleeveless floral summer dress and low-heeled tan sandals, she looked as feminine as he'd ever seen her. She wasn't wearing one of those strappy getups that showed her cleavage and two-thirds of her thighs, though Britt wouldn't have complained if she had. Her outfit looked like something Audrey Hepburn would have worn. Feminine, elegant, enticing.

"Going out, or headed home?" He would rather have told her how beautiful she looked, but her expression did not welcome compliments.

"On my way home." She brushed her hand over her skirt. "I attended a fundraiser in Asheville."

"What kind of fundraiser?"

"Political. One of my college friends is running for state office." She scanned his entryway. "Not really my thing, but Natalie begged me to attend."

"Can I get you something to drink?"

"Got any beer?"

"I'm a Steele. We always have beer at the ready."

When he closed the fridge door, he found her circling the edges of the living room, squinting at family pictures and picking up knickknacks. Her inspection of his personal items was unnerving. What did she think when she saw the picture of him and his siblings? Most of his pictures were more than twenty years old, when times were more fun, carefree. He didn't have a single picture of him and his entire family together in the past decade. The realization created a hollow feeling in his heart.

Holding out a bottle, he said, "Here you go."

She accepted the beer and took a long draw before resurfacing.

"Better?"

Nodding, she glanced around as if wanting to sit.

Dammit. Where were his manners? His mother would not be pleased.

"Have a seat." He indicated the soft brown leather

sofa. Once she was comfortable, he asked again, "What brings you out here so late?"

"I'm sorry to bother you. Your light was on and I didn't see any other vehicles in the drive, so I decided to give it a shot."

"Give what a shot?"

"See if you'd invite me in."

"Why wouldn't I? I told you earlier this week that I had nothing against you." He lifted his bottle to his mouth and tilted his head back. "As much as I cared for your mother, I blame Barbara, not you, for our predicament."

"Speaking of predicament, have you made any headway in raising the necessary funds?"

And just like that, the air cooled to thirty-two degrees.

"I still have until tomorrow."

"Yes, but the buyer's attorney contacted me today. He's going to stop by tomorrow, and I'd like to give him my answer." She searched his features. "Surely, you know by now whether or not you can get a loan or find a sponsor."

Helpless anger blurred Britt's vision. He pushed it back and concentrated on diluting their conversation down to a cold-blooded business transaction. No emotion, nothing to lose. "If I add my savings, cabin, property, business, and truck to the money the bank is willing to lend me, I'll be close—"

"Your cabin and truck? Your business?" she asked, horrified. "Why would you give up everything of value to save Mom's property? I don't understand."

"Because I made her a promise." *And because I am the wolves' last hope.*

"No promise is worth the kind of sacrifice you're suggesting."

"Normally, I would agree with you. But, in this case, it is."

"I can't do 'close,' Britt."

He bolted from his chair, startling her. At the moment, he didn't care. She was one comment away from leaving, and he couldn't think of a way to stop her. His mind sparked in a thousand different directions. Staring out the picture window, he saw nothing of the towering cluster of trees or the dilapidated shed. He saw only his reflection, his failure.

If he'd been Grif, he could have charmed her over to his side. Jonah could have waved a wad of cash to win her over. Reid could have…God only knew how, but the devil would have managed the situation. Britt had—nothing. Not a single special quality he could employ.

A light touch on his sleeve brought his attention around to an insanely beautiful pair of green eyes. How many times had he lost himself in their depths? Had wanted her to see him as a man and not just a patron? Had wanted to gather her into his arms and kiss her until they clawed at each other for release?

"There's something more going on here than a mere promise," she said in a tone one reserved for wild animals. "Tell me."

His gaze dipped to her mouth for an aching second before returning to the outdoors. Complete darkness had set in, making their reflection even more pronounced. Impenetrable.

Could he trust her with his most valuable secret?

Could he afford not to at this point?

Barbara hadn't done so. Wouldn't a mother confide in her only daughter?

Probably not, given their estrangement.

Dammit, he didn't want to make an irrevocable mistake. So much rode on the wolves remaining invisible.

He sought her gaze in their reflection. The glass barrier could not disguise her compassion, her strength, her honor. Trust budded through his veins, strengthening with every inch traveled until his spine snapped straight with his resolve.

He took a Mount St. Helens-sized leap of faith.

"An endangered species lives on the property."

"Plant or animal?"

"Isn't it enough to know one exists?"

"No. North Carolina has nearly fifty species of plants and animals listed as endangered. Due to its pristine nature, I don't doubt the property contains one or more on the list."

"If you know this, why consider selling to someone else?"

"Part of the buyer's mission is wildlife conservation. Seems a good fit to me."

"There are many levels of wildlife conservation. Many of which your mother did not approve."

"Then she should have willed the property to you. But she didn't, so it's left to me to figure out the best course of action."

A nugget of hope rattled the cage of Britt's growing despair. Not many people could recite the number of endangered species in their state. Hell, he only knew because of the research he'd been doing in the last year. So, why would Randi—someone who'd shunned the environment for more than a decade—know such a thing?

"In 1980, the U.S. Fish and Wildlife Service declared the species extinct in the wild. Through a successful reintroduction program, the species has made a small comeback, but none have been known to exist this far west since the late nineties. Until now."

Randi sucked in a sharp breath. "A canid?"

"Yes."

"Red wolf." Awe wove between the two short words. She didn't ask him to confirm or doubt her answer. "A breeding pair?"

"And a litter this year."

She covered her mouth with shaking hands, then lifted her wonder-filled gaze to his. "Show me."

CHAPTER TWELVE

RANDI HIT THE ALARM BUTTON as soon as the sound of ocean waves and seagulls began at 4:00 a.m. the next morning. Excitement vibrated through her veins. She was going to see the fabled red wolf in the wild today—and pups!

It had taken her forever to fall asleep, knowing what lay in store for her today. When Britt had said to meet him at 5:00 a.m., she hadn't even blinked. She would have gotten up at three, if he'd asked.

Turning on the shower, Randi shed her pajama bottoms and T-shirt while waiting for the water to warm up. How had the wolves survived so long? Her mother had often mentioned the challenges the red wolf faced—mixing with coyotes, lack of protected land, laws that allowed livestock owners to kill them.

Randi couldn't even guess how many letters her mother had sent to the U.S. Fish and Wildlife Service, urging them to put more resources toward the wolves' protection. Despite all that, a full-blooded breeding pair had survived the defunct Great Smoky Mountain program.

There must be more. How else could the pair she was about to see exist? If memory served, the Smoky Mountain program closed down in the mid-nineties. Which meant more purebloods might be in the area.

She threw on tan cargo pants, a dark blue cami, and an olive-green button-down long-sleeved shirt. She laced up her Columbia hiking boots before dabbing on some mascara and a bit of under-eye concealer and foundation. Natural beauty she was not.

She tossed a hairbrush, ponytail holder, small fleece blanket, first-aid kit, binoculars, and an extra pair of socks into a rucksack. From the kitchen she added four power bars, four water bottles, her wallet, phone, solar charger, tin of mints, and ball cap.

She peered into the pockets of her stuffed rucksack, feeling as though she was forgetting something important. This sort of thing used to be second nature to her, but time and neglect had made her rusty.

Shrugging, she cinched up all the openings and stuck her keys inside the leg pocket of her lightweight pants before heading out the door. If she forgot something, she would have to do without. It wasn't as if she were embarking on a multiday hike along the Appalachian Trail. Anything she needed was a short drive away.

Randi pulled down Britt's driveway with five minutes to spare. She took the opportunity to brush her wild hair and secure it in a ponytail holder before slapping her favorite lid on top.

Exiting her vehicle, she swung the rucksack over one shoulder. Exhilaration made her light on her feet and a strange rightness settled over her. Feelings she didn't quite understand and didn't have time to explore.

Britt emerged from his cabin, wearing similar attire and gear, sans ball cap. He was gorgeous in an earthy, masculine way. A way that appealed to her so much more than slick city guys.

After giving her an appreciative once-over, he nodded toward his truck. "Jump in."

She placed her rucksack on the floorboard between her legs before fastening her seatbelt. He threw his backpack in the extended cab seat behind them, where he'd already stored his antenna and tracking equipment. Realization hit.

"Last week, when I found you near the creek, you'd just come from visiting the wolves."

"Guilty."

"Why the deception? Why not tell me about the pack then?"

"Only those who need to know about the Steele-Shepherd pack know about them."

For some reason, the exclusion hurt. The logical part of her mind mocked her to get real, the elemental side screamed for acceptance—even if unearned.

Britt pulled off the main road and drove down a narrow track. With the sun still behind the mountain, she couldn't tell how visible the road was from the main drag.

"Do you have trouble with others driving down this road—or whatever you call it?"

"No. We're on Steele property now."

In other words, no one messed with the Steele family.

"It's good you wore long sleeves and pants. Bug spray would give away our location."

"I hate the stuff, anyway."

He drew to a stop and turned off the truck. "So I noticed."

Heat smothered her cheeks. Well, if she'd had any doubts about him seeing her with her pants down, his comment had just obliterated that fantasy. Thank goodness he couldn't see her reaction in the dark.

"How long until we reach the den?"

"About thirty minutes." He flipped on his flashlight. "Ready?"

It was then that Randi realized what she'd forgotten. She had pretty good night vision, but the terrain appeared rugged and no telling how much moonlight filtered through the dense canopy. She would just have to wing it.

"Lead the way."

"No flashlight?"

"With a partial moon?" She'd read an autobiography of a Delta Force operator who never used a flashlight because it ruined his night vision. Sounded good to her. "Not necessary."

He glanced down at his flashlight, then turned it off. "We'll try it your way."

Surprised, Randi smiled, eliciting one of his render-a-female-speechless grins in return.

The terrain was indeed challenging, though Britt managed to guide them around some of the more hazardous areas, using the precious sprays of moonlight that lit their path at different intervals. She'd expected the woods to go silent upon their arrival. However, the insects and tree frogs continued their melodic, pulsing hum without interruption. Almost as if they'd accepted them into their home.

For a quarter hour, they said nothing. Conversation became taboo, unnecessary. They used hand signals to warn each other of danger. The only sound between them was the crunch of forest debris beneath their boots.

Randi opened her senses in a way she hadn't allowed herself in a long time. Beyond the deafening hum, she detected the mournful cry of a bobcat and the soulful hoot of a great horned owl. A hundred scents assaulted her nose at once—damp, loamy earth, spicy pine resin, and sweet flowering raspberry.

Tension she'd lived with for weeks now drifted away on the gentle breeze weaving through the trees. The occasional annoying mosquito failed to diminish her enjoyment.

She missed this. Missed the freedom, missed the thrill of discovery. Missed...her mom, her family, her old life.

Emotion stung her nose and eyes, yet no tears fell. She would not allow nostalgia to ruin this morning's adventure. She would absorb every minute. It could be a long time before she ventured into the sticks again.

Britt paused, motioning her forward. Leaning close,

he whispered into her ear. "We're not far from the den." The humid warmth of his breath sent a shiver of awareness all the way to her toes. "Be more mindful of where you step."

She lifted her gaze to his, intending to nod her acknowledgment. What little light penetrated the canopy shone behind him, casting his face in shadow. Which meant hers was not.

Three seconds of agonizing, breath-stealing stillness ticked by before he lifted a hand and smoothed the backs of two fingers down her cheek. Anticipation licked along her flesh. Randi ached to lean her body into his, longed to run her fingers over the fine hairs at the back of his neck.

But she did none of those things, because he turned and, on soundless feet, continued down an invisible trail.

Randi released an unsteady breath. Twice now, his touch had driven her into a state of mindless, burning need. Twice, he'd walked away as if unaffected by the contact. Twice, she'd simply watched him go, gobsmacked.

Hefting her rucksack higher on her back, she followed as soundless as he, though the curses firing through her head could have awoken a hibernating bear. If she hadn't feared stepping into a hole or off the edge of a bluff, she would have flame-fried his broad, retreating back with her stare.

Finally, Britt motioned for her to slow down. He bent at the waist, shrugging out of his backpack while he inched closer to an unseen object. Randi followed suit, her eyes straining to see.

When Britt went down on hands and knees, then slithered the last few feet military style, Randi dropped to her knees. She struggled to keep the contents of her rucksack quiet while she shuffled forward on one hand and two knees. Britt had made the maneuver look so effortless, damn him. The moment she finally belly-crawled up alongside him, she sent up a silent prayer that she hadn't given their presence away.

Once again, Britt spoke close to her ear. The faint scent of his soap reached her before his words. "Still too dark." He nuzzled her earlobe, and Randi angled her ear toward him for greater contact. "Listen."

Listen? How could she hear anything past the pounding of her heart?

Randi pushed her senses to go beyond the man beside her. It took several seconds before she heard the excited play of wakening pups below them. She smiled at the happy noise—part impish yips, part fierce growls.

She itched to pull her binoculars from her bag, but the sun was only now starting to crest the mountain. So she lay there with her eyes closed, listening. Doing her best to ignore the large male body next to her.

"Randi."

He said her name in a low, thick voice. The kind a lover uses when on the verge of release. She sent him a sidelong glance, though her attention never made it beyond his full, achingly close lips. She wanted to taste them, nip at them, drink from them.

Pluck a biscuit. She was going insane. Lust-induced insanity.

He tilted her cap back, and his amazing lips drew closer and closer until they molded hers into a warm, erotic embrace. Randi did not allow herself to think. In that direction lay only sexual frustration.

Instead she pushed into his kiss, taking it deeper, more demanding. His tongue swept inside her mouth, teasing hers to come out and play. She did. The kiss became bolder, yet neither moved to touch the other. Only their lips and tongues made contact. Luscious, hot, soul-stimulating contact.

Sunlight sprayed across their faces, warming their flesh, their blood, their breaths. Try as she might, she could not break away or stem the need pulsing through her veins.

Britt's willpower proved stronger than hers. He slowed the kiss, bringing it to a sweet end. Then he rested his forehead against hers, their labored breaths mingling with each other's.

Pressing his lips against her forehead, he asked, "Did you bring binoculars?"

She nodded, unable to form words against the tightness in her throat.

"Now would be a good time to put them to use. Skooch up a bit more, then look to two o'clock. The den is at the base of a giant oak tree."

After moving closer to the bluff's edge, she unbuckled the front pocket of her rucksack and retrieved her binoculars with a shaky hand. She snapped off the lens protectors and positioned the soft rubber eyecups against her face.

Finding the focus wheel, she rolled the knob until the landscape below became crisp and so close it felt like she could reach out and touch the leaves on the ephemerals below. She scanned the area Britt indicated in a methodical back-and-forth motion until she located the exposed roots of a large tree, a two-foot dark hole tucked within.

"Found it," she whispered. "But I don't see the pups."

Britt peered below with his set of binoculars. "They might have gone back inside. Right now, they don't venture too far from the safety of the den."

No sooner had he spoken the words than a pair of pups crept to the opening. Their little faces, so innocent and curious, surveyed their surroundings with an intentness learned from observing their parents. Deeming the area free of danger, they moved a few more feet into the clearing. One of the pups crouched down, following his sibling. When the other pup came within a few feet, the crouching pup pounced.

They rolled and ran and cried and glanced around. Their energy had no limits, and soon the other pups joined their antics. When an adult came into view, their joy trebled.

"That's the breeding male," Britt whispered. "Apollo."

An adult emerged from the den. "And that's the breeding female. Calypso."

The two greeted each other, nose-to-nose.

Randi had no idea how long she lay there with her eyes glued to the red wolves. It could have been hours or only minutes, so mesmerized was she. When Britt tapped her on the shoulder and motioned for her to back away, Randi's chest contracted painfully against the loss.

She snatched one last, long look before saying good-bye.

The trip back to Old Blue turned out to be as silent as their hike to the den. Britt had expected Randi's obvious pleasure at having viewed the wolves to have intensified after leaving their perch at the top of the bluff. He waited for her to pepper him with questions about their research or when the pups would start hunting on their own. Anything. Hell, he wouldn't have minded if she'd brought up that mind-blowing kiss. But she asked nothing. If she had any thoughts on what she'd witnessed, she kept them to herself.

As for him, a million probing questions sat on the tip of his tongue. Somehow he managed to keep them from emerging in order to give her time to process whatever was troubling her.

When they stopped in front of his cabin, he couldn't take it any longer. "Well?"

"Well, what?"

He gripped the underside of the steering wheel, hard. "What did you think about the pack?"

Her serious expression transformed into a grateful smile. "I never thought I'd see red wolves in the wild. Thank you for sharing such a precious gift. I'll never forget it."

"Does this mean you'll sell the property to me?"

The moment her smile faded, Britt's stomach crashed to the ground.

"Do you have the funds now?"

"Dammit, you know I don't." He threw his door open with such force that the entire truck shook. "Nothing's changed since yesterday. Not my financial situation, or your cold heart."

Randi grabbed her belongings and rounded the truck, pausing near the front fender—a good distance away from him. "I'm sorry, Britt. I wish I could give you the time. I have my reasons. And they're important. Believe me, this isn't an easy decision."

The red haze clouding his thoughts obscured the sincerity in her words. "Unless you really screwed the pooch with your business, the amount I can offer you should more than settle your debt. So I can only assume you're motivated by greed."

"What do you know about the state of my business?" Fury shook her words.

"I have as many friends in this town as you do." Only a slight exaggeration. He had very few true friends, but many acquaintances. "People talk. Especially when a business as successful as yours suddenly goes down the drain."

As if struck by buckshot, her eyes squeezed shut and her hand rubbed one side of her chest. Britt's anger dissipated enough to grasp the harshness of his comments. *What a dick.* He never spoke to women in that kind of tone. His bluntness was reserved for idiots and his brothers. Since Randi was neither, she didn't deserve such merciless treatment. If his mother ever caught wind of this...

He drove a hand through his hair, staring at the ground. "I'm sorry. I shouldn't have said those things—"

Something hard smacked against his forehead and flopped to the ground. "Ow!" Britt blinked hard at the item. "Did you just brain me with a power bar?"

"Yes, and I've got three more."

He held up a staying hand. "Not necessary."

She marched over to her Jeep and swung her pack inside, then paused. "Did you hear about my business from Carlie Beth?"

"No!" Dammit, he was an idiot. "I won't tell you who I heard it from, but I promise you it wasn't Carlie Beth. She's your friend. She wouldn't betray you."

"Maybe she said something to Grif who conveyed the information to you."

"The state of your business didn't come to me via Carlie Beth." He moved closer. "Say you believe me."

She nodded. "I didn't think so, but I've only confided in her and Aunt Sharon. So I suppose that leaves the gossip to either my creditors or vendors." She scrubbed her temple against the hand she'd braced against the Jeep's door. "I did, you know."

Britt's mind scrambled through their conversation for context. "I don't follow."

"Screwed the pooch with my business."

With her body in profile, he had to strain to hear her. He inched closer. "How?"

"Sank all my capital into a really bad investment." Still she would not look at him. "My financial advisor assured me the transaction was safe. Only a little risk— less than I normally operate within."

"All your capital?"

"And then some." She dug her fist into her stomach. "At first, I refused. Several times, in fact. Something about it triggered my radar. But he kept sharing stats with me until I could no longer remember why I was so against it." Finally, she met his gaze. "So it's not because of greed that I'm selling to the highest bidder, it's survival."

Self-loathing, fear, and regret marred her beautiful features. The sight made him reach for her. "We'll figure something out."

"No." She climbed into her vehicle and shut her door. "I've made my decision. At three o'clock today, the

Carolina Club will hand over a check that will save my business." Tears glimmered in her eyes. "There are too many people counting on me. Failure isn't an option." She turned over the engine. "I'm truly sorry. But I've run out of time."

So have the wolves.

CHAPTER THIRTEEN

BRITT STORMED INTO HIS MOTHER'S house.

Every second that had ticked by since Randi left his place two hours ago gonged in his head like an out-of-control ball peen hammer against a sheet of metal. He took the stairs two at a time and swung right after he reached the second floor. Throwing open the second door, he paused a moment to allow his eyes to adjust to the absolute darkness. They never did.

He groped the wall until he found the light switch and flipped it on.

A well-toned arm snaked out from beneath the covers. An insistent hand waved toward the switch. "Light. Off."

Britt picked his way around piles of clothes, game controllers, beanbags, and intimidating stacks of illuminated electronics. He whipped back the thick dark curtains to let in some natural light.

"Not. Better."

"Get up, little brother. I have a favor to ask."

Jonah's head popped out from beneath the covers. "*You* need a favor from *me*?"

"And the sky's not even falling. Up, lazy ass."

Glancing at the clock, Jonah said, "I've only been in bed for five hours."

"Then you've had enough beauty sleep." Britt opened

the closet door and rummaged through his brother's clothes. Once he found what he was looking for, he twisted the wire hanger and hooked the items on the closet doorjamb. "Take a shower and put these on."

"Should I go with Iron Man underwear or Superman?"

"Whatever's going to make you look and feel like a billion bucks."

Jonah's smirk disappeared. "What's all this about?"

"I'll explain everything in the car." He snatched a key fob off Jonah's desk. "Tesla?"

Jonah nodded, eyeing him warily.

"See you downstairs in twenty minutes. I'm driving."

"Twenty minutes?" Jonah rubbed the several-days-old scruff covering his jaw. "It'll take me that long to shave this off."

"You built a multi-bazillion dollar empire within a few short months. I think you can handle a beard in five minutes."

Jonah threw off the covers. "This had better be good."

I hope so, too, little brother.

"You want me to do what?" Jonah asked, nineteen minutes later.

Britt hit his turn signal and rolled to a stop at the end of their mom's drive. "For someone whose IQ is off the charts, you can be thick, sometimes." A minivan with a carry case fastened to the top toddled down the highway at a speed that would make a turtle look like a speed racer.

"Only when I'm being fed a bunch of garbled crap. Speak in ones and zeros, then we've got a conversation."

Britt drew in a fortifying breath. "I need you to act the billionaire who's in desperate need of a diversion. You overheard a conversation about the Carolina Club at a recent party and decided to check it out."

"What kind of club is it?"

"They claim wildlife conservation. To what degree, I have no idea."

Jonah pulled out his phone and started tapping away.

"Would you mind putting that thing down until I'm finished?"

"I'm looking up Carolina Club online."

"Don't waste your time. You won't find anything listed on their website beyond wildlife conservation and education."

Jonah clicked the screen off and shoved his phone back in his pocket. "So I'm going in blind."

Britt tapped his thumb against the steering wheel, debating how much to share with his quirky brother. He was taking a big risk just inviting him along. Jonah could be unpredictable, at times. Unlike Britt's predictably boring life. In the end, he decided to lay it all out.

"I suspect the club is a front for either avid hunters or unscrupulous trophy hunters. Both have access to a great deal of money."

"How do you know?"

"Trust me on this one, little bro."

"Why do you care?" Jonah pulled at the tie around his neck. "Sounds like a godsend for Miranda Shepherd."

Again, Britt grappled with how much his brother needed to know about the situation. Conveying his thoughts on the potential buyer was one thing, revealing the location of a critically endangered species was another. He decided to keep it vague. "Barbara and I were working together to protect an endangered species on the property. I'd like to continue on with our project."

As he'd hoped, Jonah's eyes crossed the moment Britt started talking about conservation.

"And you think they're misleading Randi about their intentions for the property?"

"I do." Britt pulled into the club's parking lot. "Even though Randi doesn't have the same love of the environment as her mother, I don't think she would want to see something so precious destroyed."

"So we're here to collect evidence to support your theory?"

Britt didn't have every piece of the puzzle locked in yet. At the moment, he was operating on sheer instinct—and desperate fear. Something continued to niggle at him about the club's appearance so soon after Barbara's death, but he couldn't put his finger on it. He prayed he'd learn something useful during this impromptu meeting, because his backup plan was unthinkable.

"Sounds about right."

"Have you considered what you're going to do if this club is legit?"

"Yes."

"Aaaannd?"

"Let's take this one step at a time." Britt cut the engine. "Ready?"

Chapter Fourteen

"I WISH YOU WOULD HAVE given me more time to study up on trophy hunting."

"You grew up around hunters—both family and friends. You know how hunters speak and what excites them. Take that knowledge and tie it to an obsessive-compulsive collector." Britt slanted him a glance. "What would you do to get your hands on the original Luke Skywalker lightsaber?"

A flame of comprehension lit Jonah's eyes. "Let's do this."

They rolled out of the Tesla and strode up to the lodge's massive entrance. The doublewide wooden doors depicted a hunt scene in which a pack of snarling dogs accompanied several men on bucking horses. The bloodthirsty group cornered a large fang-displaying wolf.

"Looks like we're in the right place." Jonah pushed open the door. "I think I'm going to enjoy this."

Britt raised a brow and followed his brother into a cavernous forest, er, foyer. Every square inch was covered in green shrubbery. Taxidermic animals were displayed at strategic locations to give the visitor a feeling of submersion into a forest.

The lifelike exhibit was strangely beautiful yet deeply disturbing. Britt located no less than seven endangered and critically endangered species scattered about the small space. Never would he understand the collect-at-all-costs mentality of some hunters.

"Good morning." A man of about half Britt's height and twice his girth entered the foyer. "How may I help you gentlemen?"

Jonah held out his hand. "Jonah and Britt Steele. We've come to inquire about membership."

"Jonah Steele, you say?" The little man's eyes sparkled with recognition. "Of Steele Trap Entertainment?"

"Formerly. I sold the company," Jonah said in a refined voice that made Britt do a double take. "You're familiar with our product?"

He shook Jonah's hand, vigorously, then Britt's. "Not just familiar, sir. I'm a huge gamer. It's an honor to welcome you to Carolina Club."

The guy didn't look like any gamer Britt had ever seen.

"We didn't make an appointment," Jonah said. "I hope that's not a problem."

"Not at all, Mr. Steele. I would be happy to give you a personal tour and answer any of your questions." He smiled. "By the way, my name is Hugh Donovan. I do whatever needs doing around here."

"Sounds like we're in good hands, then."

Britt threw a who-are-you? glance at his brother, who merely smirked and followed their tour guide.

"The club has been in existence for nearly one hundred and twenty years. Descendants from our founding fathers are some of the most influential families in North Carolina."

"My brother would be interested in meeting these descendants." Britt forced his most charming smile. "He has some plans in place for the upcoming year and is interested in connecting with the right businessmen. He hasn't built a billion-dollar empire by having the wrong people at his side."

Donovan's body began to vibrate at the mention of

billion-dollar empire. "Indeed, sir. You are in luck, as a few of our distinguished members are lounging on the veranda at this very moment."

"Sounds like karma's on our side," Jonah said. "Lead the way, Mr. Donovan."

Their tour guide led them into various rooms labeled after the prominent trophies displayed within—Ursid, Bovid, Canid, Felid—before taking them outside onto an expansive flagstone patio. Thick wooden pillars separated by black cable railing allowed the observer to enjoy an incredible mountain landscape in the distance.

"Good morning, gentlemen." Donovan approached a small cluster of casually, yet expensively dressed members. "I'd like to introduce you to Jonah Steele, of the famed Steele Survivor." At the members' blank stares, Donovan cleared his throat. "Mr. Steele is the former owner of Steele Trap Entertainment and the man who saved Canyon Ridge from financial collapse."

Mild interest transformed into avid, focused attention. The group consisted of the club's president, three board members, and two regular members. Although they did not greet the brothers as effusively as Donovan, they left no room for misinterpretation of their welcome.

"What brings you to Carolina Club?" President Jack Bennett asked.

The president matched Jonah in coloring and height, however there was a toughness about him that bespoke military training.

"My brother and I learned about your organization quite by accident," Jonah said. "Intrigued, we decided to come investigate."

"I take it Mr. Donovan has given you the grand tour and answered all of your questions," the president said.

"Yes, he has."

"What did you discover, Mr. Steele?" Bennett asked.

"The club is financially stable and operationally sound."

"Indeed, we are."

Britt released a slow breath. They had decided to stick to the truth as much as possible, but with Jonah, there were no guarantees of what would emerge from his mouth.

"I'm curious about your display in the entry hall," Britt said.

"Oh?"

"I noticed several endangered species."

"Ah, yes. Many of those specimens were harvested decades ago—well before the Endangered Species Act came into existence."

"Does that mean the club no longer supports hunts involving endangered species?"

"There is plenty of game to be had without harvesting protected species."

"Yes, but that didn't really answer my question."

The president's smile dimmed. "As a general rule, no. However, on occasion, Carolina Club, along with many other similar clubs across the U.S., is invited by a foreign nation to bid on a permit to hunt an endangered species."

"How is that legal?" Jonah asked.

"Because the foreign government is in need of revenue," Britt said. "They sell permits to kill black rhinos, elephants, lions, leopards, whatever, to support their initiatives, conservation or otherwise."

"You are correct, Mr. Steele," Bennett said. "Often to fund Rangers who protect the very species they've allowed to be harvested. Ironic, no?"

"Doesn't our government stop the hunters from bringing in an endangered species trophy?" Jonah asked.

"Not if he has a valid permit," Britt said.

"That's messed up," Jonah said, dropping his refined disguise.

No one could argue that simple fact.

"You are both hunters?" a member with a short-trimmed beard and blunt, wide nose asked.

"To varying degrees," Britt said. "My brothers and I

spent our childhood hunting and fishing all over Western North Carolina. However, over the last decade, we've been distracted by careers and family. Now that we're all together again, we mean to get back to our roots. Hence our visit today."

"To approve membership without a sponsorship from a current member would be inconsistent with our past practices," one of the board members said.

"Yes," Bennett said, "but if the Steeles prove acceptable, I don't see that as a great obstacle."

An elegant, almost effeminate board member crossed one leg over the other, then flicked the ash off his slender cigar. Mild discontent kept his features just below neutral. "Canyon Ridge was lucky to have such a wealthy family in residence."

Jonah hitched his mouth into its cockiest, most confident smile. "Couldn't agree more."

"I hear that the residents are less than pleased about the town's name change. Arrogant, many say."

"What would you rather endure?" Jonah asked. "A name change or taxes so stiff you'd be forced to move away?"

"A tax hike wouldn't disturb my pocketbook." The board member stared at the glowing end of his cigar. "A more altruistic person would've saved the town without the additional turmoil."

"Ah, but I'm not altruistic in the slightest. I'm a businessman."

Britt could not have been more proud of his baby brother. He played the part of arrogant, confident rich guy to a T. If he hadn't known Jonah, he would be equal parts in awe of and disgusted by him. But no one in this room knew about Jonah's penchant for giving a good portion of his fortune to charities every year, or of his fondness for handing out hundred-dollar bills to kids on the street and vagrants huddled under tattered blankets.

"I understand we might be neighbors soon," Britt probed.

"Oh?" The president glanced at the other board members. "What do you mean, Mr. Steele?"

"The Shepherd property."

"A magnificent piece of land. One of our members spotted a twelve-point buck at the edge of the woods a few months ago." His voice lowered. "Such a shame about Barbara Shepherd. Although she and I didn't always see eye-to-eye on wildlife conservation, I respected her a great deal."

"Do you have plans for the property?"

"Hunting, of course. Our members like to have a variety of locations in which to test their skills." The president focused on something beyond Britt's shoulder. "According to our finance director, we should have the daughter's acceptance of our offer later today."

"Good morning, gentlemen," a smooth voice interrupted.

A vaguely familiar gentleman with a small entourage stood a few paces behind Britt. He wore the sickening smile one reserved for hosts who failed to pick up their dog's crap before an outdoor party. What did these men do for a living? They all either owned their own businesses or lived off their family's wealth. Britt would have to work Saturday and possibly Sunday to make up for today's escapade.

"I hope we're not interrupting an important meeting."

"A potential member," the president said, his tone stiffening. "Jonah and Britt Steele, I'd like to introduce you to Mr. Norwood, our director of finance, board member Mr. Ferguson, and members Mr. Ito, Mr. Taylor, and Mr. Watters."

Murmurs and nods followed the introductions. The two groups of men stayed as they were. No comingling, no guy quips, no backslaps. Nothing but an uncomfortable though civilized standoff.

That was when Britt put a face with a face. He'd seen Norwood at Randi's bar a few days ago with Superman. A puzzle piece slid into place.

"You've made quite a name for yourself in Canyon Ridge," Norwood quipped, eliciting chuckles from his entourage. "What does it feel like to have a town named after you?"

"Too late to the pun, Norwood," Jonah said, boredom lacing his words. "That ground has already been covered by your board member."

"We were just discussing the Shepherd property," Britt said, watching the man.

Norwood's keen gaze scanned the president's and the other members' faces. "How so?"

"President Bennett mentioned the club's looking to purchase the land to add to its hunting acreage."

"No need to worry, Mr. Steele. Our members will learn the boundaries in short order so as not to step onto the Steele Conservation Area."

"We have measures in place, so we don't have to worry about such trespassing." Somehow Britt didn't think their reputation would be shield enough to protect them from members of this group, but he enjoyed a good bluff. "But I am curious about the club's decision to purchase such a large tract of land, especially for the price tag. Besides twelve-point bucks, do you have another compelling reason for the purchase?"

"Carolina Club is membered by gentlemen with a great deal of wealth and time. If we elect to spend millions of dollars for the privilege of harvesting a sizable buck, we can do so without a moment's concern." Norwood's assessing gaze steadied on Britt. "Your family's wealth is new. It'll take a while to erase your blue-collar mentality."

"Interesting perspective," Jonah mused. "I assumed the club catered to intelligent businessmen, not spoiled playboys."

"Your original assessment is correct, Mr. Steele," the president said. "Not all the membership's philosophies are aligned with Mr. Norwood's. Our interest in the Shepherd property is because land is always a good investment and because we want to expand our holdings in the area."

Something very close to hatred entered Norwood's eyes as he gazed at the club's president. "I'll leave you to your invigorating discussion."

"Any word from Miss Shepherd?" the president asked.

"I'll have more to report later today. Gaviston has a meeting scheduled at three o'clock." Norwood pivoted, slicing down the middle of his entourage to head back inside.

An awkward silence fell over the veranda as Norwood's group left.

"I gather all is not rosy in the Carolina Club?" Leave it to Jonah to stir things up.

It took a second for the president to tear his attention away from Norwood's disappearing back. "My apologies, Mr. Steele. The club offers entertainment, skill challenges, and camaraderie like any social organization—to varying degrees."

He didn't expound on his meaning, though it didn't take a PhD to read between the lines. Not everyone got along. Just like high school, but on a much larger, more expensive playground.

"We have taken up enough of your time," Britt said.

"Do let us know if you're still interested in joining us. I'll find you a sponsor."

Jonah held out his hand. "Thank you, Mr. Bennett."

Britt and Jonah didn't say another word until they closed their car doors.

"Well?" Jonah asked. "Did you get what you wanted?"

"Yes and no." Britt set the vehicle in motion. "As I suspected, they're a hunting club. A very different type of wildlife conservation than what their attorney portrayed to Randi."

"Some states use culling as a wildlife management method."

"When populations are far greater than is healthy for

the animals or when disease, such as chronic wasting disease, is creeping toward uninfected populations, culling can be a powerful tool—for the welfare of the whole." Britt rubbed the back of his neck. "But clubs like the one we just left only care about preserving animal populations in order to ensure their next kill."

"Don't you still hunt?"

"One deer each winter."

"So what makes you different from them?"

Britt gave his brother a quelling sidelong look. "What I shoot, I eat. I don't display the heads of my kills on the walls of my home like some conquering hero. And I don't keep a record book on the number and types of trophies I've taken."

"That last part. You think the Carolina Club does?"

"I'd bet Old Blue on the fact that at least some of their members keep scorecards. Norwood and his cronies being at the top of the list."

"I've never seen you this worked up over an issue before." Jonah stared at Britt's profile for a good half mile. "You've trusted me this far. Why not share with me what's really at stake here?"

Britt recoiled at the notion of more people learning about the wolves. But given the current direction of things, the wolves didn't have long to live in the sanctuary, anyway. So Britt filled his brother in on the research that he and Barbara had conducted, on the pups' progress, and on the intricacies of the will. When he finished, Jonah sat silent, pensive.

Then Jonah said, "I have an idea, but you're not going to like it."

CHAPTER FIFTEEN

AFTER RANDI LEFT BRITT'S CABIN that morning, the minutes had ticked by like a glacier's slow advance across the Arctic Sea. Randi had glanced up at the clock above the recliner in her office so often that she started to get motion sickness.

In a way, she couldn't wait for three o'clock to come and go. She wanted to put this time in her life well behind her. The thought of her decision forcing the red wolves out of their home, after the struggle their species had endured, made her heart sad.

If there were any other way to ensure their safety and save her business, she would do it. But she'd spent hours trying to conceive another plan, only to fall back on the Carolina Club's offer. No way would she allow Britt to sink his entire savings and his personal possessions into the purchase of her property. She would never be able to live with herself. The guilt of knowing she'd saved her business but ruined Britt would haunt her forever.

Thank goodness he hadn't been able to gather the full amount. If he had, she would have been tempted to give him what he wanted, even with the consequences. The pain her refusal had caused him was almost as unbearable as the guilt she would now have to live with.

Unable to tolerate the four walls of her office any longer, Randi ducked out the back door of Blues, Brews, and Books and made her way down the alley until it emptied into Mill Street. She hadn't eaten much for breakfast and didn't want anything now. But her blood sugar was already plummeting. Time to feed the machine.

The sound of wind chimes reached her ear, and Randi read the display on her phone. Her aunt. Hitting the silent button, she dropped it back in her purse. Putting on the happy wasn't in her repertoire at the moment.

She found her Jeep, turned up the volume on her radio, and guided her vehicle eastward. Rather than stay downtown, she decided to take a drive and see where the road led. For the next however many minutes, she didn't want to think about anything important. All she wanted to do was feel the bass, enjoy the melody, and sing out of tune.

Ten minutes later, she spotted Serenity Cafe in a small strip mall. Perfect. Known for its excellent food and peaceful environment, the Thai-inspired restaurant catered to the more reflective, intellectual crowd. New Age instrumentals and sounds of the Orient streamed into the sconce-lit room. Private booths and cozy nooks dotted the space, creating productive workspaces for local businessmen and women and soothing, intimate corners for friends or lovers.

Randi slid into one of the booths and regretted that she didn't have her laptop with her. She could get more done in one hour here than in five hours at work, where her staff interrupted her concentration on a regular basis. She would swear that some of them had screw-with-Randi radar. No sooner would she get deep into entering figures in a spreadsheet than a knock would sound on her door.

When the server came around, Randi ordered Tom Yum Goong, edamame, and ice-cold water. She'd been trying to drink more water, but the only way she could tolerate the stuff was by flooding it with ice.

Looking for a distraction, she scanned the room. She

loved people-watching. One would think she'd get enough of it at the bar or coffee shop, but no. Facial expressions, body language, clothing styles—they all told a story. She wondered if the story she read was anywhere near the truth.

The gentleman in the booth behind her started talking. It only took a few seconds of listening to his one-way conversation and his shuffling of papers for her to realize he was using a Bluetooth device. Randi clenched her teeth, wondering how ticked off the server would be if she asked to be moved to a different table.

The murmur of the guy's conversation crystallized into individual words, phrases, sentences. Something in his voice—an inflection, an oddly pronounced word, something—caught her attention and held it. She lounged against the booth's back cushion, placing herself closer to the stranger.

Heat rolled up her throat while she eavesdropped on his conversation. The subject matter interested her not at all. It was his identity she was determined to ferret out. The more he spoke, the more certain she was that they'd met. By slow degrees, a name rose to the conscious part of her mind. She ran through the alphabet letter by letter, trying to force the cobwebs from her memory.

And just like that, the call ended. Any chance of locating his name disappeared. Randi blew out a breath of frustration. She ached to turn around and look at the guy, but the back of the booth rose at least two feet above her head. The much-needed privacy the cozy area afforded her moments ago, now seemed confining.

"Here you are." Her server set down a plate in front of her. "Tom Yum Goong soup and edamame." The server glanced over the table. "Did no one bring out your ice water?"

"Not yet," Randi said in a low voice.

"I'll be back with that in two shakes. Need anything else?"

Randi shook her head.

With the guy quiet behind her, Randi spooned up a straw mushroom. Ginger, lemongrass, and chiles exploded in her mouth. She soon found out the knots in her stomach had masked a rather large appetite.

Halfway through her soup, Bluetooth Guy's phone rang.

"Gaviston speaking."

Randi's fork paused midway to her mouth, and her heart thunked against her chest. *Surely not.*

"Not yet. My appointment's at three o'clock."

She placed her fork beside her plate and leaned back. Her pulse careened through her veins like a caffeinated kid buzzing around the schoolyard.

"I understand, sir. Trust me to win her over."

Keith Gaviston, attorney for Carolina Club. The voice, the name, the appointment time—there could be no doubt. Of all the freaking restaurants she could have gone to, she'd picked the one in all of Western North Carolina that Keith Gaviston frequented. The odds had to be Power Ball worthy.

"Given her current situation," Gaviston said, "she would be an idiot to pass up such a lucrative deal. No one else has the means to save her business. Miss Shepherd didn't strike me as the unwise sort."

What the hell was going on? Britt and now Gaviston. How had they found out about her financial situation? Had somebody blogged about the investment scam online and named her? In today's technology age, pretty much anything seemed possible. But how could they have found out about her? She had never come across anything that had listed the victims. And she'd looked. Hard.

Was the entire town aware of her impending financial doom? That she was about to lose her business? About to lay off over a dozen people?

"Do I have your authorization to sweeten the deal by twenty percent, if necessary?"

Scalding anger burned deep into her stomach like a big glob of wasabi. The delicious food she'd eaten tasted like dirt on her tongue. Who the hell were these people? And why did they want her thousand acres so badly?

She was missing something. Something important, and it annoyed her to no end.

"Very well, sir. I'll give you a call after the meeting."

The space behind her went silent. Then papers shuffled and the hollow sound of glass thudded against the table. Leather squeaked a moment before Randi saw the figure of a man out of the corner of her eye.

She busied herself by digging around in her purse, counting to *one, two, three, four, five* before lifting her head and looking toward the exit. Yep, even from the back, she recognized Keith Gaviston's long, lean elegance. Such sophistication would be right at home in the boardrooms glutting Wall Street.

Realizing Gaviston was on his way to meet her, she glanced at her phone and released a slow breath. Plenty of time. She would give him a ten-minute head start so there would be no possibility of running into him as she left the restaurant. He could just wait for her on the other end.

What to do? As much as it irked her, he was correct. She'd be stupid to turn down the club's offer with no other viable buyer lined up. If only she had enough time to put it on the market and see what other offers came her way. But she didn't, which meant her hands were tied if she wanted to save her business and protect her employees. Which she did.

But Gaviston's arrogance gnawed at her common sense and logic. Tore at them until raw emotion reared its impulsive head. How she'd like to take the club's lucrative offer and shove it into Gaviston's pretty mouth.

The need to chuck it all—the offer, the responsibility, the guilt—and move to some remote location and do nothing more stressful than mix drinks was strong. What would her life be like if she didn't have Triple B consuming her thoughts 24/7? Would she actually be able to have fun from time to time? Unfortunately, her getaway plans would bore the hell out of her after a few months.

Decision made, Randi paid her bill and left the restaurant—only to come face-to-face with Gaviston, when she stepped outside.

His intelligent emerald-green eyes glanced between her and the restaurant, adding two plus two. A damn flush crept up her neck.

"Miss Shepherd." He greeted her in a diamond-edged voice. "Did you enjoy your lunch?"

"I did. Be sure to try the Tom Yum Goong soup. It's the best in the area."

"I've already dined, thank you." His attention sharpened. "I forgot my sunglasses inside. Did you notice them when you left your booth?"

She could barely think beyond the rhythmic pounding in her ears. Why did she feel like she'd done something wrong when he was the one plotting against her in such a public place? "Booth? Not here. They're rather dark and gloomy, don't you think? I chose one of the window seats that face the courtyard. Much more enjoyable."

"Ah, well, I had best go find them. They're my favorite pair, and I don't want to be late for an important meeting I have at three."

Pasting a teasing smile on her face, Randi said, "Indeed not. See you soon, Mr. Gaviston."

Could anyone's luck be worse than mine? She hadn't fooled him one bit. Even if he bought the booth BS, all he had to do was set those jewel-toned eyes on their server, ask a few innocent-sounding questions, and *wham*, he'd know she lied.

And what would he do with that knowledge during their upcoming conversation?

When she returned to Triple B, she barely had time to stash her purse in a side drawer of her desk before a harried Kris McKay skidded inside.

"Where have you been?" Kris asked. "I've been calling you for over an hour."

"Sorry, Kris. I set my phone to silent. What's up?"

"Sometime last night the cooler housing the food shut down."

"Shut down? How?"

"The electricity went out."

"What about the backup system?"

"The electrician is checking it now."

A stampede of wild horses raced over Randi's chest, kicking the air from her lungs, filling her mouth with dust.

"None of the staff noticed the problem until now?"

"The new staff we've taken on for the summer aren't in tune with things like that yet, so they didn't notice the temperature change."

Blood drained from her face, and a cold slap of failure threw Randi into the nearest chair. Her heart stuttered to a stop before it began a slow slog to life again. Her hands shook and her stomach soured.

"What's the damage?"

"Health Department said it's a total loss." Kris crossed her arms over her middle. "I'm sorry, Randi."

A total loss.

No way could she recover from this. She'd already been hanging off the ledge by her fingertips.

Her business, her employees' jobs, her livelihood—gone.

Randi peered at the clock on her computer.

2:25 p.m.

Gaviston would be here soon. She recalled the unhappy lines around his mouth and the hard glint in his eyes.

Shit, shit. Double damn shit.

CHAPTER SIXTEEN

"STOP BEING A JERK." JONAH slumped down in the passenger seat of his Tesla. "I knew you wouldn't like the idea, but I didn't realize you would be this mule-headed."

Britt continued his surveillance of Triple B. His grip tightened on the steering wheel with every new word that came out of his brother's mouth. "I could never pay you back."

"That's good, because I wouldn't be buying the property for you. It's an investment. An expansion of the Steele Conservation Area."

"Grif would not agree."

"Probably not." Jonah yawned. "But that doesn't mean it's not a sound decision."

Britt propped his elbow on the window ledge and pinched the bridge of his nose as if that simple action could make everything clearer. It didn't, though the pressure did dull the throbbing.

"Jonah, if you keep throwing millions of dollars away on this town, you're going to wind up a damned pauper before you're forty."

His brother laughed. "You have no idea of my net worth, do you?"

Of course he did. He didn't call him the baby billionaire for nothing. Even so, at the rate Jonah was spending money, his stash would eventually run out, wouldn't it?

"What about you?"

"What about me?" Jonah folded a piece of gum into his mouth.

"Aren't there other, I don't know, technology things you'd rather purchase?"

"Dude, I have everything I need and more. If there's something I don't have, I'll buy it. I just finished designing something that will make me even more money. Adding a few acres to my assets won't stop me from getting things I don't need."

"It's more than a few acres, Jonah."

He sent Britt a cocky grin. "Have I mentioned that I'm filthy rich?"

"Shithead."

"Don't you know it."

An unholy mixture of dread and excitement poured over Britt. If he accepted Jonah's offer, he would feel beholden to his little brother for the rest of his life. Not accepting would place the Steele-Shepherd pack in the hands of trophy hunters. Pride versus salvation. Was there really any choice?

"Jonah, I—"

"There's something else," Jonah interrupted, resting a hand on the back of Britt's seat. "Something you're going to like even less."

Dread surged, dousing his excitement to a low hum. "Spill it."

"I've been thinking about the future of the conservation area."

Britt angled his head around to face his brother. He did not like the tone in Jonah's voice. When the town had purchased the property for the sports complex, they had taken on ten thousand additional acres with grand plans for future expansion. Twenty thousand acres in total.

However, his brother Reid had no desire for

expanding the center beyond its original footprint. With everyone's attention focused on the center's renovation, the conservation area, as Jonah had dubbed it, had taken a back burner. To everyone except Britt. He'd spent the past six months exploring the land, getting to know its contours and inhabitants.

Grif had made it clear that the extra acreage was nothing more than a bleed on Jonah's finances. None of his brothers were active outdoorsmen like Britt. They liked the occasional fishing, camping, or hunting excursion, but none of them gave nature a second thought when their outing was over.

So Britt had been careful not to get too attached. With the area's uncertain future, he'd have been a fool to do so. A real fool. Finding the wolf pack on the property changed everything.

"Grif has been speaking with a number of developers," Jonah said, confirming Britt's fears. "He's leaning toward a proposal to construct a hotel and a mini mall. Thinks it'll create a more attractive package for the center's participants, especially since we don't have lodging established."

"He's always had an eye for the big picture." The words cut like diamonds over his tongue. "If you're set on buying the Shepherd property, I would appreciate it if you'd build your hotel on the far east side, away from the wolves." It would help, but in the end, the red wolves would move on. At least he'd maintain their sanctuary for a couple more years before mankind yet again pushed them out.

"Yeah, he's annoyingly accurate, sometimes." Jonah stretched the bright green gum over his tongue and drummed his fingers against Britt's seat. "But I don't think the center will suffer if participants have to commute the mile and a half to the Bayberry Spa and Inn, which has a convenience store within walking distance. We could work out a shuttle system with the inn." He blew a bubble until it popped. "Or we could just build the damn thing adjacent to the center. Reid had safety concerns with the hotel's original placement, anyway. What would it take? Twenty acres? Thirty acres, at the most?"

"What does this have to do with the conservation area?"

Britt was pretty sure his heart stopped beating while awaiting Jonah's answer.

"Even before today, I had balked at destroying the conservation area for development purposes. Our meeting with those pampered rich boys reaffirmed my decision to protect the ten thousand acres." More finger drumming. "And I think it needs a research center."

Britt stared at his brother, uncomprehending. "For what?"

"How should I know?" Jonah flicked his hand in Britt's direction. "Whatever it is you wildlife people research."

Yep, his heart had stopped, because after Jonah's comment, the organ jolted back to life with a powerful kick to his chest.

Jonah continued, "You can do what you always wanted to do, and I can get a nice write-off at tax time. Win-win."

The opportunity Jonah presented was too enormous for Britt to process. All he could think to say was, "I've had no formal education or training. Everything I know is self-taught or through volunteer opportunities I've landed."

"You forget I never went to college either, and yet my self-taught skills have allowed me to amass a fortune." He grinned again. "You're aware that I'm filthy rich, right?"

"You're also a damned genius. I'm not."

"But you're passionate about conservation and too stubborn to fail."

"And you're a reckless idiot with no financial acumen."

"Guilty. The very reason I surround myself with good people, so they can advise me—and I can ignore them when I want."

Britt frowned at his brother. "You're frightening, you know that?"

"Does that mean you'll do it?"

"I'll have full authority over the construction and operation of the center?"

"Just like Reid has over the training center."

"You want no say in how your money is being spent?"

"Grif will bring the major purchases to my attention." He pulled out his phone. "Outside that, I trust you to make the decisions."

"Why?"

Jonah gave him one of those *WTF are you talking about?* looks. "I told you why—"

"Don't feed me your tax bullshit. Grif, Reid, and now me. Why?" Frustration, anger, and a million other emotions buzzed through Britt's veins. He didn't understand them and didn't care. But the answer to his question seemed vitally important in that moment.

Smartphone forgotten, Jonah stared out the passenger side window. His expression appeared lost. Not in thought, but in being. Like a part of him was missing.

Britt swallowed hard against a familiar though rusty emotion. "Forget it," he said in a thick voice. He grasped the back of Jonah's neck. If they weren't parked on Main Street in the middle of the afternoon, Britt would have pulled him in for a bear hug. "You don't have to explain." He gave his brother's neck a squeeze and released him. "Your offer is too generous, but I accept. For the wolves." His gaze turned toward Triple B. *And Randi.*

A giant hand thwacked him on the chest. "Good decision, bro. Hand over my key."

With some reluctance, Britt relinquished the Tesla's key fob to his brother.

Jonah's cocky grin was back. He nodded across the

street. "I'll leave it to you to break the news to Randi." He exited the vehicle and shut the door. Resting an arm on the open window ledge, he peered inside. "Don't screw it up. I'll be back in thirty." He smacked the inside of the door and flipped him off before strolling away.

"Jonah?"

"Yo?"

"Try not to pop your gum in anyone else's ear."

Jonah jettisoned the gum like a spitball. Given the size of Jonah's grin, you'd think he'd been given a behind-the-scenes pass to the filming of the next *Star Trek*.

"The birds, Jonah."

His brother's full-of-himself smile sagged. He peered up and down the sidewalk before retrieving his gumball from the pavement.

"Good, bro."

Jonah flicked the gum at Britt's head.

"Damn punk," Britt grumbled, but his gaze followed his brother's retreat.

Jonah carried with him a host of secrets, masking them all behind a distracted, can't-be-bothered-by-life mien. Though they tended to forget, every one of the Steele clan was aware of the emotional scar Jonah carried. They bore the same one, but none so deep as Jonah's.

After checking his sideview mirror, Britt push the door open and made his way inside Triple B. He spotted Kris McKay cleaning off a table in the lounge area.

"Hey, Kris."

"Hey, Britt. How's it going?"

"Not too bad." He glanced around the coffee shop. "How about you?"

"Our main cooler failed overnight."

"What happened?"

"The electricity shut down. A faulty wire or something."

"Just to the cooler?"

"Yeah, it's on a separate system from the rest." Kris sent a worried look toward the back of the shop. "I thought maybe a mouse got into the wiring, but the electrician didn't think so."

"What's his theory?"

"The wire didn't look gnawed on, and he didn't find a fried rodent. The electrician's choosing his words carefully, but it sounds like someone might have tampered with the wire."

"Any idea who?"

"No, everyone loves working for Randi."

"Isn't there a warning alarm on the cooler?"

"A very loud backup generator. But the gas tank was empty."

"Any sign of forced entry—damaged lock, broken window?"

"Everything looks normal—except the ruined food and broken wire."

"What's the damage?"

"We lost all our food stock. The insurance adjuster is on his way. Grady said they'll probably investigate, given the electrician's assessment."

Which meant no payout for a while.

"How's Randi?"

"Upset, but she's already working on a solution."

"She here?"

"Next door meeting with some hottie in a suit."

Britt checked the time. *2:40.* He'd cut it close, but what attorney was thirty minutes early? *Shit!*

He raked a hand through his hair, fighting the urge to barge into her meeting. If he did, he risked embarrassing her and she might tell him to get lost. If he didn't do something rash, the red wolves would lose. Big time.

"Everything okay, Britt?"

He stared at the wall separating Randi's coffee shop and bar, undecided. Peering down at Kris's concerned face, he said, "I have something important to discuss with her, something that could affect her decision in that meeting."

"Would you like me to get her a message?"

"I would owe you a huge favor, if you could."

A sexy, impish grin appeared. "I like having one of the Steele boys in my debt. Give me a moment while I dump this stuff behind the counter."

"I'll do that." He took the tray from her. "See if you can get Randi to meet me in her office. What I need to say should be in private."

"Her office door is probably locked."

"I'll wait in the hallway."

"Let me see if I can pull her away."

"Try hard, Kris."

"You're going to owe me a *very* big favor for this."

"Done. Now haul ass."

She hurried away, laughing.

Britt took the tray of mugs and plates to one of the baristas and made his way to the back of the shop. In the same hallway he'd used to find Randi in her stockroom last week he came across another stockroom. She probably kept her supplies for the coffee shop and bar separated. He wondered if that meant she had two different accounting systems going, or if it was just easier on her staff to find what they needed.

He twisted the handle on Randi's office door. Locked. He considered searching for the cooler and taking a look at the wiring. But staring at a repaired wire wouldn't do him a bit of good. Besides, he didn't want to take the chance of missing Randi.

Had someone sabotaged her business by destroying her perishables? He'd never heard an ill word said about her, which said a lot considering the tough stance she had to take with some of her drinking customers. He made a mental note to talk to the electrician. Maybe the guy would open up to him—tradesman to tradesman—in a way he wouldn't be comfortable doing with a client.

Randi came around the corner. He couldn't tell from her expression if she was relieved or peeved. All he could really see was a bone-deep fatigue weighing on her features.

She gave him a thorough once-over that sent his mind straight to their kiss, to the feel of her lips moving over his with excruciating tenderness. He couldn't recall now who had made the first move and, in all honesty, he could give a shit. But his body had been yearning for the warmth of her breath on his face again.

Unlocking the door, she motioned for him to enter. "Kris said you had something urgent you needed to tell me. Did something happen to the wolf pups?"

"No, not that I'm aware of." He set his hands on his hips, unsure how to proceed. This whole day had been surreal, otherworldly. He kept waiting for something to blow up in his face.

"Kris told me about the cooler. You've had a run of bad luck."

She laughed. A tired sound, a defeated sound. "Can't say I care much for this year so far."

"I'm sorry for interrupting your meeting."

"You didn't. We had concluded our business right before Kris arrived."

A vine of desperation wrapped around Britt's throat, squeezing. "Was the *hottie* in the suit from the Carolina Club?"

She eyed him questioningly, but nodded.

Britt barely got his next words out over the constriction in his throat. "Did you accept?"

"They offered another twenty percent." She grabbed water out of the small fridge and threw it to him, then pulled one out for herself. "Only a fool would have declined."

"*Dammit*, Randi! When they find out about those wolves, they're going to hunt them into oblivion."

"And you know this how?"

"I paid them a visit today."

"You did *what?*"

"Invaded their inner sanctum. They're not conservationists in the sense you're familiar with through your mother. The club preserves the land and wildlife in order to maintain their sport."

"If they're into preservation, why do you think they'll hunt the wolves into extinction?"

"Because they're not just game hunters, they're trophy hunters. They live and breathe checking animals off their kill list. Rare red wolves would be an unexpected gift to them."

Something flitted across her features. The shift happened so fast that Britt questioned whether he saw it at all. She didn't help matters when she turned her face away to open her water bottle.

"Well, I guess it's good that I'm a fool."

Britt froze. "What'd you say?"

"I said I'm a damned fool."

"You refused the club's offer?"

"God help me, I did." Facing him, she pressed the cool plastic against her forehead. "I've never done anything so irresponsible in my life." Terror-filled eyes glared at him. "And that statement includes the poor investment I made that got me into this unholy mess."

A joy he hadn't felt in way too many years replaced the heartbreak that had threatened to buckle his knees. The wolves were safe. *Safe!*

"Are you truly smiling about this situation?" she asked. "Do you have any idea of the untenable situation in which I just placed my business and employees?"

Britt closed the distance between them, losing his bottle of water along the way. He cradled the rigid edge of her jaw with his palms and planted a celebratory kiss on her lips. What he'd intended as a quick *Hallelujah!* smack lingered.

When she didn't knee him in the nuts, he deepened the kiss, sweeping his tongue against hers. Drawn to her sweet hotness. The moment her tongue surged against his, seeking, needing, demanding, their exploration turned into a tension-releasing inferno.

He couldn't get enough of her.

He allowed the kiss to go on for a while longer before the questions whirring in his head distracted him from the pleasure of her lips. Why had she declined the club's offer? From her reaction, she didn't have a better plan. Could the city girl still be her mother's daughter, an environmentalist at heart?

Putting the wolves' safety above saving her business took an enormous amount of courage and selflessness. Would he have made the same decision given what was at stake? The same sacrifice? He didn't know.

Easing away, he traced every beautiful curve of her face. Memorized them. Held them close so he would never forget this moment.

"Why?" he asked.

She dropped her gaze, silent.

"Why, Randi?"

She shrugged. "I couldn't do it." She looked everywhere but at him. "The wolves deserve a chance. They've already been through so much." Another shrug. "I just couldn't."

So many words of gratitude pushed to the tip of his tongue, though none could adequately convey the sentiments singing in his heart.

"Courageous girl."

"Foolish."

"Never." He tipped her chin up until her eyes met his. "Your mother would be so proud."

She pushed out of his arms. "Do not speak to me about my mother. I'm furious with her right now." She sat down on the edge of the recliner and dropped her head in her hands. "I have absolutely no idea of how to get myself out of this mess."

"I do."

"I'm not taking your life savings."

"How about my brother's spare change?"

She stilled, then lifted her head, one disbelieving inch at a time.

"I spoke to Jonah. He's asked me to extend an offer."

Her expression never changed. She didn't blink. He wasn't even sure she was breathing.

"Did you hear what I said?"

"Of course I did. Do I look deaf to you?"

His lips twitched. "Deaf, no. Dumb, yes."

A pillow bounced off his stomach.

"No more worries," he said quietly.

Tears sparkled in her eyes, and he ached to pull her into his arms and shower her with soothing words and calming caresses.

"But you didn't want to be indebted to your brother."

"We've both made sacrifices to ensure the pack's safety."

Her gaze roamed his features, studying every inch as if searching for a hint of emotion. A futile effort. He'd spent years hiding his thoughts.

"I don't know what to say," she said, sounding lost.

"*Yes* would be a good start."

Rising, she held out her hand. "Please tell Jonah that I accept his generous offer. Though I have no idea of the details."

He grasped her outstretched hand. "We could discuss them over dinner." With gentle pressure, he drew her closer.

"It's Friday."

Closer. "Yes."

"I work Friday nights."

"Did someone call in sick?"

"No."

"Then why do you need to be here?"

"To work. To fill in the gaps."

Closer. "Maybe the boss will give you the night off."

Confusion flared in her beautiful eyes. "But it's our busiest shift." Her attention fixed on his mouth.

A mere three inches separated their bodies, and Britt

forced himself to go slow when all he wanted to do was back her into the nearest wall and slam into her heat. "Are you short-staffed?"

She shook her head.

Lowering his mouth to her ear, he whispered, "Then be with me."

Her shuddering breath fanned over his neck, cooling his heated flesh. Britt's lips grazed along the outer shell of her ear. "Please."

Angling her face toward him, she covered his mouth with hers while her fingers burrowed into the hair at the base of his skull. He took that as a yes and curled one arm around her waist. Having her body pressed against his from head to knee made his gut quiver. Every inch of him strained to be closer, deeper.

When she arched into him, his mind exploded in color. The tenor of the kiss changed. Wild desperation replaced controlled hunger.

Britt eased his hand beneath her top. Conscious of the rough callouses on his palm, he glided his fingertips over smooth perfection. He'd never felt anything so soft and silken and warm.

Putting some space between their entwined bodies, Britt followed the edge of her bra until the backs of his fingers made contact with the underside of her breasts. She arched nearer, and he palmed both mounds, plumping them while he drew her bottom lip into his mouth.

Britt's thumbs raked her hard nipples, eliciting a groan of pleasure. His mouth watered with the need to replace his thumbs with his tongue. He wanted to taste her so damned badly that his hands shook.

What the hell had gotten into him? He'd never felt on the verge of losing control with a woman before. Always, his mind was three steps ahead of his actions. In the past, sex had been about release and, at times, simple human companionship.

Never before had he wanted to consume his partner.

Burrow beneath the covers and love her all night long. Everything about Randi felt like home, salvation, happiness. He couldn't explain his feelings, though he'd known there was something special about her since that first day in the woods.

The day when, in a fit of frustration, she'd mooned him. It had taken every molecule of willpower he possessed not to call her out on it, not to burst out laughing. No doubt her impulsive action had caused her no small amount of embarrassment after her anger had worn off. Then again, maybe not.

In Randi, he sensed a kindred spirit. When he was with her, he didn't feel so alone, so adrift, so much a failure. The connection he felt with her made no sense. Before Barbara's death, they'd barely spoken two words to each other. After her death, their exchanges had been terse and wary. Except for the short time they'd spent watching the wolves. Then, they'd become friends.

During that short half hour, their complicated human world had melted away, leaving them immersed in birdsong, loamy soil, pine-scented air, and sun-kissed leaves. Britt feared that if he didn't explore this thing with Randi, he would regret it. And now that his little brother had come to the rescue, he could get to know Randi better and look after the wolves.

He needed to muster the courage to share his feelings with Randi. To hang on to her with all of his strength. To pursue the happiness that was now within his reach.

Could he do it? Could he add another layer of responsibility to the stack?

Indecision clogged his chest, making it difficult to breathe. Britt stepped away.

CHAPTER SEVENTEEN

ONE MOMENT RANDI WAS WEAVING between clouds of sensual bliss created by Britt's long, drugging kiss. And in the next, she stood alone, cold, a silo in an empty winter field.

Her eyelids fluttered, blinking away the final remnants of her pleasant haze. She studied the object of her desire and her confusion.

A flush covered his neck and face, and light glinted off his plump, thoroughly kissed lips. His chest rose high with each breath and his hair stuck out in different places from her greedy fingers.

The only thing that didn't fit the take-me-now bill was his bloodless fists and squared-off shoulders. Where her body felt limp and pliant, buzzing with anticipation, Britt appeared tense and fight ready.

Without taking her eyes off Britt, she tugged down her shirt until it wrapped around her waist once again. The action caught his attention, and hunger hardened his features.

"Did I do something wrong?" she asked quietly.

"No."

Relief swept over her like one of those airport body scanners, only warmer, less clinical. But the consolation didn't last long. What had spooked him enough to end one of the hottest kisses she'd ever enjoyed?

Heat scorched her ears, and her eyes widened as a horrible possibility occurred to her. Could he be in a relationship? She'd never seen anyone attached to him for more than a few hours. But that didn't mean there wasn't someone special in his life. Each time they'd kissed it was as if they'd both gotten swept up in the moment.

"A-are you seeing someone?"

"If I was, this"—he waved a finger between them—"wouldn't have happened. And I certainly wouldn't have asked you out to dinner."

At his tone, Randi's spine snapped to attention. "I'm trying to understand."

He clasped one hand around the back of his neck and stared at the ceiling. Seconds ticked by, and Randi began to fidget with her thumbnail. She would have to trim it soon.

"Me, too," he said, dropping his hand.

Lost. Although he was attracted to her, he didn't know what to do with her any more than she knew what to do with him. What fine lovers they made.

She reached out and ran her hand down his forearm until her fingers nestled inside his palm. "How about we take this day by day?" She sent him a tentative smile. "Starting with dinner tonight?"

His hand tightened over hers, and Randi's heart lifted at the small reassurance.

"But it's Friday night," he said.

"I'll talk the boss into giving me the night off."

He brushed the backs of his fingers over her cheek, and she could tell he wanted to kiss her again. She wanted him too, badly, though she made no move of encouragement. A long time ago she'd learned that personal demons could not be battled by committee. Knowing someone cared and supported you helped, gave you strength, but the sword could only be wielded by the one under siege.

"I'll pick you up at seven." He turned to leave.

"Give me a second and I'll write down my address."

"I got it covered." The door closed behind him.

Randi wondered what to make of his statement. Did he already know where she lived? How? Had Carlie Beth told him? Grif? Or had he wanted to escape and knew he could get the address?

For someone who protected her privacy with a vengeance, she found herself caring little about the answer. Rather than concern, she felt only mild curiosity.

Dragging her thoughts away from Britt Steele, Randi peered down at her desk, at the stack of unopened bills, at the payroll she wouldn't have been able to pay an hour ago. Her throat closed, and the despair that had been riding her for weeks dissipated.

She'd done it. Saved her business and her employees' livelihoods. Saved herself from crushing guilt and unfathomable failure. She could not believe her good fortune, but she wouldn't dwell on it.

Randi sat down and pulled up her financial software, checking which vendors she could afford to pay off now while she waited for her check from Jonah Steele.

She began making lists, putting a plan in place. Her pen hovered over her notepad, the numbers blurred out of focus as Britt crept back into her mind. He'd accepted his brother's offer of help. Not just for the wolves but for her.

Would he come to resent his decision? Would he blame her? Would his resentment turn to hate?

Somehow she would make sure that didn't happen.

Somehow.

CHAPTER EIGHTEEN

RICHARD NORWOOD CONTEMPLATED THE attorney sitting calmly in front of him. He didn't allow the rage welling up inside him to show. No one, not even his colleagues scattered about the room, had seen the volatile side of his nature. Medication helped him keep the most damaging aspects under control, though he grew tired of hiding behind a wall of drugs and civility.

More and more, he'd depended on hunting, on the Kill List, to assuage his bloodlust, his need to defeat. The greater the challenge, the higher the reward.

Keith Gaviston wouldn't understand such cravings and, therefore, couldn't represent his interests to the depth necessary. It was time to find another voice for his cause.

"You are certain the Shepherd girl's mind cannot be swayed to sell?" he asked the attorney.

"She appeared quite settled with her decision." Gaviston's gaze moved about the room, fixing on each of the members present. "At the conclusion of our meeting, I overheard one of her employees announce Britt Steele's arrival. Perhaps she received a more lucrative deal from the Steele family. It would make sense, given the eldest son's association with Barbara Shepherd and the proximity of their two properties."

Richard's fingers tightened on the snifter he held. To

cover his reaction to the missed opportunity, he whirled the single malt scotch around the glass before taking a sip. He allowed the whisky to coat his tongue, enjoying the full-bodied, smoky flavor before swallowing.

Setting down his snifter, he gave the attorney a direct look, one that would leave no room for misunderstanding. "It seems we are no longer in need of your firm's services, Mr. Gaviston."

Gaviston nodded. "I'll let you know if Miss Shepherd changes her mind."

"You don't understand. Your services are no longer needed. Ever."

"By your decree, or the club's?"

"Is there a difference?"

Gaviston didn't get angry or make excuses and he didn't ask annoying, useless questions. His features gave nothing away to the observer. When Gaviston rose, he stood at easy attention and his movements remained smooth. He exuded confidence in the face of disaster and disappointment. The attorney could be seething with fury or melting in relief.

Richard experienced a twinge of regret for his decision. Notwithstanding Gaviston's failure on the Shepherd case, the attorney had served the club's interests well over the past three years. But Richard couldn't abide failure. Of any kind.

"If you'll excuse me, gentlemen?"

Richard inclined his head, and Gaviston shut the door with a soft thud behind him.

"Why'd you let the solicitor go?" Angus Ferguson asked, his brogue more indecipherable than usual.

"He lacked the necessary negotiating skills." Richard rested his elbows on the chair's arms and steepled his fingers together. "We need someone who will keep the club's best interests in the forefront of his mind."

Neil Watters brushed a nonexistent speck of dirt off the sleeve of his Ermenegildo Zegna suit jacket. "Do you think Steele added the Shepherd acreage to his empire?"

"Those Steele boys sniffing around here earlier couldn't have been a coincidence," Samuel Taylor drawled. "They were measuring up their competition."

"What did they learn that could have been used to outbid us?" Jun Ito asked in a low voice, his steady gaze sliding from one man's face to another.

"Damned if I know," Samuel said. "We talked about membership. No harm there."

"The billionaire's brother, Britt, accompanied him?"

"Yes," Richard answered.

"Did Hugh give them a tour?"

"Of course."

"Did they venture into the Canid Room?"

Richard's attention traveled to the gray wolf display, then to the empty mount next to it. His jaw clenched and he snatched the phone off the receiver. His finger stabbed at a series of numbers. "We'll soon find out."

"Good afternoon, Mr. Norwood. How may I assist you?"

"Send Hugh Donovan to me." He hung up. To think they'd welcomed the Steele brothers into their exclusive sanctuary and they'd used what they saw or heard to outmaneuver them was unimaginable. Unforgivable.

A few minutes later, Hugh strolled in, a smile on his fat face. "Daniel said you were looking for me?"

Richard did not ask him to sit down. "Tell us about your tour with the Steele brothers?"

As the steward became aware of the tension pulsing inside the room, his smile faded. "They arrived without an appointment. Since I had nothing pressing, I answered their questions and gave them a tour."

"Did your tour include this room?"

"Yes, we spent a bit of time here. The older brother seemed particularly fascinated with the specimens in here."

"You may go," Richard ground out. "Payroll will forward your final paycheck next week."

Confusion mixed with beads of sweat on Donovan's forehead. "You're firing me?"

"Obviously."

"But why, sir?"

"Not only did you allow spies to breach our walls, you gave them a grand fucking tour."

"Spies? What are you talking about?"

"The Steele brothers were here on reconnaissance."

"Why?"

"To take our measure and use it against us."

"Use what against us? I don't understand what you're accusing me of."

Richard shifted forward in his chair. "Let me be plain, then. The brothers saw the missing red wolf display on their tour. They used that information to talk Miranda Shepherd into selling her property to them."

Donovan licked his plump lips, leaving a gut-roiling shine behind. "Red wolves?"

"Good day, Mr. Donovan."

The steward sent a desperate glance to the other gentlemen, looking for salvation. He found none.

Into the silence that followed the steward's departure, Neil said, "Hugh's been here for nearly thirty years. He had plans to retire this fall."

"He cost us valuable resources today. I couldn't let that go unpunished."

"Gaviston's comment about the Steeles purchasing the Shepherd property was only speculation," Samuel drawled.

"Can either of you think of another reason why the Shepherd girl turned down our lucrative deal?"

Silence.

"Will the president agree with your decision?" Jun asked.

"Do not worry about Jack Bennett. I will deal with him."

"Bloody hell, what a mess," Angus grumbled. "Where do we go from here?"

Richard sipped his whisky. "Simple. If we cannot buy what we want, we'll take it."

CHAPTER NINETEEN

BRITT PULLED UP IN FRONT of the single-story bungalow sandwiched between two McMansions. Steele Ridge wasn't unlike many places across the country where wealthy property owners were buying small older homes and tearing them down. No one would blink an eye at that except the new owners used up every bit of land zoning would allow to erect their three- to four-thousand-square-foot structures. The new construction looked ginormous beside quaint homes like Randi's.

Anxiety about seeing Randi again battered his body. At his urging, Jonah had directed Grif to send Randi a deposit to hold the sale while the paperwork was being drawn up. The influx of cash would help her restock her cooler and pay off her vendors, keeping Triple B afloat for the length of time it would take to execute the sale. For once, Grif hadn't grumbled about Jonah spending his fortune. He seemed oddly excited about the additional acreage.

Lost in thought, Britt didn't notice Mrs. Lancaster until her age-worn voice caught his attention.

"Britt Steele, what brings you to Sunset Boulevard?"

At least eighty, probably nearing ninety, Mrs. Lancaster walked sure-footed down the sidewalk, accompanied by an enormous red Doberman pinscher. The dog had to weigh as much as its owner and the

Dobe's head hit the woman at chest level. Yet the well-trained canine seemed content to prance on tiptoes at her mistress's side.

Not waiting for an answer, she eyed Randi's house and sent him a knowing smile. "About time someone showed that girl a good time. She works way too hard. No play makes a woman age." She raked a hand down her diminutive body. "As you can see, I had my fair share of fun in my day." Behind her thick blue-framed glasses, she waggled an eyebrow, causing her enlarged eyes to appear more than a little wonky. Then her expression turned serious. "Treat her with respect though, or answer to me"—she waved a hand at the Dobe, whose brandy-colored eyes bore through Britt's skull—"and Pansy."

Pansy? More like Xena.

Because she seemed to be waiting for some sort of acknowledgment, Britt fell back on his Southern upbringing for a reply. "Yes, ma'am."

That was the thing about living in the same small town all of your life—everyone had a hand in raising you. Even when you were a thirty-four-year-old man. Rather than be irritated by the fact, Britt smiled at the old woman's gumption. He hoped he had that much fire flowing through his veins at eighty.

"How's your mom?"

"Spry as always."

"And your sister, Evie?"

"Killing it in college."

Mrs. Lancaster's eyes sharpened. "What about your other sister? I never hear mention of her."

Because my family's secrets are none of your damn business.

"Breaking hearts as usual." A canned answer, a factual answer. But not in the way most people took the comment.

"That a girl."

Pansy decided to take a dump in Randi's front yard, redirecting her mistress's attention.

Britt released a heavy breath and shoved aside the ancient memories clawing to the surface. He had enough to worry about right now besides his estranged little sister. When Pansy finished her business, he almost bent and gave the dog a hug for saving him—until he realized what his mother's upbringing would force him to do next.

Mrs. Lancaster removed a plastic bag from her pocket and moved to pick up Pansy's crap.

Dammit. Something like this would never happen to Grif.

"Here, Mrs. Lancaster. Let me get that for you."

"Not necessary, my boy. You're all dressed up."

Grabbing the bag, he said, "I'll be sure to wash my hands before kissing the girl."

The old woman cackled while Britt turned the bag inside out and scooped up the warm pile. After he tied the bag handles together, Mrs. Lancaster took Pansy's trophy from him.

"In my day, we called men like you good eggs."

"Thank you, ma'am."

"Remember what I said about treating Randi right." Mrs. Lancaster patted her Dobe's head. "Heel, Pansy." She carried on toward her own bungalow, two doors down.

By the time he reached Randi's porch, she stood in the open doorway, leaning against the frame. Wearing one helluva sexy outfit. A sleeveless midnight-blue dress wrapped around her body, revealing hidden curves and breasts any hot-blooded man would admire. Open-toed black shoes with killer spikes topped the ensemble—or so he initially thought.

The real icing was her bemused smile. Something about the tilt of her lips clamped around his chest and squeezed like hell. It was a genuine smile. Warm, teasing, sensual. He could wake up to that smile alone, every day. The realization swiped the last of his breath right out of his lungs.

"She's got quite the spunk, doesn't she?" Randi asked, her grin widening.

"Does she vet all your guy friends?"

"Every single one."

An image of Randi inviting other men to her house dampened his good humor. He refused to let it ruin his evening, though. Lord knew he was no saint when it came to female companionship.

"I see I misjudged dinner attire." Her gaze raked down his body, taking in his black button-down shirt, jeans, and cowboy boots. "Give me a few minutes and I'll put on something more appropriate."

"Don't you dare." He made to snatch her wrist to prevent her from disappearing inside, then pulled back at the last minute, remembering the load he'd picked up. "I'll be the envy of every man in Chick-fil-A."

"You're going to make this painful for me, aren't you?"

He could think of many more ways to describe tonight, but *painful* wasn't one of them. Unless he counted the ache building in his pants. Having Randi, in that dress, within reach all night could be debilitating.

"I have the perfect place for us."

"Would you like to wash your hands while I get my things?"

"Saw my poop-scoopin' abilities, did you?"

"Indeed I did." Her teasing smile softened. "Very gallant of you, Britt Steele."

"Mom would've tanned my hide had I stood there and watched."

"Big guy like you afraid of his mama?"

"Every Southern boy is afraid of his mama."

Laughing, she retrieved a small black purse while he made use of her powder room. When they left her house, she slid her hand into his. The act was so natural, as if they'd done this same thing a thousand times, that Britt didn't think twice about leaning in and pressing a soft kiss to her lips. In those dream-worthy heels, she almost stood nose-to-nose with him.

Perfect.

When he opened Old Blue's door, she hesitated a moment, no doubt assessing the most ladylike way of climbing into his pickup.

"Would you care for a suggestion?"

"Would you care for a stiletto to the forehead?"

He laughed, lifting her into his arms and setting her inside. "You can work out the logistics next time—when I'm not starving." He shut the door on her curses.

Thirty minutes later, they arrived at Urban Grille, a contemporary restaurant decorated in grays and black and lots of natural stonework. The place had an upscale vibe with a down-to-earth feel. A perfect place for worn jeans and boots or cocktail dresses and heels.

"This is amazing," Randi said as they waited to be seated. "How'd you find this place?"

"Grif." His brother had a knack for finding all the unique, worth-your-money shops and restaurants in any area he visited.

The hostess showed them to an intimate table for two adjacent to a low-burning fireplace that was more for ambiance than warmth. A tea light candle flickered on their tabletop.

Britt pulled out Randi's chair for her before taking the seat next to her.

The hostess handed them their menus. "Enjoy your dinner."

Randi opened her menu. "Any suggestions?"

"I'm a steak kind of guy. Big, juicy, bloody."

She made a face. "Not helpful."

Britt kept his attention on his menu, even though he knew before they'd arrived what he would order. The next hour would be agony. He would rather have taken her on a hike or a drive along the Parkway. With those two options, he could have discussed various points of interest.

Everything they might talk about over a meal—the wolves, her bar, her mom—would be a forbidden, open wound. Did she have hobbies? Favorite places to visit?

Chancing a peek over his menu, he studied her. What did she do with her precious few hours of freedom? TV? Movies? Books? Music? Or maybe she preferred to sit on her porch with an iced tea while watching the sunset. Or tracking her nosy neighbor up and down the street.

She wore her hair down. He couldn't recall ever having seen her wear it that way before. She seemed to prefer taming it into a ponytail or a sloppy ponybun. Tonight, her blond strands appeared animated in the firelight. Like silken flames dancing on a woodland breeze.

Woodland breeze? What the hell?

Britt slapped the menu onto the table. He couldn't even blame his brothers for putting such poetic nonsense in his head. Phrases like *silken flames* and *woodland breeze* didn't show up in Jonah's graphic novels or Grif's financial e-zines. And who knew what Reid read for enjoyment. Probably survival guides or how-to-take-your-badass-gun-apart-in-ten-seconds-or-less mags.

"Everything all right?" Randi asked.

"Of course." He nodded toward her menu. "Did you find something?"

"I found a lot of somethings. Deciding on one is the hard part."

"Hey, there," a masculine voice said over Britt's shoulder. A young man with icy-blue eyes parked his well-honed body at the end of their table. "Welcome to Urban Grille. I'm Blake and I'll be your server tonight. What can I get y'all to drink?"

Randi closed her menu and smiled up at the guy. "A sangria, please."

Blake moved closer to Randi. "Red or white?"

"What do you suggest?"

"Red. Definitely red."

It was hard for Britt to tell at this angle, but he was almost certain the waiter's gaze lingered on Randi's mouth.

"Bud Light for me," Britt cut in. He glanced at Randi. "Ready to order?" Anything to keep this guy from ogling his date one more minute.

Randi nodded. "I'm torn between the cedar-planked tilapia and chicken marsala. Any recommendations?"

Britt clamped his mouth shut as he listened to the two go back and forth. When Blake finally turned to him, he gave the twenty-something kid a hard look. "Prime rib. I want it hopping on the plate."

"Got it," Blake said, unaffected. "I'll be back with y'all's drinks in a sec."

Randi crossed her legs and sat back. "Do you know our server?"

"No."

"Would you prefer he'd been a she with her breasts bursting out of the top of her too-tight T-shirt?"

Her words slapped away his bad humor. "It would have been more pleasurable on my part."

"And less on mine."

"Have I mentioned I'm territorial?"

"Territorial? A trait you picked up from the wolves?"

"A trait I picked up around *you*."

"For a woman you barely know?"

His voice lost its teasing tone. "I know you, Miranda Shepherd."

"How is that possible? We'd barely spoke to each other until a week ago."

Britt couldn't tell her the truth about his Friday night visits to her bar. Lord only knew what she'd think of a thirty-something guy who hadn't dropped a large enough set of balls to ask her out. And he certainly wasn't ready to admit he'd never been territorial with any other woman.

"Your mother spoke of you often."

"My mother knew less than nothing about me. All of her attention was focused on her work, her causes." She let her gaze roam over the other guests, visibly collecting herself. She attempted a smile, no doubt trying to direct him away from her too-revealing words.

She'd made other vague references to her relationship with Barbara. She was dealing with abandonment issues, whether perceived or real, he didn't know. In the time he'd spent with Barbara, she'd never let on about the state of her relationship with her daughter.

In fact, she seemed to know a great deal about Randi's personal and professional accomplishments. She was never shy about praising her daughter. He'd been intrigued well before their chance meeting at his mom's sixtieth birthday party six months ago.

Their brief conversation had him entering her bar the very next Friday. Though he'd seen her only a few days before, he hadn't been prepared for his first glimpse of Randi in her element. Outfitted in a powder-blue V-neck top with bootcut jeans and cowgirl boots, she'd fit the mold for most small-town working-class girls in North Carolina. But her sloppy ponybun and fresh-faced appearance had tantalized him all night. She'd zipped around the bar for hours, always sparing a comment or smile for her customers. Never tiring, never disappearing, never looking his way.

Triple B was Randi and vice versa. Her stamina and focus put him—and everyone around her—to shame. No one on her staff could keep up with her. No one commanded the same attention.

The more he'd visited her bar, the more he'd wanted to get to know her. Not her public persona. The real Randi. The Randi who broke open a bottle of wine behind closed doors. The Randi who wore sweats and read books in her living room. The Randi who smiled a genuine smile at her friends.

His life wasn't exactly complicated, but it was full. He had no idea how to work a romantic relationship into his schedule. Still didn't, especially with this new project Jonah had laid at his feet.

Women liked attention—a lot of it, and it had to be delivered in various unfathomable forms like flowers, phone calls, movies, meals, kissing but no sex, touching but no sex, and then sex, sex, *I love you.* The sheer volume of need blew his mind. And if he didn't deliver…silent treatment.

Love. He'd never experienced an inkling of the emotion. Maybe because most of his relationships had only lasted a few months before either they or he got bored and wanted to move on.

What a mess. Here he was, pushing for the next step, yet he had no idea if he was even prepared for it. Maybe his next step didn't match hers. Maybe they had nothing in common. Maybe her interest in him stopped at physical companionship. Having a boyfriend might be the furthest thing from her mind. Could he settle for a sex-only arrangement? He'd done so in the past, but every time he considered that kind of relationship with Randi, his mind shied away from the idea. Something vital would be missing. Off. Way off. Lost for hours kind of off.

"Here we go." Blake set down their drinks. "Your meals will be out in a few minutes." He trotted off, leaving silence in his wake.

"Should we discuss the details of my agreement with Jonah?" she asked.

The first stirrings of failure formed low in his gut. He'd hoped this evening would end in her agreement to see him again. But that plan had just taken a right turn toward the big R.

"There's really not much to discuss. He's purchasing Sagebrook for a price agreeable to you both."

"No caveat? No exceptions? No contingent-upon clauses?"

He shrugged. "Jonah likes to keep things simple."

"What is he getting out of this besides additional land? Does he know about the wolves?"

"He does now."

She shook her head as if the pieces of the puzzle refused to click into place. "Your brother is that wealthy? That he could purchase a thousand acres just to save a pack of wolves?"

"And he won't even feel a dent in his wallet."

"He must love you very much."

It took several seconds for Britt to force the words through his tight throat. "He's a good kid—when he's not a pain in the ass."

She smiled. "I always wondered what it would be like to have a brother or sister."

"I have a few you could borrow. Free for a decade."

"You'd miss them too much."

"I have an amazing ability to ignore my own needs. I'll survive."

"Wait until I see Grif. I'm sure he'll be interested to know that his older brother was trying to barter him off."

"You're right. Grif would never let me execute the deal for free. He'd make sure I got a fair—more than fair—price for him."

Her laugh echoed across the room. A pure, contagious note that made his mouth cock into an answering grin.

"You are all sorts of wrong. I wouldn't have taken you for a wicked card-carrying member."

Leaning back, he toyed with his fork. "What membership did you think I held?"

"Staid. Brooding. Controlled."

Britt raised a brow. "By all means, take your time and think about it awhile."

"What? You don't like my assessment?"

"I'm not sure. Sounds like you're calling me boring."

"When you come into my bar, you and your brothers always have people around you. Yet most of the time, you appear to be observing, not participating."

Interesting. She'd watched him as much as he'd watched her. Maybe the Big R of rejection had ducked behind the bend.

"I'm not much of a conversationalist." Britt cringed. Way to sell himself to the hot chick.

"Really? I don't recall there being any awkward moments between us."

Britt reviewed their previous conversations and discovered she was right. Even during some of their more difficult discussions he hadn't been at a loss for words. Tonight was no exception. He'd sat down dreading how he would make it through the meal. How he would keep things interesting when so much of what they had in common would be off-limits. But they'd been here a good fifteen minutes, and he was enjoying himself.

"Must be you."

"I doubt it. You might be one of those people who express themselves better one-on-one, rather than with a group of folks."

"Did you major in psychology?"

"No, but I should have. Running my own business is as much about building healthy relationships with and between my staff as it is increasing revenues. Both take time and a whole lot of patience." She took a sip of her sangria. "You know what I'm talking about. Aren't you a contractor or something?"

"Simple handyman."

Her eyes strolled over his face, neck, and chest. "There's nothing simple about you, Britt Steele."

The way she said his name made his gut tighten. If they hadn't been in this restaurant, he would have had her sprawled out beneath him on a bed, floor, island, anything horizontal. The need to feel her wrapped all around him was becoming an obsession.

"*Au contraire,*" he said. "I live in the woods, in a four-room cabin. I have no wife to answer to, no kids to screw up, no employees to disappoint. My client changes on a weekly, sometimes daily basis, and if I don't like him or her, I walk away. Simple."

An emotion flitted across her beautiful face, but it fled before he could poke a finger at it. "What about friends? Or…female companionship?"

"I have a select few friends whom I trust and who've

known me since I was a rugrat. When it comes to companionship with the opposite sex, I'm"—he held her gaze—"selective."

"No commitments?"

"None."

"No hard feelings?"

"Friends to the end and after." His mouth slid into a smile. "You should know, I don't do flowers or morning-after calls."

"Now that's too bad." Her expression turned solemn. "That might be a deal-breaker."

Sonofabitch. He started to tell her he'd make an exception when her straight face started crumbling.

"Have you heard the expression 'paybacks are a bugger'?" he asked.

She craned her neck around, searching.

"What are you looking for?"

"Anyone who might have captured your expression on camera. I would give up my Jeep for a copy."

"Why do I get the feeling you're going to be trouble?"

She winked. "I haven't the slightest idea."

He weighed the wisdom of his next statement. A hefty caveat to the arrangement their banter was creating. His time with her could disappear in a blink. Or it could be the beginning of something really special.

Oh, hell. He had to go all in on this or he'd regret it. "There's one more thing you should know."

She stilled, hearing the change in the tone of his voice. "Go on."

"I'm not looking for sex alone."

Confusion scrunched the area between her eyebrows. "I'm listening."

"I want to be with you, hang with you, laugh with you."

Her features relaxed. "I believe they call that friends with benefits."

"That works for me."

"Me, too."

The air sizzled around them, and Britt didn't know if he'd make it through supper without dragging her across the table for a hard, tongue-dueling kiss.

"Here you go," Blake-the-bad-timing-server bleated with a charm-filled grin. "Cedar plank tilapia with chimichurri sauce." He set a plate before Randi before dropping Britt's in front of him. "And jumping-on-the-plate prime rib."

Britt's stomach growled. He ignored it. Ignored bleating Blake. Ignored the voice warning him to take it slow, to be the turtle. *Be the turtle, be the turtle, be the damn turtle.* His eyes traveled to Randi's, settled, asked. Her answering nod, infinitesimal.

"Can I bring you anything else?" Blake asked.

To hell with the turtle.

"Yes," Britt said. "Carryout boxes."

CHAPTER TWENTY

ANTICIPATION LEAPT ALONG RANDI'S NERVE endings as Britt steered his truck down the gravel drive leading to his cabin. Their conversation had dwindled with each mile he'd put between them and the restaurant. Words gave way to long, promising looks, to charged silence, to driving, aching need.

The only thing that kept her from ripping free of her skin was Britt's tight hold of her hand. Upon entering his vehicle, he'd tangled his fingers with hers and hadn't let go. How had he known that she needed the comfort of his touch, the connection of his flesh against hers?

He turned the truck off and faced her, an easy smile on his lips. A smile that belied the hunger in his eyes. "Come on, I'll buy you a drink." Squeezing her hand, he released her, then came around to open her door.

She couldn't help but be charmed by his attempt to set her at ease. Beneath his watchful, brooding facade existed an easygoing, down-to-earth guy who appealed to her on a scary level. He was like warmed peach cobbler on a chilly summer night, like a pair of well-worn leather boots supporting you on a rugged hike. And wedged beneath all that brooding and easygoingness beat a big compassionate heart.

After assisting her down, he set her hand in the crook of his elbow. Such a sweet, gallant gesture that seemed as natural to him as breathing. Using the uneven terrain as an excuse, she pressed against his arm and soaked up the firm strength of his big body.

He hit a switch, and a side table lamp cast a soft glow over the small living space. His cabin looked like a bachelor's pad in many ways. Dirty dishes teetered on the counter, and an empty beer bottle sat near a leather recliner. A faded blue ball cap, a red flannel shirt, and a ring of keys hung from a pegboard near the door.

But dust didn't cover every surface, and the cabin didn't smell of stale food. In fact, a woodsy, faint lemony scent blanketed the air. A laptop and several thick books occupied the small breakfast table, and newspaper clippings, graphs, and a U.S. map covered a corkboard on one wall.

She saw no sign of a television or music system. His cabin felt like a home and command center all in one.

Britt paused, scanning the interior as if seeing it for the first time. "I, uh, didn't expect company tonight."

His confession warmed her. In her office earlier, he'd, intentionally or unintentionally, tapped into her loneliness to entice her to dine with him. Although she hadn't been 100 percent sure of where they'd end up after supper, she'd prayed it would be his bed—or hers.

But he had not made any assumptions about how things would end tonight, which further confirmed his statement about this thing between them not being just about sex. Something she hadn't completely believed at the time. Now she did.

Randi released his arm and strolled around the room, unabashedly snooping. Angling her body over the breakfast table, she read the header of one slender book.

International Journal of Natural Resource Ecology and Management.

Her gaze moved to the next book.

The Secret World of Red Wolves.

Every tome littering his table explored something about the natural world. Not one handyman how-to guide or operating manual. He lived and breathed wildlife and land management.

A stack of papers atop a large manila envelope caught her eye. *Application for Anti-Poaching Foundation…Green Army—*

"Let me clean this up." He snatched the papers and books from the table and stashed them on a small desk tucked against the living room wall.

"May I ask you a personal question?"

He speared her a wary look. "Sure."

"Why did you pick your current profession rather than the one that's obviously so close to your heart?"

"No degree, no biologist position."

Although his explanation was straightforward, Randi detected an aching regret underlying his words. "Have you considered taking night classes?"

A whisper, barely a touch, grazed along the zippered seam at the back of her dress. Her breath caught, waiting. But the release of her zipper never came.

"I've taken a few night classes," he said. "At this point in my life obtaining a degree for career reasons doesn't make sense."

"Why do you say that?"

His fingers skimmed over her hair, soothing her scalp. "Most biologists have five to ten years under their belt by my age. In the time it would take me to get my degree, those same biologists would have their eye on retirement."

"All the better for you to take their place."

He chuckled. "I'm too old to learn a young man's science."

She twisted around. "Nonsense." She pointed toward the stack of books. "You've educated yourself. All you need now is field experience."

"I was working on it."

Understanding widened her eyes. "Is that why you were working with Mom?"

"In part." He stared at his desk, at the mound of papers. "Lord only knew what, but Barbara saw something in me."

"It's not too hard to figure out what."

A smile appeared on his handsome face, thankful, sad, defeated. He trailed a finger along her cheek. "Optimist."

She shook her head. "Someone has done a number on you, and I suspect the guilty party's standing right in this room."

"Meaning, I'm my own worst enemy?"

"You wouldn't be the first to fall into that destructive mindset." Her voice drifted off. "Or the last."

He brushed a stray tendril away from her eye. "Sounds like we're both a mess."

"Yes." If only she had the right words, the perfect morsel of wisdom to awaken him to his potential, to set him free from his self-imposed chains. Maybe her mother struggled with the same thing and that was why she began mentoring him.

Action versus discussion.

Her attention dropped to his mouth, fixed there. *Action. Action, action, action.*

"If you continue staring at me like that," he warned on a ragged breath, "I'm going to show you an effective distraction technique."

She rose on tiptoes, slipping her hands inside the collar of his button-down shirt. Her cool hands a balm against his heated neck. "Like this?" A mere half-inch away from his lips, she paused and glanced up at him.

Stepping closer, he brought her body flush against his, covering her mouth with a hungry, openmouthed kiss. He tasted of beer and oranges and danger.

She carved her fingers through his hair, pulling him closer, deeper. When she ground against his hardness, he groaned and flexed his hips, driving them both mad. Too many clothes separated them. She hooked her knee around his thigh.

Understanding her demand, he grasped her hips and lifted until she locked her legs around his waist. Their lips never parted as he picked his way to the bedroom. Once he reached the bed, he released her bottom and allowed her feet to slide to the floor. Breaths pulsed, hearts collided in an ancient rhythm.

Randi could not think beyond the next second. Desire guided her every thought, every sense, every move. She could *smell* him. An intoxicating blend of masculine arousal and woodsy soap.

"If you're going to change your mind," he said. "Now's the time."

"Not a chance." She clasped her hand over his and kissed his palm. "Unzip me?"

He gave her a hard kiss before stepping behind her. Smoothing his hands down her unbound hair, he gathered the mass and laid it over one shoulder. With the greatest care, he opened the back of her dress. The rush of cool air against her overheated skin marking his progress. He continued his slow journey until the zipper terminated at the base of her spine.

Closing her eyes, she prayed he wouldn't be disappointed by her choice of underwear. Cotton and comfort were her preferred style. However, she had a couple of satiny special occasion sets, though they still veered toward comfort. No thongs or otherwise up-your-crack panties—just plain old bikini cut. Black.

The tips of Britt's fingers traced up her back, then down before inching their way under her dress to smooth over her flat stomach. His big body heated her flesh as he kissed the side of her neck, nuzzling her ear. His tongue toyed with the soft lobe, sucking it into his hot, wet mouth.

The area between her legs clenched, wanting his attention to move ever downward. Not knowing what to do with her hands, she shimmied one arm out of the dress and grasped the back of his neck. The other rested over his arm beneath her clothes.

Releasing her earlobe, he trailed kisses along her jaw until she angled her head around to accept his kiss. His tongue plunged inside at the same time his fingers curled into her hot, wet center. A tremor started at the core of her body as she waited for the glide of his finger along her burning center. But contrary man that he was, his finger remained tantalizingly, achingly still.

She began to squirm against the onslaught of raw need. His other hand cupped her breast, anchoring her to the earth. The hard, long length of him nestled in the crease of her bottom. She was aware of every inch of him, yet couldn't think of what to do next. So she covered his hand between her legs and flexed her hips, encouraging him into a rhythm she knew would blow her mind.

He didn't move. The only parts of him in motion were his lips and tongue.

"Britt, please," she whispered. The ache between her legs became painful, deep, elemental. She found it hard to breathe.

His hands eased away, ceasing their torture, and Randi mourned their loss. Emptiness filled the space. Until he began easing off her dress. It floated to the ground, pooling around her high heels.

Slowly, she faced him and nearly melted with relief at the look of appreciation on his gorgeous features.

"Better than my dreams," he murmured, reaching for her.

Randi lifted a staying hand. "Your turn."

"Why do I feel it's payback time?" He unbuttoned the cuffs.

"So harsh." She freed several buttons. Her mouth watered with each inch of bare skin revealed. "For me"—she opened his shirt and pressed two lingering kisses to the center of his chest—"this is reward time."

He muttered something unintelligible before clamping his jaw shut. Randi smiled when his hands gripped her sides. She would enjoy this.

To keep Randi from seeing his hands shake, Britt

held on tight while she began her torture. Sweet torture.

He'd used up the balance of his control when he'd discovered how wet and hot she was for him. *Him.* How many times had he envisioned this very moment over the past several months? So damned many he had the steps memorized—until Randi decided she wanted a taste of him as much as he wanted her.

The soft pads of her hands explored his torso with excruciating thoroughness. She pushed aside his shirt with her nose to reach his nipple. Her breath fanned over his skin a second before her tongue laved the hard nub.

His grip on her waist tightened as his cock pulsed with driving need. "Randi," he said between broken breaths. She gave no indication she heard him. "Sweetheart, I promise you can play next time." He cradled her face again, forcing her to look up at him.

The sight of her heavy-lidded eyes and damp lips was too much. He kissed her again, wishing he could give her the time she needed, but knowing he was nearing the end of his control.

He shrugged out of his shirt and unfastened his jeans. Sitting on the bed, he removed his boots and socks, tossing them to the side. While he was occupied, she'd removed her sexy shoes. He hated to see them go, but was glad he didn't have to worry about getting spiked in the ass during their first time.

She came to stand before him, all creamy skin and black satin. With a featherlight touch, her fingers smoothed over his shoulders and trailed down his arms to his hands. One encouraging tug had him standing, his jeans gaping open to reveal his erection. He never wore underwear with jeans. Way too confining.

Drawing her bottom lip into her mouth, she reached for him, wrapping her small hand around his girth. Britt held his breath, needing her touch, fearing he would shame himself with one pump of her hand.

But she didn't squeeze or pump. She explored. Soothed the beast raging inside him. He pushed his jeans down and eased away long enough to open the drawer on the bedside table. Grabbing a condom, he ripped its packet open and slid it on. When he turned back, she'd removed the rest of her clothes and climbed onto the bed.

Britt swallowed. She was so unbelievably beautiful and, at least for tonight, she was all his.

Randi's mouth went dry at the predatory gleam in Britt's gaze. He stalked on hands and knees across the bed until he covered her. His kiss was long and lush, not fevered and frenzied. He restrained her hands above her head and nudged her legs apart with his knee.

"This won't be an all-star moment for me," he warned. "I've wanted you too long. But I promise to make it good for you."

"I hope to do the same."

"You already have, sweetheart."

Without preamble, he covered her left breast with his mouth, teasing her nipple and plump flesh. Then she felt the first probe at her entrance. Randi lifted her legs. The tip slid over her wet folds before pressing deep, then deeper, so deep her breath stopped. She pushed against him until she could feel him touching the very heart of her core.

"Let me go," she demanded.

"Not yet," he ground out.

He kissed her again while he withdrew by slow degrees. Pleasure built below and above as his tongue and cock set a body-shattering rhythm. Soon, she realized her hands were free and she pressed them into the area where his spine and bottom met, encouraging him into greater, faster, deeper thrusts.

When she felt the first stirrings of orgasm, she hooked her legs around his waist and rode out the earthshaking storm. He sensed the end was near too, because he stopped kissing her and glanced down at where they were joined before adjusting his position and awakening her sweet spot.

Brilliant light exploded behind her eyelids and she cried out.

"Thank you, God," he said between clenched teeth before giving in to his own release.

The air around them crackled with the scent of sex and silence. Britt lifted his head and studied her features, searching for what, she didn't know.

So she smiled, settling on reassurance. When he gave her a lazy grin in return, her heart clenched against an unfamiliar ping of emotion. He kissed her and rolled off, stomping toward the bathroom, not bothering to turn on the light. Seconds later, he returned, all warm flesh and full-of-himself stretches.

"What would you like to do now?" he asked, nuzzling the underside of her jaw.

She glanced at the bedside clock and stopped short of groaning. Tonight might be the quickest date she'd ever been on. Two hours from pickup to after-sex awkwardness. Just the thought of rolling out of bed and putting on her skintight dress made her plop back on the pillow.

"Something wrong?"

She palmed her forehead, staring at the ceiling. "You mean other than me having to squeeze back into that dress and drive home?" She chuckled. "No, nothing's wrong."

"Do you want to go home tonight?"

She peered up into his face and noticed his guarded expression. "Don't you want me to?"

He slid one leg between hers and leaned close. "No." He kissed her temple. "In fact, I think you should stay the night, then go camping with me tomorrow."

"Camping?" She reared back to see him better. "Or glamping?"

"What the hell is glamping?"

"What will our accommodations be like?"

"Our *accommodations* will be a two-person tent complete with individual sleeping bags or, if you prefer, one large sleeping bag, and a pop-up stove." He raised a brow. "Is that glamorous enough for you?"

Randi covered her eyes with one hand. "I haven't been camping since I was ten years old."

He peeled two of her fingers away. "Then it's time for you to sleep beneath the stars again."

"I am sleeping beneath the stars." She pointed to the ceiling. "They're right up there."

He nipped at her bare shoulder. "Don't be such a city slicker. You'll enjoy camping in the woods." Sliding the sheet down, he bared her breasts. The cool air and his attention made them harden. He took one ruched nipple between his finger and thumb and rolled the tip. "You have my word."

CHAPTER TWENTY-ONE

BRITT ADJUSTED HIS BACKPACK AND picked his way down the narrow rocky trail. After a two-hour hike, they were now descending and making their way back to their campsite.

The view had been spectacular. Not a cloud in the sky to obscure the surrounding landscape. If it had been July, a humid haze would have reduced their visibility. He couldn't recall the last time he'd hiked this mountain. It felt good to explore other areas.

For the past six months, he'd been focused on the Steele Conservation Area. Beautiful property, but even ten thousand acres can seem confining after a while.

"I like this direction much better," Randi said from behind him. "My thighs thank you."

"Don't thank me yet. Pretty soon your shins will be screaming."

"Lovely," she grumbled. "Next time, wait until I start complaining about the pain before revealing the reason. Now I'm going to spend the next several minutes anticipating splintering shins, thank you very much."

Despite her words, she had yet to complain about their commune with nature. She'd been a good sport about it, though he knew she hadn't gone on a hike of this magnitude in a long while. Hell, he'd gotten winded toward the summit and he explored this kind of terrain on a weekly basis.

"If I hadn't said anything, you'd be griping at me later for not forewarning you."

"You have a point. I guess you'll have to pick your poison."

Britt shook his head, smiling. Ever since their lovemaking last night, they'd settled into an easy banter, something he'd only ever enjoyed with his siblings and Deke.

They came across a large boulder jutting across the trail. Britt climbed atop it and held out his hand for Randi. She clasped his fingers, and he hauled her up.

From their vantage point, they could see the winding, rugged nature of the path ahead of them.

"Remind me again of why we took the more advanced route?"

"Because the family-friendly route would have bored you to tears. This way is far more exciting."

"So I see." She wedged her thumbs beneath the arm straps of her rucksack. "I'm going to sleep like a rock tonight."

He jumped down. "No, you're not."

She opened her mouth for a retort, but she must have caught the heat in his eyes. Her attention lingered on his mouth a moment before scrambling off the boulder.

Dog that he was, Britt had been unable to stop thinking about the feel of Randi wrapped around him, warm, inviting, and so damned responsive. They'd made love twice more, once as the sun crested the horizon. He would never forget the small ray of morning sunlight that edged between the curtains to land on Randi's profile. Beautiful and surreal.

If he were more of a religious man, he might have believed God had delivered an important message. Instead, he'd soaked up every second and, right before she awoke, he'd realized, hands down, this was the happiest he'd been in ages.

A throat cleared behind him. "When can we go see the wolves again?"

"Tomorrow, if you're a good girl tonight." Where the hell were these sexual innuendos coming from? He couldn't recall ever teasing a woman like this before.

"Didn't you say something about wanting more out of this relationship than sex?"

He didn't have to turn around to see her brow arched in query. "Which should not be confused with no sex at all."

"I can tell I'm going to need a playbook to navigate the tricky maneuverings of Britt Steele's mind."

"All you need to know is that I'm a simple man of simple needs." Pausing, he angled around to look her in the eye. "And my body needs you."

Shock widened her eyes. Britt couldn't blame her. He hadn't meant to make such a declaration, but his damned tongue was speedier than his brain. This thing between them was new to her. She had no way of knowing that he went to Triple B to see *her*, not to hang with his family and friends and listen to good music.

Feeling too exposed, he continued down the mountain. Too bad life didn't include a delete button for stupid comments. He'd be banging the hell out of that key right now.

"May I ask you a personal question?" she asked.

If the terrain hadn't been so uneven, he would have closed his eyes and prayed for lightning to strike him dead or a crevasse to open up before him or a mountain lion to leap on him from the bluff above. Well, maybe not the mountain lion scenario. Having his throat ripped out wasn't on his top ten list of ways to die.

He knew of a way to scare her off the scent. "If I can do the same."

Her agreement was slow in coming. But it came. *Dammit.*

"All right."

Loose stones littered the trail for several yards. "Be

careful here," he said. "Remember to position your feet at a ninety-degree angle to get the best traction."

"I'm well aware of how to traverse steep terrain. Don't try to distract me."

"You wound me." He put a hand over his heart. "My thoughts were only on ensuring your safety."

"Gag me."

The trees opened up, and she paused to take in the view. Layers of velvet green painted the foreground, and a fine mist of blue hovered in the background. Beneath it all, the mountain swam across the landscape like the Loch Ness monster's sleek body cresting expansive Scottish waters.

"Why have you never married?" she asked. "And don't give me copout answers like 'I'm too busy' or 'I haven't found the one.'"

"Tough interrogator." Britt scoured his mind for a legitimate reason she would accept. It was true that he hadn't come across a woman who encouraged him to think beyond the next date. Over the years, he'd enjoyed keeping company with, having sex with, or taking walks with, different women. But none had ever occupied his thoughts at strange, unexpected times, nor had he ever been interested in them beyond a superficial level. "I doubt you'll like my answer."

"That's not important. I'm interested in hearing why."

"No spark."

She frowned. "As in, the women you've dated weren't upbeat?"

He shook his head. "I won't be able to articulate this."

"Just say what you're feeling."

"The others…they didn't spark anything inside me." He tried to find inspiration in the blue mist flowing over the mountaintops in the distance. But everything that came to mind sounded so overdone. "I don't expect fireworks, but I'd like to experience some excitement or anticipation when I'm around my future wife. Especially in the honeymoon phase of a relationship. If I'm two weeks into seeing someone, I sure as hell want to feel something besides mild interest." Behind him, the silence lengthened. He released a self-conscious breath. "Told you I wouldn't be able to explain it well."

A slender hand curled around the back of his neck. "You articulated it perfectly." She tightened her hold. "I hope you find your spark."

Maybe I already have. The words trickled through his mind like a slow-burning line fire along the forest's floor. Could Randi really be the one? The one who would make him smile with nothing more than a sideways glance, make him stir to life with a single caress, make him think of the future with a whispered wish?

The trickle of awareness became a raging storm of certainty.

He snaked an arm around her waist, bringing her body flush with his, and kissed her. "Come on," he whispered. "Let's get back to the site before the sun sets. Making camp in the dark isn't much fun."

She nodded, and they spent the rest of the hike lost in their thoughts. Other than setting up the tent to air out and rolling out their sleeping bags, they'd done nothing else to make their campsite habitable before heading up the mountain.

Britt pulled two bundles of firewood from the back of his pickup and tossed them down next to the fire pit. Then he hunted the edge of the nearby woodland for kindling.

Meanwhile, Randi dragged the large red-and-white cooler from the truck and set it on the picnic table bench. As with many park picnic tables, initials from long-ago lovers were scratched into the thick layers of brown paint covering the surface.

Soon they had a roaring fire and brats sizzling on a cast iron griddle. With the sun dropping below the horizon, their comfortable June day turned into a chilly early-summer evening. Randi exited the tent, shrugging into a dark blue fleece jacket and carrying a long-sleeve flannel for him.

"Thanks." He accepted the flannel, marveling at the naturalness of this small domestic scene. Neither of them had to be told what to do, they just did what needed doing.

"I'll get the plates ready."

Britt knelt down to check the brats. Using a fork, he rolled the links onto their uncooked side and debated his next move. He didn't want to ruin their easy camaraderie, but he also had a compulsive need to know every detail about her.

"Would you rather sit by the fire or at the picnic table?"

"Either works for me. You decide. The brats will be another minute."

She brought over two folding chairs and set them up around the fire pit. "The fire feels nice."

"Got a plate or bun for me?"

A bun materialized over his shoulder.

"How do you like your brat?" she asked. "Plain or with all the fixin's?"

"All the fixin's."

He forked one of the brats into the bun and handed it to her. She traded him for an empty bun.

Removing the griddle from the grate, he set it aside to cool. If he'd been alone or with his brothers, he would have had a small pan of baked beans heating up as well. Somehow beans and second date didn't seem like a good idea. He'd settled for bringing BBQ chips and a tub of potato salad.

By the time he made it to the picnic table to load up his plate, she'd already buried his brat beneath a mound of kraut, sliced tomatoes, onions, and mustard. His mouth watered.

"Look okay?" she asked.

"Couldn't have made it better myself, thanks."

He added a couple spoonfuls of potato salad and a

handful of chips to their plates. Grabbing their utensils and drinks, they headed back to the fire.

Hungry from a long day of activity, they dug into their food, making satisfied groans along the way.

"Back at your cabin," Randi said between bites, "I saw a half-completed application for the Anti-Poaching Foundation. I looked it up. Sounds like a great opportunity. What date are you shooting for?"

The brat burned in his stomach. "I've had seconds thoughts on the trip."

"You don't want to go now?"

"Timing's not right."

"Is someone in your family sick?"

"No, why?"

"Then the rest can wait."

"It's not that easy, Randi. Between my business, overseeing the training center's renovations, and now Jonah wants to build a wildlife research center in the conservation area, there's no time for assisting conservation efforts in another country."

"A research center? That's wonderful!"

Her genuine happiness for him made the whole thing finally feel real. He'd been dying to tell her since yesterday, but couldn't think of a casual way to bring up the topic.

"It is. Jonah's a good kid, and he's determined to make his entire family happy. But there's so damn much to do."

"Take it from me, the time will never be right." She swatted a fly off the rim of her bottle. "Set aside the time and go. You never know when life's going to throw you into a gut-twisting tailspin. I'm the perfect example of everything toddling along great, then *bam*. I almost lost everything in the time it took Pansy to unload in my yard. Don't wait, Britt."

No one, besides Evie, had ever taken an interest in ensuring his happiness. His family loved him and wanted the best for him. But no one had ever ventured inside his life enough to insist he make time for himself.

Britt reached over and drew her mouth to his. He slid his tongue along the rim of her upper lip, and she opened, giving him access. She tasted of beer and brats and heaven. It was a chickenshit way of conveying his gratitude, his growing affection. One day, he would find the right words. But not tonight. Tonight, he would show her.

When he eased back, she asked, "What was that for?"

"For giving me something to think on."

"I'll have to come up with a few more things to occupy your mind."

He laughed, and they settled into an easy silence while staring into the flames.

The fire died down, and Britt got up to add a few more logs. He took the opportunity to ask the question that had been stabbing at his curiosity for days.

"My turn for a question."

She sent him a don't-screw-with-my-serenity look. He ignored her.

"What happened between you and your mom?"

Her longneck slipped between her fingers, though she caught it before the bottle hit the ground. "Pardon?"

"Like your mom, you're a good person. Both caring, smart, funny." He took a drink. "I've been trying to figure out what drove you apart."

"Britt, it's been a great day. I don't want to dampen it by talking about my mom."

"We had a deal, remember? Question for a question."

A deep sigh erupted beside him. "It's complicated."

"We've got all night."

"Our estrangement wasn't caused by any one thing." She set her plate aside. "It was more like a lot of small events that wedged between us, creating a gaping chasm neither of us could—or would—cross."

The indifferent tone to her voice made him want to pull her onto his lap and rock her to tears. Because no matter what control she had over her emotions right now, she needed to let go. To mourn her mother. To grieve for the mother-daughter relationship she secretly yearned for, but was now lost to her.

"What kind of events?" he asked.

"That counts as a second question." She sent him a steady sideways glance. "Are you sure you want to continue our question for a question game?"

Britt bit back a curse. He'd allowed himself to forget how her beauty masked a savvy businesswoman, one who knew how to barter and get what she wanted.

All in.

"I don't consider this a game," he said in a low voice. "I'm trying to figure you out, share with you. If quid pro quo is the only way I can achieve my goal, so be it."

Her expression turned guarded, and she returned her attention back to the fire. "Until I was about eight or nine, I enjoyed a full, loving family life. Then my mother got a position with International Wildlife Conservation and everything changed."

"Didn't she work before?"

"Oh yes, she'd always held a job. A single-income household wasn't an option for us."

"What was it about the IWC position that changed everything?"

"She traveled—a lot. When not at work, she volunteered. She rescued animals. She mentored college students." Randi broke off a dandelion leaf near her foot. "Her position with IWC triggered an almost manic need to save everything—except her family."

"Where was your father in all of this?"

"My father did his best to make up for my mother's absence. But some things, like braiding my hair or glamming me up for a school play, were beyond his skill set." She tore the leaf apart, bit by bit. "I miss him."

"How'd he die again? Barbara said something about a heart condition."

"Massive heart attack. My dad hated going to the doctor, so he ignored my repeated requests for him to get his swollen ankles and numb fingers looked at. One day he was at the dinner table and the next, he wasn't."

Not knowing what else to do, Britt smoothed his palm over her back in large circles. "I'm sorry, Randi."

She sent him a small smile. "It was a long time ago."

"But no less painful."

Dropping the shredded leaf bits, she asked, "What about your dad?"

He set his empty plate on the ground and picked up her half-full one. "Finish your supper while I share the Steele family saga."

"Are we setting caveats on answering each other's questions now?"

"Just this one time." He pointed to her food. "Eat."

She picked up her fork. "Yes, sir."

"The situation with my dad wasn't much different than what you experienced with your mom. Except for one thing. Your mom stuck around." Britt rested his arms on his knees and stared into the fire. "Not long after Evie was born, my dad started spending weekends at an almost uninhabitable cabin. Weekends turned into weeks. Weeks turned into months. Months into years. Every great once in a while, he'll make an appearance at a family function. But for the most part, he's cut himself from our lives."

"Why?"

"Nobody knows. Any time we ask him about it, he disappears again."

Randi reached out and clasped his hand. "I'm so sorry."

"Don't be. Everyone in the family is past it. I feel bad that Evie never had her dad in her life for any solid time. But I've tried to make sure she didn't feel the loss too much."

"You're a good brother." She rubbed her thumb over his knuckles. "I can't imagine how hard it must have been for you."

"Me? I had more time with him than my brothers and sisters."

"You became a father figure overnight. In ways you probably don't even realize, you lost parts of your youth."

"Maybe. Maybe I have a different relationship with my siblings than I would have had if my dad had stuck around. But given the same situation all over again, I'd take care of them as best I could."

"From what I can tell, the Steeles are a happy, good-hearted family. In large part due to you."

"The credit goes to Mom. She's the heart of the family. All I did was keep her kids from killing each other."

"I suspect you contributed far more to the family than curtailing death and dismemberment."

Britt leaned over and used his thumb to wipe off a dollop of mustard at the corner of her mouth. Without thinking, he licked it from his thumb. "And I suspect you redirected this conversation away from answering the rest of my question."

She snatched her paper napkin from beneath her plate and swiped it over her mouth, cheeks, and chin.

Britt sat back in his chair and stretched out his legs and waited.

"I held out hope for six long years, expecting that she'd get tired or fired and return to us." She rinsed down her brat with some beer. "Mom never did. Had I not known how good it could be, I probably would have adapted to the new regime." She stared hard at the bottle in her hand. "But I knew. I prayed and prayed and prayed for my mom to come back. But she put her job before her family, and I don't think I'll ever be able to forgive her for taking something so precious away from me."

Little wonder she'd detached herself from nature. In her mind, it was the reason she'd lost the close bond with her mother and it eventually broke apart her family. Britt slid his hand down her arm and curled his fingers between hers. "I know you might not be ready to hear this, but Barbara loved you."

Randi picked at her potato chips.

"She did," he insisted. "Every moment we had together that allowed for idle conversation, she spent those minutes praising your accomplishments."

"Britt, please. We've been through this." Absently she rubbed the pad of her thumb, hard, against his forefinger. "Other than knowing about Blues, Brews, and Books, my mother knew nothing of my hopes, dreams, wins, or failures. And honestly, knowing about Triple B was not impressive. The whole town's aware of my ownership."

In as conversational tone as he could muster, he recited the first story that came to mind. "On your eighteenth birthday, you spent the day visiting your top two universities rather than hang out with your friends."

Her thumb paused in its quest to rub a hole through his skin.

"On your twenty-first birthday, you chose to drive your Aunt Sharon to the women's clinic on the fifth anniversary of her cancer-free status, because you couldn't bear for her to get the mammogram results alone."

"Hardly a sacrifice. Aunt Sharon's one of my best friends. She's always been there for me when I needed her. How could I not do the same?"

"You'd be surprised at the number of people who would have chosen differently." Angling toward her—a difficult feat in a folding chair that was barely wide enough to support his ass—he sandwiched her hands inside his. "She saw you graduate summa cum laude."

"What do you mean 'she saw'?"

"With her own eyes. In the audience."

Her face began to crumple. "Why didn't she find me afterward?"

"She didn't say." He softened his voice. "Would you have welcomed her?"

Tears glistened in her beautiful eyes. "No," she whispered. "No."

She closed her eyes, fighting emotions pent up far too

long. He expected to see tears flow down her cheeks, but none appeared. With a will made of steel, something he'd admired many times over the months but hated witnessing now, she pushed and stomped and punched every vulnerable feeling into a cold coffin of self-preservation.

A forced smile appeared on her strained face. "Could we unveil the rest of my screwed-up life at another time?" Need shone in her eyes. Need for him. "I think it might be time for us to warm up our sleeping bags."

Britt wanted to better understand her and share so much more with her. But he dared not. She looked drained and fatigued, and despite his awareness that her offer of sex was, at least in part, a seductive ploy to redirect his efforts from her mind to her body, her suggestion sent fire through his veins.

What was the Hollywood expression? Ah, yes. Baby steps. He would take this—them—one small, clumsy step at a time.

CHAPTER TWENTY-TWO

RANDI'S BODY ACHED. BONE DEEP, body and soul.

Spending the night on the hard ground was only part of the reason. Britt had accepted her offer of pleasure with unexpected intensity. She'd lost track of the number of times he'd awoken her with kisses and caresses. Close to morning, he'd curled his body around hers, entering her, though not taking them to climax. Two bodies merged. One being, one thought, one need. She had slept more soundly in those few hours before dawn, with him inside her, than all the nights of her life combined.

After spooning down some oatmeal and packing up their campsite, they returned to Steele Ridge to check on the red wolves. A thick fog had gathered in the trees, making long-distance visibility impossible. Randi made sure she stayed within ten feet of Britt's broad back. The disorienting fog didn't seem to faze him at all. He attacked every meter of invisible trail with a sure foot and confidence few achieved in broad daylight when hiking the woods.

Rather than enter via the Steele Conservation Area side, Britt chose to set off from her mother's property, so Randi could locate the Steele-Shepherd pack from this vantage point. Whether he intended to do so or not, their hike took them by the bluff that had claimed her mother's life.

Randi had not been here since the authorities had hauled Barbara Shepherd's broken body up the cliff. She'd arrived on the scene in time to see the last few minutes of the recovery effort. Five minutes that would be forever etched her in mind.

Britt guided her to the edge. "This is the place?"

She nodded, staring down at the steep embankment to the wide stream below. "A young man who'd wandered onto our property fly fishing spotted her. If he hadn't come along when he did, Mom could have lain out here for days."

It was unnecessary to explain to Britt what could have happened to a fresh corpse in this area of North Carolina that supported coyotes, bears, wolves, and a multitude of other scavenging creatures. A cramp took hold of her stomach.

"Have the authorities determined what caused her to fall?"

"No evidence of wrongdoing. Nothing beyond what logic dictates—she had a moment of inattention, something spooked her, she tripped, slipped, the possibilities seem endless."

Randi turned away from the scene of her mother's last moments on earth. The same questions pounded in her head. Had she died instantly? Had she suffered for hours before finally succumbing to her injuries? Randi would never know. The only person who could tell her had plummeted to her death. "Mom knew the dangers of hiking alone. She died doing what she loved most in the world."

Even after bleeding out her emotions to Britt last night, she still couldn't hold back the bitterness. The landscape she'd been admiring only moments ago now appeared exactly what it was, gray and bleak.

"How much longer until we reach the den?"

"Another twenty minutes or so." He wrapped his

hand around hers. "Did anyone ever approach your mom about selling her property?"

"Not that she ever told me. Why?"

"Nothing. Just a random thought."

Randi's focus turned inward, scouring her mind for a stray comment made by her mom or aunt that meant little to her at the time but now held relevance. Her steps slowed.

"A few months ago, my aunt said something about my mom having a run-in with a solicitor. I assumed she meant a lawn care service salesman or something similar." She covered her mouth. "Could it have been the Carolina Club's attorney?"

He squeezed her hand. "It's hard to say. But I'm growing suspicious of your stream of bad luck."

A corkscrew dug into the center of her heart. Could Britt's suspicions be right? Could the Carolina Club be the architect behind her mother's death, her financial advisor's earnest recommendation, her failing business?

"Why would they go to such lengths? For a plot of land? The property is a naturalist's dream, but a hunter's?"

He kissed her temple. "Don't mind me. I have a dozen nefarious plots running through my head at any one time. I shouldn't have said anything."

Without another word, he led them away from the bluff. A chill tapped down her spine. Tucking her chin into her chest, she shoved her hands into her fleece jacket pockets. She followed Britt for several minutes, her mind full of nothing and everything. The glow of their night of lovemaking long gone. The closeness, the warmth, the joy seemed ages ago. A different Randi, a different time.

Craaack!

Britt stopped.

With her body hunkered against the chill, Randi didn't react to the sound as quickly as he and plowed into his solid back. He didn't grunt in pain, simply reached back and steadied her.

"Gunfire?" she whispered.

He nodded. "Close, too. Had to be on Steele or Shepherd property."

Grasping her hand, he continued along the trail for several more minutes before bending down on his haunches to inspect something on the ground. Peering over his shoulder, she noticed red liquid smearing several leaves on a low-growing New Jersey tea bush.

"Is that blood?"

Breaking off a leaf, he held it up to his nose. "That would be my guess." He tossed the leaf away and rose, scanning the area. "Stay put. I'll be back in a moment."

"Wait, no—"

"I can track the blood trail faster and stealthier alone." He squeezed her hand in reassurance. "The shot came from ahead of us. You'll be safer here." He kissed her fingertips. "Stay here, Randi." His gaze met hers. "Please."

She had yet to see this commanding side of him. Being the eldest of six children and with an absentee father, he'd probably had to take control often over the years. And that six-lettered concession he tacked on the end of his directive felt a little rusty.

Nodding, she said, "Be careful."

He disappeared into the fog far too soon, leaving an eerie, desolate silence in his wake. Randi scanned her surroundings, though nothing besides the bloody leaves looked out of place. The fog was so dense, even wind could not penetrate the moist barrier.

A hundred scenarios ran though her mind as to what the presence of the blood meant. The more she thought about it, the more sinister the scenarios became. She shook her head with enough force to rattle her brain. Dramatics weren't her thing. The most likely reason for the blood was a rabbit, or some other unfortunate creature, coming into contact with a wolf.

Above her, a twig snapped. She studied the edge of the cliff above and caught a glimpse of color. She backed up a step for a better look. But nothing was there. No furtive movements, no shadowy figure, no predatory eyes.

Leaves rustled on the path behind her. Randi whipped around. Empty. Her heart fluttered inside her chest like a bird trapped in a cage. Fog had a way of amplifying noise, making music playing a half mile away sound as though it were in your backyard.

She knew this, yet she still found herself backing away, one foot after another. Toward Britt, toward safety. With nothing more than a half-cocked smile and a few words of reassurance, he would return her mind to its rational, logical state.

As she continued her careful retreat, she split her attention between the cliff above and the path behind her. The hairs on her arms and neck rose to attention. Someone—or something—hovered above her. Watched her. Or maybe she had too many scary movies under her belt. Or maybe Britt's comments about the Carolina Club carried more truth than fiction.

Either way, she was getting the hell out of here. She took three frantic backward steps before she realized she could become hopelessly lost out here without Britt. Navigating the woods wasn't a problem for her once she'd explored the area a few times. But she'd never ventured this deep. Even if she had, the fog changed the looks of everything.

Damn. Damn. Double Dog Damn.

Then she heard it. The distinct, rhythmic sound of feet on forest floor moving toward her, from the direction Britt had disappeared. Relief cascaded over her like a waterfall of warm water. Before she even saw him, he calmed her. Embarrassment heated her cheeks at the way she'd allowed her imagination to run amok. All because of a little creepy fog.

Working in a bar for as long as she had, she'd dealt with some pretty tricky—and many times, scary—situations. Drunken university guys with rocket-fueled testosterone, domestic disputes turned physical, and jealous screeching, scratching, and punching triangles. She'd jumped into the fray of each of those situations without blinking an eye. Each time, her actions were driven by the basic desire to stop the violence and save the bar.

But none of those people saw her as a late-morning snack. There were few things that truly terrified her in this world, but being eaten, alive or otherwise, sat at the top of her I-Never-Want-To-Experience-This list.

As she pondered what two-inch canines could do to her flesh, Randi's subconscious remained on the approaching footsteps. Something about the cadence was off. Something she couldn't put her finger on, but a mere second before a black bear cub appeared, she knew it couldn't be Britt.

The cub shuffled closer. Given its size, Randi guessed the bear's age to be around six months. Panic held her immobile. She didn't dare move, breathe. Where was the cub's much bigger, much stronger, fiercely protective mother?

A cub so young and vulnerable did not set out on its own. Unless the sow had driven off her babe to save it from a persistent male bear sniffing around. Or maybe an unscrupulous hunter had killed her. Or a vehicle. Or a hiker in self-protection. So many possibilities.

The horrific bear scene from *The Revenant* skirted across her mind. *Oh, crap. Britt!*

Did he have a run-in with the mother? Was that why the cub was alone? Could Britt be lying injured somewhere? Needing her?

The cub let out a keening, mournful cry, and Randi stopped short of shushing it. If the mother came loping through here and found her not thirty feet from her cub... Randi broke off the thought before the gruesome images took shape again.

Randi had no place to hide. Her only hope was staying still and praying the cub would pass her by. Then she recalled the feeling of being watched. Could it have been this little guy or gal? Surely not. The cub seemed oblivious to her presence.

When the cub came parallel with her, though still a good fifteen feet away, Randi regulated her breathing and lowered her eyelids to slits. The cub continued to amble on its way, releasing a pitiful cry every few feet.

The sight broke Randi's heart. She had to find the mother and somehow reunite the two. If the mother was dead, then she would contact a local rescue. An unprotected cub wouldn't last for more than a few days with a pack of wolves so close by.

She waited another full minute before creeping ahead on the path, intent on finding Britt. Wary of the baby doubling back or mama making an appearance, Randi kept peering over her shoulder until the fog hid the cub's whereabouts.

Rounding the corner, she came toe-to-toe with mama bear.

Britt slammed to a halt at the sight of Randi facing off with a black bear. In the distance, he heard the baleful cry of a cub, and terror like nothing he'd ever experienced before rose up to suffocate him.

Randi slowly backed away. The bear huffed and swatted her paws against the ground.

"Stop, Randi! You're headed toward her cub." Britt waved his arms wide. "Over here, Mama." He stuck his tongue against his teeth and delivered a piercing whistle. "Over here."

The bear swung around at the new sound, snapped her jaws.

Britt held his ground, keeping one eye on the bear while surveying Randi's options. To her right rose a steep bluff. To her left, an even steeper cliff. The mother bear stood between him and Randi.

"Mama, come away. Over here, girl."

"Britt, no!"

"Be quiet, Randi. The moment she turns my way, get the hell out of there."

Britt took three harsh breaths like a pole vaulter right before takeoff. Then he marched toward the anxious bear. She gave him five steps before she charged.

Tossing away all his experience, he turned his back on the bear and ran, hoping she would follow. She did for all of three seconds. When the crashing of pine needles and branches behind him faded, Britt whipped around in time to witness the worst nightmare he could possibly imagine.

Mama bear had reversed her charge and was now headed for Randi. Stuck between the agitated bear and the cliff, Randi had no place to go but down. She caught his gaze, and he saw the mountain of fear behind her decision.

"Don't you do it, Randi! Don't you do it!"

"Run, Britt. Run!"

A split second before the bear reached her, Randi stepped off the ledge.

CHAPTER TWENTY-THREE

MAMA BEAR ROARED HER TRIUMPH while watching Randi plummet down the mountainside.

Panic overwhelmed him, crippling his thoughts. He had to remain calm, nonthreatening, or the bear would never take her cub and move on. Every second seemed like an eon sliding by, every minute felt like a death knell.

The black bear paced along the edge of the cliff, making sure the threat to her cub didn't return. He backed away, putting distance between him and the cub. Out of the corner of his eye, a thick oak appeared. Could he get behind the tree before the female remembered him? He had to try.

Keeping his backward momentum even and quiet, he edged around the tree and fell against the trunk, his legs shaking, his heart blasting in his ears.

The cub bleated out a cry, and Britt froze, listening for the loping run of a pissed-off bear. When no crash of underbrush reached his ears, he peered out from his hiding place.

Mama bear's protective gaze zeroed in on him.

Shit!

Ducking behind the tree again, he waited. And waited. He waited until he couldn't stand it anymore. This time when he shot a look around the tree, the bluff's edge was clear.

He found them lumbering along the path he and Randi had taken earlier. Every few feet, mama bear would throw a glance behind her.

Keeping part of his attention on the retreating bears, he marched over to the edge of the bluff. The fog was even thicker below, though a two-foot-high band of visibility rode along the ground. Enough for him to pick out Randi's rucksack hung up on a granite outcropping.

He shrugged out of his backpack and retrieved a roll of bright yellow flagging tape. Tearing off several feet, he intended to tie the length around one of the nearby trees. A message to any rescuers should the worst happen.

But mama bear must have caught his scent or heard his frantic movements. Foam flecked from the sides of her mouth and her enormous claws dug into the forest floor, heading right for him.

Dropping the tape, Britt stabbed his arms into the backpack's straps and sent up a prayer before following Randi.

For the first fifty feet, Britt managed to control his descent by tapping into decades of hiking up and down the mountains of Western North Carolina. He even managed to nab Randi's rucksack on his way down the cliff. But soon, gravity fed his movements and he flew faster and faster and faster. So fast his boot slipped on some loose earth. After that, his descent turned ugly.

His body bounced off every hard-surfaced or sharp-edged object making its home on the mountainside. He slid, he tumbled, he rolled, he cursed. He cracked a rib, maybe two. Finally, he flip-flopped to a halt.

Not giving his body time to spotlight his injuries, he jolted upright and began his search for Randi. Whirling in a circle, he scanned the area in all directions. Not a single sign of her stubborn blond head.

Cupping his hands around his mouth, he bellowed, "Randi!"

Silence.

"Randi!"

The tingles tracked down his spine, cutting and scraping, one vertebra at a time. He yelled her name, again and again and again.

He found her wrapped around a thick tree.

Heart in his throat, he set two fingers on the side of her neck. Nothing. He repositioned his fingers. Nothing. He pressed his pads against the fine bones of one wrist. *Thump, thump. Thump, thump.* A weak pulse, but there.

"Randi, wake up." With a gentle yet firm hand, he peeled her away from the tree. "Sweetheart, open your eyes."

When he got no response, he tapped her cheek. "Randi." She remained unmoving. He smacked a little harder, cringing at the sight of red blossoming on her pale cheek. He hated causing her pain, but he hated the idea of her dying even more.

"Miranda Shepherd." He infused as much authority into his voice as possible while he searched for any signs of head trauma. When his fingers came across a lump behind her right ear, he cursed. "Wake your stubborn ass up. I don't have time to coddle you all damn day."

Her eyelids fluttered.

"That's it. Open your eyes." Britt scrambled for something to help her shake off the fog of her head injury. "If you don't wake up, I'll have to take over Blues, Brews, and Books. I've got a few modifications I'd like to make."

Her eyes opened, then shut again.

Britt brushed her hair away from her face. "My first official duty as CEO would be to get rid of the utensils. People can use their fingers."

A line formed between her brows.

"And then I'll bring in peanuts. Patrons can shuck them right onto the floor."

"Not in my bar," she croaked out. "Allergies."

Britt smiled, sending up a prayer of thanks. "Welcome back." She tried to sit up. "Not so fast. I need to figure out where you're hurt."

After a quick inspection, he found no protruding bones or deep gashes. But he did locate several scratches and a bruise forming on her right jaw. "Everything looks okay from the outside. Let's see what your body thinks about an upright position."

She sat up, with his assistance. A groan escaped her, and she clamped her hands around her head.

"You may have a concussion." He peered up, noticing the fog had lifted somewhat, but the distance to the bluff's edge was daunting even for able-bodied hikers. "I'm calling nine-one-one."

"No," she said. "Just give me a moment to adjust."

Now that the immediate danger to Randi had passed, Britt's body's aches and pains were making themselves known. He straightened to ease the sharp pain in his ribs.

"A concussion is nothing to mess with, Randi. You could have bleeding on the brain and not know it for several hours."

"I've been conked on the head a time or two without any lasting damage. The benefits of having a thick skull."

"Setting your thick skull aside, we're going to need some help climbing back up."

Her eyes flared, and she scanned his body. She smoothed her thumb over his chin and came away with blood on the pad. "Are you all right?"

"I'm fine." He grasped her searching hands, afraid she'd connect with his sore ribs.

"How'd you get down here?"

"Same as you."

"Good Lord, are you insane?"

"No more than you."

"I, at least, had a motivating reason."

"So did I."

She stared at him, hard, as though trying to read the meaning behind his words. Britt wouldn't enlighten her. Neither of them were prepared for that kind of conversation.

Her color returned by slow degrees.

"How do you feel?"

"Like I rolled down a mountain." Her crooked grin faded when she took in his expression. "I'm okay." She slid her hand over his, where he clasped her fingers in a death grip. "Just a headache and a few bruises. My body takes on a lot more damage during my Pilates class." She patted his hand. "Help me up, please."

Britt grimaced when he leveraged himself to his feet.

"You're hurt," she accused. "Stand back, I'll do this on my own."

"It's nothing. A bruised rib, maybe." He held out his hand to her. "Nice and slow."

He helped her up, steadying her when she wobbled a bit. She took a few tentative steps, assessing her body, part by part.

Britt took advantage of her preoccupation and assessed his injuries. Everything seemed to have survived, except the left side of his rib cage. He hoped it was just a severe contusion, but he had his doubts.

"Let me see." Randi motioned for him to lift his shirt.

"It's nothing."

She raised a brow, waiting.

Britt didn't like to be fussed over. But he could see she wasn't going to let this go. He released a long aggrieved sigh before lifting his shirt.

"A bruise is forming, already." Her finger skimmed over the area, making him flinch. Not in pain, but from the sheer gentleness of her touch. "Did I hurt you?"

Britt shook his head. He couldn't stop looking at her. His chest hurt. His mind kept chanting, *Thank God, thank God, thank God she's alive.* He couldn't have borne any other outcome.

"Other than the bruise, I don't see anything alarming. How's your breathing?"

Her earnest expression shattered his silent prayers—and his irritation. Attentions he normally found annoying when performed by his mom or Evie seemed endearing coming from Randi. Britt tested out a few deep breaths and was relieved to only feel a slight twinge on the inhale.

"I'll survive."

"You're not just saying that, are you? I've heard broken ribs can puncture lungs."

"If you want complete honesty, I probably have a cracked rib, but I don't think it's broken."

"How can you be sure?

"Because it feels like the time Reid head-butted me."

"I don't know how your mother survived raising four rambunctious boys."

"Lots of spinach."

She gave him a wan smile, rubbing her temple. "Did you find the source of the blood?"

"No." Thank goodness he'd trusted his instincts and cut short his tracking. If only he'd listened to his gut sooner, he might have been able to save Randi from a two-hundred-foot tumble. "After we get you checked out at the hospital, I'm coming back to follow the trail. I don't care for the direction it's headed."

"What do you mean? Where's it going?"

"Right now, the trail is on a straight path to the wolves' den."

"Do you think one of the wolves has been injured?"

"It's one possibility."

"And another?"

"Could be a fresh kill one of the wolves is carrying back to the den."

She studied him a moment. "You don't believe the latter theory."

"I find it less likely. But given the fact I couldn't find a single print—animal or human—any scenario is possible at this point."

"Time for us to stop dithering. Let's find the best place to crawl to the top."

Britt eyed Randi. She had that woman-on-a-mission aura-thing going. "When we get out of this valley, I'm taking you straight to the hospital."

"Maybe later." She set her hands on her hips. "First, we need to figure out whose blood you found."

"Have you forgotten that I found you unconscious?"

"My memory is still intact." She glanced behind them, at the distant sound of flowing water. "How about we walk along the riverbed for a while to see if we come across a creek or seepage draining into the river. The terrain there might provide for better footholds."

"Your mind's set, isn't it?"

"Yep. We'll go to the doctor together—once we solve the blood mystery."

Something unlocked in Britt's chest. It was as if a pressure valve released, and decades of suppressed feelings coursed freely once again. Warmth that had nothing to do with the weather penetrated every fiber of his body.

Brushing the backs of his fingers over her jaw, he startled her from her battle planning. He kissed her. A slow, possessive kiss. Every raw, unfiltered emotion flowed from him to her. For the first time in his life, he didn't hold back. He left himself open, vulnerable.

Randi must have sensed the shift. When she drew back, her face revealed a blend of wonder and wariness. Who could blame her? Even under normal circumstances, people complained of not being able to figure him out. Toss in a volatile situation, toss in volatile emotions, and chaos ensues.

Grasping her hand in his, he said, "Come on. Let's see if we can find a way out of here."

"If?"

"Don't worry, I know survival tactics. Grubs don't taste as bad as they look on TV."

Randi allowed Britt to lead her along the riverbank, grateful to lose the I-don't-hurt-like-hell mask for a few minutes. Her head felt like a pack of angry forest

Brownies had attacked it while she'd been unconscious, and her vision blurred around the edges.

She likely had a concussion, at least a mild one, but her fear for the wolves outweighed her desire to seek medical attention. By the careful way Britt moved, he was doing his best to shield her from the extent of his wounds, too.

What had he been thinking, to hurl himself off the bluff? It was nosebleed steep at that location. She at least had a strong reason—avoiding really long teeth and claws. His only inducement was…her.

"You put your life at risk for me." Her fingers worried the shoulder straps of her rucksack. The enormity of what he'd done made her break out in a cold sweat. "I appreciate it. Really, I do. But don't ever do such a harebrained stunt like that on my behalf again."

"Do you really think I had a choice?"

"Of course you did." Her gaze narrowed on the back of his head. "Since no emergency personnel showed up, I take it you didn't call for help before barreling down the mountain. What if you'd been knocked unconscious, too?"

"Someone would have eventually come across my truck and scoured the area."

"Eventually."

He faced her. "Look, I get that I didn't act with strict logic. It was kind of hard to with an angry bear coming at me."

"She charged you, too?"

He nodded. "I was desperate to get to you and didn't wait long enough before approaching the spot where you disappeared." He swiped a hand through his already disheveled hair. "When I saw you step over the edge, something snapped in my mind and I operated on pure instinct. All I could think about was getting to you. That I'd left you alone too long—and put you in danger." He threw up his hand. "Dammit! I couldn't think beyond the possibility you were either dead or dying at the bottom of a mountain and it was my fault."

"You couldn't have known a mama bear and her cub would happen by my location. Had I remained still, she might have passed me by, just like her cub." She tunneled her fingers into his clenched fist. "This wasn't your fault. Sometimes bad things happen. We're both alive and mobile. Focus on that fact."

He placed two fingers beneath her chin. "Your pupils are slightly dilated. I think you're in more pain than you let on."

"I'll take some ibuprofen at the first opportunity. Until then, let's get to your wolves."

He kissed her. A soft, possessive, slow kiss, before setting off again. Randi's heartbeat stormed inside her chest, and her pulse hammered against her already pounding temples.

When Britt had tried to redirect the mama bear's attention away from her, Randi's fear had trebled. No one had ever put her life above their own before. She was humbled and confused and turned on. He'd been fierce but calm. Strong and sure. Like her very own superhero.

A wave of dizziness hit, and she stretched her hands out for balance. She swallowed back the bile that rose in her throat and focused on Britt's back, on staying upright, staying lucid. For both their sakes, she hoped Britt found a kiddie hill for them to climb rather than a black diamond.

She dug into her rucksack for her sunglasses, even though the sun hadn't burned off all the fog yet. They helped reduce the light and, therefore, the pain.

It took another thirty minutes before he found a place for them to ascend with minimal physical effort. By the time they made it to the top, they both heaved great lungfuls of air.

He studied their surroundings. "No more talking from this point forward. We're close."

"I couldn't, even if I wanted to."

Adrenaline pumped through Randi's body, giving her a second wind while blowing off the top of her head. She needed some relief from the constant, debilitating pressure on her skull. *Soon,* she kept telling herself. *Soon.*

When they finally reached the ledge overlooking the den, all the mind-paralyzing pain evaporated, making room for incredible excitement—and a bit of apprehension. Britt hadn't been able to pick up the blood trail again, so they had no notion of what to expect at the den below.

Randi held her breath as she peered through her binoculars. Everything around the den seemed unremarkable. Two of the pups stood inside the opening, their gazes intent on something to their left.

Then a set of baleful cries and yip-barks reached her. She lowered her binoculars and noticed Britt had slid forward in order to get a better vantage point. "What's going on?"

"I'm not sure." He scooted forward until his head and shoulders draped over the edge. "The wolves are pacing around something." He advanced another six inches.

Randi grasped his calf as if she could stop him from pouring over the side.

"Sonofabitch."

"What? What do you see?"

He eased back beside her. Granite etched his features. "One of the wolves is lying motionless near a boulder. I think it's Mellow."

"Mellow?"

"One of the juvenile pack members."

"Is he injured?"

"If not for the way the pack is acting, I would have said he's napping. It's one of his favorite spots." He stowed away his binoculars. "I've got to go down there."

Fear crammed into her throat. "What about the others? Will they try to protect Mellow from you?"

"Not likely. Red wolves have a strong fear of humans. They'll disperse the moment they see me."

"Then I'm going with you."

"I don't think that's a good idea."

"Why not? If it's safe for you, it should be safe for me."

"I'm not sure how the injured wolf will react. I'd rather not have to worry about you getting attacked."

"No need to worry about me. I'll be standing behind you."

He stared at her a moment, then shook his head. With a resigned air of defeat, he asked, "Will you at least do what I say, when I say?"

"Of course. I'm not stupid, you know." She grinned and was pleased to see his return smile.

"Come on, Shepherd. I have a feeling this is going to be unpleasant."

All amusement fled at the thought of Mellow's suffering. Finding a natural ladder of limestone slabs and earth mounds, they made their way down to the creek bed. With precise movements, they inched toward Mellow's location.

The breeding male noticed their approach first and alerted the others. The juveniles scattered and the pups ran to the safety of the den. The breeding female paused halfway between the den and Mellow. Apollo eyed them until they were within fifty feet before deciding it was time for him to back away.

Poor Mellow didn't stir at all.

When they were a few feet from the motionless wolf, Britt held up a hand to Randi. A silent demand for her to stay behind. From this distance, she couldn't tell if Mellow was breathing or not. She sent up a rusty prayer, hoping they made it in time to save the sweet fella.

Britt knelt down near the wolf's rear end, visually examining the canid from head to toe. With the boulder in the way, he couldn't approach the wolf from behind. He would have to assess the situation from a safe distance before moving into biting distance.

When the wolf didn't lash out, he inched closer, speaking to the animal in low tones. Still nothing. Randi moved to the side until she could see Britt's expression.

Still too far away from the wolf to see any small rise in his torso, she would have to depend on Britt's reaction for news.

He reached out a careful hand to rub the tips of his fingers through the wolf's red-blond fur. Not even a twitch.

Sadness spiked in her chest, filling her throat. She glanced at the other wolves, who were pacing a distance away, eyeing them with wary suspicion.

Britt monkey-walked until he crouched beside Mellow. He set a hand below the wolf's armpit, a pulse point. A moment later, he closed his eyes, his chin dropping to his chest.

Randi's hand shook as it came up to cover her mouth. "Is he—?" She couldn't finish the sentence.

Brushing his hand over Mellow's side, he said, "Yes." His palm came away covered in blood. "Shot."

"Oh, Britt." She shuffled forward and grasped his shoulder. "I'm so sorry." She took in Mellow's buff coat with red splashed behind his tall, pointed ears and wondered how anyone could end such a beautiful life. "What do you suppose happened? Could a hunter have mistaken him for a coyote?"

"Any responsible hunter can distinguish a coyote from a red wolf. There's a good thirty- to forty-pound difference in their sizes, and their coloring and features are distinct." Britt drew a hanky from his back pocket to wipe the blood from his hand. "Though that doesn't stop some hunters, and more often livestock owners, from claiming they can't tell the difference so they can harvest or remove a wolf."

Randi remembered what she'd wanted to tell Britt. "Right before the cub and mother bear arrived, I got this eerie sensation of being watched. When I searched the bluff above me, I caught a glimpse of movement, a splash of color that didn't belong. Orange, I think. At the time, I thought my imagination was wreaking havoc on my senses, but now I'm not so sure."

"Can you recall anything at all about the figure? Man? Woman? Animal?"

"No, I'm sorry. The image was so fleeting and the fog was so thick. Even now, I worry that it was a branch blowing in the breeze or a trick of the fog. I could be making way too much out of it." She revisited that moment in her mind's eye, recalled the way the hairs along her neck and spine unfolded like the wings of an eaglet before its first flight. "It's probably nothing, though something on that cliff put my instincts on high stalker alert."

"Then I'm sure it wasn't a branch or something the fog conjured."

An unnamed emotion gripped the back of her throat. His matter-of-fact statement hinted at a level of trust that surprised her. How could he have that kind of faith in her when she doubted herself? It was a humbling moment.

"What do we do now?

"I'm in uncharted territory," Britt admitted. "My gut urges me to remove Mellow from this area. A dead member this close to the den could cause the pack unnecessary stress and force them to relocate."

"Where should we take him?"

"I'll carry him into the woods and look for an abandoned burrow or hollowed-out downed tree."

"He must be seventy pounds. How are you going to lift, then carry, that amount of dead weight with a broken rib?"

"I'll figure it out." He peered down at Mellow's lifeless body. "I can't leave him here."

The pain would be excruciating. No way would her conscience allow her to stand by and watch him struggle with the wolf's corpse. "I'll do it."

"Do what?"

"Carry Mellow to his resting place."

His assessing gaze raked over her.

"If I can unload cases of booze, I can manage this."

"You might be carrying him for several hundred feet."

"If need be, I'll pause to rest."

A battle waged inside him. She could see the conflict playing across his features. He was used to handling things, taking charge. Depending on someone else was not part of his repertoire.

For him to be considering her offer meant he was hurt worse than he'd let on. Randi doubted a little discomfort would stop him from taking care of Mellow. But knee-buckling pain might be more than even a tough guy was willing to risk.

"What about your head injury?"

"I still have a headache, but the dizziness has passed."

The muscle in his jaw flexed. It was as though any words of agreement were stuck in his throat. Randi took pity on him and knelt down, assessing the best way to lift the wolf in her arms.

Britt crouched on the opposite side. "I don't like this."

"I know." She caught his gaze. "Let me do this for you. For the pack."

Restless, agitated sounds from the pack reached them.

He pulled in a deep breath and winced. "I'm going to help you lift him."

"Are you sure?"

"Yes." He rubbed the backs of his fingers under his chin. "Once he's in your arms, I'll support either his front end or back end, whichever will help more."

Randi nodded. It was a good compromise, and she would likely welcome the help after fifty yards or so.

Working together, they managed to settle Mellow in her arms. The process wasn't much different than picking up an oversized sedated dog. Britt took the wolf's hind end, which helped balance the weight.

They walked a great distance into the woods before finding a large uprooted tree. By the looks of it, the maple had tipped over many years ago. Probably the same year this part of North Carolina had experienced record rainfalls. When the soggy ground could no longer support the top-heavy tree, the whole thing had upended, taking a half ton of dirt with its root system.

The deep indentation left behind would make a nice burial site for Mellow. With a bit of maneuvering, they laid him down, then covered him with foliage and rocks. They stood silent at the edge of the burial site for several seconds. Randi slid her hand into Britt's, needing the connection and hoping to erase the disturbing set to his features.

When his fingers didn't curl around hers, she studied his profile. "What are you thinking?"

"I can't figure out how they found them."

"They, who?"

"Whoever it was that hunted down my wolves and murdered one."

"You think someone trespassed to hunt the wolves?"

"I can't come up with any other reason why someone would risk the Steele family wrath." He was silent a moment. "Only a handful of people know about the Steele-Shepherd pack."

Disbelief pushed against Randi's heart. Every muscle stilled. The closeness she'd experienced while working with him to care for Mellow's body vanished in a cloud of hurt and disappointment. She removed her hand from his slack grip. "I didn't share your secret."

"The pack has lived here unharmed since their discovery over a year ago." He turned cold eyes on her. "You think it's a coincidence that the day after I revealed the den's location to an outsider one of the wolves wound up dead?"

Outsider.

"Coincidence or not, I told no one about the wolves."

"Not even the slick attorney for the Carolina Club?"

"Especially not Keith Gaviston."

"What reason did you give him for not selling to the club?"

A volatile mix of fury, suspicion, pain, and guilt roiled in his dark eyes. Randi did her best to focus on the pain and guilt. Britt and her mother had assumed the huge responsibility of watching over the pack. So much so that Britt had been willing to take his personal finances to the brink of collapse to protect the wolves.

While his accusation sliced down the center of her heart, she tried her damnedest to consider it was his guilt lashing out, his belief that he'd failed to protect the pack. She wanted to believe that when he no longer had the grime of death and loss on his hands he would realize that she would never break such a precious confidence. She wanted to believe that in the calm of the aftermath he would trust her.

The logical side of her mind kicked in. Could she really expect so much from someone with whom she'd grown close in only a week? Couples could spend a lifetime together and be shocked by a secret or an unforgivable action. A week meant nothing.

A heavy weight lowered on her chest, making it difficult to speak.

"I told Gaviston that the club's and my goals for the property didn't line up."

"And he just packed up and left. No attempts at persuasion?"

"Of course he tried. He would be a lousy attorney if he hadn't."

"Might you have told him about the wolves to make him back off?"

"I didn't need to," she said between clenched teeth. "I have worked in a bar for most of my adult life. Some have been full of randy, aggressive boy-men. Some full of successful, charm-you-out-of-your-underwear gentlemen. I've had many good-looking guys try to *persuade* me into their beds, dinner, weekend getaway, or simply to hand over my number. But those surface elements don't tempt me. They never have."

When his hard stare remained intact, the last of Randi's hope fled on an uneven heartbeat. "Britt, I can see that you don't believe me. And I can't think of anything else to say that will change your mind." She turned away. "Make sure you see a doctor when you're done here."

"Where are you going?"

"Home."

"Give me a minute and I'll walk you out."

"No need." She kept moving, not daring to turn back. "I'll find my way out."

"How will you get home?"

She pulled her phone from her back pocket, amazed it hadn't shattered into a million pieces on her mad flight down the mountain. Waving it in the air, she said, "I'll call someone to pick me up."

"Like hell you will."

Randi angled around him, refusing to touch him or even brush against him. As mad as she was, she might break another one of his ribs. Damned man. She'd been honest and where had it gotten her? He didn't even believe her.

"Randi," he said, "I'm taking you to the hospital."

"No, you're not." She whirled around to face him. "You've all but called me a liar. I c-can't"—she pulled in a choking breath—"be with you right now."

"At least let me take you home." He stepped closer, gentling his voice. "Please."

Against her will, her body responded to the tender concern in that one little word. The fight went out of her, and she nodded.

Without another word, he guided her out of the woods and drove her home. He rolled to a stop outside her bungalow. Neither of them moved. Neither spoke. They both understood that the moment she stepped out of his truck would be the end of their short-lived relationship. Sadness clutched her throat and wouldn't let go.

She grabbed the shoulder strap of her rucksack, preparing to leave. "I'm deeply sorry about Mellow. But I promise you, I didn't reveal your secret. I could never have done that to them—or you."

The walk to her front porch seemed to take hours. The closer she got, the blurrier the red door panels got. By sheer force of will, she waited until the door closed behind her before she let the tough girl act fall away.

How had she allowed herself to get so wrapped up into Britt Steele in such a short amount of time? It defied logic. Defied the evolution of every other relationship she'd ever had. Everything about him appealed to one sense or another. His quiet watchfulness, his understated humor, his friendship with her mom, his care of the wolves, his love of his family. He did nothing by half measure. When he committed to something or someone, he poured everything into the connection.

Pushing away from the door, she moved to the front window, expecting to see an empty road. But Britt's truck still idled at the curbside as if he was afraid to cut the final thread holding them together. The sight made mincemeat of her knees. She grasped the back of an armchair to steady herself.

Should she go to him and try to talk some sense into his thick Steele skull? Or did he need time to process everything that had happened? Would she come out on the winning side? Would he realize she could never betray his trust?

Questions soared through her mind with blinding speed, making her dizzy. "To hell with this." If she didn't try to make him see reason one more time, she wouldn't be able to sleep tonight. Or tomorrow night. Or the next night. She marched to the door and threw it open only to watch Old Blue ease away from the curb.

Randi closed her eyes and melted back into her house. She dropped her rucksack onto the floor and began peeling away her clothes. Stepping into the shower, she endured the cold spray of solitude and, later, the scalding rush of heartbreak.

CHAPTER TWENTY-FOUR

BRITT PICKED HIS WAY AROUND construction debris at the building site of the training center. Pieces of metal and wood and chunks of masonry littered the outside yard, giving it a post-hurricane appearance.

Pushing open the front door, he was glad to see the disorganized chaos outside did not extend inside. From the looks of it, the contractors had wrapped up their work on the interior today, as promised.

"Reid!"

After he'd left Randi's place, he'd driven around for over an hour. His mind had seethed with other possibilities of how the wolves had been discovered. He'd even called Jonah and Deke to see if they'd discussed the wolves with anyone. Thank goodness he'd asked them over the phone rather than in person. Neither were too happy with him at the moment.

He didn't believe in coincidences, yet he'd seen the truth in Randi's eyes when she said she hadn't divulged the den's location. But people accidentally revealed secrets all the time. It was near impossible to be aware of every word said, especially in times of high stress or when rushed. Mouths spewed shit every day. Marriage counselors would be out of work, otherwise.

On his third pass of the construction site, he'd spotted Reid's F-150 and another possibility had occurred to him. The more he'd considered the idea, the more likely it seemed. In many ways, Reid would be the guy you'd want at your side. Once he committed, he was like a damned leech. He either had to be cut off or burned off.

But other times, Reid had the mentality of a twelve-year-old. No common sense—or, if he did, he ignored it.

"Reid!" Britt stomped his way into the cavernous gym. No sign of the pain in the ass. "Reid, I need to talk to you!"

Britt gritted his teeth and searched for his brother, room by room. He found him on the back patio, sitting in a bag chair with a longneck dangling from his fingers. The image was so not Reid that all he could do was stare.

"I knew I should have pulled my truck around back," Reid said without turning around.

"Did you hear me calling your name?"

"Brynne probably heard you downtown. From inside her damned shop." He took a drink. "What'd I do now?"

In the back of Britt's turmoil-drugged mind, he noticed something was off with Reid. But Britt's own issues elbowed their way to the fore. "Have you been war-gaming on the north side of the conservation area?"

"I haven't been war-gaming on any side of the conservation area."

"Have you been hunting?"

"Not since the last time the four of us went out."

"Did you give your friends permission to hunt the conservation area?"

Reid set down his beer and gave Britt his full, unwavering attention. "Are you out of your flippin' mind? What's this all about?"

"Answer the question first."

"Fuck off."

It was the exact wrong thing to say to Britt in his current mental state. From one breath to the next, the two of them squared off face-to-face. Britt stood shoulder-to-shoulder with Reid, though his little brother knew how to kill a man in a hundred different ways.

"Answer the question," Britt demanded.

"Tell me what's going on first. If I'm going to be accused of something, I want to know why."

He knew to his core that Evie hadn't divulged the pack's existence and his quick phone calls to Jonah and Deke told him they weren't the culprits. Now that someone had found the wolves, he didn't know what to do about it. Did he relocate them? Did he let things play out? Did he hire security to keep an eye on the den?

Letting more people in on his secret that was becoming less of a secret made every cell in his body rebel. He stared down his brother, wanting to believe Reid had nothing to do with Mellow's death, even indirectly.

Something flickered in his brother's eyes. "Does this have anything to do with what you and Evie've been whispering about for months?" Reid caught his surprise. "It is. So you have a secret you'll share with a twenty-something college student but not me? A Green Beret?" Reid shook his head and sat back down. "Freaking priceless."

When put that way, his reluctance to tell Reid about the wolves seemed ridiculous. Yet outside his military experience, Reid had proven time and again that stupidity really did run in the Steele gene pool. Out of all his siblings, Reid was the one he'd never managed to connect with. They were oil and water—responsible vs irresponsible, introvert vs extrovert, beer vs whisky.

"What did I ever do to you to make you not trust me?" Reid asked.

"I trust you."

"You sure got a funny way of showing it, bro."

Maybe he'd put too much weight on their differences. Maybe he should have been looking for common ground rather than all the ways they differed. His brother might be an ass, but he was an honorable ass.

"Look," Britt speared his fingers through his hair,

"you're not the only one I've kept in the dark about my project. Evie's the only one in the family I've told. Partly because she's the only one who has ever had an interest in what I do and partly because my former partner and I decided to keep the in-the-know circle small."

"Former partner?"

"Barbara Shepherd, a passionate wildlife conservationist and my mentor while she was alive."

"Randi's mom?"

"Yes. Randi learned about the project after her mother's death. That's how quiet we kept it."

"So the secret project is in the woods, on conservation area property."

"And on Randi's." Britt eased down on the top step of the patio, careful of his injured rib, and rested his back against the cedar column bracing the pergola above. "A little over year ago, I came across a den of red wolves."

"Wolves in North Carolina?"

"They were reintroduced to the state back in the late eighties, along the coast. Later, the federal government tried to establish a cell in the Smokies."

"I'll be damned."

"When the program out here collapsed, about thirty wolves were never located. The feds believed that they either died from starvation or bred themselves out with the local coyotes."

"Until you found your merry rogue band."

"They're purebloods." Britt shook his head, still amazed at their resiliency. "Somehow they've managed to resist coyote temptation all these years. It's an amazing discovery."

He peered up at his brother, expecting to find boredom etched over every plane of his face. Instead, he found genuine interest. So much so, Reid had leaned forward in his chair while Britt spoke. The sledgehammer lifted from his chest.

"You and Barbara Shepherd have been monitoring the den ever since?"

"Yes." Britt smiled. "The pack had pups this spring."

Reid's lips quirked upward. "Congratulations, Papa."

"Funny."

His brother's expression sobered. "How do I factor into all of this?"

"Randi and I found one of the juveniles dead this afternoon. Shot."

"You think I killed one of the wolves?"

"Not on purpose. But I wondered if you and your friends were out horsing around. Maybe one of them thought they were targeting a coyote."

"No way. Not me. Not my friends. They know better than to go near the conservation area."

"I didn't think so, but I had to ask." He released a frustrated sigh. "For over a year, the wolves have lived in peace and now one is dead due to human interference."

"You said that you and Randi found the dead wolf. Who else knows about the den?"

"Me, Randi, Evie, Jonah, Deke, and now you. Barbara Shepherd, of course, but she's gone."

"Jonah?"

"Only yesterday. He's buying the Shepherd property."

"Damn, you've been busy."

"You have no idea."

"I don't know Randi well. Could she have blown the den's location?"

Britt bit his tongue, unable to 'fess up to the fact that he'd all but accused her of giving in to Gaviston's charms and selling out the wolves.

"Went down that tricky road, did you?" Reid tried to suppress a grin and failed. "Didn't work out well, I take it."

"No. It did not." Britt rubbed the heel of his palm against his forehead. "I reacted to a fleeting suspicion before thinking the damn thing through."

Reid clutched his chest. "Where's my calendar?" He pulled out his phone, tapping away. "I need to make a note of this. *Britt Steele reacted without brooding something to death.*" He clicked his screen off. "There, a historical moment recorded for me to pull up and mock at a later date."

"Has anyone ever told you that you're an ass?"

"Every day of my life, bro. Sometimes twice on Tuesday."

Britt nodded toward the cooler sitting at Reid's side. "Got an extra in there?"

Snapping the lid open, Reid grabbed a beer and tossed it to Britt. "Not your normal weapon of choice."

"Not a normal day."

"From your boo-fuck-hoo face, I take it Randi's important to you."

"We've...grown close." Britt scraped a nail over the label on the beer bottle. "I need to make this up to her."

"Buy her an ice cream cone."

"What?"

"Ice cream. Chicks love that kind of thing. Sweet and romantic."

"Does Brynne agree with you?"

"Don't know. Haven't tried it with her yet." He stared down at the blue-and-gold label on his bottle. "But I'm gonna keep it in my back pocket."

"Trouble already?"

A muscle flicked in his jaw.

"Reid?"

"I almost lost her, and it scared me shitless."

"A little overprotective, are you?"

"So she says."

"Welcome to the world of Britt."

Understanding darkened Reid's face. "We've never thanked you for taking care of us after Dad left."

The air valve in Britt's throat closed. He looked away. "Don't start now, or I'll have a damn heart attack on your construction site."

"Can't have that. Mags will insist on a full-scale investigation, which will put us even further behind."

"Prick."

"Back atcha."

An easy silence fell between them, one the two of them hadn't experienced in years. Decades, maybe.

"Do me a favor, would you?" Britt asked.

"You want me to help you track down who's hunting the conservation area?"

"How'd you know?"

He flashed one of his grins. "There's more to me than amazing good looks, bro."

Britt shook his head. The old Reid was back. "I would appreciate the help, thanks."

"Sweet." Reid popped out of his chair. "Ready?"

Britt eased to his feet, downing the last of his beer. He set the empty bottle inside the cooler, then clapped a hand on his brother's shoulder. "Let me know how the ice cream thing goes."

An uncharacteristic flush entered Reid's cheeks.

Britt laughed, ruffling his brother's hair like he used to when they were much younger. "Come on, dickweed. Let's find out who killed my wolf."

Snap!

"*Sonofabitch!*" Reid's whole body arched as he jumped away from the iron jaws of the illegal trap. "That makes four." He rubbed a hand over his chest. "I'll never get used to the sound of a sprung trap. Can't even imagine what that must feel like on a paw."

On the way to the conservation area, Reid made a stop at the urgent care clinic so Britt could have his ribs checked out. All the pain turned out to be nothing more than a helluva contusion, which suited Britt just fine. He wondered if Randi had gone to see her doc yet.

At the conservation area site they scouted for any evidence of who had killed Mellow and whom, or what, Randi had seen on the bluff right before her encounter with the bear. So far, they hadn't found anything of a personal nature that might help them identify the trespasser. However, they had found a number of set traps that might carry the owner's fingerprints.

The find confirmed Britt's opinion that Mellow's death hadn't been an accident. He'd been hunted. Somehow, the wolf had eluded his hunter and sought the safety of the den. So the question remained—had the trespasser killed the wolf for fun, sport, or profit?

Britt grabbed the trap. "Randi and I got lucky when we were out here earlier. One misstep and we would have gotten nailed by one of these." He shoved the iron torture device into his backpack, noticing for the first time how low on the horizon the sun sat. "We're losing our light. I'll come back tomorrow to finish the search."

"It just so happens that I'm a free man tomorrow."

Britt grinned and clasped Reid's shoulder. "Thanks, mutt."

"You're welcome, Tarzan."

"You up for a little Name That Tune?"

A slow smile stretched across his brother's face. "Do I get to kick some ass?"

"Quite possible."

"I'm in."

After leaving the conservation area, they piled into Britt's truck and drove for an hour before pulling into Carolina Club's parking lot. Britt backed into a parking stall and cut the engine.

"So what's the plan?" Reid withdrew his Sig Sauer from beneath his lightweight jacket. He gave it a once-over, checking the chamber before re-holstering the weapon. Noticing Britt's tension, he said, "Don't worry. It'll stay concealed unless they go stupid on us."

Britt nodded, resting his wrist atop the steering wheel. "We wait."

"Then what?"

"When Norwood and his cronies come out, assuming

they're still inside, we confront them about the traps and shooting."

"That's your plan?" At Britt's nod, Reid asked, "Where does the ass-kickin' factor in?"

"The second they tell one lie too many."

"You don't really expect them to 'fess up to trespassing on our property, do you?"

"No. But I'm hoping I can tweak Norwood's ego enough to make him careless." Britt spotted three figures emerging from the lodge. The gentleman who walked ahead of the others bore Norwood's tall, fit physique and receding brown hairline. "Let's see if we can make one of them sing."

Calm settled over his brother as they followed the three club members. The transformation from Reid's normal can't-sit-still-self to the laser-focused-soldier was something to witness. He'd seen this shift in him once before, when Brynne'd had a run-in with a drug trafficker.

The sight elicited a strange combination of emotions in Britt. Seeing that his brother's character was made up of more than the one-dimensional pain in the ass made him proud, yet this side of Reid terrified him a little. What sort of experience had he gathered under his belt to bring such calm before facing an adversary?

They intercepted the trio as they reached the cluster of luxury vehicles awaiting them. Guessing Norwood would claim the largest one present, Britt planted himself between the leader and a Cadillac Escalade. "Norwood."

Reid positioned himself at an angle where he could catch visual cues from Britt while also keeping tabs on each of the hunters.

Norwood studied Britt. "Steele, right?" At Britt's nod, his gaze leveled on Reid. "Although you resemble the billionaire, you don't have his height"—he took in Reid's gray T-shirt, black cargo pants, and military boots—"or his boardroom polish."

"Answer my brother's questions and you won't have to witness my superpower."

"Now that your ruffian brother has set the tone, to what do I owe this unusual meeting?"

"We've found evidence of illegal hunting on Steele property." Britt paused, letting his statement sink in and watching for any flicker of awareness from the trio.

"Illegal hunting takes place every day, all across the state. I don't follow why this news should be of any interest to us."

"Because no one in Steele Ridge would dare trespass on our property, let alone set traps so deep within our territory."

"Traps?" one of the men behind Norwood drawled before spitting on the ground. His large cowboy hat, white button-down shirt, jeans, and big country attitude screamed Texan. "Those are not the tools of a true hunter."

"Sounds like you have a fur trader picking from your land," the third gentleman said in a Midwestern accent.

Britt's gaze flicked to his brother's. He'd been so focused on the club and their reasons behind their too-generous offer for Randi's land that he hadn't stopped long enough to consider other, more logical possibilities. Could Mellow have been killed by a trapper? With lightning speed, his mind flew through the events of the past twenty-four hours.

If a trapper had wanted Mellow's pelt, he would have found a way to lure him into one of his traps so he could suffocate him or strangle him with a snare. Bullet holes in pelts reduced their value. Although he couldn't explain the traps, the individual who shot Mellow wasn't a fur trapper.

Norwood plastered an unaffected, knowing smile on his face. "Now that we've helped you crack the mystery of your trespasser, perhaps you'll step aside." He waved a hand toward his SUV.

"I don't think so." Britt widened his stance and, out of

the corner of his eye, caught Reid honing his trouble radar. "The animal was shot."

"Desperate times call for desperate measures, Mr. Steele. Who better to understand such a concept than your family? The saviors of Canyon Ridge."

Until that moment, Norwood's unflustered facade seemed unbreakable. But a note of cynicism had entered his voice, revealing one of the cards he held. Now Britt had to figure out the rest of his hand.

Britt propped his elbow atop his forearm. He tapped his fist against his mouth, contemplating his foe. "Since you have such a keen interest in Miss Shepherd's property, I'm left to wonder why your club didn't bail out Canyon Ridge, so that you could have access to such prime hunting grounds."

A fissure crackled its way across Norwood's control, leaving a blackened, jagged trail in its place.

Britt smiled. "You tried, but my little brother outbid you. Or was it that the club denied your request?"

"My club is run by idiots—" Norwood caught himself. "Jonah Steele's motivation was a great deal more personal than the club's interest."

"In what way?"

Too late. Britt didn't see the trap coming until Norwood's eyes brightened right before he pounced, landing a perfect punch.

"Jonah wanted to ensure gainful employment for all of his brothers."

Reid took two menacing steps toward Norwood. Britt's hand shot out, stopping his brother.

"We've all done just fine without Jonah's help," Britt said.

"That might be true for Griffin and even you, to some extent, if one could say banging nails all day was a lifelong ambition." Norwood nodded toward Reid. "However, the Beret's injury took away his future—until his baby brother came to his rescue."

It was the wrong nerve for Norwood to poke.

Reid surged toward Norwood again. "You don't know shit about me."

"On the contrary, I've come to learn a great deal—about all the Steele brood." Unconcerned about a pissed-off Green Beret bearing down on him, Norwood caught Britt's eye. "Seems the Steele family has a few delicious secrets tucked away in the closet."

"Reid, hold up—"

His command came a second too late. One second Reid was charging toward Norwood and the next, he was on the ground. Behind him stood a slender Asian man decked out in a dress shirt, dinner jacket, gold medallion, and slacks. He was the epitome of sleek elegance—like a black leopard sporting a diamond collar.

"Gentlemen, may I introduce you to Jun Ito. He holds a black belt in a number of hand-to-hand combat disciplines, as you see."

Reid rolled to his feet, preparing to strike back, though Britt could see his brother favored his injured leg. Ito had known where to strike. Norwood hadn't been bluffing about his knowledge of the Steele clan.

"Reid, stand down."

"Fuck that. I'm going to show this guy what a proper greeting looks like."

"We'll deal with this another way. Head to the truck."

Britt willed his headstrong brother to listen to him just this once. Although Britt had no doubt that an uninjured Reid could take on Jun Ito, he didn't have the same confidence about the Reid who stood before him. The brother who'd spent the past several months in physical therapy, strengthening his knee. He would do what he had to do to protect his brother. Even if it was from himself.

Jun Ito neither smiled nor smirked. He simply stood before Reid, awaiting his opponent's next move. Reid backed away from the fight, but not without sending Britt a you'll-pay-for-this glare.

"Wise decision on your part," Norwood said. "Jun is quite lethal to his enemies—and his prey."

"How about we set aside the drawing room bullshit?" Britt said. "If I find you or one of your members on Steele or Shepherd land, I'll have you arrested for trespassing and poaching."

"What could possibly be on your land that would entice us to break the law?" Norwood mused. His cronies chuckled behind him. "It wouldn't be that lovely pack of endangered red wolves, would it?"

CHAPTER TWENTY-FIVE

RANDI DRAGGED HERSELF OUT OF bed around eight the following morning. For many, this was still early. For her, she'd just wasted half a day. But after her falling-out with Britt, she couldn't make herself care about all the things she wouldn't be able to get done now because she'd slept in.

No matter how many times she reminded herself that Britt's accusations had been formed in a vapor of grief, they still hurt. Did he trust no one?

Pulling her favorite coffee from the cupboard, she replayed his harsh words for the hundredth time while rubbing at the dull headache in her temple. He didn't believe in coincidences. Neither did she. So there had to be another explanation for how Mellow was discovered. Something they were missing. Her mind kept returning to the Carolina Club and her sudden streak of bad luck.

The thought that they could've orchestrated all the chaos in her life seemed fantastical. But she had to consider the possibility. What good would that do her, though? The police had found no evidence of wrongdoing at her mom's accident site. How would she go about proving that the club had influenced her financial advisor? She was no PI, and the police would need more than her and Britt's suspicions.

She hit the brew button on her coffeemaker, and soon

a stream of scalding dark liquid splattered into a large mug containing French vanilla cream.

After indulging in her guilty pleasure, she showered, dressed, and headed into town to run some errands.

Stopping at Blues, Brews, and Books first, she checked in to see how things were going with the morning crowd.

"Good morning, Miss Shepherd," said her handsome new barista, Brock Blackwater, the moment she came through the door.

"Morning, Brock." Scanning the storefront, she checked for tables that needed to be bussed and signs of unhappy customers. She found none. Beautiful. "Did Kris tell you we're on a first-name basis around here?"

"Yes, ma'am." He poured milk into a metal cup. "It'll take awhile for me to break free of my grandfather's teachings and military training."

With his close-cropped black hair, wide-set brown eyes, honey-brown skin, and endearing manners, Brock had become a customer favorite, especially with the ladies.

"The café looks wonderful."

"Thank you, ma'am."

Smiling, she made her way to the grocery store. She didn't enjoy traversing the gargantuan store when she only had a few items to purchase, but she loved the place for her big Sunday shopping excursions. So many choices, and the place had a pick-up-your-dinner-and-go café. Heaven for a single woman.

Grocery cart full, she dodged traffic in the parking lot. When she paused to make way for an RV-wanna-be pickup truck, she spotted Britt's broad shoulders and blond hair weaving through the rows of vehicles. She adjusted her sunglasses to make sure it was him and not something her bruised brain had conjured.

She took in his shaggy, sun-kissed hair and square jaw. Yep, that was the real deal. Seeing him so soon after their argument made her throat clog.

She wanted to call out to him, but had no idea of what to say. Rather than risk the awkwardness, she made a beeline for her Jeep. She braced herself against discovery, certain he would try to intercept her. Or worse, ignore her—like she was doing to him. *Ignore* wouldn't be the right term. More like *avoid*, not that the word choice made the action any more palatable.

Throwing her groceries into the back, Randi held her breath until she pulled out onto the road, leaving the store—and Britt—behind. Before heading home, she stopped to get gas and cash at her bank's ATM. By the time she drove down her street, her heart and nerves were back under control.

Britt and his brothers frequented her bar quite often. She couldn't allow something like this to turn her into a fleeing coward. Wading through the first dregs of a breakup was not new to her, though this thing with Britt affected her on a different level than all the other guys before him.

Randi straightened her shoulders, promising herself that any future Britt sightings would be handled with a great deal more maturity than she'd displayed this morning. At least that was what she told herself until she saw Britt propped against the side of his truck, waiting for her return home.

"Pluck a biscuit!" She sent a frustrated glare heavenward. "Did you really need to test my mettle this soon?"

Britt pushed away from his truck and gave her a tentative smile as she drove past to pull into her driveway. His uncertainty gave her the courage to throw up her hand in a quick wave.

Absent a garage, she pulled into her normal spot in front of the metal shed that sat adjacent to her bungalow. Jumping out, she peeked out the rear window in search of Britt under the cover of retrieving her bags.

"Need a hand with those?"

Randi startled, bumping her head when she reared

back. Stars sparked, blinding her. This morning's breakfast did the wave in her stomach. She reached out to steady herself, and a big hand grasped her wrist.

"Whoa." Britt took the bags from her hands. "You okay?"

Sweat broke out on Randi's forehead an instant before all the blood drained from her face, leaving an icy path behind.

Britt angled around to see her face. "You're pasty white." His expression hardened. "You promised, Randi. You promised to go see your doctor."

Although he'd barely raised his voice, his words carved a path right through her skull, making her shrink away.

"I'm sorry," he whispered. "Let's get you back into your Jeep, and I'll drive you to urgent care."

"No. I'll take a couple ibuprofen and be fine."

"You're worse today."

"I hit my head on the car. It'll pass."

He guided her away, taking slow, careful steps. "I didn't mean to scare you."

"It's okay. I didn't expect you by my side so fast."

"Figured you might need some help."

"Oh? Why?"

"Saw you leaving Hoffman's and it looked like you'd stocked up for the week." He held up the bags. "Seems I guessed right."

"Thank you." Had he planned to come here before he saw her at the grocery store? He didn't seem upset, but Britt had a way of masking his feelings. Did he come here to break it off? Or to apologize?

Unlocking the front door, she motioned for him to enter. "You can set those on the counter, if you like."

He did so, then started unloading the bags.

"Britt, you don't need to put away my groceries."

"It's the least I can do for causing you to hit your head. I'll take care of the perishables while you find something to take for your headache."

Although it was a sensible suggestion, she got the impression that his assistance had as much to do with stalling their conversation as it did with saving her milk. Under normal circumstances, she would have scolded him for ordering her around. But not while the pounding in her head threatened to turn her stomach inside out.

A quick glance in the bathroom mirror revealed that she looked as haggard as she felt. Not much she could do about it. She reached into the medicine cabinet, praying the pills kicked in ASAP.

Returning to the kitchen, she asked, "How are your ribs? Any broken?"

"I got lucky—just badly bruised."

"I'm glad to hear it." She couldn't stop herself from inspecting his body. Not that she could see past his clothes. Outside of a few scratches on his face and arms, he looked well. "Can I offer you something to drink?"

"No, thanks." He glanced around the room, anywhere but at her, then up at the clock. "Did I come at a bad time?"

"Not at all. I'd planned to hang out at home for the rest of the day." In an even voice, she asked, "What's up?"

Bracing one hand on her small island, he raked the other through his hair. "Look, I suck at apologies. The words never come out right." He caught her unsympathetic gaze and released a breath. "I'm sorry for insinuating that you'd shared the location of the den. At the time, my mind couldn't wrap around any other alternative, even though I knew, *knew* you wouldn't do so." Both hands now gripped the edge of the island. "I thought you might have accidentally said something that led a hunter to the wolves. When you denied the possibility, I should have believed you."

"And now? Do you believe me now?"

"Yes."

The hurt Randi had been living with for the past twenty-four hours slowly evaporated. She understood how emotion could clog reason. It had happened to her more than once. If their roles had been reversed, she might not have been able to get beyond the fact that all had been well until she'd trusted someone new with her secret.

Reaching across the island, she covered one of his hands with hers. "Thank you for stopping by. I didn't like the way we left things yesterday."

"Neither did I." He turned his hand over, and she splayed her palm over his. "What can I do to make this up to you?"

What can Mommy do to cheer you up? A semi rolled over her chest, crushing her organs, shattering her bones. Her mother's voice echoed between them.

In the early days, when her mother had tried to be an attentive parent, she would coax Randi out of her mood with that simple question. The tactic had lost its effectiveness many, many years ago. Her mom's world had revolved around protecting the environment. All else took second place. Even her daughter.

Randi could not go back there. It had taken her years to understand that her mother's frequent absences had nothing to do with her and everything to do with her mother's priorities. The knowledge still stung to this day. But the heart-wrenching lesson had formalized into one unbreakable promise to herself. She would not settle for the number two spot again. Especially not with the man with whom she would share a bed, a life, a family.

She stared into Britt's soulful brown eyes and saw the devastation he could cause her by putting his interests before their relationship one too many times. A black cloud blanketed her kitchen, snuffing out every bit of light, every bit of joy, every bit of hope.

Bracing her feet apart, Randi withdrew her hand and straightened her spine. "Your apology is enough." Her gaze dropped to the tan, cream, and black swirled pattern in the island's granite countertop, collecting the right words until it became clear that there would be no perfect way to deliver her message. "I've enjoyed our time together. Very much. However, this incident with the wolves has made me recall a long-ago promise I made to myself."

He shifted his stance and it was as if a powerful vacuum sucked up every trace of vulnerability he'd displayed during his apology. "Which was?"

"When I found a guy I might want to be with, I would be number one in his eyes."

What had been hard, cold angles on his features seconds before were now contours that burned with determination. He strode with predatory slowness around the island. His attention riveted on her face.

Arms at his side, he stopped a hand's width away. "If you wish it, nothing will ever come between us."

Randi couldn't hear her voice over the fireworks in her heart. "But that's just it, you put your work with the wolves before your belief in me. If you can do that at this stage, what will our relationship be like in fifteen years?"

"I made a mistake. My grief overrode my good sense." He lifted his hand to cradle her cheek. "I didn't put my work before you, though I did give you a good glimpse of my flawed self." He palmed her other cheek. "If you're going to give me the ax, do it because I was an idiot and didn't think things through before reacting—not because you believe I value the wolves more than you. Nothing could be further from the truth." Angling his head the tiniest bit, he bent closer until their breaths cleaved together. "Do you believe me now?"

He lobbed her words back at her, in challenge or plea, she couldn't be sure. Randi swam in a fog of uncertainty and desire. More than anything else in that moment, she wanted his mouth on hers, his body against hers, his feelings matching hers.

How did she feel about him? Her connection to him had definitely grown into something special, something intense. Months of watching him come into her bar, together but somehow apart from his family, had caught her attention. Months of sensing his gaze on her, but neither of them managing to say more than a few words, had intrigued her. Months of wondering about the quiet, watchful Steele brother had primed her for this moment.

Ah, hell. What a twisted, sadistic joke her life had become. Of all the men her heart could have settled on, the fickle organ picked the man who would freaking break it the fastest.

But a lifetime of avoiding everything that was important to her mom could not be erased by his heart-reviving declaration. The pain of wanting a deep, loving connection that would never come to fruition had embedded itself into every fiber of her young girl's soul. Was she brave enough to step into a relationship with a guy who possessed all the same obsessive passions as her mom?

"I do believe you," she whispered.

Satisfaction lit his features, and he moved to cover her mouth with his.

"However"—she reached between them and placed an index finger against his chin, stopping him—"I need some time to think this through." The pad of her finger traced the edge of his lower lip. "From the second we crossed paths in the woods, my world has been spinning at a dust devil rate. I haven't had a moment to blink, let alone evaluate what I want from this thing between us." She smiled a little. "If you want a stripped-to-the-bone truth, I was just getting used to the idea of our friends-plus agreement."

His expression shifted from satisfaction to wariness to a sort of resigned understanding.

"While you're searching that brilliant mind of yours for answers, remember this." He kissed her, starting soft and slow before building to an unchecked tangle of lips, tongues, hands, and grinding hips.

Need tore through Randi, even while her mind tried

to put on the brakes. But Britt's warm mouth, big body, and intoxicating scent all conspired against her reason. She wanted him. She wanted him *now*.

Her hands flew to his belt buckle, and his fingers fumbled with the single button and zipper of her capris. After peeling off her panties, he lifted her onto the island, sending fruit and canned goods in all directions.

Their lips never parted. Not once.

Not when he entered her, not when she wrapped her legs around his lean waist. Not when he drove into her again and again and again. Not when she dug her nails into his flexing bottom, not even when she groaned her pleasure.

With their foreheads pressed together, they struggled to regain their breaths.

"Did I make your headache worse?"

"What headache?"

"Not funny, Randi. You could have a concussion."

"It's already feeling much better." And it was. She kissed him again. No amount of pain would keep her from him. *This.*

"Hang on."

Randi tightened her noodle-limp legs at the same time he lifted her from the counter. For a moment, she thought he would carry her to the bedroom and finish removing their clothing. But he just stood there, embedded inside her, his face huddled into the crook of her neck. Holding her.

The intimacy of the moment was beyond anything she'd ever experienced before. She had no words to describe the warmth that flooded her from the inside out. She wanted to stay like this, in his arms, forever.

Lifting his head, he met her gaze, and Randi knew what she felt for this man would last forever. She hoped she could survive the devastation he would wreak upon her one day.

An unapologetic grin formed on his thoroughly explored lips. "I only meant to leave you with an unforgettable kiss. Though I can't say I'm sorry for the outcome."

Randi gave him an answering smile and nuzzled his nose. "Neither can I. Maybe we should give it a retry." She clenched her inner muscles and felt an answering shift deep inside her.

"I do like the way you think, Shepherd." He took a step toward her bedroom and his eyes widened and flashed before his left arm gripped her hard and his right hand whirled blindly to the side. He arched his back, twisting, catapulting himself—and her—over the back of her sofa.

They landed in a heap, their breaths whooshing from their lungs.

Randi peered down at Britt's scrunched-up face. "Are you all right?"

"Yes," he wheezed, holding his side. "Just…give me a second."

"Britt, your ribs!" She tried to scramble away, but he held tight. "Let go, so that I can get off you."

"Not a chance." With effort, his face cleared. "Did you jar your head?"

"I'm fine. A little disoriented is all. Did I hurt you?"

"It'll take more than a little thing like you to damage me."

"I'm far from being little." When she tried unlocking her ankles beneath him, he lifted his hips, lodging himself deeper inside her. Randi closed her eyes a moment. She forced back the deep ache and straightened into a sitting position. They were still locked at the waist. "What happened?"

At the rustling sound behind her, Randi twisted around to see Britt's boots fanning back and forth, his jeans and briefs anchored around his ankles.

Eyes wide, she turned back to him. "Are you sure you didn't strain something?"

"On the contrary"—his lips quivered and his eyes sparkled—"I'm feeling quite acrobatic."

She contracted her inner muscles again. "Impressive."

Britt groaned and rolled his hips, lengthening, pulsing, seeking the very center of her need. "I'm going to show you why it's not a good idea for us to be friends anymore."

CHAPTER TWENTY-SIX

"THIS IS MAYBE A SORE subject between us," Randi said, "but I have to ask. Did you find out who killed Mellow?"

Britt flipped a thick patty over, careful not to splatter grease on his bare stomach, and added a square of provolone. After another bout of lovemaking, they'd hauled themselves out of bed and raided Randi's kitchen for something to eat. At the island, Randi was busy cutting up vegetables for her salad while Britt went with a tried-and-true hamburger.

"Reid and I made a pass through the woods. The only thing we found were several traps."

"Traps? For the wolves?"

"And anything else unlucky enough to step in the wrong place." Britt scraped the medium-rare burger out of the skillet and transferred it to a bun. "Including people."

"Do you think the person who killed Mellow also set the traps?"

"My gut tells me no." Setting his plate down, he piled lettuce, bacon, tomato, pickle, onion—he glanced at Randi and decided against the last condiment—onto his burger. Then slathered the top bun with mayo and ketchup before adding it to the pile.

Randi raised a brow.

"What?"

"Quite the masterpiece you've got there."

"Hamburger-making is an art form in the Steele household. Or, at least, in this household." He nodded to her salad. "Please tell me you don't eat like a bird all the time."

She laughed. "No, but I do try to watch my calorie intake."

"Good." He carried his plate and a glass of ice water over to the breakfast table. "I can't take all that chirping."

Shaking her head, she sat next to him. She wore a long cream-colored sweater over a light green cami and darker green pajama bottoms. Her feet were bare and her beautiful hair was confined at the back of her head.

Most men would have preferred to see their new lover dressed in satin and lace and showing a whole lot more skin. But Randi's casual after-sex attire made him feel welcome, at home. He hadn't experienced any awkwardness while he was making himself comfortable in her kitchen. Everything seemed familiar, yet new and invigorating.

"Why do you think the trapper and hunter aren't one and the same?"

"For the most part, they have two opposing interests. Traps are generally used for preserving pelts for resale, relocating an animal, or medical evaluations." He bit into his burger.

She jabbed her fork into her salad. "Whereas, a hunter's intention is either to kill for food or remove a nuisance animal."

"Or to display the kill as a trophy."

"Do you think the Carolina Club might be behind the incident?"

"After Reid and I met with them, I'm more sure than ever that they wanted your property in order to access the wolves. How they found out about them remains unanswered. But Mellow's death—I'm not sure. They're all seasoned hunters. It seems unlikely that they couldn't track an injured wolf."

"Why did you visit the club?"

"I hoped their egos would force them to brag about their exploits, but I underestimated Norwood and his cronies. Though he did confirm my suspicions about the property purchase, I suspect he did so to convey a threat more than anything else."

"What sort of threat?"

"He wants me to know that he's aware of the wolves' existence."

"But doesn't that give the police something to go on?"

"Knowledge does not equal action. I'll need more than a taunt to take to Maggie."

"Maggie?"

"Sheriff Kingston. My cousin Maggie."

"Ah, yes. I don't think of her as Maggie."

"And I have a hard time thinking of her as anything other than the little tyrant Maggie."

Her smile turned nostalgic. "Having such a big family must be wonderful."

"Sometimes. Other times, it's like having gnats flying around your head all day."

"Y'all love each other, though." She moved cubes of tomatoes and squares of meat around her bowl. "That's something to cherish."

Britt covered her free hand with his. "I know what it's like to lose a parent, even when they're still alive and breathing. I had more time with my dad than my siblings did and I remember what it felt like to be loved by him." He caressed her knuckles with his thumb, hoping he wasn't botching this. Advice wasn't his forte. "However, he's broken my trust in irrevocable ways." His hold tightened. "I mourn him in the same vein you mourned your mom before she died. But we can't allow the disappointments of the past to shape our future, to stop us from living the life we deserve."

Randi's chin quivered and her lips thinned. Tears

gathered in her eyes. "Other than what I pried out of you the other night, you haven't spoken much about your dad."

"I've spent almost two decades of my life angry and searching for a reason for his reclusiveness and, ultimately, his abandonment." Britt raked the back of his finger down her damp cheek. "Not until you did I have the courage to set it all aside."

"Me?" she whispered.

"You." How to explain what he'd only recently discovered? "I saw in you—the hurt, the anger, the confusion—everything I struggled with for years, and realized none of it made a bit of difference. I still don't know why my dad made the choices he did and probably never will. And for the first time, in a very long time, I'm okay with that." He stared into her glistening green eyes. "Because all my energy, all that I am belongs to you. If you'll have it. Have me."

Britt's mind shut down while he waited for Randi's response. Not a single synapse sparked, and he didn't replay his words, editing every syllable *ad nauseam*. He waited in suspended silence. Though he might have sent up a little prayer; he couldn't recall.

He willed her to say something, anything. But nothing emerged. She stared. He waited.

Her continued lack of communication jumpstarted his brain and doubt crept in. "Randi?"

"You've left me unable to form a single word. A first, I think."

If he explained to her what other women might have said when their partner professed his feelings, he would be suspicious of any affirmative response. No one wanted a coerced profession of affection. And she wouldn't appreciate being nudged into saying something so important if she didn't feel the same.

What to do? What to do?

Acting as though he'd never laid his heart out on the kitchen table seemed the safest option. He nodded toward her half-eaten salad. "All done?" Not waiting for an answer, he headed to the sink with his dirty dishes.

"Britt—"

The chime of a dying organ echoed through the house. Randi squinted toward the front door.

"You expecting anyone?" he asked.

"No."

A knock followed the doorbell. "Britt, I know you're in there. Open up. I need to speak with you."

"Who is it?" Randi asked.

Britt bit back a curse. "Jonah." He marched into the bedroom and threw on his jeans. "I'll get rid of him." He opened the door enough to speak with his brother, but not enough for Jonah to see Randi. "What?"

"This is longer than a thirty-second conversation." Jonah adjusted the wide strap cutting across his torso. "Let me in."

"Not good timing, Jonah. I'll catch up with you at my cabin in thirty minutes."

Jonah eyed his bare chest and feet. "Sorry for interrupting, but this can't wait. Randi should hear what I have to say."

Jonah appeared as unaffected by the world around him as ever, but the hint of concern hardening his features gave Britt pause. "This had better not be some prank Reid put you up to."

"Reid doesn't even know I'm here." Jonah craned his neck to look over Britt's shoulder. "Randi, will you tell stud man to let me in? I have something important to share with you."

"Britt, it's okay."

Stepping back, Britt pushed open the door. "Remember, I know where you live."

"Yeah, yeah, yeah."

Without saying a word, Jonah dug his laptop out of his messenger bag and placed it on the kitchen table. He retrieved his AC adaptor and plugged it into an outlet, then his computer. Next came a wireless mouse.

Britt slid into the chair opposite Jonah. "Make yourself comfortable."

Jonah didn't acknowledge his comment. His fingers flew a thousand miles an hour across his keyboard.

"Can I get you something to drink?" Randi asked.

"A glass of water. Tap is fine."

Britt thrummed his fingers on the table. Even during the best of times, he wasn't a patient man. When he had a declaration hanging in the air like poisonous gas, his threshold for interruptions and silence reached a gut-sinking low.

"Jonah, out with it."

"Ten more seconds."

Randi set Jonah's glass of water down before taking the seat next to Britt's. They shared a glance, and Britt shook his head. He should be grateful for his brother's arrival. Jonah had saved him the humiliation of Randi's response. *"You're a nice guy and all, but it's way too soon to know if this is love."*

No shit, Sherlock. Although he'd been aware of her for months, she'd only come to know him in the past week or so. *Sweet Pete.* She must think him insane.

A small hand moved down his thigh to rest on his knee. Warmth penetrated his jeans, awakening a part of him that should not even be alive after their bout of lovemaking. He sent Randi a questioning look. She gave him a reassuring smile.

He squeezed her hand in return. "We've waited well past ten seconds. Spill it now, or I'm going to tell Mom you're the one eating her caramel sea salt ice cream, not Reid."

"That's low, man." He tapped the enter key. "Once you see this, you're going to be a lot nicer to me." He flipped his laptop around, facing them.

Britt stared down at the small screen, not comprehending what Jonah wanted him to see at first. Then he noticed the play symbol in the midst of a busy background.

Giving his brother a dark look, Britt said, "If this isn't legit, I'm kicking your ass all the way back to the Hill."

Rather than be intimidated, his brother rolled his eyes. "One of these days, you're going to wake up and see I'm not a kid anymore."

Randi reached forward, moving her finger over the trackpad until the cursor lined up with the Play button. She glanced at Britt, and he nodded.

The video began to play, the grainy green image indecipherable at first. Then the camera adjusted, and Britt could make out a wooden lean-to in the background and patchy grass in the foreground. The camera panned out, and he could see a chain-link fence enclosed the entire area. Inside the fence, a pair of canid eyes reflected back at him.

Randi sucked in a breath.

Britt's teeth clamped together so hard he feared they would break. His gaze shot to Jonah's. "What is this?"

"Live video feed of a red wolf."

"Where's the broadcast coming in from?"

"That's the million-dollar question."

"How did you come across this video?" Randi asked.

"I hacked into the Carolina Club's network. They need to get a new IT person. Their firewall was scary easy to breach."

"Why?" Britt asked.

"You mentioned that some of the members kept scorecards of their trophies." He shrugged. "That made me curious, so I poked around their website until I came across a Members Only login." He took a drink of his water. "Locks and Do Not Enter signs on the Internet are like tubs of caramel sea salt ice cream. Too tempting to resist. So I don't."

Covering his mouth with one hand and leaning back in his chair, Britt folded an arm over his middle while he followed the wolf's anxious pacing. The kennel appeared to be about ten by ten, and from the condition of the turf and the makeshift den, this wasn't the first time the kennel had been used to hold an animal captive.

"Did you find the scorecards?" Britt asked.

"Yep. Looks like anyone who hits six hundred kills becomes a Master Marksman."

"Six hundred animals?" Randi asked.

Jonah nodded. "Norwood's one kill away, and several others are on his tail."

"I can't even imagine."

"Do you think that's one of our wolves?" Randi asked.

Her use of "our" lightened his heavy heart for a brief moment. "The video quality is such that I can't be a hundred percent, but I'll venture a guess and say yes."

"Britt, I'm so sorry." She placed a comforting hand on his arm. "Is the wolf limping?"

His stomach roiled. "Looks like Reid and I missed a trap."

"Hit the escape key," Jonah said.

Randi did so and the video contracted to a small square in the center of a page. A page detailing how members could bid for the opportunity to hunt a rare female red wolf.

Reducing the size of the video improved the quality. Britt leaned in, squinting. He slammed his fist on the table. "Those sons of bitches."

"What?" Randi asked, focusing harder on the wolf. "What do you see?"

"Calypso. One half of the Steele-Shepherd breeding pair."

Horrified, Randi's gaze cut from Britt to the detested video. "The pups' mother?"

Grim-faced, Britt nodded.

"I don't understand."

"Auctions bring in a lot of revenue for hunt clubs,"

Britt said in a low, dangerous tone. "I've read some statistics where over sixty percent of the operating fund comes from auctioning off permits to hunt rare or endangered animals."

"What do we do now?" she asked.

"According to the page, members have until three o'clock tomorrow afternoon to place their bids. Then the GPS coordinates of the release point will be sent to the winner's phone." Britt gripped the back of his skull with both hands. "Without the coordinates, we're dead in the water."

"There must be something we can do," Randi insisted, her heart aching for both Calypso and Britt. "Why don't we hunt down a list of all the properties owned by the club."

"Assuming they snatched Calypso within an hour of Reid and I visiting the den site, they've had a good twenty-four hours of drive time. That's a vast expanse of property to search."

"Do you think the pups have been without food for that long?"

"They've been spending more and more time outside of the den, which means Calypso was beginning to wean them. If the pack hasn't already started doing so, they'll introduce them to solid food through regurgitation."

"Dude, you could have stopped at 'solid food.'" Jonah's thumb tap-danced across his phone's screen.

"Please tell me we're not just going to sit here." Randi had never seen Britt so indecisive, so defeated. It broke her heart, and she could feel desperation bubbling in her stomach.

Britt rocketed from his seat and paced the small confines of her kitchen. "There's not much I can do. Without a lead on the release location, I have no direction to follow. I could go to Norwood, but intimidation doesn't work on the bastard."

Jonah swiveled his laptop back around and typed a few commands before closing the lid. "The way I see it, you have two options."

Randi tore her eyes away from Britt and focused on his brother. At first glance, one could easily dismiss Jonah Steele. He had many of the typical millennial generation characteristics—disconnected to those around him, technology dependent, bored to the point of rebellion. However, when he spoke, he commanded attention. His intelligence, without question. His focus, laser-sharp. His curiosity, no equal.

"Well, one, really," Jonah continued, "but I'll share the second option just for the sake of giving you a choice."

A growl erupted from Britt's throat.

Standing, Jonah stowed his laptop in his bag. "One, you can stay here and pace all night, emitting a few savage sounds as your frustration builds. Or, two, you can head to the Hill and help us locate the wolf."

Britt halted. "Us?"

"Reid, Grif, Evie, Brynne, Carlie Beth, Mom, and anyone else who answers my text for action."

"Text?"

"While you were growling and pacing, I was texting." He slung his bag across his torso. "A good deal more productive, I might add."

Randi's eyes widened as Britt stormed over to his brother, who started backing away.

Britt pulled Jonah into a brief, hard, back-slap hug. "Thanks." The single word came out low, rough. He cupped the back of Jonah's neck. "I know you're not a kid anymore. But you'll always be my baby brother." He pushed him toward the door. "Deal."

An ache caught deep in Randi's throat. The two brothers annoyed each other and were as opposite as opposites could be. But at the heart of their relationship, they loved each other and would do anything for one another. A gift she hoped they never took for granted.

"Don't dally, stud man." Jonah glanced back at them, giving his big brother a pointed look. "The clock's ticking."

"I'll be there in twenty minutes."

After throwing a puzzled look her way, Jonah left them alone.

I'll be there in twenty minutes. I not *we.* The exclusion hurt. A lot.

Her inability to navigate the maelstrom of emotions that had hit her when she realized Britt was telling her that he loved her may have destroyed the best moment of her life.

How could he love her after spending mere days in her company? How could she return the sentiment? It made no sense. The rapid advancement of her feelings smacked of blind, irrational lust, and it frightened her. How could she love him when in all honesty she knew him so little? And what little she knew reminded her of her mother, which was not a good comparison.

The silence between them stretched, became deafening. Every comforting, reassuring phrase that came to mind sounded flat and idiotic. She longed to walk up behind him and knead the tension from his square shoulders. But Britt Steele held a large, flashing sign over his head that said, "Don't mess with me right now."

Instead of smoothing away the hurt she'd caused, Randi slid from her chair. "I take it I'm not invited to join you at the Hill." When he said nothing, Randi rubbed at the knot forming in her chest. "I see." She strode to her bedroom door on Pinocchio legs. "I hope you find Calypso in time, Britt. I really do." Locking her bathroom door, she shed her clothes and stepped into the shower.

The frigid spray did nothing to stop the scalding tears from falling, nor the shattering impact of the front door slamming on yet another failure in her life.

CHAPTER TWENTY-SEVEN

BY ROTE, BRITT PARTICIPATED IN the chatter around him, half his heart thrown into plans for saving Calypso while the other half remained in a bungalow on the opposite side of town.

Why in the hell had he put Randi on the spot like that? He'd considered trying to joke the words away, but that would have made him look like a bigger lunatic or, worse, a liar, both of which he hadn't been able to stomach. He'd ruined one of the most momentous days of his life, with his schoolboy impetuousness. Worse, he couldn't think of a way to repair his mistake.

And dammit, he missed her. They'd been separated for less than an hour, yet those minutes seemed like weeks.

"What do you think, Britt?" Grif asked.

Adjusting his focus, Britt caught the empathetic glances of his brothers and their mates. He glared at Jonah, whose face was buried in his laptop. His brother couldn't have missed the tension between him and Randi, and he must have remarked on it to this gang. With his mother puttering in the kitchen, he was saved from enduring her commiserating gaze. But Carlie Beth's condemnation could have cleaved his head in two. Where was Evie? He needed to have at least one ally in this house.

As soon as Britt had strolled into his mother's house, Reid had settled into his familiar Green Beret tactical mindset and dubbed Jonah's suite of rooms as the War Room. Amid Jonah's electronic command center, Reid taped pictures of Norwood, Ito, Ferguson, Taylor, and Watters to the wall. He also posted several large sticky notes on the wall. One note contained various preserve-type settings in the area that would be large enough and private enough to host an exclusive, illegal hunt. Another note identified the steps they would take to locate Calypso once they hit the ground.

"I'm sure Deke would offer us a hand," Britt said, answering Grif's question. "He might even be able to scatter up some of his buddies at the U.S. Fish and Wildlife Service."

Jonah was muttering beneath his breath.

"What d'you have, Jonah?" Reid asked.

"A worthy opponent." His gaze narrowed, focused. His fingers hit the keyboard harder, faster. "The IT person who set up their main website isn't the same as the one who secured the inside of the members-only site. The latter geek knew what he or she was doing."

"Do we have a plan if Jonah's not able to hack the site?" Brynne asked.

"I'll hack it."

"Brynne has a point," Carlie Beth said. "Let's say Jonah gets in, but the information we need isn't there."

"What is it with the two of you?" Jonah complained. "I'll search until I find what we need to save Britt's wolf. Now stop distracting me."

Carlie Beth and Brynne raised matching eyebrows, not used to Jonah's take-charge side. Britt sympathized with their confusion. His brother was usually absorbed in one device or another. However, this afternoon Jonah seemed possessed by the desire to annihilate the Carolina Club for daring to mess with his family.

Jonah would succeed. It was only a matter of when.

Even if they failed to reach Calypso in time, Britt

would never forget Jonah's determination today. How his brother had worked so hard to stop a terrible act he didn't particularly have a passion for one way or another. How he worked until his fingers cramped for one reason and one reason only—because the issue was important to Britt. Period.

Glancing around the room, he'd never felt closer to his family than he did right now. Rather than Britt shouldering the entire burden of Calypso's kidnapping, each person in this room had taken a piece.

And just like that, years of resenting his big-brother, man-of-the-house status peeled away like a rattlesnake's skin, leaving him...content. Truly content for the first time in memory.

The only rough patch in this field of new spring grass was Randi. He wished she were here so he could share this moment with her. After the way he'd excluded her from this meeting, he'd be lucky if she ever spoke to him again. *He* would never speak to himself again if their roles were reversed.

Though he hadn't seen her expression, he'd heard the pain in her voice. The acceptance. Something about that last part made him angry. Didn't she care for him at all? Love might not have crossed her radar yet, but a deeper connection existed between them. They enjoyed each other's company, they shared a love for the environment, and they desired each other. He hadn't misread those cues, and Britt knew without a doubt they were just the beginning.

Carlie Beth clicked off her phone and stood, snapping Britt out of his reverie. "Brynne and I have an errand to run."

"We do?"

"Yep." She grabbed Brynne's hand and pulled her out of the cocoon made by Reid's arms. "Text us when Jonah locates Calypso."

After a flurry of kisses and good-byes, the ladies left, leaving four bewildered men behind.

"Anyone know what that was about?" Britt asked.

"No," Reid said, "but I doubt it bodes well for one of us."

"My money is on Britt," Grif said.

Reid moved to stand before the list of potential locations. "We're missing something."

"Like what?" Britt asked.

"The only acreage we have listed that's owned by the Carolina Club is the five hundred housing their headquarters." Reid asked Britt, "Didn't Donovan tell us they owned thirty-five hundred, statewide?"

Britt sat forward. "Sounds right."

"Where are the other three thousand acres?"

"I'm on it," Jonah grumbled. "Would you like me to order you a damned pizza while I'm at it?"

"And miss Mom's fried chicken and homemade gravy?" Reid asked. "Not a chance."

"Look for sizable, contiguous acreage," Britt said. "This particular hunt will require privacy."

"What about their headquarters?" Grif asked.

"My gut tells me this auction is the work of a small faction within the club. If I'm right, they won't risk the other members finding out about their illegal hunt."

"I hope Jun Ito's one of them," Reid said. "He and I need to finish getting acquainted."

"If he is," Britt said, "you're not going to get within a hundred feet of him."

"That dictate's going to be hard to follow while I'm stomping his ass."

"Reid, he could undo months of healing."

"Thanks for the vote of confidence, bro."

"Who's Jun Ito?" Grif asked. "Besides the obvious."

"One of Norwood's cronies who likes to attack from behind," Reid said.

"Then I agree with Britt. Stay away from him."

"Just once, I'd like for one of you to take my side in an argument."

"When you start using your head instead of your pride, I'll have your back," Britt said.

Jonah snatched a sheet of paper from the printer. "Here's a list of parcels owned by the Carolina Club. All of them are over one hundred acres." He grabbed another printed sheet. "This map shows where those parcels are located in relation to Steele Conservation Area."

"Looks like we can rule out three of the seven," Britt said. "Too far away."

"That leaves us with four properties and thirteen hundred acres to scour in"—Reid checked the monitor displaying the live feed of Calypso and a countdown clock—"twelve hours and eleven minutes."

"Maybe we're going about this all wrong." Grif stared out the window, overlooking the backyard.

"What do you mean?" Reid asked. "We're looking at this from every angle possible."

"Every *legal* way."

A thread of excitement wove around Britt's chest. "What do you have cooking upstairs?"

"We're burning a great deal of energy searching for the secret location of the wolf."

"Are *we* now?" Jonah tossed in. No one paid him any mind.

"What if we set aside the wolf's location for now and concentrate on the players."

"I'm listening," Britt said.

"Who do you think masterminded this auction?"

"It's gotta be Richard Norwood," Britt said. "The guy taunted us about the wolves. He wanted us to believe they weren't safe anymore."

"Then we'll hit his bank account," Grif said.

For the first time in over an hour, Jonah stopped typing. Reid's jaw fell open, and Britt's lungs collapsed.

"When you say 'hit,'" Britt said, "what do you mean, exactly?"

"Look for entries in his account that hints at a secret he wants kept or something he doesn't want destroyed."

Grif said the words in such a matter-of-fact tone that

you'd think he suggested ruining someone's life on a daily basis.

"Like an affair or a secret baby?" Reid asked. "Or funding a terrorist group?"

"Something like that. I hadn't really thought it through yet."

"Finding it—whatever *it* is—could take more time than we have," Britt said.

"There's another way," Jonah said.

"How?" Grif asked.

"Relieve his personal account of funds. Much faster."

"No fucking way." Britt pointed a finger at Jonah. "Get that shit right out of your head. Hacking into a bank account is a lot different than an auction site. You'd violate a thousand different federal laws. We're not going there."

"For every fifteen minutes the wolf is missing from her pack," Jonah continued, "we extract ten thousand dollars from his account."

"Damn, Jonah," Reid said. "Remind me never to piss you off again."

"If you get caught," Britt said, "you'll break Mom's heart."

"Then I'll be sure not to get caught."

Britt looked to Grif, who stood silent by the window. "Will you talk some sense into him?"

"Not a single byte left behind to mark your path, Jonah."

"Got it."

"Grif, you can't be serious!"

"I've done it before," Jonah said. "When I was fourteen and Reid wouldn't pay back a hundred-dollar bet."

"You thieving shit."

"It's not thieving when you owe the money."

"What kind of twisted genius logic is that?"

Britt dropped his head in his hands, his pulse raced off the charts. As much as he wanted to save Calypso, he couldn't do it at the expense of his family. He wouldn't take the chance of losing another family member.

He lifted his head, his gaze locking with Grif's, then Reid's. "We can't risk it."

They both nodded.

"Too late," Jonah said. "Hacking already in progress."

"Jonah, no!"

His brother stopped typing. "I'm already in and need to concentrate." He met Britt's gaze. "Let me do this."

For you.

Even though his little brother didn't say the words, Britt read them in his eyes. For Jonah to risk so much for something important to Britt made his nose sting and his throat close. Damn stupid genius was going to give him a heart attack.

Britt gave Jonah a hard nod, and his brother's fingers took off like rockets.

"If you get caught, I'm joining you." Britt rose, no longer able to sit still. "I'd rather face prison than Mom's disappointment." He picked up a beanbag ball off Jonah's desk and began tossing it from one hand to the other. "What if we're wrong and Norwood's not the mastermind behind the auction?"

"Then Jonah can put the money back," Reid said.

"I'm pretty sure it won't be that easy," Grif said, "but we can go with that approach for now."

"Does anyone want to know what I think, since I'm the one committing the crime?"

"No," all three brothers said in unison.

"What's our plan?" Britt asked.

"After Jonah siphons off the first ten thousand dollars of Norwood's fortune, you call him and explain our proposal," Grif said.

"Me?"

Grif rubbed a finger over his bottom lip. "You have the most emotional investment in seeing the wolf's safe return. Norwood won't question your motivation. When he sees ten thousand dollars slip away from his account, he won't doubt your resolve—or your resources."

"What are we demanding in exchange?" Reid asked. "The wolf? Or the wolf's coordinates?"

"Wolf," Grif said. "Norwood could send us in circles long enough for the bidding to close."

"If they release Calypso, we might never find her," Britt said. "Or find her too late."

"Let's say our plan's successful," Reid said. "We will have made a powerful, dangerous enemy."

"As will he," Jonah said.

Britt lifted a brow. Reid grinned.

Grif said, "Spoken like a true hacker."

"Jonah, let us know when you're ready," Reid said.

"Ready."

"You've already hacked into Norwood's account?" Grif asked.

"Bank accounts are easier to pick than Reid's high school locker."

"What the hell is wrong with you?" Reid asked. "Is nothing of mine off-limits?"

"Haven't come across anything yet."

"What's taking so long with the auction website?" Britt asked.

"I'm dealing with a pro on that site."

"Now that's comforting," Reid said.

Jonah frowned. "I'm close."

Britt retrieved his phone from his front pocket. "Got a number for me?"

Jonah rattled off Norwood's private number.

The line rang three times before a clipped voice answered. "Norwood."

"You took something that doesn't belong to you."

"Who is this?" Norwood demanded. "How did you get this number?"

"Before today's over, you'll be surprised at the information I can get my hands on with a few clicks of a mouse."

"Steele," Norwood spat.

"Here's how this is going to play out." Britt moved to stand behind Jonah. His brother pointed to the opposite screen. "For every fifteen minutes the female wolf isn't safely within her own territory, your bank account ending in 4325 will make a sizable donation to the Red Wolf Alliance Fund." Britt squeezed his brother's shoulder, and Jonah smiled and his index finger depressed the enter button.

"You wouldn't dare."

"To show you my sincerity, I have made your first charitable contribution of ten thousand dollars. Please check your account."

An unnatural silence flooded the opposite end of the phone, followed by furious clicking.

"Bastard. I'm calling my bank to report this."

"I don't suppose President Bennett and some of the other more straight-shooting club members know anything about your hidden auction site, do they?"

"What do you want?"

"Drop off the female wolf at the two-track located a half mile north of the training center construction site. You have one hour."

"That's not enough time. I'll need double that amount."

"Are you sure? Because your generosity to the Alliance doesn't stop until I see for myself that the wolf is unharmed."

"You and whoever you're working with will pay for this."

"Not as much as you. The Alliance thanks you for your contribution, by the way."

"An hour and a half," Norwood growled.

"Come alone, Norwood, or your contributions will double." Britt clicked off his phone.

"Daaamn," Reid said, "Maybe you and Jonah should have joined my unit."

"You know Norwood's bringing backup, right?" Grif asked.

"Without a doubt."

They both looked to Reid.

A grin broke out on his face. He clapped his hands, rubbing them together. "Finally, some action."

Britt glanced from brother to brother and prayed he'd be able to keep them safe. He'd never faced off with a threat like Norwood. The guy was a seasoned killer. Almost six hundred kills. Could someone like that shift their lust for conquering animals to humans?

Something told Britt he was about to find out.

Chapter Twenty-Eight

"FUCKING REDNECK!" RICHARD NORWOOD SENT his twenty-four-inch monitor crashing to the floor. "He won't get away with stealing from me."

"What's got you in a lather?" Samuel Taylor drawled.

"The Steeles." Richard paced his spacious office within the east wing of the club's lodge. "For every quarter hour we hold the bitch, they're going to donate ten thousand dollars of my money to charity."

Angus Ferguson whistled. "Bold devils."

"Can your IT expert block their attack against your bank account?" Neil Watters asked.

"Yes—in time. But they're sending the money to a damned nonprofit. The longer this goes on, the trickier the explanation."

Hands clasped behind his back, Jun Ito asked, "Should I put a halt on the auction?"

"That'll raise too many questions among the membership," Samuel said. "I've already heard murmurings about the legitimacy of our hunting permit."

"I would suggest a server error," Neil Watters said. "Puts the blame elsewhere and it'll explain the lack of video."

"So we're handing over the wolf and tucking tail?" Angus asked, incredulous.

"No. Each of them will forfeit something important. Something they will mourn."

"Do you think all four Steele boys are involved?" Samuel asked.

"Two for sure. The animal lover and the computer genius."

"The Green Beret, too," Jun said. "He would not miss an opportunity to prove his prowess."

"They're nothing but a pack of wild animals. You can bet Griffin's involved as well."

"Five against four," Samuel said. "Good odds."

Richard scrolled through his phone's contact list. "First, we take down the club's server." He set his phone to his ear. "The Steeles will either see it as a signal of good faith or it will send them into a state of wariness."

"Either reaction works in our favor," Jun said.

Richard spoke into the phone. "Shut the server down. Yes, down. All the way." He covered the receiver with his hand and caught Angus, Jun, and Samuel's gazes. "Find their weaknesses, make them pay."

CHAPTER TWENTY-NINE

RANDI DREW HER PONYTAIL THROUGH the opening at the back of her purple *Moosin' Around* ball cap.

After Britt left, she'd skulked around her bungalow in a state of numbness. Rather than stay and talk things through, he'd bailed. He'd run off to save the wolf, leaving her behind. The irony was beyond measure, and she only had herself to blame.

She should have listened to the Nagging Nellie voice warning her not to get involved with a damn tree hugger. She'd known it would end in heartbreak. She'd freaking known it!

Grabbing the empty cookie sleeve, she tossed it into the trash. Some people drowned their disappointments in alcohol. Not her. She pigged out on Thin Mint cookies. Every winter, like clockwork, she'd buy a dozen boxes. She ate one box right away, and the rest she pulled out of the freezer when the mood struck.

While snarfing down an entire sleeve, she'd come to two important conclusions. One, men were jerks. Two, she wouldn't sit here and take this being-left-behind crap like she'd been forced to do all those years ago with her mother.

No, she would run Britt to ground, confess her feelings, and make him promise never to leave her again.

And there would be some lovemaking involved, too.

But first, she had another mission to accomplish.

She snatched several water bottles out of the refrigerator and nabbed a handful of power bars. The doorbell chimed, and Randi froze. She stared at the solid oak door as if she could see through to the other side.

Drawing in a fortifying breath, she eased the door open and found three stunning women on her porch, each rolling in a kaleidoscope of excitement, wariness, and determination.

"I obviously got your text," Carlie Beth said, "and rounded up the troops, as requested."

"Thanks for coming on such short notice, ladies." Randi backed up a step and the trio filed in, giving her a hug as they passed by. "Can I offer you something to drink?"

"Beer," Carlie Beth said.

"Water would be great," Evie said.

"Nothing, thanks," Brynne said.

Randi waved toward the small breakfast table. "Have a seat."

"Don't leave us hanging," Brynne said. "What's up?"

Randi set their drinks down in front of them, but didn't join them at the table. "How much do y'all know about the wolf auction?"

"Carlie Beth and I were present while the guys were plotting how to recover Calypso," Brynne said. "We filled in Evie on the way over."

"Jonah's hacking into the club's server in order to retrieve the coordinates of the video feed," Carlie Beth said. "He'll do it, though he might be too late."

"Or he might run into a glitch," Brynne said.

"They're sinking all of their efforts into a technological solution." Evie's sweet features melted into a thoughtful expression. "Technology isn't foolproof and it can be far more destructive than intended."

"We tried to get the guys to consider developing a Plan B," Carlie Beth said.

"But they were having none of it," Brynne said.

Randi paced the area between the breakfast table and island. "I have an alternate plan."

Her guests perked up.

"It's dangerous."

"Can't be worse than a stalker," Carlie Beth said.

"Or a pissed drug trafficker," Brynne said.

They all looked to Evie.

"What? I haven't had anyone try to kill me yet. Though Teddy Bendicott tried to slip me the tongue in seventh grade."

Randi took a deep breath, hoping they wouldn't think she was crazy. "We follow the club members."

Her friends shared a look.

"'Follow' as in spy on them?" Brynne asked.

"Just like 007."

"Why, exactly?" Carlie Beth asked.

"To see if they'll lead us to Calypso's location." Randi picked up a pen off the island and began flicking it back and forth. "I can't stand the thought of Britt's wolf penned up and under Norwood's thumb. Who knows if the asshole's giving Calypso water or food. And her poor pups." She threw the pen down. "I can't imagine what this must be doing to Britt."

"I'm in," Evie said.

"Me, too," Carlie Beth said.

Brynne hesitated. "What happens if these club members catch us trailing them?"

"We'll put on the dumb blonde act," Evie said.

"You mean dumb brunette," Brynne said.

"Huh?"

"Ninety percent of blondes are brunettes in disguise."

Evie smiled. "Touché."

"From what Britt told me," Randi said, "Norwood and the others are intelligent, cunning men. I'm not sure they'll fall for the innocent act."

"Brynne's good at persuading bullheaded men," Carlie Beth said.

"Yeah, if she can win over Reid," Evie said, "Norwood and those guys won't stand a chance."

"Wouldn't it be best if you got the authorities involved?" Brynne asked.

"I have my cousin, Maggie, on speed dial," Evie said. "If things get hairy, she'll be at our side in a snap."

"You follow them, find Calypso, then what?" Brynne asked.

"We call Britt."

Brynne still hesitated. No doubt thinking about the last time she and Evie went sleuthing and she wound up confronting a drug trafficker on her own.

"If you're not comfortable with this plan," Randi said to Brynne, "you don't have to come."

"I could probably ask my mom," Evie put in, "just to make sure we each have a partner. Safety in numbers, you know. Mom likes to kick it up, from time to time."

Brynne's eyes widened. "No need to bother Mrs. Steele. Count me in."

Evie smiled, and smugness danced along the edges.

"I played right into that one, didn't I?"

"She survived four older brothers," Carlie Beth said. "One boutique owner doesn't stand a chance."

"Are we sharing our plan with the guys ahead of time?" Brynne asked.

"You're kidding, right?" Evie asked. "They'll go ballistic."

Doubt shoved aside Randi's joy at her friends' support. "Ballistic?"

"Don't let a little Steele anger scare you off," Carlie Beth said.

"We didn't part on a good note earlier, and now I worry this will make things worse."

"If it'll make you feel better, I'll bring Jonah in on our scheme," Evie said.

"Let's work out the details first."

"In the short time I've been accepted into the Steele clan," Brynne said, "I've learned one important lesson."

She held Randi's gaze. "If you want to maintain a certain level of control and independence while dating a Steele, you need to establish boundaries from the get-go." Her features softened. "Britt and his brothers might not like our plan. They might yell a bit. But those boys will still love us. So, if we believe in our plan, then we execute it and hope for minimal yelling."

"I'm not sure Britt feels for me the same way Reid feels for you. Especially after this morning."

Evie snorted. "He's been moping around my mom's house since he arrived." Her expression turned serious. "Of all my brothers, I'm closest to Britt." She slanted a glance at the other two ladies. "Don't tell Grif or Reid." She turned her attention back to Randi. "I know Britt's moods. I know his dreams, and I know he has never cared for a woman the same way he cares for you."

Hope clutched Randi's chest. "I d-didn't say the words. I was…afraid." Speaking became difficult, air wouldn't come fast enough. "He left angry." She clasped a hand over her eyes, embarrassed. "He left. He left *me*."

Carlie Beth stood, wrapping an arm around her. Evie cursed her brother.

Randi blinked away traces of moisture from her eyes. Dammit, she would not cry. She couldn't recall the last time she'd indulged in a good, hard cry. Maybe not since realizing she'd lost her mom in all the ways but on paper, over a decade ago.

To cry now, in front of people who loved Britt, was beyond mortifying. She forced herself to smile.

Brynne rubbed her back. "It's the Steele men. They bring out the best—and worst—in us."

Evie joined the three of them at the island. "It might be hard to believe this now, but Britt isn't a runner." She sent Randi a pained younger-sister look. "He's steadfast and present—for everything. To a sister, it's annoying. But I'm sure you'd find it reassuring or hot. He's probably just as confused about his feelings as you are about yours and needed some alone time to sort things out."

Could she be right?

Randi found it hard to believe anyone's mind could be as screwed up as hers. She and Britt had both been under a lot of stress lately, thanks to her mother. She filled her lungs with familiar determination, and focused.

"Okay, ladies. Here's what we're going to do…"

CHAPTER THIRTY

THE SECOND NORWOOD AND ITO entered the woods, Randi and Carlie Beth scrambled to follow. After Randi's phone's GPS revealed the winding, gravel drive they'd been traveling down led to a dead end, they'd decided to ditch her Jeep along the roadside and hoof it the rest of the way.

They paused at the edge of the tree line, allowing their eyes to adjust to the shadows. Deep in the woods, Randi could see a set of stationary lights.

"Is that a house back there?" Randi whispered.

"Not sure." Carlie Beth pointed to her left. "There's a footpath."

"Let's go."

"Wait."

"Don't lose your nerve now."

"I don't like this."

"The forest isn't my preferred environment either, but this could be the place they're hiding Calypso."

"I'm not worried about traipsing into the woods. My instincts are clanging together like two empty beer bottles."

"Beer bottles?"

"You know what I mean. Any time I don't follow my instincts I generally wind up in trouble."

"They're getting out of visual range. Make up your mind."

"Okay, but I'm updating Evie and Brynne." Carlie Beth tapped out a short message and nodded.

Randi bent low and ran toward the biggest tree she could find. She caught a glimpse of a camouflaged back. They leapfrogged from one tree to another before coming to rest behind an enormous thick-leaved rhododendron where the woods met the cabin's tattered front yard.

"Doesn't look like much of a rich man's retreat."

Randi took in the faded green shutters hanging askew and the weathered and bowed wraparound porch. "I get the feeling they don't spend a lot of time here."

"You take one side and I'll take the other?"

Randi agreed with the wisdom behind her friend's words, though she didn't like the idea of them splitting up.

"Let's regroup in five minutes around back."

"Got it."

She followed Carlie Beth's furtive movements until her friend disappeared into a vat of darkness. Randi pushed out of her hiding spot and hurried to the opposite side of the cabin. Two windows came into view. Heavy plaid curtains blacked out the first one and the other glowed like a lighthouse beacon.

She headed toward the light.

With her back against the cabin, she gathered her courage before digging her fingertips into the windowsill and rising on tiptoes to peer inside. The brightness momentarily blinded her, leaving her exposed and vulnerable. Her vision cleared, and she found herself looking into a kitchen. Several plates and some silverware sat in a drying rack and an array of empty liquor and beer bottles lined the sink's edge.

But no Norwood or Ito.

Easing away, she made her way around the back of the cabin. Where the front yard looked rundown and unkempt, the backyard appeared immaculate. Nestled in one corner of the flagstone patio sat a jumbo Jacuzzi tub along with several cushioned rocking chairs. The other side sported an outdoor kitchen and stone fireplace. A lush, weed-free lawn spanned out in all directions, with one area terminating at a picturesque red barn.

A hand smoothed down her arm, and Randi caught the shriek in the back of her throat.

"What the hell!" Randi whispered.

Carlie Beth put a finger to her mouth and motioned for her to follow. They skirted the edge of the manicured lawn until they reached the barn.

"What's inside?" Randi asked.

"I don't know. I was waiting for you before I went in."

Carlie Beth eased the door open and got halfway inside before a low, guttural warning growl met her intrusion. Another joined in, and another, creating a chorus of fear. Randi grabbed the back of her friend's denim shirt, yanked her out of the barn, and slammed the door shut. Claws tore at the door and the dogs howled their anger.

"Damn, that was close."

When her friend's knees turned to jelly, Randi wrapped an arm around her waist and forced her to run. "Come on, we're blown."

They made it into the woods and began the long trek to her Jeep when Randi caught another sound. She stopped, tilting her head to listen.

"What's wrong?"

Randi held up a finger, straining to hear.

There.

A mournful howl mixed in with the guard dogs' low, forceful barks.

Calypso.

"She's here."

"Where?"

Randi rotated in place, pinpointing the wolf's location. "Behind the barn."

"You're not thinking of going back?"

"I've got to chance it. I need to make sure." Fear kept

her friend immobile. Little wonder. Having someone you care about try to kill you and your daughter could have lasting mental repercussions. "Stay here. If something goes wrong, run for Britt and the others." She dug her car keys out of her pocket. "Take these."

"I'm not hiding in the woods while you go sneaking around."

"I got this, Carlie Beth. Take a breather."

The near miss with the dogs must have shaken up Carlie Beth more than Randi realized, because the tough-as-nails blacksmith stopped arguing and gave her a sharp nod.

"Look, confirm, and get your butt back here."

"Yes, ma'am." Randi took off.

Once she hit the rear of the barn, she slowed her frantic pace. The paradise established at the front of the barn didn't extend to the back. Weeds of all sizes crept their way right up to the barn. Gravel and concrete chunks dotted the area and a rusted tractor would soon become part of the natural landscape.

Jutting out from the center of the building was a tall chain-link dog run. Inside the run paced a large, anxious canid.

Calypso.

The wolf's ears perked up as if she heard the silent call, then the breeding female scurried beneath the lean-to.

Wanting to set the wolf at ease, Randi moved closer, speaking in low tones to the scared animal. "It's okay, girl. We're going to get you out of here."

Calypso didn't take her eyes off Randi or seek her comforting touch. She stood, staring, her tail wedged between her legs.

Randi's attention shifted to the pen door. She didn't see a lock. Could she be so lucky? Could she lift the latch and set Calypso free? Would the wolf find her way home? Or would she roam the mountains lost and alone?

The floodlight outside the pen clicked on, startling

Randi and forcing her to squint as she dashed for the woods.

"Leaving so soon, Miss Shepherd?" a bemused masculine voice asked.

Randi stumbled to a halt, searching for the man behind the voice.

With measured, nonthreatening steps, Norwood approached until he stood a dozen feet away.

She scanned the area behind him. No Ito.

"Why are you holding this wolf captive?" A lame stall tactic, but that was the best she could come up with in her fear for Carlie Beth.

"I'm sure you're quite aware of why we're holding the bitch." He readjusted the rifle sling until the weapon rested in his hands. "Though I could be persuaded to release her."

"How?"

"Give me what I want, and I'll give you the wolf."

"Which is?"

"Your property."

"I've already given my word to another buyer."

"Your lover's brother will understand."

Nausea crept into her throat. How could he know about her and Britt?

"If I sell you the property, you'll hunt the wolves."

"Of course."

"Why would you when there are so few left?"

"They're extinct already. The U.S. Fish and Wildlife Service is only prolonging their inevitable demise."

"How can you be so coldhearted about their plight?"

"How can you be so naive?"

"I would rather be naive than uncaring." Anger straightened her back. "Besides, I'll be damned if I sell my property to the man who killed my mother."

Norwood sighed. "Worked that out, did you?"

"So you don't deny it?"

"For the record, I didn't kill Barbara Shepherd. That was the handiwork of my hotheaded Scottish friend."

"You don't seem too upset about it."

"I would have preferred that he stuck to our original plan, but Barbara would never have sold to us. Ferguson simply hurried things along to Plan B."

"Plan B," Randi repeated. "Me?"

Norwood smiled. "So trusting."

"The bad investment scheme was you."

"Again, I cannot take the credit. Watters is our financial genius. He had a nice chat with your financial advisor."

Humiliation scored Randi's cheeks. How could she have been so stupid? Why hadn't she listened to her instincts?

"So who are you?" she asked. "The puppet master who hides behind the curtain?"

The smirk he'd been wearing since stepping out of the shadows disintegrated.

"I'm the one who is going to make your boyfriend and his family pay for their interference, but not before I slaughter the entire wolf den before his eyes."

"Fucking monster."

"Careful, Miss Shepherd." Norwood lifted his rifle until the barrel stared her down. "Ito, join us."

A shuffling sound behind Randi tore her attention away from Norwood. Ito appeared. One arm clamped around Carlie Beth's torso, the other around her mouth.

"Now, Miss Shepherd, you have two options. One, sell your property to the club and we all walk away with what we want. Or, two, stick to your stubborn convictions and you'll send Miss Parrish into the cage with the hungry bitch."

CHAPTER THIRTY-ONE

USING THE LAST SPEARS OF the setting sun, Britt picked his way from the two-track to the den, giving his gut the reassurance it needed before meeting with Norwood. He had a full hour, more than enough time.

Since learning of Calypso's capture, he hadn't been able to stop thinking about her pack. Had Apollo moved the den? Had Norwood poached more than Calypso? Had any of the wolves been killed during the attack?

Reid had argued with him for several precious minutes about hiking to the den alone. Not until Britt had armed himself with a rifle, sidearm, and ankle knife had his Green Beret brother relented.

Britt made it to the bluff overlooking the den in record time. His heart kicked against the wall of his chest while his binoculars swept the valley below. Not a single wolf stirred.

Each second blasted in his mind like an endless line of artillery guns.

Then he heard it. In the distance. The excited yip-barks of a wolf pack returning to the den. Britt refocused his lens and caught sight of several wolves loping through the forest. He trained his binoculars on the den's entrance, waiting, barely breathing.

Several glute-clenching seconds later, a tiny nose emerged from the shadowed opening. Then another and another, until all the pups appeared. They stretched and yawned and stared in the direction of their approaching kin.

Britt dropped his forehead against the back of the hand holding the binoculars, taking a second to absorb the relief pouring into his body. Tension had threaded around his muscles for so many hours the release was almost painful.

Lifting his head, he observed the pack's reunion. And frowned. Something about their behavior was off. They appeared agitated rather than excited. Apollo stood away from the pack, his attention focused on the direction in which they'd arrived.

Britt set his binoculars back in place and scanned the woods. At this distance, he had a clean line of sight for a couple hundred feet in every direction. To the west, the landscape moved. Greens, yellows, and browns shifted, marking the progress of an approaching human storm.

Two figures dressed in full-on camouflage appeared. A tall, barrel-chested man and a shorter blond man trudged their way toward his location. Each carried a small animal crate—and a rifle at their back.

"What are you boys planning on doing with those?" Bold-ass shits.

Widening his search, he scanned the area for more poachers and found none. Britt fired off a text to his brothers before scrambling down the bluff.

He stayed low, using wide tree trunks and wiry shrubs for cover until he circled around and came up on their rear flank.

Britt recognized both men from his visit to the Carolina Club. Neil Watters and Angus Ferguson.

"Are you sure this is the right way?" Watters asked.

"I'm following Harvey's directions. This is the way he took while tracking down the male wolf that was stalking his livestock."

Harvey.

The only Harvey Britt knew was Harvey Griggs, the

sheep farmer on the west side of Steele Conservation Area. A decent, God-fearing family man and, evidently, the one responsible for shooting Mellow. If he'd been having trouble with the wolves, why hadn't he contacted him or Jonah?

Harvey wasn't a hunter. He probably thought the animal was a coyote, and the law allowed open season on coyotes, all year long. The farmer would've thought nothing about killing a coyote to protect his spring-born lambs.

Britt understood now why he hadn't been able to track the person who'd shot Mellow. If it were Harvey, he wouldn't have bothered to trail the injured animal far, especially on Steele property. Outside of their work dogs, livestock farmers saw most animals as revenue or a nuisance. Lord help any who fell in the latter category.

Trespassing didn't follow hunting seasons either, and Harvey would have to answer to Maggie when this poaching business was over.

"Going somewhere, gentlemen?"

They whirled around, their empty crates crashing into the side of their legs.

"Who are you?" asked the behemoth with a Scottish brogue. Ferguson's eyes narrowed against the deepening gloom. "Steele."

"You're trespassing on private property, Ferguson."

Taking in Britt's rifle and holstered handgun, Watters set down his crate.

"Drop your crate, Angus," Watters said.

"Now why would I want to do that?"

"Either set your crate down and leave, or I call the sheriff and you'll be arrested for poaching," Britt said.

The Scot looked down at his empty crate. "Oh? What did you see me poach?" When Britt said nothing, he laughed. "Stand aside. I might as well have a look at these troublesome wolves."

Ferguson's lack of concern set off Britt's alarm bells. Most people reacted with either fear or belligerence when confronted with an armed landowner. The Scot's amused indifference conveyed an inappropriate amount of confidence. Which could only mean—

"Put down your weapon," a voice behind him demanded.

Ferguson smiled. Watters's jaw hardened.

If he surrendered his weapon, everything would flip onto its backside. He could see it in the Scot's glittering gaze. Their offense of poaching would become assault—or even murder.

Most poachers killed for either food or greed. Others, for the pleasure of ending a life. The Scot's rabid expression told Britt which category he fit in.

Britt's hold on his rifle tightened.

CHAPTER THIRTY-TWO

JONAH TAPPED OUT A TEXT message before hitting Send. He waited for *Delivered* to pop up before zapping another ten grand from Norwood's account. The thirty thousand he'd already redistributed had barely made a dent in the hedge fund manager's fortune.

Norwood had millions stashed in banks around the world. Even the hundreds of thousands he'd spent over the years traveling to remote locations to kill exotic wildlife had no more effect on his finances than a grocery store stop.

His phone dinged, and he read the response.

Thanks for the heads-up, cuz.

Jonah didn't pause long enough to enjoy his relief. Now that he no longer had to worry about Evie and the other ladies, he could get back to his cyber war. Evie would make him pay for his interference later, but he didn't much care.

His fingers flew across the keyboard. He battled harder against his opponent on the other side of Norwood's server, especially after everything went black minutes ago.

No longer was he fighting against a system programmed to respond to actions in prescribed ways. He was now in hand-to-hand combat with the server's guardian. For every punch Jonah delivered, his opponent erected at least five more shields and seemed to be able to anticipate his next move well in advance.

At this moment, Jonah couldn't care less about the wolf. His entire focus was centered on winning the most challenging game of his life.

He ignored the call of Mother Nature for as long as he could. But things started getting painful. He shot down the hallway to the only bathroom on the second floor and took care of business. His thoughts zigzagged back and forth, discarding move after move like a player considering a high-stakes chess game.

His mind thrived on solving complex puzzles. They made him feel alive, invincible, even when he feared he couldn't win. Many years ago, he'd shared this exhilaration with Micki, but that all ended when she played hero, then abandoned him. He shook his head, dislodging the old, painful memory.

A repetitive sound snapped him back to attention. How long he stood there, lost in his head, holding his dick, he couldn't be sure. A thud followed by screeching, cartwheeling metal, over and over. Had one of the gutters detached from the house? Or, had the wind tossed a lawn chair across the yard? No, whatever had hit the ground had some weight to it.

Zipping up, he stepped into the oversized tub to look out the window. Not a single leaf stirred. Everything below appeared clear, though he had a limited perspective from this high of an angle. Heading back to his room, he passed the stairwell leading to the main floor, and paused. He cocked his head to listen. The only noise he heard came from the family room TV blaring out his mom's favorite DIY show.

He continued on to his bedroom. When he stepped inside, a light, cool breeze drifted across his face. A window stood wide open. He never opened his windows.

Slowly, Jonah pivoted, scanning the large space. Everything looked as it should, except for his desk. A cast-iron ball dropped in his stomach at the sight of the four dust-free spots on his desk where his monitors used to sit. Gone. The CPUs and backup system, too.

No!

"My apologies about your impressive computer system," a voice said, echoing across the room. "I'm sure someone of your interests can grow quite fond of such inanimate objects."

With the sun setting, shadows filled the corners of his suite of rooms. After Reid moved out, Jonah had knocked out a wall to create an office area or command center, as everyone liked to call it. Now the area seemed too large, too empty, too threatening.

"Who's there?"

"Someone who has a keen interest in your activities."

"How'd you get past our security?"

After an incident with Carlie Beth's daughter, Reid had installed a high-end security system, complete with video-monitoring.

"My family is successful in more areas than real estate. All those homes and businesses must have a state-of-the-art security system. All systems have weaknesses."

Real estate?

Jun Ito.

Shit.

He was screwed.

Jonah might have had a chance with one of the other poachers. But Ito was the lightning rod who'd taken down Reid before he knew what had hit him. Their patrols hadn't stood a chance.

Backing toward the window, Jonah glanced out and found the backyard eerily quiet. The only thing that disrupted his view was the bits of mangled metal and shattered monitor screens all over the place.

He cursed his stupidity. *Of course* the bad guys would come for the lone, helpless computer geek. Classic Hollywood.

Why hadn't he stopped long enough to consider the

possibility? He'd been too wrapped up in winning against the machine that he hadn't paused to think about the flesh-and-blood consequences. By getting caught up in his own world, he'd failed Britt and the wolf. And maybe his mom.

A wave of unexpected calm washed over him. "Time to stop hiding, Ito."

From behind one of the two thick columns separating Reid's former bedroom from his, the shadow transformed into arms and legs of a lean but fit Asian man.

"Where are the rest of your cronies?"

Ito's features remained neutral. Except for his eyes. They tilted up in a way that announced, *I'm going to enjoy this next part.*

"Busy taking care of other business."

Shooting a look toward the door, Jonah prayed his mother was too absorbed in her show to notice what was going on upstairs.

"Concerned about your dear mother?"

"What have you done?"

Ito smirked.

Jonah stormed across the room, intent on finding his mom.

The other man blocked his way. "I think not."

"Get out of my way, or I'll break your fucking neck."

"Your brother tried and failed."

"I'm not my brother."

"True." Ito eyed him. "The Green Beret is driven by pride. Pride destroys. However, you are compelled by something far more dangerous, I think."

Jonah's insatiable curiosity nearly got the best of him. He wanted to know what Ito meant. But he forced himself to keep the question behind his teeth.

"Back away from the door," Jonah said.

"If you leave this room, you are ensuring her death. I'm sure you do not want that on your conscience."

The bastard stepped aside, giving him an impossible choice.

"She's still alive?"

"For now."

"If you've harmed her in any way, you won't survive the Steele family's wrath."

"Perhaps it would be best to see how many of you survive this ordeal before making such bold statements."

"Poacher to murderer—your parents must be so proud."

The blow was swift and hard. Jonah's world spun and he slammed down on one knee.

Ito grabbed a handful of Jonah's hair. His features remained unchanged as he snarled his threat. "Mention of my family shall never pass through your ignorant mouth again." Ito released him. "Sit down."

Jonah shook his brain back into working order. "Then what?" He rose, massaging his pain-racked jaw to make sure it wasn't broken.

"We wait."

"Why? Mission accomplished. You destroyed my ability to find the wolf."

"I have always found your kind to be resourceful. It is best if I remain here until I receive word it is done."

"What's done?"

Ito said nothing.

Jonah sank into a deep leather chair. Worry for his brothers, Evie, and the other ladies made his stomach roil. He had to play it cool for now. Keep Ito's mind off his mom below while figuring out a way to get word to Britt.

"Why are there extremists in every group?"

"I don't know what you mean."

"Let me clue you in. Stealing an endangered wild wolf, placing her on auction, detaining my mom, throwing my equipment out the window, doing God-knows-what to my brothers—don't you think that's a bit much for the pleasure of killing a scared, defenseless animal?"

"Wolves are not defenseless."

"When up against a high-powered rifle? Yes, they are."

"You obviously don't understand the sport."

"Sport would be if you and the wolf were on an equal playing field. What you're promoting is senseless murder—just so you can fill empty counter space at your club."

"Such a naive young man. When our country goes to war—and it will in our lifetime—you will be thankful for hunters like me. Men who can protect and provide for do-gooders like you, who were more concerned with preserving every living creature instead of using them as a training ground."

"You're a sick puppy, Ito."

"One day, you will understand."

"Understand what?"

"You chose the losing side."

CHAPTER THIRTY-THREE

"DROP YOUR WEAPON, WOLF MAN."

The blunt end of a gun barrel dug into the back of Britt's skull. Two poachers in front of him and, at least, one behind. How many more?

The barrel pressed harder. "Best not to test me."

Gritting his teeth, Britt placed his rifle on the ground. His phone vibrated in his pocket.

"And the handgun."

Snapping his .40 caliber free of its holster, he laid his Sig Sauer next to the rifle.

"Watters, check him."

The blond, who appeared as though he'd rather be anywhere but here, conducted a thorough enough search that he couldn't have missed the knife strapped to Britt's right ankle, though he didn't confiscate it. He did, however, take a boot heel to Britt's phone.

"He's clean." Watters avoided Britt's gaze.

"Looks like we have ourselves a bit of a problem here, gentlemen," the poacher behind him drawled.

"Samuel, shouldn't we contact Norwood?" Ferguson asked.

Samuel Taylor, the Texan.

"He already has his hands full."

"Why don't we tie this guy up, grab the pups, and get out of here," Watters said.

"Do you see any rope?"

"There's another option," Britt threw over his shoulder to the man who was clearly in charge.

"What's that, wolf man?"

"Let me go before this can't be explained away as a misunderstanding."

"He has a point, Samuel," Watters said. "We all agreed to the risks associated with taking the female wolf and even her pups. With our connections, the worst punishment we would have faced if caught was a stiff fine. This"—his index finger spun in a circle between them—"will go well beyond a fine."

A message passed between Ferguson and Taylor, and Britt braced himself against the decision he saw reflected in the Scot's cruel eyes.

"You've not been with the League long enough for us to entrust you with the list of our Top Ten."

Watters glanced between his two colleagues and Britt. Blood seeped from his face. "You can't be referring to people."

"Not just anyone, but specific classifications of people," Ferguson said.

"I don't understand."

"At this stage, you weren't meant to," Taylor grumbled. "But the Steeles stuck their noses in our business, forcing us to fast-track your orientation."

Cold, damp heat scoured Britt's body. "What part of me will become your trophy?"

"Nothing grand," Ferguson said. "The danger of discovery is too great. A rib will do."

Britt's midsection contracted.

"What human classifications do you have?" Watters asked in a voice that conveyed both fear and disgust.

"Warriors such as the Maasai or Sentinelese, a member from each of the United States Armed Forces—"

"Why not serial killers and mass murderers?" Britt interrupted. "At least then your list might make sense."

"Because they're cowards, spineless and weak," Taylor said. "Like the animals we hunt, our human prey have battle scars. They have honor, intelligence, courage."

"You think I fit this bill? Someone you've met twice?"

"Yes, or you wouldn't be here protecting a pack of endangered wolves no one wants. And you have the added bonus of being a fucking Steele."

Ferguson smiled. "Double the fun."

"Don't worry, wolf man," Taylor said. "This will all be over quickly. We don't have the luxury of time for a chase."

"So this will be cold-blooded murder? You're not even going to give me a fighting chance."

Taylor jabbed him with the barrel so hard that Britt felt warmth trickle down the back of his head.

"I told you. We don't have time."

Not once had any of them used his name. Much easier to detach from a heinous act if they boil their victim down to an object or thing, rather than a living, breathing individual with feelings, thoughts, and family.

"Strip," Taylor ordered.

"Why?"

"Convenience and confusion."

"You lost me."

"Convenience for us because we won't have to undress you to retrieve our trophy. Confusion for when the authorities eventually find your carcass."

"Stop this," Watters demanded. "You're talking about murdering a *person*. I cannot let you kill him and I won't be a party to this."

"Then the League disavows you," Taylor said.

Ferguson drew his sidearm and blew a hole in Watters's head.

The blast rocked through the forest, and Britt knew then that he would die in these woods.

But not without maiming a few of his enemies.

"Strip, wolf man."

Britt's hands curled into fists and his gaze locked with the Scot's. The sick bastard smiled, anticipating Britt's fight-or-flight instincts. The poacher's expression said he didn't care which action Britt chose.

A splatter of bright yellow paint smacked Ferguson in the face, splashing into his eyes.

"What the hell?!" Ferguson rubbed at his eyes, blinking and cursing and trying to keep Britt in view, but unable to hold his eyelids open for more than a second.

Taking advantage of the distraction, Britt rolled away, grabbing the knife Watters had ignored in his search. A shot rang out. Britt took aim and his knife ripped into Taylor's right shoulder. The poacher's rifle crashed to the forest floor.

Taylor fumbled with his holster, and Britt slammed his shoulder into the Texan's gut, taking them both to the ground. Britt's weight emptied the air from Taylor's lungs, leaving the bastard gasping for breath and giving Britt time to toss his handgun out of reach.

"I'll take it from here, Britt."

Britt reared back to find Sheriff Maggie Kingston hovering over him, her Glock pointed at the heaving poacher's head. Getting to his feet, Britt whipped around, preparing to deal with the cursing Ferguson. What he found had him shaking his head. Literally.

Evie and Brynne, legs braced apart, stood opposite Ferguson, guns aimed at his chest.

"Beautiful timing, ladies, though I'm wondering what the hell you're doing here."

"Doing something besides watching Jonah fight a cyber war." Not taking her eyes off Ferguson, Evie asked, "Are you okay?"

"Yes, thanks to the three of you."

"Looked like you had it under control."

"Either that, or I was about to get my ass beat."

Maggie forced Taylor to roll over, a rather hard feat with a knife protruding from the poacher's shoulder.

Taylor wailed like a newborn while Maggie clamped his wrists together.

Britt divested Ferguson of his weapons before forcing him onto his stomach. Maggie tossed him a second pair of handcuffs and began relaying instructions into her shoulder mic.

"Are those Reid's new paintball guns?"

"Not his most recent purchase," Brynne said. "Those monsters are under lock and key."

Evie's smile lit up the forest. "Not bad for forty yards, huh?"

"You made the shot?"

Maggie rose to glare at both ladies. "Against my explicit orders."

Never one to be cowed, Evie waggled her eyebrows.

"Let's see how cocky you are after I speak to your mother." Maggie let out a loud, aggrieved sigh, one that indicated she'd had more than one run-in with her little cousin. "I'm just glad Jonah tipped me off to what you girls were up to."

"Jonah told you?"

"He thought you might be in over your head." Maggie inspected the scene. "He was right. I don't even want to think about what would've happened had I not caught up with you before you entered the woods." She sent her cousin a warning look. "Next time, I'll lock you in my cruiser to make sure you follow my direction to stay back."

The joy of adventure drained from Evie's face. Britt felt the familiar urge to comfort her, but he agreed with Maggie on this. Her sleuthing could have had fatal consequences.

"What is all of this about?" Maggie asked. "Jonah said something about a kidnapped wolf."

"A faction of the Carolina Club are extreme trophy hunters," Britt said, rising. "These three, plus at least two others, decided they wanted to add a critically endangered red wolf to their kill list."

"Looks like they've upped their game to people now." Maggie's eyes narrowed on Britt. "Three to one? Where are your brothers? And why didn't you call me?"

"None of us expected this." Britt waved his hand toward Watters. "I came over here to check on the pups, see how they were faring without their mother."

"And your brothers?"

"Jonah's back at the house. Grif and Reid should be headed to the two-track where we're to meet up with Richard Norwood, the leader of this murderous group." His hand slid inside his pocket for his phone before remembering Watters had destroyed it. Bending, he picked up the pieces and threw them into his backpack. "What time is it?"

Maggie told him.

"Norwood will be arriving soon with the female wolf."

"You got him to give her up?"

Britt winked. "With a little incentive."

Maggie shook her head.

"We should go," Brynne said, looking uncomfortable. "Randi and Carlie Beth followed Norwood and Ito. If these guys are capable of killing a member of their group, no telling what Norwood will do if he finds them out."

Britt's insides churned at the thought of Randi under Norwood's power. "Dammit, Evie. Why were y'all trailing these crazy-ass hunters?"

Evie flinched, her gaze dropping to the ground.

"We thought they might lead us to Calypso," Brynne said quietly, putting an arm around Evie.

That admission earned the ladies another severe sheriff scowl. "All of this could have gone wrong ten ways to Tuesday, Evie. I hope you see that now."

Evie nodded. "We just wanted to help. The wolves mean so much to Britt—and to me. I couldn't stand the thought of Calypso caged and alone."

Maggie curled a hand around the side of her cousin's

face and kissed her on the head. "You brought a paint gun to a fight with a hunter, really?" Not waiting for an answer, she heaved Taylor to his feet. "Time to go to jail."

"What about my wound? I need a hospital!"

"Paramedics are waiting by the road. They'll decide where you go first." Maggie gave him a little shove. "Now stop your whining and move."

Evie wouldn't meet Britt's gaze. He didn't like seeing her upset. Never had.

Putting on his best shit-eatin' grin, he nudged Ferguson with his boot. "How do you tough guys feel about being taken down by a college girl with a paint gun?"

Evie's eyes widened and her sweet laugh danced all around them.

Noticing several sets of flashlights making their slow progress through the woods, Britt asked, "The cavalry?"

Maggie glanced over her shoulder. "Looks like." She confirmed via her radio, then snapped on her small flashlight, waving it in the air.

"I gotta get to the two-track."

"Go," Maggie said.

"You'll be okay?" he asked Evie and Brynne.

They both nodded.

"Be careful," Evie said.

To Maggie, he said, "Let Grif know I'm on my way? And have Reid head back to the Hill to check on things there."

"Sure thing."

"Evie, contact Randi and Carlie Beth." He checked both prisoners' bindings before collecting his Sig and rifle. "Tell them to disengage and go home. If they dig their heels in, let them know what's happened here."

She nodded, tapping in her password.

"You ladies did well tonight. Very well. Thank y'all."

They each gave him a grateful, beaming smile.

Britt secured his weapons and pack and took off at a

speed his legs hadn't attempted since high school track. He had to get to Grif before Norwood arrived. And he hoped to God Evie got ahold of Randi in time.

"Britt!" Evie yelled.

He jarred to a halt. "What?"

"I have several texts from Carlie Beth. They found Calypso at a cabin off Choctaw Road."

Some of the aching tension eased from Britt's chest. "That's great. Tell them to get out of there. I'll take care of Calypso. You and Brynne head back to the Hill."

"Oh, no. No, no, no!" Sweet blue eyes bleak with guilt and fear slammed into him. "Norwood has Randi."

CHAPTER THIRTY-FOUR

BY THE TIME BRITT REACHED the two-track, he was breathing fire and his feet throbbed from the brutal pace he'd set. Grif paced beside his Maserati, Louise.

Catching sight of Britt, he asked, "What the hell's going on? Maggie gave me some cryptic message about staying sharp until you arrived."

"Some major damn shit, that's what." Britt raked the sweat off his forehead.

"Hit me with the short version."

"I met up with Ferguson, Watters, and Taylor near the den. They got the upper hand. Ferguson killed Watters because he didn't want to kill me. Evie and Brynne took down Ferguson with a paint gun. Maggie arrested the others."

"All of that happened in the last hour?" At Britt's nod, he asked, "Why didn't you fucking call me?"

"Watters destroyed my phone."

"Anyone besides Watters hurt?"

"The ladies are fine and the other two club members sustained minor damage."

"What about you?"

Britt waved him off. "There's more bad news."

"Let it rip."

"Evie, Brynne, Randi, and Carlie Beth decided to

follow Norwood and his cronies to see if they would lead them to Calypso."

"You're shittin' me, right?"

"I wish."

"Where're Carlie Beth and Randi?"

Britt struggled to form a single syllable, his worry for Randi paralyzing the words in the back of his throat.

Grif clamped a hand on his shoulder. "Just spit it out. You don't need to clean it up for me."

"Randi and Carlie Beth found Calypso."

"And?"

"Norwood found Randi."

"What about Carlie Beth?"

"Her phone's going directly to voice mail."

"*Fuck!*" Grif strode away, phone to his ear. The moment stretched. He ended the call. "What's the plan?" His words were thick.

Britt had had a long time to think about strategy on the run over. "We wait for Norwood."

"What if he doesn't show?"

"Then we head to Norwood's cabin on Choctaw Road, where Randi and Carlie Beth found the wolf. See if there's anything that'll lead us to Norwood."

"What about Maggie?"

"She'll send a deputy as soon as one frees up."

"Sounds like a shitty plan."

"Got a better one?"

Grif grasped his head with both hands, one still held his phone. "I can't lose her."

"I know the feeling."

Grif swiveled around. "You and Randi?"

Britt gave a sharp nod.

"'Bout damn time."

"Amen, bro."

"How can you be so calm? I feel like my flesh is peeling off my bones."

Lifting his hands, Britt unclenched his fists. They shook like a two-day-gone addict's. "I'm anything but calm. Norwood's group has advanced to killing people for sport. Those bastards have Randi now."

"And Carlie Beth."

"It's been a long time since I feared failing my family. That I wouldn't be able to protect them," Britt admitted, eyes burning down the two-track, willing Norwood's vehicle to appear. "I'm in over my head on this one."

"I'll call Reid. Have him check on Mom and Jonah."

"Already done." Britt's jaw hardened. "I should never have gotten y'all involved in this. If something happens to any of you—"

Grif wrapped a hand around Britt's neck, the same act Britt had performed a hundred times on his younger brothers when they were struggling with something.

"These assholes are nothing but bullies."

"With guns."

"We dealt with our fair share of guns and bullies over the years. Together, there's nothing we can't handle. We're Steeles."

Mirroring Grif's brotherly embrace, Britt stood there, in the dark, feeding off his brother's strength, his confidence, his reassurance. He couldn't recall depending on any of his siblings before, not like this. When strength was needed, he gave it. When comfort was needed, he provided it. When ass-kicking was needed, he kicked it.

Giving his brother's neck a grateful squeeze, he pushed away. "Thanks for the pep talk." His fingertips dug into his forehead. "The 'what-ifs' are destroying my mind right now."

"I'm here for you, Britt. We're all here for you. There's no need for you to act the father figure anymore. If anyone tries to hurt our family, they have four Steele boys to deal with now."

"Five Steeles. Evie deserves a ranking after the shot she landed on Ferguson's smug mug."

A smile creased Grif's face at the same time light arched over his body. Britt turned to find a vehicle approaching. The quarter moon didn't provide enough illumination to identify the vehicle.

"If that's Maggie, Norwood's going to bolt." Britt shrugged off his backpack. "Did you bring a weapon?"

"Do I look like I cart around a gun? I thought we were coming here to pick up a wolf."

"I'll put my rifle in the front seat of Old Blue." Britt sent him a sidelong glance. "You do recall how to pull the trigger, Slick?"

"Shut it."

Glad he'd had the foresight to point his truck down the two-track, Britt deposited his rifle and flicked on his headlights, then sidled up next to his brother. "Let me borrow your phone."

Grif handed it over.

Britt punched in a number.

Evie answered on the second ring. "Hey, Grif."

"It's Britt. I don't have much time. Can you call Deke, explain what's happened, and ask him to head over to Choctaw Road to check on Calypso?"

"Of course. Everything okay there?"

"Norwood's coming down the track. Tell Deke to take extra precautions." Britt clicked the phone off and passed it back to his brother before Evie could ask more questions.

"Looks like an SUV. Dark," Grif said.

"Can't be Maggie's cruiser."

"Norwood then."

The silhouette of a single figure in the vehicle's front cabin came into view.

"Where's Ito?"

"You told Norwood to come alone."

"That was a lifetime ago. Everything's up for grabs now."

The SUV pulled to a stop.

"You want me to handle Norwood?" Grif asked.

Britt considered his brother's offer. Grif had far more experience in negotiating volatile situations, and not knowing where Randi and Carlie Beth were only added to the already high stakes. But Britt couldn't hand this problem over. He'd gotten them all into this and he would damn sure get them out it. "I got this."

Norwood exited the vehicle and paused near the front fender. "Steele."

"Norwood." Britt peered through the vehicle, searching for a set of canid ears. "Did you bring the female?"

"Of course." Norwood gestured to the back of the vehicle. "Shall we?"

Britt shared a meaningful look with his brother, who nodded his understanding, before following Norwood to the back of the SUV.

Norwood pressed a button on his remote and the back hatch lifted. What couldn't have been more than three seconds seemed an eternity.

A large metal crate took up most of the SUV's trunk compartment. Inside the locked crate laid Randi, bound and gagged.

Still as death.

CHAPTER THIRTY-FIVE

BRITT LUNGED FOR NORWOOD, GRABBING the poacher by the throat and lifting him up on his toes. "Get her out of that fucking cage. Now!" The fury pouring into his muscles overrode the pain caused by his bruised rib.

"Easy, brother." Grif grabbed his wrist. "Don't snap his neck before we get the key." More quietly, he added, "And Carlie Beth."

Norwood didn't flinch at Britt's reaction, though his red face turned a satisfying blue. The bastard had anticipated his rage, hoped Britt would lose his shit when he saw Randi's motionless body.

Dear God, he couldn't tell if she was dead or alive. "Is she breathing, Grif?"

His brother bent close to the kennel. "Yes, the hair over her face is rising and falling with her breaths."

"Be glad that's the case, Norwood." Britt loosened his grip, but didn't let go. "The key."

"We have a few things to negotiate before I set your friend free."

"I don't negotiate with brutes and senseless killers." To Grif, he said, "Get the bolt cutters out of the left side compartment." He kept a pair in his truck so he could take down old or unnecessary barbed wire fencing, which helped keep migrating wildlife from getting tangled in the wires.

Norwood glanced over Britt's shoulder, catching Grif's eye. "Perhaps you could talk some sense into your brother. After all, it's your girlfriend's life on the line, not his."

In the next instant, Grif shoved Britt aside and hammered Norwood in the jaw, knocking him to the ground. Norwood came up spitting blood. "What have you done with Carlie Beth?"

"I thought at least one of you would be levelheaded. Looks like I'll have to adjust my communication style to that of caveman."

"Enough of your games, Norwood," Grif said in a cold, emotionless tone, one Britt had never heard his brother use before. "Where's Carlie Beth?"

"Safe for now."

"We're going to wipe your accounts clean for this, even the hidden ones," Britt said.

Norwood checked his smart watch. "I believe you'll find such an undertaking impossible now that Jun Ito's disabled your brother's hacking operation."

Britt's gaze snapped into the direction of Tupelo Hill, where he'd left Jonah and their mother. Alone. Had Reid made it back in time to protect them?

"Don't believe me?" Norwood flicked a hand at Britt. "Go ahead, call him. Then we will discuss *my* plan for this evening."

Jonah picked up on the second ring.

"Everything okay there?"

"Jun Ito trashed my computers."

"Are you and Mom all right?"

"We're good. The Green Beret saved the day. Ito's down."

Relief nearly buckled Britt's knees. *Thank you, Reid.*

"The bastard didn't find my laptop, though."

Britt paced away. When he was certain Norwood couldn't see him, he winked at Grif, setting his brother at ease.

"Time's up, Steele," Norwood warned.

"Do you need backup?" Jonah asked.

"Maggie's on the way. Gotta go."

Britt tossed the phone back to Grif.

"Such a shame about young Jonah's computers," Norwood said. "Though I don't suppose it'll be a hardship for him to replace everything."

"Ito failed."

"Your mind game won't work on me. I received confirmation from Ito ten minutes ago."

"He missed Jonah's laptop."

"An easy fix." Norwood hit a button on his smart watch. "Ito?"

"No, shit for brains." Reid's voice carried through the small speaker. "Karate Dude is trussed up like a peacock."

Britt vowed to buy Reid drinks for an entire year.

Norwood disconnected. "This turn of events hardly matters." He sent a superior smile to Grif. "I'll secure your cooperation through the lovely Miss Parrish." To Britt, he said, "I hope you weren't too attached to those wolf pups. I've decided they'll make excellent future sport for our members."

"The good thing about narrow-minded, obsessive people is that they're predictable," Britt said. "The pups aren't going anywhere."

"I do hope you've stationed more than one protector. If not, he will have his hands full very soon, if not already."

"You lose again. Watters is dead. Ferguson and Taylor are in custody."

"Dead?"

"Shot by Ferguson."

"You lie!"

"Call your friends," Grif said. "They might have a hard time answering their phones, but I'm sure Sheriff Kingston won't mind assisting."

"Down to one," Britt said. "Now tell us where you've stashed Carlie Beth."

The arrogance that had been present on Norwood's face since he'd stepped out of his vehicle now faltered. His attention shifted from Britt to Grif as he put distance between them.

"Don't even think about running," Grif warned. "There's nowhere you can hide that I won't find you."

Norwood ripped open his jacket.

"Get down!" Britt pushed Grif away and reached for the weapon holstered at his side.

But his brother was having none of it. Grif recovered and slammed into him just as Norwood fired his gun. Grif's body jerked.

"Griffin!"

Britt eased his brother to the ground.

Another blast from Norwood's weapon and the bullet lodged in Britt's shoulder blade, pitching him forward.

"Sonofabitch!" That hurt like a mother. Torn between chasing after Norwood, calling 911, and grabbing the first-aid kit, he yelled at Grif, "Where are you hit?"

Grif pointed to his side.

"Exit wound?"

His brother nodded. "I'll live."

"I need to go after him."

"You're in worse shape than I am."

"Watch over Randi. There's a first-aid kit in my truck."

"Dammit, Britt!"

Britt took off after Norwood. Even wounded, he began making headway on the slower, older man. As blood drained from his body, his face turned cold, his fingers grew numb. His vision blurred.

Norwood glanced over his shoulder. His eyes widened at Britt's close proximity. Desperate, the poacher fired a shot at him. The bullet went wild. Norwood lost his balance, slipped, and he stumbled, his arms cartwheeling to keep himself upright.

Surging forward, Britt threw his good shoulder into Norwood's back, tackling him to the ground. Pain sliced through Britt's side. Norwood went down hard, his breath punched from his lungs by the packed dirt. His pistol went flying into the brush.

Unable to move, Britt allowed his two hundred and twenty-five pounds to immobilize Norwood. He lay there, atop the bastard, like a damned beached whale. He hoped Grif couldn't see him from this distance. Living something like this down would take years.

"Britt, you okay?" his brother yelled.

"I'm fine. Norwood's down."

Norwood squirmed. "Get the hell off me, redneck."

Britt slid more fully atop his prisoner and crammed his forearm into the back of Norwood's neck. "Where's Carlie Beth Parrish?"

"Fuck you."

"Wrong answer." He pressed harder. When he did, he noticed an active mound of sandy dirt. "Last chance to do the right thing, Norwood." Britt shook off the black spots crowding into his peripheral vision.

"And lose my chance of watching you and your brothers dance around like headless chickens? You stole from the wrong man, Steele. Happy hunting."

"Don't say I didn't warn you." Britt scooped up a handful of the mound and dumped it on Norwood's head. It took a few seconds for the ants to recover. When they did, Norwood screamed.

With his hands lodged beneath him, Norwood couldn't fend off the attack. Britt had no idea if the ants were biting the poacher, or if it was just the sensation of having bugs crawl over his face and into every available orifice that turned the arrogant brute to a wailing child. Either way, the ants had him singing like a soprano.

"She's in my vehicle!"

"That's Randi. Where's Carlie Beth?"

"My truck. Tied up on the back floorboard."

"You'd better not be lying."

"See for yourself." He spat out an ant. "Now let me up."

Britt started to roll off his prisoner, but stopped as an idea formed. "I have a few more questions."

"What?" He gagged. "What for God's sake?"

"Did you, or one of your cronies, kill Barbara Shepherd and sabotage Miranda Shepherd's business?"

Norwood howled with laughter between hacking coughs.

"Time for more fun." Britt forced Norwood's chin around and up so he could see the mound of ants he still had to work with. "I've got plenty of friends who are itching to play."

The poacher struggled in earnest, almost knocking Britt off his roost.

"Confess, and I'll spare you my friends' happy dance on your face."

A stream of violent, life-threatening oaths flowed from his captive's lips.

"All right, but I tried to keep this civil."

Britt scooped up a handful and slowly poured the ants on Norwood's head. A few made a run up Britt's arm. He ignored them.

Norwood shrieked. "Yes, damn you! Ferguson killed the old bitch when she wouldn't sell, Watters set up the bad investment, and Taylor cut the power to the cooler."

"All under your direction?"

"No! I had nothing to do with the Shepherd woman's death."

Satisfaction and sadness sent Britt's forearm into the poacher's neck, forcing the bastard to gasp for breath.

Before he did something that would send him to prison, Britt rolled off and came face-to-face with a fender. With the racket Norwood had been making, he hadn't heard the squad car's approach.

The deputy peered over the hood. "Evening, Britt."

"Hey, Deputy Blaine. Did you catch his confession?"

"Sure did. So did my dashboard camera." He nodded toward the anthill. "Effective device."

Dashboard camera. Fucking great. "After he's bug-free,

could you take care of him? I need to check on my friends."

"Yes, sir. Sheriff Kingston already filled me in. Said to do what I could."

Britt got to his feet, splaying his right hand out to steady himself. His tussle with Norwood had jarred his injured shoulder so badly that the entire left side of his body was numb.

"Can you check Norwood's pockets for a key? It's for a lock."

The deputy cuffed Norwood, ignoring his prisoner's pleas to free his hands. Blaine dug into each of the poacher's pockets, finding nothing. "Sorry, sir."

"Where is the key, Norwood?"

The stupid bastard looked like he was going to refuse to answer. Until Britt eyed what was left of the anthill.

"Driver's side visor."

"Smart man." Britt made his way back to Grif, who was trying to operate a pair of heavy bolt cutters to free Randi. But he had lost too much blood. "Hold up. Let me get the key."

"Where's Norwood? Did he say where he'd left Carlie Beth?"

"He's with Deputy Blaine." Britt flipped open Norwood's visor and the key fell into his palm. He opened the back door. "Check the floorboard."

Grif stumbled around to the side of the vehicle. As soon as he looked into the SUV, the ferocity marring his features softened. "Found her."

Jamming the key into the crate's lock, Britt twisted it one way, then the other until he heard a click, felt the release. Swinging the door open wide, Britt untied Randi's arms and legs. Her eyelids fluttered open. Britt released a shaky breath.

"Randi," he coaxed. "Try to sit up."

"What happened?"

"You had a run-in with Norwood."

Panic flared in her groggy eyes. "Carlie Beth?"

Peering through the SUV, Britt watched his brother

remove Carlie Beth's gag and restraints. He spoke to her in soft tones, his movements slow and gentle.

"Grif's got her. She'll be fine."

"Thank goodness." She squinted at her surroundings. "Am I in a dog crate?"

"Come on." He held out a hand. "Let's get you out of there."

"Britt, I—"

He kissed her softly on the lips. "Save your explanation for later. I want to inspect your wounds right now."

"You're not mad?"

"Of course, I am." *Angry, terrified, guilt-ridden.* He touched a trembling finger to her cheek. "Let's take this one step at a time."

She noticed him favoring his left arm. "Are you hurt?"

When he didn't answer, she scrambled out of the vehicle to inspect his body. She sucked in a sharp breath. "You're bleeding! Dear Lord, there's so much blood."

"I'm okay." Britt coaxed her into the crook of his good arm. "It looks worse than it is."

"Norwood got him while he was trying to play hero," Grif threw out.

Britt glared at his brother.

"Have you called for an ambulance?" she asked.

"Not yet."

"Are you serious?"

"I've been a little busy."

By the time the gang arrived a few minutes later, he and Grif had managed to get their bleeding under control, with the ladies' help. The strain of blood loss had them both sitting on the edge of the tailgate next to Randi and Carlie Beth, who were still fighting the effects of some kind of knockout drug.

Maggie sized up the entire scene in one thorough glance. "All of this to save a wolf?"

"Not just any wolf," Randi said. "A critically endangered species, a breeding female, a mama snatched away from her pups."

Concern twisted in Britt's stomach when he saw Evie and Brynne trailing behind Deke. He couldn't see any visible injuries, but the two women were subdued. No doubt shaken to the core by their skirmish with Ferguson and the others.

"Does Aunt Joanie know what you boys have been up to this evening?" Maggie asked.

"Some of it," Grif said. "If you fill her in on all the details, I'll lock you up in your mama's chicken coop again."

"Touchy, touchy." Maggie gave Grif a pointed look. "Need a ride to the hospital?"

"Clean exit wound. I'll take care of it later."

"Let me know if you're successful in hiding your wound from Aunt Joanie."

Grif turned to Carlie Beth. "I really don't like her."

"I do."

"How about you?" Maggie asked Britt.

"I'm not going anywhere until I see that Mom, Jonah, and Reid are all right."

"What's happened?" Brynne asked, concern breaking through her somber mood. "Is Reid hurt?"

"He derailed Ito's plan for knocking out our"—Grif shot Maggie a wary glance—"um, Internet project."

"Sweet Mary," Maggie said with a shake of her head. "Don't tell me."

"When I spoke to Jonah, he said everyone was safe." Britt eased off the tailgate and moved closer to Brynne and Evie. "I just need to see for myself."

Brynne nodded, though the news didn't seem to provide much comfort. "I'm going with you."

He set an arm around Brynne's shoulders. "We'll be out of here in two shakes."

Pressing her head into his chest, she hugged him hard before moving to sit by Randi.

Evie sucked in a sharp breath, noticing his blood-soaked shirt. "You're going to the hospital."

"After I check on things at Tupelo Hill."

"But—"

He brought Evie in for a big brother hug. "Trust me."

Britt caught Maggie's eye, indicating Randi and Carlie Beth. "They need to be checked out, and Grif needs some stitches."

All three shook their heads.

"When you go, we go," Randi said.

"It could be awhile."

Randi and Carlie Beth crossed their arms and Grif raised a what's-your-next-move? brow.

Their support made his heart hurt. Time and again, during this ordeal, his family and friends had been there for him. For the first time in years, the burden of responsibility wasn't his alone to carry.

Maggie nodded toward Norwood sitting in the back of her deputy's squad. The man's hair stood on end and he kept rubbing his head on the seat back. "Who's the psycho?"

"Richard Norwood," Britt said. "He's the ringleader, too, and the one who kidnapped Randi and Carlie Beth and shot Grif."

"And Britt," Grif said.

He glanced at Randi. "Deputy Blaine can fill you in on the rest."

Maggie's features hardened and her hand settled on her sidearm.

"Calypso's fine. She has a gash on one of her legs, but nothing a vet can't fix," Deke said, shifting his gaze away from Evie. "I'll grab the proper equipment and return her to her pack."

"Thanks for the help. I owe you."

Deke tapped his fist to Britt's. "Damn straight you do." He peered into Evie's face. "You were brave tonight, Squirt."

"It was a team effort." Evie aimed a wobbly smile at him. After giving Britt another squeeze and receiving a kiss on the head in return, she moved to stand near the other ladies.

"What happened?" Deke asked. "She wouldn't discuss it with me."

"She saw a man murdered tonight."

"Sheezus." Deke scratched-massaged the back of his neck. "Anything I can do?"

"Not at the moment. She just needs some space and time for the shock to wear off. I'll keep an eye on her."

"They stole from me," Norwood yelled through the squad window. "All I've been doing is defending myself. You should be arresting them, not me."

"I'll get right on that," Maggie said with her characteristic dry humor. "I'm going to send a deputy over to Aunt Joanie's house to pick up Ito."

"Thanks for the help tonight."

"Anytime." She backhanded his good arm. "Just make sure it doesn't happen again."

Maggie stopped to speak with Deputy Blaine before sending the young officer off to the Hill. After performing a five-point turn, she headed back down the narrow two-track, branches scraping the sides of her cruiser. Ferguson and Taylor slumped in the rear seat. Watters was no doubt on his way to the county morgue.

Deke said his good-byes and assured Britt that he'd take good care of Calypso.

Britt took in his ragtag group. Breathing became difficult. Every one of them had put themselves in danger to save Calypso. The depth of their generosity and love overwhelmed him. How he would ever be able to repay them, he didn't know. But he would start by getting them the hell out of here.

Ten minutes later, their caravan rumbled up the long drive of Tupelo Hill. They'd passed Deputy Blaine's vehicle, carrying a blank-faced Jun Ito.

The screen door flew open, and Mom rushed down the steps, analyzing each of them. She zeroed in on the blood coating the front of Grif's shirt and beelined in his direction.

Grif groaned.

"Good luck," Britt said under his breath.

"Shut it."

"Mom," Britt said, noticing her gauze-covered wrists. "What happened? Did Ito tie you up?"

"Nothing for you to worry about. My baby boys took care of that Ito fellow."

Jonah and a bandaged Reid appeared on the porch.

Britt's throat tightened.

Randi made soothing circles on his back.

"I'm sorry, Mom. I should have—"

"Britt Steele, don't say another word. This wasn't your fault. You can't be in three places at once. No matter what your father told you before he wandered off, you're not responsible for everyone's welfare."

As much as he loved his mother, she was wrong. Protection was the only damn thing he was good at. The only thing he could contribute to his family.

"Brynne!" Reid called. "What's that in your hand?"

Brynne lifted his old paintball gun as if she'd never seen it before.

"Ruh roh," Evie tucked her pilfered gun behind her back.

Too late. Reid had already clapped eyes on all his toys. He marched toward Brynne. A mix of incredulity, anger, and all-out fear tormented his features.

"Please tell me you didn't go after those hunt club guys." He yanked the paint gun from Evie's grasp. "Jonah, lock these away."

"Bro, chill out."

Ignoring his brother, Reid grabbed the barrel of Brynne's paint gun, intending to take her weapon, too. She held tight.

"They're dangerous men, Brynne," Reid said. "This was no time to play girl power."

"That's enough, Reid," Britt said.

"Stay out of this, Tarzan."

Britt stiffened. His heart hurt so damned much. He waited for it to explode.

"I know where your mind's going and you need to shut it down," Grif said. "Or I'll beat you bloody right here in front of Mom. We all contributed to and agreed to the plan. There was no way for any of us to see the true evil that lurked within the club members."

"I should never have brought y'all into this. I should have handled it myself."

"And you would've gotten yourself killed. Do you think any of us would have wanted that outcome?"

Despite his brother's assurances, Britt still rocked with shame.

"We're not kids anymore," Jonah said, joining them. "We make our own decisions, good or bad, and live with the joy or the consequences."

As if he spoke philosophical drivel on a daily basis, Jonah continued, "Besides, I haven't had this much fun since designing Steele Survivor." He held up the paint gun. "Should we shut down the Green Beret before he says something Brynne can't forgive?"

They all glanced at Reid where he continued to harangue Brynne and Evie for placing themselves in danger. Brynne braced her feet apart and folded her arms across her middle, indicating her breaking point was near.

When Britt made to take the gun, his mom swatted his hand away. "I've got this." She prepared the ball for launch like a pro.

Stunned, Britt caught Evie's eye and nodded at their mom. She elbowed Brynne when Reid paced away.

Mom lifted the gun, but the end of the barrel shook. No doubt her nerves were as frayed as everyone's. Jonah steadied it with one hand, earning him a grateful smile.

"Thank you, son."

"Anytime, Mom." He winked. "On the count of three. One. Two. Three."

She pulled the trigger, hitting Reid square in the back.

Britt flinched, knowing just how much the hit would hurt.

Reid spun around, eyes wide. Mom loosed three more, lighting Reid up like a canvas in a Nickelodeon art class. He cursed and bowed and bent against the assault. The last ball sent him to the ground.

"What the fu—?"

"Language, Reid," Mom said. "Now apologize to Brynne and Evie."

Rolling to his back, he asked Brynne, "What'd I do, babe?"

Still holding her paint gun, Brynne stared down at Reid for several awkward seconds. Then she sighed and held out her gun to Evie.

"Come on, Reid," Brynne said. "I'll explain when we're in private. Apologize to Evie first."

Getting to his feet, Reid said, "Sorry, Eves. Didn't mean to go off on you like that."

"Don't worry about it." She glanced at Brynne. "I understand."

Reid sent his mom a wounded look.

"Don't give me that, Reid Sullivan Steele. You know better than to yell at women, especially the ones you love." Her voice softened. "No matter how afraid you are."

Britt stepped toward his brother. "Thanks for taking care of Mom and Jonah. I should never have left them unprotected." Words became difficult. "I owe you. Big time."

Reid glanced away. A muscle in his jaw jumped several times before he shifted his attention back to Britt. "You don't owe me anything. We're family. We watch out for each other." His eyes narrowed. "Now get yourself to the damn hospital." He set off after Brynne, who was already turning her vehicle around in the driveway.

His mom lifted Grif's shirt and saw the white bandage. Her lips thinned into an unhappy line.

"Randi and Carlie Beth," Mom said, "escort my two stubborn sons to the hospital so they can get stitched up—or whatever they need." She turned toward the house. "I've had enough excitement for one night. Come, Jonah. Walk your mother home."

Jonah held out his arm. "You'd make a great character in a video game. Mad Mama. Mind your manners or get mowed down with Mama's machete."

"Machete?"

"Paint gun's too boring."

"Evie," she called. "Come save me from your brother's shenanigans and fill me in on your latest escapade."

Grif assisted Carlie Beth into his Maserati.

"You okay to drive?" Britt asked.

"I already lost that battle," Carlie Beth said.

"Side wound beats out head wound." Grif peered up at Britt. "Coming?"

"We'll be right behind you."

"Make him sit down before he falls down," Grif warned Randi.

She winked and waved him and Carlie Beth off.

The drone of insects cocooned Britt and Randi in an intimate yet awkward cone of silence. The events of the past two hours seemed almost unreal in the wake of the normality that followed. Reid was an ass, Mom brought about order, Jonah developed a new video game character, Evie consoled her mama, and Grif was, well, Grif.

Only one enigma—Randi. Their relationship was a long way from normal.

"Eventful night," he said taking a step forward.

"Let's get you to Old Blue."

"Not yet."

"I'm sorry about the kidnapping or hostage-taking or whatever you call getting drugged, trussed up, and thrown in a cage." Randi crisscrossed her arms into a protective barrier.

"Mind telling me what you ladies were about tonight?"

"We wanted to help you save Calypso."

"So you decided to split up and follow the club members?" He moved closer.

"Seemed like a good idea."

"How did Norwood get ahold of you and Carlie Beth?"

"We followed him and Ito to a cabin, where we lost sight of them. After snooping around the property, I found Calypso in a kennel on the backside of a barn. And that's when Norwood arrived."

"How did you manage to get word to Evie?"

"Carlie Beth had a moment to update Evie while I verified the yip-barking I heard belonged to Calypso. If I'd had another minute, we could have avoided being drugged and hog-tied."

"Did he—?"

"No."

"How can you be sure? Some men are sick bastards and wait until the woman's unconscious to—"

"I would know, Britt." Conviction burned in her eyes.

"You're certain?"

"I am." She shook her head. "I can't believe they would kill a breeding female and steal her pups."

He let the topic go, not wanting to upset her. Later, he would attempt to talk her into a physical exam. "After Norwood and the others moved on to more exotic two-legged prey, killing a wolf would mean nothing to them."

"I can't even comprehend such evil."

"I hope you never do."

From one breath to the next, he moved until they were a whisper apart. He reached for her hand. She didn't flinch away.

"They won't hurt anyone, or anything, again, thanks to you."

Shaking her head, she glanced away. "I made a muck of it."

"Your spying might have taken a ragged turn"—he smoothed his thumb over her knuckles—"but you stopped Norwood from retrieving Calypso. Given what I now know, I'm confident he would have killed her rather than give her up."

"Sweet Mary, I really dislike that man." She swallowed hard. "Carlie Beth helped."

"What is it that makes women deflect compliments?"

"You're trying to paint me as a brave warrior," she said in a harsh tone. "I'm not. I came up with a flawed plan that nearly got my friend killed."

"Yet you did what y'all set out to do—found Calypso."

"Wasn't pretty."

Britt smiled. He couldn't help himself. She was adorable when trying to downplay her heroism. Misguided heroism, but heroism all the same.

"What?"

"Nothing."

"About earlier," she said, her voice tentative. "In my kitchen. You said some things, and I kind of clammed up. I want you to know—"

"Don't feel like you need to explain yourself or say anything you don't mean with your whole heart." He lifted her hand to his chest. "I shouldn't have put you on the spot like that. I'll wait. For as long as it takes."

"What if the feelings never come?"

That…hurt.

Britt pushed the knife out of his chest and focused on the goal—win Miranda Shepherd's love.

"We'll walk that path *if* the time comes." He curled a hand around her cheek. "Fair warning—Grif's not the most stubborn one in the Steele family. I hold that honor. And I'm going to charm, pester, and seduce you until you find me irresistible."

CHAPTER THIRTY-SIX

"YOU'RE QUICK," RANDI SAID.

"Am I?"

Randi's heart beat so fast she thought she might pass out. Speaking of passing out—sweat beaded on Britt's brow and, for the first time, she heard a note of strain in his voice.

"It's time to go to the hospital."

"A few more minutes." His gaze skimmed over her head. "Unless you're feeling worse."

"My drowsiness doesn't come close to your bullet wound."

"It could be days before we're alone again." He slid his fingertips over hers. "Please."

Unable to deny him, she clasped his hand and guided him to a wooden bench placed next to a colorful display of phlox, butterfly weed, and coreopsis. "Let's at least sit while we talk."

Britt eased down on the seat, careful not to lean back. He released a long breath. "Let's hope I can stand up when the time comes."

"Your mother is going to kill me."

"She knows better than to put the blame on you."

"Five minutes, Britt."

"Deal."

Although she'd enjoyed the sisterhood aspect of her plan to follow the club members, she didn't care for the unknown danger part. She'd had enough of the terrifying unknown when she'd been on the verge of losing everything.

Upon awakening in a dog kennel, she had been disoriented and confused—until she realized Britt had been injured. Terror like nothing she'd experienced before had sucked the air from her lungs and jolted her into action.

When she'd finally browbeat Britt into removing his T-shirt, the sight of blood oozing from a black hole in his shoulder blade struck her immobile for several awful seconds. Then her first-aid training had kicked in and she'd done what she could to contain the bleeding. With the bullet lodged against the bone, her options had been limited.

Randi stared at Britt's profile, unable to organize the maelstrom of emotions flooding her mind. Did he truly love her? The unconditional, forever kind of love? Would he tire of her or of the long hours she worked? Could she make him happy?

"What's going to happen to the pack now?"

"Thanks to my brother, the pack will have a safe place to roam free."

"But people know about their location now."

"They'll be protected through the Steele-Shepherd Wildlife Research Center."

"Shepherd?"

"Seemed a fitting name—after the woman who found the pack."

"My mother."

"Barbara might not have won any Mother-of-the-Year awards, but she loved you."

The hard casing protecting her heart against her mother's neglect splintered open. Like a stern parent turned roll-on-the-floor grandparent, her mother had done for Britt what she hadn't been able to do for Randi. The realization brought warmth to her heart, rather than icy resentment.

Britt smoothed his fingers along the curve of her cheek. "Randi, I need to share something with you. Something difficult. Painful. But I'm not sure how to go about it."

"Just say the words."

"Norwood and the others...They're responsible for Barbara's death and your financial issues and the cooler incident. They've systematically tried to ruin you so you'd sell your property to the club."

"I know."

"You do?"

"Norwood practically gloated about his accomplishments. However, I didn't think to ask him about the cooler." She burrowed her hand in his. "How did you get him to confess?"

"I produced an incentive." He squeezed her fingers. "I'll save that story for later."

Two fat tears fell on the bench between them, then two more, and two more. The grief she'd been holding in for weeks, years, spilled over until exhaustion silenced her.

An image of her mother's last, terror-filled minutes replayed in her mind. Randi would never forgive herself for not being there when her mom needed her most. But another emotion rose to the surface, one she didn't quite comprehend, but recognized all the same. Pride. She was proud of her mom for standing up to Norwood and his bullies. Proud she fought for what she believed in.

If only the ending could have been happier.

"You okay?" Britt asked.

"I will be. Right now, I just miss my mom."

"I miss her, too. She was brave. Like you."

Randi's throat had grown so dry, she couldn't swallow the lump that welled up there.

"Ready to put the past behind us?" Britt asked. "Are you up for it?"

Could she do it? Put the past behind her? She wanted to. Wanted to so badly. The constant hurting and anger had taken its toll on her. She was ready to let it go. Ready to forgive her mom. But could she forgive herself?

Maybe with Britt by her side she could. Maybe she could finally shake off the burden of her past and step into her future.

Their future.

"Together?"

He leaned closer. "Together." His tempting lips, a whisper away, curled into a weak smile. "I think you'd better haul my ass to the hospital now."

EPILOGUE

Twelve weeks later

BRITT OPENED HIS CABIN DOOR to find Grif on the other side. Dressed in a charcoal-gray suit, white shirt, and a deep ocean-blue tie, his brother would be the best-looking guy at the groundbreaking ceremony.

"What are you doing here?" Britt asked, his mood souring.

"Making sure you don't attend the ceremony in steel-toe boots."

"Nothing wrong with boots."

Grif gave him a once-over. "I see Randi already got her hands on your attire."

"It might surprise you to know that I've been dressing myself since I was ten years old."

"Exactly why I'm here."

"Morning, Grif." Randi sidled up to Britt. "You're looking dashing as usual."

When Grif bent to kiss her cheek, he winked at Britt. "You're quite beautiful yourself." He nodded toward Britt. "Nice job cleaning up the lumberjack."

Randi curled an arm around Britt. "I only helped with the tie."

"Take that, asswipe." Britt shut the door in his brother's face.

"Britt!"

"We haven't hugged all day." He pulled her into a full embrace, loving her jasmine scent and the feel of her in his arms.

"Not true. We hugged quite a bit a few hours ago."

"How about we blow off this waste-of-everyone's-time ceremony and go back to bed."

"Tempting, but no. Are you nervous?"

"What's to be nervous about, getting up in front of hundreds of people and making a fool of myself?"

"You're going to do great."

"Public speaking isn't my thing." He paced away, grabbing his wallet, readjusting his tie. "Everything I've come up with sounds like pandering mumbo jumbo."

"Tell them about your goals and objectives for the center."

"I'll put them to sleep."

"Stick to the layout of the building. Discuss your ideas about what types of projects the center will undertake."

"The people who give a damn about the center's projects have already been informed. The rest either won't care or they'll complain about the Steeles taking over yet another part of the town."

"Only you would make a five-minute photo op into a Spanish Inquisition." She grasped his chin and guided his gaze down to hers. "Speak from the heart. Tell them about the plight of the wolves. About the importance of protecting them and other endangered species. You won't fail to capture their attention or interest."

He tapped her on the nose. "How do you know so much about people?"

"I'm a bartender. I observe people for a living."

Grinning, he said, "Pay you five bucks to do it for me."

"Come on, big guy. All you have to do is flash that

killer Steele smile and they'll be groveling at your feet."

When his grin broadened to show his pearly whites, she shook her head and led them from the cabin. "Won't work on me now. I'm on a mission."

By the time they arrived, the build site was overrun with milling guests.

In typical Grif-plan-it and Jonah-pay-for-it style, they had made a simple stick-a-beribboned-shovel-in-the-dirt into a grand affair. An enormous tent stood center stage with rows and rows of white acrylic chairs beneath. At the back of the tent, a caterer set up rectangular tins of food on tables draped in royal blue. Delicious aromas wafted across the field, making his mouth water. A bluegrass band had set up shop on a forty-foot trailer attached to a five-yard truck. Cotton candy vendors and balloon sculptors worked the crowd, and large conceptual plans of the center and surrounding property lined one wall of the tent.

"Holy Mother," Britt muttered when he turned off Old Blue. "This is going to take a lot longer than five minutes."

"Chin up, Steele." Randi's lips twitched before she jumped out of the truck. "Game on."

Hand in hand, Randi and Britt made their way to the front of the tent where the rest of the Steele clan had already gathered. The moment Joan Steele clapped eyes on her eldest son, tears gathered in her eyes. She strode into his arms, squeezing him tight.

"I'm so proud of you, son."

Emotion clogged Randi's throat when Britt rested his chin atop his mother's salt-and-pepper head. She experienced a pang of regret for lost moments like this that she would never share with her mother. They had missed so many opportunities to make memories. If she were ever lucky enough to have a child, she would not make the same mistakes with her second chance at happiness.

"I think your baby boy deserves your tears," Britt said. "He made all this happen, with his generosity."

"Jonah and I have already had our mother-son moment." She leaned back. "It'll be your handiwork that'll make this facility successful." In perfect Mom Steele tradition, she adjusted her son's tie and swiped off nonexistent lint from his camel-colored sports jacket. "Now, go get 'em."

Before taking the stage, he bent to kiss Randi. "Twenty bucks?"

She smacked his behind. "Get up there."

Britt shook his brothers' hands, giving Jonah a man hug before kissing Evie, Brynne, and Carlie Beth's cheeks.

Randi smiled at his procrastination technique.

Finally, he climbed the stairs and took the stage, tapping the live mic a little too hard. A loud *thump* blasted through the large speakers. Everyone quieted.

Britt's mom urged Randi down beside her and held her hand. They both waited in tense anticipation for the man they both loved to break his silence.

"Thank y'all for coming today. Your support for this project means a great deal to me and my family." He retrieved a crumpled, folded piece of paper that Randi had never seen before from an inner pocket of his jacket. Using his palm, he smoothed out the paper.

For a long time he stared at the words he'd written. Joan glanced at Randi, worried. Randi mustered a reassuring smile she didn't feel.

She wanted so badly to climb up on the stage and put an arm around his waist and whisper words of encouragement. But she knew that kind of help would only cause him embarrassment.

After raking a hand through his hair, Britt mumbled something beneath his breath before cramming his speech back into his pocket.

"Listen," he said. "Many of you know me well enough to realize that I'd rather be eating a bowl of snails right now than standing up here." Laughter erupted through the crowd. His gaze sought Randi's, and she gave him a you-can-do-it nod. "Thanks to my brother Jonah, Steele Ridge's wildlife research center will participate in a nationwide effort to safeguard the critically endangered red wolf. Now that the breeding female has been reunited with her pack, the center is set to partner with a dozen environmental agencies to ensure the red wolf, and other endangered species in Western North Carolina, won't sink into extinction."

Joy filled Randi's heart as she listened to Britt forge on, his voice growing stronger with each spoken word. His passion for the wolves rippled through the crowd.

"The Steele-Shepherd Wildlife Research Center is dedicated to my good friend and mentor, Barbara Shepherd. Without her amazing knowledge of the environment, I wouldn't be in the position I am today to help the wolves. I miss her sharp wit and infectious passion for the natural world. I'm only sorry she couldn't be here to celebrate this moment, with me and her daughter, Miranda Shepherd."

Emotion clogged Randi's throat. She wished her mom could be here to cheer Britt on. He'd worked hard to get to this moment. His passion and honor were his guiding force. When he finished speaking, applause thundered inside the tent, and Britt's stoic features lightened in a way she'd never witnessed before.

Once the congratulatory handshakes and back pats ended, Evie sent her an excited eye-widening head bob. Randi wove her fingers through Britt's and guided him away.

"Where are we going?"

"You'll see."

She escorted him to a sheet-covered easel. Evie joined them, her whole body vibrating with anticipation.

"What are the two of you up to?"

Evie's smile broadened.

Wariness crept across his face.

"Don't tense up, knucklehead," Evie said. "You're going to love our surprise." She glanced at Randi. "Now?"

"I think you'd better."

Evie carefully removed the sheet, uncovering a large foam board beneath. The board depicted a beautiful illustration of the History of the Red Wolf, starting from the days before the settlers arrived, when wolves were plentiful and roamed the entire southeastern part of the United States, to the present, when fewer than fifty reintroduced wild wolves called the Alligator River Wildlife Refuge and Steele Conservation Area home.

Britt stared at the artwork, a muscle twitching in his cheek.

She and Evie shared an uneasy glance.

"We thought this would look wonderful painted on a wall in the center's main lobby," Randi said. "So all who visit will learn about their courageous fight for survival."

One blunt masculine finger reached out to trace the female wolf surrounded by her pups.

"Do you like it?" Evie asked, a note of uncertainty in her voice.

"You did this...for me?"

"Deke provided the historical facts and the artist we hired turned it into a story."

Leaning close, Britt studied the young blond man and older long-haired woman sitting on the bluff's edge overlooking a den of wolves below.

"Is that—?"

"You and Barbara Shepherd," Evie blurted out. "The moment the two of you found the Steele-Shepherd pack."

From the moment Evie lifted the sheet, Britt's eyes had not left the beautiful rendering. Other than the muscle flicking in his jaw, he displayed no other emotion.

"If there's anything you'd like changed," Randi said,

"we can have the artist tweak the image or the historical narrative."

"No, it's perfect," he whispered.

The pressure on Randi's chest lifted, and she sent Evie a relieved smile.

"We have one more surprise for you." Evie held out a letter-sized manila envelope. "Open it."

"This is too much."

Randi smoothed the backs of her fingers over his clean-shaven cheek. "No, it's not."

He covered her hand with his and kissed the inside of her wrist.

"Save it for later," Evie said. "Open the envelope so I can go flirt with Deke."

"Find someone your own age," Britt said without heat.

He slid a finger beneath the envelope's flap. Reaching inside, he pulled out several sheets of paper. His eyes wove back and forth as he read the top page, an e-mail confirming his participation in a three-week-long wildlife conservation program in Zimbabwe.

"You'll patrol the reserve with the park rangers every day, learning how to find snares and how to use smartphones to ensure poachers are prosecuted." Evie bounced on her toes. "The program also works with the local community, educating them on ways they can provide for their family without poaching." She arrowed her hands over her nose and mouth. "Why am I telling you all of this? You probably know it by heart. Call me excited!"

Swallowing hard, he asked, "How did you manage this?"

"I swiped the completed application off your desk and colluded with your sister," Randi said. "She shared with me your long-held desire to visit Africa and do something to help save the rhinos and elephants."

"So we mailed the application for you," Evie said. "A plane ticket's inside the envelope."

"You leave within the week."

"But the construction—"

"Will hobble along without you. It's all paperwork right now anyway, and your brothers and sister have agreed to watch over everything until you return." Randi tangled her fingers with his. "No more excuses."

"That's my cue to scram." Evie flew into his arms. "Go, Britt. Do this for yourself. We'll take care of things here." Rising on tiptoes, she kissed his cheek, then winked at Randi before making good on her promise to flirt with Deke.

Britt thumbed through the sheets of paper. "There never seemed to be enough time—and in the early days, money—to go." He looked up. "You wave your magic wand, and—*bam*—I'm on my way." He shook his head. "It's all happening so fast."

"For once, somebody—or several people, in this case—is taking care of things for *you*." She tugged the packet out of his grip and clasped his hands in hers. "You deserve time away, doing something you love."

"But—"

"No buts. There's never going to be a good time. You must carve out moments for yourself and enjoy them."

"There's only one ticket. If I'm going, you're going."

"As I told Evie, who'd insisted I go too, this getaway is yours, and yours alone." She smiled. "I'll tag along on your next adventure." She smoothed a thumb over his knuckles. "Take lots of pictures."

"I don't know what to say."

"Say you'll go. If not for yourself, for Evie. She's been so excited and anxious about this surprise that she hasn't slept for two days. She wants you to be happy."

Inhaling one long breath, he released it, slowly. He drew her closer, urging her arms around his waist. She caught the slight tremor in his hands when he traced his fingertips along her jawline.

"I love you." His words came out on a raw whisper.

It was Randi's turn to be rendered speechless. Ever

since taking down Norwood, they'd spent every available second together, though neither had said those three words to each other.

She'd been certain he would grow frustrated by the long hours she kept and the times she was too tired to make love. But he hadn't. At least not that she could tell. He'd adapted.

Some mornings he would stop by her coffee shop, order a large black coffee, kiss her temple, and head out to a job site. Friday nights he hung out with his brothers and their girlfriends at Triple B's bar, eating, drinking, and listening to the newest blues band. Sometimes, Randi would join them for dinner.

Lunchtime was their time. No matter where his work took him, she would bring him lunch. They would sit on his tailgate and talk about whatever came to mind as they ate their food.

Their lives had fallen into an easy, comfortable rhythm, but Randi lived in constant fear of the "It's not you, it's me" conversation.

She hadn't allowed herself to think about a future with Britt because she worried there would be none. Even so, she hadn't been able to stop herself from falling in love with her bear of a guy, more and more, every day.

Unable to stop herself, she kissed him. The warmth of his lips, the boldness of his tongue, the sweet gentleness of his hands, the solid weight of his embrace—all reassured her as nothing else could.

"I love you, too."

Something hot and possessive flashed in his eyes before his mouth covered hers. His rigid length pressed against her stomach, sending a spike of need straight to her core.

No doubt remembering a crowd of friends and family hovered nearby, he eased away. "I'm not going to make it three weeks without you."

"You must, and I expect you to enjoy every second

you're gone." She kissed him. "I'll be here when you get back."

"When I return, I'm going to ask you to marry me. So be prepared to say yes."

Randi blinked. "Did you just propose?"

"No, I'm giving you fair warning about my intentions—in case you need to warm up to the idea."

Incredulous laughter bubbled into her throat. Her eyes watered with the effort to hold it at bay. The last thing she wanted was for him to think she was laughing at him. But damn, he never did anything the prescribed way.

"I feel a hug coming on."

"We're already hugging."

"No, a *real* hug." He pressed his forehead against hers. "Randi?"

She closed her eyes, inhaling his intoxicating scent. "Hmm-mmm?"

"I found my spark."

Randi set her grin free.

MORE STEELE RIDGE
COMING IN 2017

Breaking FREE

Roaming WILD

Stripping BARE

WWW.STEELERIDGESERIES.COM

AUTHOR'S NOTE

From the moment I conducted an Internet search on endangered species of North Carolina and came across *Canis rufus*, I knew I had to share the red wolf's story through Britt Steele's eyes.

In *Loving Deep*, Randi and Evie presented Britt with a beautifully rendered mural showing the history of red wolves. Over on my website, I have painted a brief picture of their incredible fight for survival. Please go take a peek at www.TraceyDevlyn.com/RedWolves. Fair warning—the red wolf's story is equal parts compelling and tragic, and highly debated among scientists.

I hope you'll take a moment to learn more about this critically endangered species.

Be prepared to fall in love.

ACKNOWLEDGMENTS

My journey to Steele Ridge, North Carolina could never have happened without my two authors-in-crime buds Adrienne Giordano and Kelsey Browning. Their creative talent and unfailing friendship have been a constant source of inspiration and strength to me. I'm utterly amazed by the world we've created and know readers will love the Steele Ridge series as much as I do.

No thank-you would be complete without recognizing the one person who knows me best and loves me, despite my many flaws. Love you, Tim, and not just because of the surprise treats you leave on my desk.

Much gratitude to editors Gina Bernal, Deborah Nemeth, and Martha Trachtenberg for their role in polishing *Loving Deep* to its present shine. You're all amazing!

Kim and The Killion Group—your covers rock!

Huge, ginormous hugs to Dangerous Darlings Street Team and Team Devlyn beta readers. Without your enthusiastic support, I could never continue living my dream.

And lastly, my deepest appreciation to every reader who has given me a chance to pull you into one of my worlds and entertain you for a while. Whether it be in a time long past or a moment in the present, thanks for traveling with me.

TRACEY DEVLYN is a *USA Today* bestselling author of contemporary and historical romantic suspense, historical mysteries, and mainstream thrillers. She's cofounder of Romance University, a group blog dedicated to readers and writers of romance, and Lady Jane's Salon-Naperville, Chicagoland's exciting new reading salon devoted to romantic fiction.

An Illinois native, Tracey spends her evenings harassing her once-in-a-lifetime husband and her weekends torturing her characters.

www.TraceyDevlyn.com

CPSIA information can be obtained
at www.ICGtesting.com
Printed in the USA
LVOW01s1001160117
521098LV00017B/585/P